THE
ENGLISH
FÜHRER

Rory Clements was born on the edge of England in Dover. After a career in national newspapers, he now writes full time in a quiet corner of Norfolk, where he lives with his wife, the artist Naomi Clements Wright. He won the CWA Ellis Peters Historical Award in 2010 for his second novel, *Revenger*, and the CWA Historical Dagger in 2018 for *Nucleus*. Three of his other novels – *Martyr*, *Prince* and *The Heretics* – have been shortlisted for awards.

To receive exclusive news about Rory's writing, join his Readers' Club at www.bit.ly/RoryClementsClub and to find out more go to www.roryclements.co.uk.

Also by Rory Clements

Martyr
Revenger
Prince
Traitor
The Heretics
The Queen's Man
Holy Spy
The Man in the Snow (ebook novella)
Corpus
Nucleus
Nemesis
Hitler's Secret
A Prince and a Spy
The Man in the Bunker

THE
ENGLISH
FÜHRER

RORY
CLEMENTS

ZAFFRE

First published in the UK in 2023
This paperback edition published in the UK in 2023 by
ZAFFRE
An imprint of Bonnier Books UK
4th Floor, Victoria House, Bloomsbury Square, London, WC1B 4DA
Owned by Bonnier Books
Sveavägen 56, Stockholm, Sweden

This is a work of fiction. Names, places, events and
incidents are either the products of the author's
imagination or used fictitiously. Any resemblance to
actual persons, living or dead, or actual
events is purely coincidental.

A CIP catalogue record for this book is
available from the British Library.

ISBN: 978–1–80418–110–2

Also available as an ebook and an audiobook

1 3 5 7 9 10 8 6 4 2

Typeset by IDSUK (Data Connection) Ltd
Printed and bound in Great Britain by Clays Ltd, Elcograf S.p.A.

Zaffre is an imprint of Bonnier Books UK
www.bonnierbooks.co.uk

For Jack, with love

CHAPTER 1

AUTUMN 1945

Liz Lightfoot was beginning to believe that her husband would kill her.

A soft breeze drifted off the North Sea. It was early October and there was still a hint of late summer warmth in the air. Just about enough to make love outdoors. Anyway, they had nowhere else to go, and they needed each other.

Normally, they liked it here in the dunes. It was an easy ride on Tony's motorbike and, as a farmer, he had privileged access to petrol. No one would ever chance upon them, and a hollow in the sand offered some shelter from the wind. The marram grass and an old blanket softened their nest. They were warm enough because they weren't going to remove *all* their clothes, simply unbutton and unhook the necessary items. And then get on with it, like rutting animals.

He was twenty-three and she was twenty-two. They were married, but not to each other.

They hadn't been able to see each other for almost a week, so their lovemaking was frantic and hurried. Then, at last, they lay in each other's arms in silence. And yet she felt ill at ease because something wasn't right. Some sort of tension in the air. Something that she couldn't articulate to Tony. Below them, on the wide beach, just beyond the barbed wire fencing that kept walkers away from the land mines and barricades and pillboxes, a colony of grey seals slept, blissfully unaware of the activity in the dunes.

The gratification of the sex was followed as always by the misery of their situation. There were many questions and no answers, so they simply avoided addressing them. How could he, Tony Hood, abandon his wife Sandra and their baby son? And how could she, Liz Lightfoot, leave her husband, Lucas, when he would undoubtedly take a claw hammer to them both if he ever found out about their affair?

Liz pulled away from Tony and stood up, shivering as she adjusted her dress, brushing the sand from between her legs. She froze. 'Did you hear that, Tone?'

'What?'

'I thought I heard a voice, down on the beach.'

'There's no one there. Just the seals snoring.'

She nodded. He was probably right. It was just her nerves playing up, the fear that this was all going to end badly. 'I have to get home. Mrs Fearon across the street will be twitching her curtains. She already gives me looks.'

Tony lit a cigarette and took a long drag. 'Old bag. Tell her you were visiting your mum.'

'To do that, I'd have to go and talk to the cow. Anyway, she'd just call me a liar and a whore or sneer at me with her arms folded across her scrawny tits. Church-going bitch.'

They had all been friends, Tony and Sandra, Lucas and Liz, since school and throughout their courting days. They always went out as a foursome, to the pub in the village and the Saturday dance in Yarmouth, and they got married within a month of each other. Tony was Lucas's best man, and Lucas was Tony's.

And that might have been that. A lifetime of dreary, respectable marriage, kids and suppressed desires.

Then along came bloody Hitler with his goose-stepping hordes. Lucas quit the railways and joined the Royal Norfolks at the beginning of 1941. Tony was running the farm after the old man's stroke and so he couldn't enlist. It wasn't a big farm, just eighty acres, but agriculture was essential war work, a reserved occupation. Putting food in the nation's bellies was just as important as shooting Germans.

Still, it wasn't easy staying out of uniform. People looked at you in the street and their hard faces asked the same question: my son's fighting, why aren't you?

Before he enlisted, Lucas had asked Tony and Sandra to keep an eye on his lass. It was an unnecessary request, because they all lived close to each other in the village and they knew their responsibilities as friends. In the event, it was Tony more than Sandra who looked out for Liz, because she needed help doing the sort of things Lucas would normally have done – fixing fuses, unblocking pipes, heaving coal. Man's work.

Tony loved those hours he spent around Liz's place. They laughed all the time. And she always saved enough rations to bake a cake when he was coming round. It didn't take them long to realise the blindingly obvious: they had both married the wrong person.

They had been a foursome because Tony and Liz liked each other's company. Sandra and Lucas were only there because, well, no one had told them otherwise. Out of habit. Optional extras. Gooseberries.

One day, back in April in the last days of the European war, while Tony was repairing a kitchen shelf that had come loose, Liz apologised and said she hadn't had a chance to bake a cake. Would Tony like anything else instead?

'A kiss would do nicely,' he said, without a thought. The words just tumbled from his mouth and then he looked embarrassed. 'Sorry,' he said. 'That was out of order. A biscuit would be fine.'

Liz took his face in her palms and kissed him on the lips. After that, nothing could have stopped them. If the air raid siren had gone, they wouldn't have heard it.

Even though Sandra was at home with a growing bump and Lucas was over in Europe mopping up Nazis, they never felt guilt, only insatiable hunger for each other's company and bodies. The strange thing was that their spouses were the good-looking ones. Lucas was tall and broad and rugged, every inch the sportsman and soldier. Sandra was pert and pretty with a warm, trusting nature. Sweet Sandra, so naive that she wouldn't for a moment imagine she was being betrayed.

The best you could say about Liz was that she was homely to look at and had a good figure. As for Tony, he had a sense of humour and was presentable for a farmer. But that didn't count for anything. Their attraction for each other was not about looks: it was a force of nature, as irresistible as gravity.

In the summer, they had talked about running away, going to Manchester or Leeds or London, simply disappearing. But the impending birth of baby Ronnie had put paid to that. They knew there was no way out.

God Almighty, this was a terrible situation.

Now, even worse, Lucas was home from the war. He'd learnt to drive heavy troop carriers in the Army and had easily found a civvy job driving lorries, a career that was bound to end in disaster one day, because the Army had also taught him hard drinking.

'Do you want a puff?' Tony said softly, blowing smoke into the breeze and cursing silently as he realised one of his fly buttons had come adrift. Sandra would notice that, but she'd believe his story that it must have come away when he was relieving himself out in the fields. Sandra wasn't the jealous type. It wouldn't even occur to her that Tony might try it on with the two land girls they'd been assigned, let alone have an affair with Liz. And if a gossip had whispered the truth in her ear, she would have dismissed it with a laugh.

'God,' Liz said, ignoring the offer of the cigarette. 'This sand gets everywhere. And I mean, *every*where.' She still felt uneasy. Even if she had been wrong about the voice on the beach, she had an uncomfortable sensation that they were not alone. Always that terror that Lucas had found out, that he could have followed them here. This place no longer felt safe.

'What are we going to do, Liz?'

'What can we do?'

'I can't live without you.'

'No.'

'But I can't do it.'

She was looking away from him, down across the dunes to the beach and the moonlit sea. 'What's that?'

'I mean I can't leave the baby.'

'No, Tone, look over there – way out to sea. What is it?' Her voice low and urgent.

Tony rose to his feet and followed the direction of her gaze. Some distance out, across the still, dark waters, out where the sea deepened beyond the sands, something vast and monstrous was rising slowly above the surface. He watched, apprehensive and bemused, as the thing emerged, throwing up a wash of foam and waves, then casting angular moon shadows across the sea as it slouched and settled.

'It must be a sub, but it's the size of a bleeding battleship,' he whispered.

'Look, there's someone on the beach, near the seals. He's flashing a torch.'

'No, there's two of them. I don't like this.' He stabbed the cigarette into the sand.

'Isn't that . . .'

'Who?'

'You know, him. Let's get out of here.'

'We can't – they'll see us.' He tried to pull her down so that she wouldn't be seen.

'For pity's sake, Tone, we have to go. If I'm not there when he gets home, he'll kill me.' She was urgent now, fighting against him. Whatever was happening on the beach or out to sea, it was the prospect of Lucas finding out about her affair that really terrified her. She pulled herself away from Tony and tugged at his arm. 'Come on.'

They crept through the marram grass, moving inland away from the shore. Her heart was pounding with unspoken terrors. Fear of punishment for sins of the flesh, fear of the the entity emerging from the depths. From the sea, amid the hypnotic sound of the breaking waves, she heard another noise – the thrum of an outboard motor.

Raising her head, she saw lights – torches – and heard voices again. One of the men was holding a mooring line from the stern of a motorboat, the other began walking towards the dunes.

Tony pushed her back down. They shuffled snakelike towards the landward edge of the dunes, hurrying to put distance between themselves and the men. He stopped her, a finger to his lips as he peered down across the trees to the old ruined church. He put his mouth to her ear. 'There's another bloke, Liz, with a van.'

She saw what he was looking at. Dear God, the man was lighting a cigarette, leaning against the bonnet of his vehicle, no more than twenty yards from Tony's motorbike, which was parked up in the shade of a tree. Perhaps he hadn't spotted the bike, but they couldn't get to it, not without being seen. And if the man was armed . . .

Suddenly, the man looked up in their direction.

Hours later, in the far distance where the North Sea deepened and just before dawn, the captain of the I-405 consulted his 55-man crew for a second and final time, and all agreed.

They had come here from Japan the long route – more than eighteen thousand nautical miles – across the Pacific, down the coast of Chile, via Cape Horn, up through the Atlantic Ocean, skirting the west coast of Ireland and passing through the channel north of Scotland known as the Pentland Firth, then southwards through the North Sea. In these difficult and treacherous waters, the precious British Admiralty charts, tide tables and tidal stream atlases had been vital. These were documents carefully collected and stored away by the Imperial Navy over many years for just such an eventuality.

Most of the way, they had travelled on the surface by night at a steady fourteen knots, resting and waiting submerged during the day at no more than three knots. At times, they had remained beneath the surface, barely moving for days on end as storms raged above them. It had been a long, gruelling journey. Water was strictly rationed, as was food. They had no supply vessel and had not been able to call into any port to take on fresh provisions.

All now were thin and enervated, but their eyes shone bright in their hollowed-out cheeks with the knowledge that they had accomplished what had been asked of them.

Their movement through the channels around the British Isles had been the most nerve-racking, because of strong tides, particularly in the waters between Caithness and the Orkneys, and clear moonlit skies all the way down the North Sea. There was a great deal of shipping, and they could not allow themselves to be seen.

And then there was the constant threat of uncleared mines, anchored at various depths. Only chance saved them.

Finally, they had arrived at the rendezvous point and had once again submerged. This had not been straightforward because the sea was desperately shallow off the coast of East Anglia and the shifting sands made the best of charts unreliable. But there was no better navigator in the Imperial Navy than Captain Takashi Ohata, and all had gone to plan.

Now they were out in deeper water again and the end was near.

The submarine surfaced and the captain and his senior officers took position on the conning tower, from whence they scanned the horizon in all directions. No other ship was seen and so they returned below-ships and the order was given to dive.

At 350 feet below the surface, all four engines were killed and the crew of fifty-five men were assembled in the main gangways, all crowded together and silent as the captain invoked the spirit of bushido, the way of the warrior, then made his farewell dedication to families, to the people and, above all, to the emperor.

To preserve water for drinking, no man had been able to wash in two months and the stink was all-enveloping. And yet every man retained his dignity and did his best to look smart in his loose-fitting dress uniform.

In his last moments, Takashi Ohata thought of that day, 6 August, when the atomic bomb was dropped on Hiroshima. Following America's conventional bombing raids on the nearby Kure naval base, the I-405 had been sheltering offshore, anchored in the inland sea a mere twelve nautical miles from Hiroshima city. His home. The place where his beautiful wife and sweet seven-year-old daughter lived.

The submarine had been on the surface, always on alert for air raid sirens and the necessity to dive, and he had been in the conning tower, issuing orders for the day. The first he knew was the silent speck high in the sky of a lone B-29 Superfortress flying at about thirty thousand feet. That was surprising in itself. Usually the American bombers came in their scores or hundreds.

Next came the blinding light, followed seconds later by the aftershock and the roar of the greatest explosion mankind had ever known. The sea rose and flung the I-405 sideways, snapping the anchor chain. And then came the cloud, a whole city rising as ash and smoke into the air.

All qualms about this mission had evaporated with the lives of his loved ones.

Now, two months later, far out in another sea on the other side of the world, Takashi Ohata bowed low and his men bowed in their turn. The charges had been set in every compartment of the vessel. He saluted with his right hand and pulled the lever with his left.

Had any other ship been in the vicinity its crew would have seen the sea light up, brilliant gold and grey, and they would have seen a great wash welling up like a hill of water. Then, seconds later, they might have heard the muffled roar of an explosion from far beneath. Soon after, they would have felt the tall wave hit them with force, pushing them off course.

But no other ships did see the end of the I-405 and its hull and its men would lie buried forever in far-flung waters, thousands of miles from home, their duty done.

CHAPTER 2

The lecture theatre was packed. The subject of the talk was 'Espionage and the Elizabethan Theatre', with special emphasis on the activities of the sometime spies Christopher Marlowe and Anthony Munday. Tom Wilde spoke with verve and enthusiasm and with plenty of humour to keep his young, gown-clad audience engrossed.

It was four years since his last lecture here and he was in his element.

'Of course,' he said, in his summation, 'there is one very obvious reason for the link between the theatre and the world of espionage. It is the nature of spies that they must be actors, concealing their true characters and motives, living in a make-believe world of illusion and obfuscation.'

As he closed the session, he took a little time to pack up his bag. It was a habit he had acquired over the years, for it allowed undergraduates to approach him with questions or simply to make themselves known to him. On this occasion, five young men and one woman came forward.

He chatted with them in turn, answering their queries, suggesting books and asking them which colleges they had joined, for they were all beginning their first year. The last one, a powerful-looking young man, held back a bit before stepping up and introducing himself as Danny Oswick. He wore a luxuriant moustache of the type favoured many years earlier by Lord Kitchener, and Wilde took him for a sportsman, either rugby union or, perhaps, a boxer like himself.

Wilde recognised the name immediately because he was on the list of undergraduates he would be supervising this year. They shook hands.

'Good to meet you, Oswick. I believe we have your first supervision in a few days.'

'Next week, yes, sir. Very much looking forward to it, sir.'

Wilde smiled. It was clear from the clipped response and the repetitive use of the word 'sir', that Oswick had recently been demobilised. 'Which service were you in?' he asked.

'Army, sir. Infantry.'

'Well, we have three years to get to know each other better, so we can both look forward to that.'

'You were recommended to me by Colonel Sir Neville Catesby. He was my commanding officer and spoke very highly of you. I suppose he has been something of a mentor to me.'

Wilde couldn't place Oswick's accent. He seemed to have the bearing of an officer, but his origins were less easy to discern. It certainly wasn't a public school voice. Wilde knew those types well enough having undergone the rigours of Harrow. He admonished himself for the very thought of judging a young man by class. Labour was in power under Mr Attlee, a new world was dawning, the old orders were crumbling. And a good thing, too. This country had been stuck in its insufferable hierarchical past too long. Queen Victoria was long dead, for pity's sake.

'Neville Catesby? I'm seeing him this evening.'

'Yes, sir, I'll be there, too. He's very generously invited me along. I trust that's not out of order, sir.'

'No, no. Well, perhaps we'll have a chat there.'

'That would be spiffing, Professor.'

Spiffing. Wilde resisted the temptation to laugh. The word seemed so incongruous coming from this young man's mouth, as though he had deliberately learnt it, as if he believed it was the sort of word officers and undergraduates should use.

Wilde strode out in the cool autumn air. As he made his way past the police station on St Andrew's Street, he spotted the familiar rotund figure of his old friend Rupert Weir exiting the building.

'Well, well, doing the devil's work today are we, Rupert?'

'Walk with me, Tom. Got to get some oxygen into my lungs. Just been chatting to the inspector. He smokes non-stop and I need to breathe.'

'Interesting case?'

'Extremely. Quite bizarre, in fact. Find me a coffee and a smoke-free room and I'll tell you about it.'

'I know just the place.'

Five minutes later, they entered Wilde's college through the ancient stone gates. The head porter tipped his black bowler to the professor and his friend.

'Any messages, Scobie?'

'Not today, Professor Wilde.'

'Coffee in the buttery?'

'No information on that, I'm afraid, Professor, but who knows what Bobby might have secreted in his larder. Proper Aladdin's cave his gyp room, so I'm told, sir.' Scobie winked. They both knew that Wilde's gyp – his college servant – had sources of his own that wouldn't bear investigating too deeply for fear of being found in breach of rationing regulations.

Wilde and Weir ambled across the wide expanse of the New Court and then the Old Court. The grass was threadbare and weed-ridden. Like the whole of Britain, it needed a lot of care and attention after six years of neglect.

They ducked into the arched entrance and climbed the stairs to Wilde's rooms. Bobby was in his own little room washing cups. He grinned and it occurred to Wilde that he had even fewer teeth these days.

'Coffee, Professor?'

'You're a mind-reader.'

'Black for the both of you?'

'I don't think that will be a problem for either of us.'

'And would you like me to lay a fire?'

'Probably not, thank you, Bobby.'

His rooms were beginning to feel homely again. The cobwebs had been brushed away, the windows polished, the calf-hide sofa dusted and buffed.

As Wilde shuffled his papers from his satchel onto his desk then briskly filed them away, Weir stood gazing at the framed painting on the wall opposite the window. A shoeless boy was gazing into the distance across a meadow somewhere in the American Midwest.

'You've seen that before, haven't you, Rupert?'

'Of course. But I've never really looked at it.'

'It's a Winslow Homer oil,' Wilde said. 'I think it's one of his earlier works, though I don't have a date for it. My father left it to me.'

'I find it terribly sad. As though something were lost that could never be retrieved.'

'Lost innocence, Rupert. I feel the same way. Sometimes it makes me want to weep.'

Wilde settled into one of the two armchairs, allowing Weir to stretch out his portly, tweed-clad frame on the sofa.

'Well, what's the case that's got you so fired up, then?'

Weir was the police surgeon. As a rule, his services were not required much in Cambridge, which was not noted for its high crime rate. There was criminal activity, of course, mainly centred on a couple of public houses in the north of the town, but even that had died down in the war years when the local felons were either called up or banged up. Most trouble these days involved black-marketeering, brawling American servicemen or vehicle crashes. Dr Weir's most common call-out from the police was to give his opinion on the inebriation or otherwise of drivers. That left him largely free for his primary duties as a general practitioner.

'Well, it's undoubtedly a murder. A body found in a ditch halfway to Ely. An unidentified man in his mid-thirties. Labourer or farmhand from the callouses on his hands and the muscles on his arms, but beyond that we have no idea who he is.'

'How did he die?'

'Ah well, that's the thing, Tom. That's what makes it interesting. His heart had been badly damaged by a powerful corrosive substance. I sent samples to the Met's toxicology boys and I've just got the results back. One of the people at Guy's suggested the victim might have been injected with phenol and so they tested for that. A simple ferric chloride colour test gave a conclusive result.'

'You'd better remind me what phenol is.'

'In its simplest form, you might call it carbolic acid, but this is a highly concentrated aqueous solution which makes a remarkably cheap and effective poison if injected directly into the bloodstream. A jab in an arm vein will kill you within a couple of minutes. One straight to the heart would kill quicker. In either case there would be a great deal of pain. That's the way our corpse was done for.'

'Extraordinary,' Wilde said. 'Heard of cyanide, arsenic, strychnine, but never this stuff.'

'Phenol. One gram – a tiny fraction of an ounce – into the bloodstream hits the central nervous system, causing cramping, spasms and sudden collapse. In the present case, there wasn't even evidence of a struggle. Chummy – that's what I'm calling him for the moment – had no other injuries and no sign of being bound. A mighty curious incident.'

'No suggestion that he could have done it to himself? Suicide?'

'No sign of a syringe, so I think it's fair to assume not. Also, I told the inspector that I am certain Chummy didn't die in the ditch. He was dumped there after being killed elsewhere.'

'Why haven't I heard of this substance before?'

Bobby arrived with a tray bearing a pot of coffee, two cups with spoons and a bowl of sugar lumps. 'Anything else, Professor?' he said after setting the tray down. 'I could rustle up a couple of digestives.'

Wilde looked to Weir, who nodded enthusiastically. 'That'll be a yes, please, Bobby.'

'Right you are, sir.'

Wilde poured the coffee while Dr Weir returned to the subject of phenol. 'To be honest, I have never heard of it being used as a murder weapon.'

'Where would your killer have got the stuff?'

'Almost anywhere. It's extracted from coal tar and is used in many industrial processes – coal tar soap for one – and also various medical procedures. It really is ridiculously plentiful and inexpensive. Many years ago, Lister used it as an antiseptic in surgery.'

'What are the police saying?'

'Have you met Detective Inspector Shirley?'

'No, I have not had the pleasure.'

'A stoat of a man, or should that be weasel. Clearly promoted way beyond his capabilities because of a wartime shortage of good coppers. Anyway, he's come down from Manchester and seems to think everyone around here is a country bumpkin while he's the big city boy. Seen it all. Solved every crime. Actually, he's utterly useless and has lost all respect among the rank and file. So I've gone behind the inspector's back and put in a call to the Met, specifically the Special Branch.'

'Well, that's all you can do. Let me know how you get on, won't you? I'm intrigued.' There was a knock at the door. 'And now here come our biscuits.'

'Glory be! Nothing finer than a digestive, Tom.'

CHAPTER 3

'Are you sure about this, Lydia?'

'Tom, I'm really not interested in Neville Catesby and his ridiculous party. I've got to go and see May.'

'Can't it wait until morning? I don't understand why you have to see her now.'

'Are you cross that I'll be using up some of our precious petrol ration?'

'You know that's not it.'

She gave him a look. Wilde sighed in resignation. When his wife had made up her mind about something, it really was a complete waste of time arguing with her. She was as immovable as Everest, and just as unconquerable.

He had thought it would be a good idea to take her along to this party. It was called The Survivors Party or, more informally, the Before We Were So Rudely Interrupted party. Catesby had organised a bash for October 1939, but had cancelled it after the declaration of war. This 'resumption' would be a chance for the fellows and families of various colleges to get together for the first time in years. No doubt there would be plenty of Cambridge alumni in evidence, along with various senior members of the Establishment – judges, bishops, generals, writers, artists, perhaps one or two members of Attlee's cabinet and a few opposition spokesmen.

And with Catesby, the ultimate Renaissance man, as host and chief spreader of rumours, there would be plenty of salacious gossip. It promised to be a big event in the life of the university.

'I spoke to May two days ago and she wasn't well,' Lydia continued. 'She said she'd call me back, but she hasn't. And when I call her, there's no reply. So I'm worried. Is that enough reason for you, Tom? Wouldn't you check up on a sick friend?'

'Of course I would,' he said, wondering where May Hinchley's own GP came into the picture. 'You're right, as always. Give her my love, won't you?'

'I will. But don't bother to send *my* love to Sir Neville.'

'And you try not to bring the lurgy home.'

Wilde realised, of course, that she simply didn't want to go to the party, and he supposed he could understand why. Sir Neville Catesby was strong meat, as were many of his acquaintances. He was a man who knew everyone (it was said he was probably unique in having met Hitler, Mussolini, Stalin, Roosevelt and even Tojo at various times during the thirties) and had been everywhere. Had he met Churchill too? More than likely but hardly worth mentioning. Only God knew how he ever had time for lecturing or supervising undergraduates.

He loved politics and he loved gossip, however trivial. There would be the usual university backbiting, the sniping at various masters, bursars, senior tutors, the conspiring and the cliques. This had always been Cambridge life and there was no reason to imagine that six years of war would have changed anything.

For his own part, Wilde had managed to rise above university politics. Perhaps it was the fact that he was American that helped. He had experienced college life in the States and the machinations there were of a very different order – more to do with personal advancement than doing others down out of sheer malevolence. Anyway, his two successful books had done wonders for his reputation. However envious his peers might be, they would be hard-pressed to undermine his academic credentials.

May Hinchley had not sounded at all well on the telephone. She felt a bit feverish and was short of breath. She said she thought she had caught something from one of the children she taught and also mentioned her village friend, Joan, who had been ill. Lydia had a horrible feeling it might be the dreaded flu.

The flu. It was such a simple three-letter word, yet it was deadly. In 1919 it had killed her own mother, along with countless others. A minuscule virus invisible to the eye, an entity that could kill more people than thousands of tons of steel and high explosives.

May had promised Lydia she would call back with an update, but that was two days ago, and it was most unlike May not to keep her promises. If her friend was ill, then Lydia wanted to help her.

She still hadn't given up on her ambition to go to medical school and train to become a doctor like her father; she had always believed she had a good bedside manner and healing hands.

It was only the arrival of their son, Johnny, at the beginning of the war and the misogyny of the medical profession that had held her back thus far.

The evening was cool and pleasant as she set off, but likely to deteriorate. Lydia felt certain that a mist would develop soon. It was that time of year. She enjoyed driving the new car. Well, not exactly *new*. With Johnny growing, they had splashed out on a slightly bigger vehicle, a six-year-old Riley. It was a little rusty around the wheel arches, but Tom had said it was in reasonable shape, all things considered. A brand new car would probably be out of the question for a couple of years until peacetime production lines were up and running.

The road out of Cambridge was surprisingly busy. Mainly military trucks, jeeps and a few big, fancy American cars. In the passenger footwell, she had a bag with one of their last bottles of wine. She knew that however rough May was feeling, she'd prefer a glass or two of claret to a bunch of flowers or grapes.

Flowthorpe was eight miles outside town, a pleasant village of about three hundred inhabitants with a shop, an elementary school, a church and two pubs. May was headmistress at the school and lived alone. She was only thirty-eight, a little older than Lydia, but she had made up her mind that she was fated never to marry.

'Look at me, Lydia,' she had said over glasses of cider in The Fox's Tail a few weeks earlier. 'Bespectacled, broad-about-the-beam and bookish. Those were my own dear father's words, believe it or not. The three Bs! How to make your daughter feel good about herself!'

'Don't listen to him, you're beautiful. There you go, another B. Anyway, there's someone for everyone. Just wait and see.'

'Well, I've been waiting quite a long time now. My best hope might have been one of the Yankee servicemen when they showed up at the airfield a couple of years back. But it wasn't to be, so no, Lydia dear, I'm resigned to spinsterhood.'

'That's a horrible word, May. You are a hard-working woman with an important job to do. Don't ever let anyone talk down to you. You put knowledge and ideas into young minds, for heaven's sake. What could be more useful than that?'

'Being a doctor, perhaps?' May said. 'Sorry, I shouldn't have said that.' She knew all too well that Lydia had been desperate to become a doctor for six years or more. Her chances were slimmer than ever, with the very real problem that women's places in medical schools were oversubscribed by a factor of twenty to one.

Lydia turned off from the main road into the narrow mile-long byroad to Flowthorpe. There seemed to be some sort of obstruction up ahead. Her headlights cut through the light fog coming up from the river and she saw that two armed men were standing in front of a lorry that was parked side on, blocking the way.

The party was already heaving when Wilde's taxi arrived at Harbinger House just over twenty minutes to the west of Cambridge. The building was a magnificent early Georgian property, one of the homes of Sir Neville Catesby. A servant took Wilde's coat and showed him through to the candlelit orangery, where a string quartet was playing Beethoven, the music barely audible above the hubbub.

He looked around, taking in the scene before spotting a waitress with a silver tray bearing flutes of champagne. Wilde gave her what he hoped was a winning smile. 'I don't suppose there's any chance of a Scotch instead, is there?'

She smiled back sweetly. 'Of course. I'll see to it, sir.'

'You're very kind. Thank you.'

He felt a tap on the shoulder and, turning, came face to face with Philip Eaton. Wilde laughed. 'Well, of all the gin joints in all the world . . .'

'Hello, Tom. I thought I might see you here.'

'I confess I wasn't expecting you, Philip.'

'We've been having a meeting at Dagger Templeman's place. Nothing I'll bore you with. And, of course, I've known Neville for years. He was a great inspiration to me when I was an undergraduate at Trinity.'

'Of course. Forgive my startled expression. But let's be honest, Philip, you haven't always been the bearer of glad tidings.'

'Don't worry, this is simply pleasure. I just thought I'd pop in briefly to pay my respects.'

'So you're not staying here at Harbinger House?'

'No, Dagger's putting me up. Actually, he's here somewhere as well. Look out for him. I'm sure he'd appreciate a quick catch-up.'

The waitress returned and handed him a tumbler of whisky, then offered her champagne tray to Eaton who tucked his stick under his arm thus freeing up his only hand to take a glass. He had lost his left arm and damaged his left leg in a road incident before the war.

Both men thanked the waitress and she drifted away into the crowd.

'You're probably wondering where all this gorgeous fizz comes from in a time of extreme rationing, Tom. The way I understand it, Neville commandeered a vineyard chateau in the Champagne region and used it as regimental HQ while driving eastwards from Normandy. On departure, he made off with several hundred bottles. Apparently, he considered it fitting reward for liberating the vineyard from the Hun.'

'I imagine the Germans had already consumed a healthy portion of the stock.'

Eaton laughed. 'Of course, but I'm told they missed the best vintages.' He held up his glass. 'Bottoms up, old boy.'

'Cheers.'

'And the delightful Lydia, is she here with you?'

'She had other plans.'

'Code for can't abide varsity get-togethers?'

'Do you blame her?'

'Not at all, Tom, not at all. Oh, and I'm desperately sorry to hear that Harry Truman has wound up the OSS. Is it a wise move, would you say?'

Eaton was a senior member of MI6. He and Wilde had worked together over the years, both during Wilde's wartime operations with America's intelligence outfit, the OSS – Office of Strategic Services – and earlier, on an ad hoc basis. Wilde had already resigned from the OSS when he'd heard just a couple of weeks previously that the agency had been shut down without warning or adequate explanation.

The fabulous people Wilde had worked with in the London bureau were stunned, because they had set up a world-beating intelligence operation in three short years. Some of the senior men like Allen Dulles and Bill Donovan and Wilde himself were not just disappointed, but alarmed. They knew that the end of hostilities with Germany did not signify the elimination of all threats.

Neither Wilde nor Eaton needed to articulate what that threat might be. They both understood that the next enemy would be their new best friend, the Soviet Union. Churchill had spoken of sunlit uplands when the Nazis were defeated, but out of the corner of his eye Wilde saw a dark cloud billowing up in the distance.

'I'm told Harry Truman called it un-American to spy on other countries. He feared the OSS would end up as a secret police. Like the Gestapo or NKVD or something,' Wilde said.

Eaton nodded. 'Churchill had similar concerns about the massive expansion of MI5 and MI6. He worried we would become overmighty and a danger to our own people.'

'Well, I take their point, Philip. But there are greater perils. And I think Truman's made a big mistake. The OSS or something like it is going to be needed – and sooner rather than later.'

'For what it's worth, Dagger and myself and many others in both Five and Six agree with you.'

Their mutual acquaintance Lord Templeman – known as Dagger for the knife-shaped port wine mark on his face – was a senior member of MI5, head of V section. It was not work he did for the money for he was extraordinarily wealthy and owned one of Cambridge's finest houses, even grander than Catesby's place.

Eaton glanced up at the clock, gulped down his champagne and handed the empty glass to Wilde. 'Well, it's been good to catch up with you, Tom, but I must circulate. Would you mind disposing of my glass? Impossible to carry the damned thing and operate the stick at the same time, I'm afraid.'

Wilde stayed him with a hand to the shoulder. 'Before you disappear, any word on our friend Borisov or Minsky or whatever he's calling himself nowadays?'

'Not a sausage. Vanished like smoke. I suspect he was worried we'd send him back to Moscow for a bullet in the head. But we'll find him.'

Wilde bade his old MI6 acquaintance farewell, then stood for a few moments, champagne glass in his left hand. While Eaton hobbled away, it occurred to Wilde that the MI6 man had seemed a little distracted, but that was hardly a rarity; his mind usually seemed one or two steps removed from present circumstances. And he must surely be worried about the disappearance of Boris Minsky, otherwise known as Sergei Borisov. The Russian was a colonel general in the Soviet intelligence organisation SMERSH and Wilde had helped him defect when he was in Berlin two months earlier. Now he very much wished he hadn't.

Sipping Scotch, Wilde gazed upon the throng, many of whom he knew and some of whom he liked. John Betjeman was there, surrounded by a crowd of admirers, while Osbert Sitwell stood alone, distractedly nursing a glass of wine. Sir Neville was a few yards away talking to a minister of state and a popular thriller writer, so Wilde waited until they dispersed to circulate before going over to extend his greetings to his host.

'Tom Wilde, you've survived the war and made it to my little do. And well done, I see you've sniffed out the secret whisky stash.'

'OSS training, Neville. We have noses like bloodhounds. May I say that I'm very happy to see that you survived too.'

'But we didn't all make it, did we? In a little while I shall be proposing a toast to our absent friends, those who fell in defence of the realm. The poor bloody soldiers, sailors, fliers and all the rest – the men, women and children, burnt and blasted on land and at sea. God rest them all.'

'Indeed.'

'But I'm not sure I would have kept my sanity without your biography of Robert Cecil to keep me company. He was my constant companion throughout the campaign.'

'Really? I had no idea you were an enthusiast.' The book about Queen Elizabeth's devious secretary of state and spymaster, son of Lord Burghley, had come out in 1939, the last year of the peace before the great conflagration. It had sold well on both sides of the Atlantic.

'Oh, yes. What a remarkable man. A study in power. As you must know, I have met all the great world leaders of the twentieth century, but I do believe that if Sir Robert were alive today he would be pre-eminent among them. It just shows what a diminutive fellow can achieve if he obeys Machiavelli's strictures, eh? Imagine if the Gunpowder plotters had had the sense to assassinate Cecil early on in their conspiracy, why it would undoubtedly have been successful.'

'Food for thought, Sir Neville. I'm glad you liked it.'

'Liked it and learnt from it, my dear fellow. I came away believing that Sir Robert Cecil understood the nature of power better than even Niccolò Machiavelli himself. Your biography is a handbook for the great dictators.'

Wilde laughed. 'Actually, I saw it as a portrait of a remarkable man, not an endorsement of his methods. And certainly not an instruction manual for tyrants.'

'Well, I don't know who Herr Hitler read, but it didn't work. Think where the world would be now if he'd had your tome to guide him.'

'Very amusing, Neville.'

'Not as amusing as the entertainment I have planned for this evening. Who will be the brunt of my humour tonight, eh, Wilde? Who would you like to see humiliated?'

'Yourself, perhaps?'

'Never going to happen, old man. I learnt at a very young age to kick the other fellow before he kicks you.'

Neville Catesby was a compact man of about fifty, known for his urbanity, his natty dress sense and, paradoxically, the snowfall of dandruff that you longed to brush from his shoulders. All conceded that he was a decent scholar and an engaging lecturer in English literature, also that he was brave, having been mentioned in dispatches in the First World War. As a distinguished Cambridge professor he could easily have sat out the second war in his rooms as plenty of others had, but instead he answered the call to join his old regiment and won battle honours when he landed in the first wave in June 1944. It was said his Military Cross was richly deserved.

It was also true that he could be entertaining, but in a way that, at times, made him seem cutting and cruel. He took delight in the misfortune of others, what the Germans called *schadenfreude*.

Perhaps he had seen too much, for he had travelled the world like some latter-day Phileas Fogg. Wilde imagined men in their clubs discussing his latest escapade. 'He's a card, old Neville,' they'd say and each of them would repeat a well-worn anecdote to much laughter. Whether any of them actually liked him was questionable, but they would not say a word against him in case it reached his ears and they in turn became the butt of his savage wit.

Wilde had his own thoughts. There was something else, something beneath the surface. It was Lydia who first pointed this out. 'He's a Claudius, Tom. Loves to play the decorated army officer one minute, the dazzling academic the next, then the roving diplomat – and I don't think he's any of them.' Wilde always listened to Lydia's character judgements, but in this case it didn't get him any closer to the hidden truth about Sir Neville Catesby, army colonel, university professor and man of the world. The only surprise was that he had never entered politics, which was strange for such a political man.

As if on cue, Danny Oswick, the moustachioed undergraduate Wilde had met after his lecture, appeared on the scene.

'Ah, Danny,' Catesby said. 'Have you made Professor Wilde's acquaintance yet? I believe he's to be your supervisor.'

'Yes, sir, I attended Professor Wilde's lecture today and introduced myself.'

'Good, good. Well, I'm sure you'll be a damned fine fit. No better history bug than your new supervisor, young man.' He patted Wilde's arm. 'Let me leave you two chaps to get to know each other a bit better, eh?'

Wilde smiled. He didn't really want to engage with his new undergraduate in these circumstances. There would be plenty of time for that in his rooms during supervisions and he liked to leave a little distance between work and socialising. If Oswick hoped to gain an academic advantage by putting down an early marker, it wouldn't work. Not with Tom Wilde.

They chatted for a few minutes. Wilde was not surprised to learn that Oswick had joined the army as an ordinary soldier but, having caught Catesby's attention, it was suggested he go for a commission. Then with the war coming to an end, Catesby told him he had a decent brain and should get a proper education, which was why he was now at Cambridge.

'And you're interested in the Tudors?'

'Very much so, sir.'

'Well, look up Conyers Read in the college library. No one does the late sixteenth century better. I'd particularly recommend Mr Secretary Walsingham. That'll give you a good start.'

'Thank you, sir.'

A gong broke into their conversation and a toastmaster announced that Sir Neville would like to say a few words.

Relieved, Wilde said he would see Oswick later in the week, and moved away to get a better position to hear the host's tribute to the fallen.

For the next couple of hours, Wilde moved through the throng, catching up with those he hadn't seen in years and meeting a few new people. He had booked his taxi home for ten, and so took his leave of Sir Neville before the promised late-night entertainment.

'Great shame you're missing the fun, Tom. I was going to perform a little comedy turn and give both barrels to that insufferable bore Mountbatten. Got some extremely juicy secrets from his short time at Christ's after the first show.'

'But he's not here is he?'

'Oh, don't worry, word will get back to him. I've made sure of that. Anyway, keep an eye out for young Oswick, won't you?' Catesby clutched Wilde's hand. 'I have great hopes for him. He didn't have much of a start in life, but he's clever. Britain will need men like him if we're ever to get back on our feet.'

Arriving home, the door was immediately opened by Lydia, as if she had been waiting for him. He could see the concern on her face. 'Lydia?'

'Tom, come in quickly. Something very strange is going on.'

CHAPTER 4

'Well, how was May?'

'That's the point, Tom – I didn't get to see her.'

They were in the sitting room. Lydia was nursing a glass of wine from the bottle she had failed to deliver to May Hinchley earlier in the evening.

'There was an army roadblock a mile outside Flowthorpe,' Lydia continued. 'They wouldn't let me pass.'

'Did they explain why?'

'They said it was a security issue. No one was allowed in or out. They wouldn't tell me any more.'

'So then what?'

'Well, I turned around and took the long route round to try to get in from the other direction. Same thing, another roadblock. No explanation. But I knew there was a bridleway, so I parked the car and tried to get there on foot. I couldn't get through – the fields and woods were all patrolled by soldiers with guns. I even heard a couple of shots.'

'They were shooting at you?'

'No, I don't think so. I don't think any of them saw me.'

'Well, you're right – it's very strange. Have you tried phoning again?'

'Yes, of course. I tried from a phone box in the next village. The line was dead. So all I could do was drive home. Then I switched on the wireless in case there was any news, but there was nothing. I simply don't know what to think, Tom.'

They stared at each other for a few moments, both knowing what the other was thinking. She laughed. 'You simply can't let go, can you, Tom? The war might be over for everyone else, but not for Professor Wilde. However, in this case I'm right behind you. Go there with my blessing, and find out what's happening to my friend.'

Wilde changed into suitable clothes: thick moleskin trousers, leather jacket, goggles and boots. He was slightly worried about his whisky intake at Harbinger House. He hadn't expected to be taking a vehicle out tonight. But it was almost midnight so there would be little other traffic on the roads. It was probably only his own life he was risking.

He wheeled out the Rudge Special. It didn't have a full tank, but there was enough to get him to Flowthorpe and back.

Within minutes he was out of town. The old bike with its 500 cc engine was getting a bit long in the tooth, but it hadn't racked up much mileage in the past six years and Wilde was very fond of it. Tonight, though, the road was slippery and the old tyres didn't give him a great deal of traction; nor did the machine's dim yellow headlight cut through the fog very well. Visibility was down to a few yards. On the plus side, the mist might be of assistance if he was to find a way past armed patrols.

He ditched the bike close to the bridleway, then moved along the path through a tunnel of dripping, autumnal trees. Every so often he switched on his torch to check the way ahead. It was a risky strategy because he could not afford to be spotted, but without it he could not be sure of the path.

Coming out of the trees, the bridleway cut straight across a ploughed field. At the far side, he saw three lights through the mist, all moving. Soldiers with flashlights, blocking the route through. Lydia had been right: the village of Flowthorpe had been severed from the outside world.

But Wilde had the fog working for him. That and his knowledge of the area. He had been here birdwatching, in the old days before fatherhood and the war intervened, and he knew that he could find a route through the woods if he took his time and dropped into the undergrowth when soldiers appeared.

Half an hour later he was through. He had passed the outer perimeter of guards and could see the lights of The George and Dragon, one of the two village pubs, on the other side of the road beyond the green and the duck pond. But there was a lot more than that. Crouching in the undergrowth, he saw that two large tents had been erected on the green. Soldiers were standing guard, rifles at the ready. Two men in white coats emerged from one of the tents, followed by a young woman in nurse's uniform. All three of them wore gas-type masks, which they pulled up for a brief discussion. Then they replaced the coverings and returned to the tents.

By the look of it, the village green had been turned into a field hospital.

On the roadway to the right, in front of a thatched cottage, he saw an American jeep with a couple of sacks hanging from a bar across the rear. A man in countryman's clothes with a shotgun under his arm approached with a string of dead animals – rats, a fox, two cats – and dumped them in one of the sacks.

Wilde heard a noise behind him, but before he could turn, he felt a sharp jab in his back and fell forward. He grunted with the shock and turned to see that two soldiers were standing behind him, pointing rifles at him.

'Get up,' one of the men said. 'Slowly. With your fucking hands in the air.'

Wilde obeyed the order, easing himself to his haunches and then his feet, his hands raised just above his shoulders.

'Who are you?' the soldier said, the same one who had spoken before. He wore sergeant stripes on his sleeve and he towered over Wilde.

'Thomas Wilde.'

'Is that all?'

'I'm a Cambridge professor – I have come to see a sick friend, May Hinchley.'

'And you didn't notice the road blocks and the patrols? This is a restricted area.'

'Yes, I noticed. But I was getting no explanation as to why the area is restricted, or what was happening to my friend.'

'Well, you're not allowed here, so you're coming with us. Don't try anything funny.'

Wilde didn't even consider arguing or trying 'anything funny'. These two soldiers were professional, war-hardened men who obeyed orders unquestioningly and wouldn't hesitate to shoot if he made any sudden movements.

They pushed him forward onto the green, past the tents. He took a quick glance and saw that the marquees were lit by hurricane lamps and were full of military camp beds – perhaps thirty in all – each occupied by a patient. He wondered whether May Hinchley was one of them, but didn't have time to look closer because he was being pushed forward across the road. A step up and he was through the front door of The George and Dragon.

To his left, the door to the main bar was open. He got a fleeting glimpse and quickly surmised that it had been turned into some sort of administration office. Three men in white coats, along with two British Army officers and two United States Air Force men were huddling over a large map spread across two tables that had been pushed together. None of the men looked up at Wilde as he was pushed past by his captors.

'In here,' the sergeant said, opening a storeroom containing a mop, a broom and various other household goods. He nudged him with the muzzle of his rifle and Wilde stumbled forward into the small space, no more than four foot square.

The door was closed behind him, and he heard the bolt sliding home.

He found himself in pitch darkness. Wilde felt the walls for a light switch, but there wasn't one. Then he remembered his torch and switched it on. The stores were pretty basic and gave him no assistance. A stock of cigarettes and matches, three cases of bottled pale ale, a shelf with spirits – London gin, Scotch whisky and Kentucky rye. And cleaning materials: a carton of Vim cleaner, some cloths, a dustpan and brush, old rags.

Well, if the worst came to the worst there was the Scotch to fall back on. He had felt pleasantly mellow at the party, now he was painfully sober. He guessed the rye was there to satisfy the requirements of the US airmen whose base adjoined the village.

He had nothing to lose by making his presence known to anyone who might be nearby, so he hammered on the locked door with his fist.

'Settle down in there.' A voice from just outside the door. Wilde guessed it was the second soldier, the private.

'Let me talk to an officer.'

'Don't push your luck, mate.'

There was nothing to be gained from arguing. Wilde lowered himself onto the cold stone floor and bunched up his knees. He killed the torch; no point in draining the batteries. In the darkness, he closed his eyes. And waited.

Ten minutes later, he heard voices. The bolt was pulled back, light flooded in and the two British soldiers were standing there, but this time they were accompanied by a United States Air Force officer, who was looking down at him with a blank expression.

'Get him up and bring him through to me in the snug, Sergeant.'

'Yes sir.'

Wilde was manhandled by the two soldiers and marched through to a small bar opposite the main bar. The officer nodded to the two soldiers. 'You can leave us now.'

'We haven't searched him, sir.'

The officer turned his gaze to Wilde. 'Have you got a gun, knife or any other weapon?'

He shook his head.

'Well, I think I'll take the man's word for it.'

'Yes, sir.' The sergeant clicked his heels and removed himself and the private from the room.

'Sit down, won't you,' the officer said, indicating a dilapidated chair by the window, several yards away from the desk. Wilde accepted the invitation while his captor closed the door, then took the chair a good distance away from his captive. 'OK, let's start at the beginning. I'm Lieutenant Colonel Broussard, US Air Force. Who are you?'

'Thomas Wilde, professor at Cambridge University.'

'Do I detect a faint accent there, Professor?'

'I'm an American citizen, half Irish. And before you ask, I'm here to check on the condition of a friend, May Hinchley.'

'You must have noticed the road blocks and the patrols? There's a security alert here – your way was barred for a reason.'

'Which made me all the more determined to find out what was going on.'

Broussard nodded grimly. He was about forty years of age with greying sideburns and a rather stiff manner. 'What did you do in the war, Professor?'

Wilde hesitated. Was it something he should be telling this man? Why not? The organisation had been disbanded and Broussard could probably find out anyway with a call to the embassy. 'I was with the OSS, London bureau.'

'Ah, one of the Oh-So-Sexy guys. You did good work.'

'We like to think so

'Bad move closing you down.'

'I won't argue with you there either.'

'But OSS or not, I'm afraid I'm going to have to hold you here while I take orders from on high about what to do with you.'

'Can you at least give me an idea about what's going on here? Has there been an accident – or is this is some kind of medical emergency?' In his mind, the sickness of May Hinchley pointed to the latter option.

'I'm afraid I'm not at liberty to discuss that.'

Wilde wasn't unaware of the weapons that all sides had been developing during the war. He had been involved in top-level discussions about such matters at the OSS. Chemical weapons, guided missiles and finally, eclipsing them all, the atomic bomb. But this was something else. 'Let me take an educated guess, Lieutenant Colonel Broussard, could we be talking about a biological incident here?'

'Think what you like, Professor.'

'At least tell me what has happened to my friend, Miss Hinchley. She's the headmistress at the local school.'

'I'll try to find out for you. In the meantime, I'm going to have to ask you to accompany me to a holding cell, hopefully rather more comfortable than the broom cupboard. Are you OK with that?'

'Not exactly. Do I have an option?'

'I'm afraid not.'

'And am I in danger of infection?'

'No comment.'

'Can I call my wife?'

'Nope.'

'You can't keep this secret, you know.'

'Oh, you're wrong about that. The British people have had six long years of keeping shtum. They know that careless talk costs lives – it's been drummed into them. And now it's in their very nature to keep their mouths shut when told to.'

CHAPTER 5

Wilde was put in a room on the airbase. It had an austere military-style bed, on which he stretched out, trying to stay awake, thinking through the events of the evening. But the effects of the whisky took their toll and within an hour he had fallen asleep. When he awoke it was still dark, but he quickly realised that that was because the room had no windows and the door was shut, probably locked.

All he knew was that he was in the USAF officers' quarters at Flowthorpe aerodrome. 'This is usually a guest room, Professor,' Lieutenant Colonel Broussard had said. 'I trust you find it comfortable. We don't have a cellblock here.'

He rose from the bed and switched on the light by the door, then knocked and called out, imagining there would be a guard outside, but no one answered. He tried the handle and it was, indeed, locked. So he returned to the relative comfort of the bed, where he lay with his hands behind his head on the thin pillow and continued his thought processes. It didn't get him very far; the truth was, he had no real idea what was happening here. Just his initial instinct that there had to be a biological element to it – the nurses, the men in white coats, May's illness.

Mostly he thought about Lydia. She would be worried sick by now. Firstly, she hadn't been able to find any news about May's condition and now her husband was missing.

An hour later, the door opened and a young soldier – not one he had seen before – entered carrying a tray with a cup of tea and some toast with thinly spread margarine.

'Ah,' Wilde said. 'Room service.'

The soldier said nothing, simply put the tray on the ground, turned sharply and departed, locking the door after him.

Wilde sniffed the tea, then sipped it and ate the toast. There was no lavatory but there was a small handbasin. He was contemplating peeing in it when the door opened again. Lieutenant Colonel Broussard was standing there, alongside the familiar figure of Philip Eaton, leaning on his stick.

'Good morning, Tom.' Eaton's voice was as languid as ever, dripping affected ennui.

'Philip, I might have known. So this is why you're up here in Cambridge.'

'We need to talk.'

'Do you think I could have a pee first? The facilities in this hotel are shocking.'

'Of course,' Broussard said. 'Forgive me, Professor, I should have had a pot left for you. Follow me, there's a john just along the corridor.'

After freshening up, Wilde was accompanied to Broussard's office. It was a tiny room with a wooden filing cabinet, a desk with two telephones, a typewriter and a lamp. The bottom half of the wall was painted green, the top half institutional cream. Wilde's gaze strayed to the window. Outside he could see aeroplanes – mostly bombers – dispersed across the wide, flat landscape.

'Are you going to tell me what this is all about now?'

'We need your word that you will say nothing about what you have seen,' Eaton said. 'The words "top secret" have been over-used these past few years, but in this case they are appropriate. If this got out there would be mass panic, and we can't allow that.'

'Well, given the presence of a field hospital, I've guessed it's a biological incident, but is it a natural occurrence or something more sinister?'

'It's not confirmed, but we believe it's a localised attack of *Yersinia pestis*. You might know it better as the plague bacteria. Several villagers and a few USAF personnel have been affected and there have been three deaths.'

'Good grief. And May Hinchley – is there any word, Lieutenant Colonel?'

'She's alive. Not well, and not out of the woods, but there's reason to hope.'

'Look, Tom,' Eaton said, 'we are desperately trying to contain this thing. We've killed hundreds of rats, mice, squirrels and cats and we're allowing no one in or out, other than in exceptional circumstance – medical staff and ministry people. This is like something out of the Middle Ages, but we are trying to apply twentieth-century science to the problem, using strict quarantine measures to contain it.'

'How did it get here?'

'No line of inquiry has been ruled out. The fact is, we simply don't know. We were fortunate to identify it so quickly. That was thanks to the local GP, Dr Fitzpatrick, who was in India for much of his career and had seen it there. He was also an old friend of Dagger Templeman and contacted him straightaway because he understood the security repercussions. That's why we were able to close down the area at such speed. Sadly, Fitzpatrick caught it himself and didn't survive, but he has probably halted the spread and saved many lives. Anyway, I'm here to decide what's to be done about you. If we let you go, are you willing to keep your mouth shut?'

Of course he was. Well, up to a point; he was hardly going to keep this from Lydia.

'Yes. I understand fully why you need to keep the thing secret. Panic could be disastrous.'

'Thank you, Tom.'

'So I don't need to be quarantined?'

'Not unless you've been bitten by a flea or if a patient has breathed over you. And I'm led to believe you haven't been close to the sick.'

'What about May Hinchley? Could I at least see her – from a distance perhaps?'

'I'm afraid not. The only good news for you is that your motorbike was found and it's outside this building. Feel free to go at your leisure. But I have to tell you one other thing: Dagger will be wanting a word with you. Expect a call later today.'

It had started with the shivering. May Hinchley had closed up the little Flowthorpe elementary school for the night and was walking the short distance to her cottage when she first felt it. Of course, she merely thought it was a chill in the air. The start of autumn proper.

But once home, having hardly eaten any of her frugal supper of two-day-old bread and a bowl of leftover soup, she quickly began to feel extremely ill. She put the back of her hand to her head and sensed heat, and so she took two aspirins and decided to go to her narrow brass bed for an early night. The preparation for the next day's lessons would have to wait.

That was when Lydia called. It hadn't been a long conversation.

'Oh, Lydia, dear,' May had said. 'Can we talk tomorrow? I don't feel awfully well and I'm just off to bed.'

'What is it, May?'

'Nothing. I'm sure it's nothing. Probably just a bug I caught off one of the children. There are always things around at this time of year. My friend Joan was a bit poorly when I saw her this morning. Anyway, if I don't feel well tomorrow, I'll call Dr Fitzpatrick.'

In the night, the fever came. She was almost delirious but had the presence of mind to realise that she needed help; the problem was she didn't have the strength to get up from her bed and go to the telephone. The heat in her body was unlike anything she had ever experienced.

Her face, her arms, the joints of her knees and thighs were so tender she could not bear the weight of the blankets and so she crawled out of the bed and onto the floor. It felt as though her skin was hardening, that her insides were swelling and exploding. She could scarcely move but nor could she remain still. Sleep – any kind of rest or peace – was impossible.

Somewhere in the delirium, she knew she would die unless she could secure medical attention. Slowly, without true comprehension of what was happening to her, she crawled down the stairs to her front room. Her heart was pounding like the pistons on a train, her breathing was short and painful. It seemed every part of her body was in a tumult of agony.

With the last of her strength, she reached up to the handle, pulled the door open and fell out onto the street.

The next she knew, she was waking on a camp bed in a tent. How long had it been? Had she been unconscious or had she simply lost her mind?

A nurse wearing a face mask was gazing down at her. 'Ah, you're with us, dear,' the nurse said. 'Don't try to say anything. Just keep still.'

Was it minutes, hours or days? She had no way of knowing. She shifted her position on the bed and screamed in pain.

'I'll give you a little morphine,' the nurse said. 'That will ease the discomfort.' She reached for a hypodermic and quickly filled it from a small vial, then jabbed May's arm. 'You're on penicillin, dear, but we're not sure how effective it'll be because it hasn't been tried on this type of thing before. Just keep your eyes closed and try not to move.'

Now, she was awake again. The morphine had worn off and she felt awful. Her body felt as if it was covered in boils and she was sure she must be oozing pus. But her mind was working at last. When the doctor came around with a nurse, May was able to make eye contact.

'Temperature, Nurse?' the doctor said.

'Ninety-nine point five. It's coming down steadily.'

May thought the doctor was smiling at her, but couldn't be sure because of the mask covering most of his face.

'What's happened to me, Doctor?' she said.

'You've had a very nasty turn, Miss Hinchley. Quite a fever. A hundred and five degrees at one point. That would have done for a woman in less robust health. We're not sure what you've got, but others in the village have had it.'

'I thought I was going to die.'

'Well, we're pretty sure you're improving. So just try to keep calm and all will be well.'

'Could you get a message to my friend Lydia Wilde, please?'

'Is she here in the village?'

'No, she's in Cambridge.'

'Then I'm afraid not. We are under emergency quarantine measures until we have worked out exactly what's going on. I'm sorry, Miss Hinchley. Try to be patient.'

She felt his plastic-gloved hand touching her arm gently and once again she was sure his eyes were smiling.

Wilde rode slowly. He considered calling home from a village telephone box on the way, but that would just have held him up and so he rode on.

It was mid-morning when he arrived back at Cornflowers. Lydia answered the door and he could see the panic in her eyes.

'Tom, for God's sake, where have you been? I've been frantic. I called the police and they were no help. I didn't know what had happened to you or what to do.'

'I'm all right, and I believe May is too.'

'Believe? What do you mean *believe*? Either she is or she isn't. What's happening, Tom?'

'Is Johnny at school?'

'Of course he is.'

'Well, this is for your ears only.'

They sat in the kitchen and he told her all that had happened. Lydia listened in silence, then said, 'I should be there helping. I should be with May, holding her hand. I need to be a doctor, Tom.'

'They won't let you in. The truth is I was lucky to get out. Flowthorpe will be cut off for days, if not weeks.'

'Is this some kind of attack?'

'No one's saying.'

'I have to go and see May.'

He shook his head. 'I'm sorry, it really is out of the question. And you can't breathe a word to anyone.'

'What then? I need to know how she is. She's my friend, I have to help her.'

'I'll be seeing Templeman. I'll make sure we are given a proper bulletin on her condition. But I did get the impression that she's over the worst.'

'I can't bear it. I thought the bloody war was finished. It just doesn't stop, does it? More deaths, more misery. What sort of world have we built for Johnny and his generation?'

CHAPTER 6

One of Lord Templeman's black Rolls-Royces arrived at noon. The young driver was dressed in chauffeur's livery and touched the peak of his cap deferentially to Wilde. 'His Lordship requests that you accompany me to his office.'

'If he wants to see me, why didn't he come here?' Wilde asked.

'That I couldn't say, sir. I just do as I'm told.'

Wilde let the driver off the hook with a smile. 'Sorry, I know it's nothing to do with you. And yes, I'll be happy to come. Just let me get my coat.'

Ten minutes later, they pulled up in the courtyard of Latimer Hall, one of the most ancient of Cambridge's buildings, the colleges aside. A footman escorted Wilde through to Templeman's study which, he thought, might more properly be called a library given that three of the four walls were shrouded in bookshelves, full of rare tomes from the Middle Ages onwards.

Templeman immediately rose from his desk and welcomed Wilde with a handshake. Wilde had mixed feelings about this room. He had been here before, under duress. MI5 had been investigating him in 1942 following his own inquiries into the death of the Duke of Kent in a plane crash. This time the reception was decidedly more convivial.

As head of MI5's V branch, Dagger Templeman was in charge of liaison between the branches and sections of the secret intelligence services. It was a role that had become vastly more complex with the huge increase in the work and manpower occasioned by the war. For Templeman, a man born to immense wealth, it was a position of power which he employed with the charm and ease born of his class and expensive education.

'Whisky, Tom?'

'Is it safe?' The last time he had been here something had been slipped into his drink, something which loosened his tongue.

'It's a fine twelve-year-old single malt. I'll join you to demonstrate its purity.'

'Then I'll say yes.'

Templeman went to his polished sideboard and poured the amber liquid into a pair of crystal tumblers, then handed one to his guest.

'I take it this is about Flowthorpe,' Wilde suggested.

'Indeed. Terrible business – and I'm extremely grateful to you for your cooperation in keeping the lid on it. But what I have to tell you is that there's a great deal more to it than Philip Eaton has told you. As a senior MI6 man, he must be included in the inquiries – up to a point – because there has to be suspicion that this disease has foreign origins. But the investigation itself is being treated as a domestic matter, and so it has been assigned to MI5 and the Special Branch. Need to know has always been my guiding principle. Vital in my position, as I hope you'll understand.'

Vital in every secret service, Wilde thought. Even before the OSS, he had understood that information was power, and must never be given away without adequate return.

'The thing is,' Templeman continued, 'we're desperately worried that this Flowthorpe affair is just the beginning – that there's worse to come. There is a very real fear that this is an attack with a biological weapon, and we know from our own research that these ghastly things have the potential to wipe out whole populations. A chemical attack can be contained, but it is far harder to control a disease, which may be passed from one infected person or animal to another.'

'An attack?'

'I pray not, but my instinct says yes.'

'Then we need to know who's behind it.'

'Quite. Who would you bet on? Nazi remnants, perhaps? The whole world believes that the beast is dead, but that's not quite true. It may be mortally wounded and in its death throes, but its razor-edged tail is still thrashing and capable of inflicting damage. Or perhaps our new best friends in Moscow? And is there a link to Unit 731? We must find the identity of the beast and strike it through the heart.'

Unit 731. It was an outfit Wilde had hoped never to hear of again. The very name made his flesh crawl. 'Ah,' Wilde said, 'so that's why I'm here.'

'I suspect that no one in England knows more about Unit 731 than you, Tom.'

'God, I don't know that much. Only what I've heard from our boys in the Far East. Surely MI6 must have information of their own. Ask Eaton. Talk to Porton Down.'

'I have. They hadn't even heard of Unit 731 until a couple of weeks ago; nor had I. Six sees it as an entirely American issue. If anyone has access to the men who worked there, it's the American military and whatever passes for a US intelligence service now that the OSS has been decommissioned.'

Unit 731. The Japanese biological warfare research laboratory based in occupied Manchuria, not far from the city of Harbin. 'Laboratory' would be too kind a word; torture chamber was more appropriate.

The researchers had used humans – Chinese or Russian captives or simply non-combatants dragged off the street – as guinea pigs. They had been infected with numerous diseases, then dissected alive. None of the captives had survived, but Wilde – through encrypted wire conversations with Bill Donovan in DC – knew at least part of the squalid story.

At its heart was a man named Dr Shiro Ishii. Surgeon general of the Imperial Japanese Army.

Unit 731 had been his idea. He supervised the building of the camp and developed a programme to harness the destructive power of a series of diseases. Crucially, he was instrumental in developing delivery systems for the foul weapons devised at the camp.

And then these weapons were taken out and used. Chinese villages and towns were deliberately infected with plague, malaria and cholera, killing thousands of people. Perhaps tens of thousands or even hundreds of thousands. If anyone knew the exact figure, they weren't letting on. Perhaps only Shiro Ishii knew the full extent of his depredations.

'You really think this has something to do with Unit 731, Dagger?'

'We have to consider the possibility, because the Japanese undoubtedly had the most advanced biological warfare technology of all our enemies. They are at the forefront of our investigation until proven otherwise.'

'But Japan has surrendered. How could their weapons have arrived in England?'

He shrugged and took a healthy sip of his whisky. 'Good question. One I would very much like answered. One line of inquiry has to be Unit 731's possible links with Nazi science.'

Had the Germans and Japanese collaborated in developing bio-weapons? It was not a matter Wilde had given much consideration now that the wars in the East and West were both ended.

He knew that various German doctors had experimented on human beings in the concentration camps and that some of them were likely to come up for trial at Nuremberg after the main event involving Goering, Hess and Ribbentrop was over. As for a link between the German and Japanese bio-laboratories, that had never been suggested as far as he knew. But there were clues. 'I wish I could give you hard information on that.'

'You hesitated, Tom.'

Yes, he had, and for a reason. 'OK,' he said. 'You may not have heard of Murray Sanders. He's a microbiologist, now part of the military set-up at Camp Detrick but formerly held tenure at Columbia University. He was aboard the transport ship *Sturgis* when it arrived in Tokyo Bay on August thirtieth ahead of the surrender ceremony. His mission was to find out what the hell the Japanese had been doing with bio-weapons because we knew they had used disease mercilessly as a weapon of indiscriminate destruction.'

'Hopefully they'll pay for their sins one day.'

'Hopefully,' Wilde agreed. 'Anyway, an Imperial Army guy named Ryoichi Naito was waiting for Sanders on the quayside and offered his services to him as interpreter. Sanders accepted the offer but, of course, he didn't believe for a moment that Ryoichi was a mere linguist. He had to be a spy. Actually, we have since learnt that he was no common-or-garden agent. This fellow was second-in-command to the big cheese Shiro Ishii.'

'Interesting.'

'There's more. Ryoichi studied in Germany before the war and he even spent time in America seeking out yellow fever samples at the Rockefeller Institute for Medical Research in NY. He was sent packing, as it happens. But it's the fact that he was also in Germany that struck me. Who was he talking to there – and why? You'd have to think the conversations between the two major Axis powers continued after war broke out.'

'I take your point.'

'It's a clear link.'

'Where is Sanders now?'

'Not sure. Could be still in Japan. Could be back at Camp Detrick.'

'Can you talk to him?'

'I don't know. I no longer have any official status. I've even surrendered my diplomatic passport. I'm a history professor – so how the hell do I get authority to talk to anyone at Camp Detrick?'

'You got on well with Bill Donovan. Talk to him. He may already know what's been happening at Flowthorpe from the intelligence section at the airbase.'

'What exactly do we want from him?'

'Well, surely the Americans in Japan have access to Ryoichi and Shiro and the other criminal bastards. Get Sanders or one of the others to ask some tough questions. Is Japan involved in this outbreak? Is there a link to diehard Nazis?'

Wilde wasn't at all sure how this would work. During the war, he had had extensive encrypted conversations with Bill Donovan across the Atlantic and, in the last months, they had got to know each other in person when Bill was working from a suite in a fancy London hotel. Donovan had been founder and director of the OSS, the top man, and they had got on well, so it might be worth a shot. The problem was Donovan himself was now out of a job. What influence did he retain?

'Will you do this? I know the American Air Force at Flowthorpe has its own interests. Biological warfare is a difficult subject for all sides, but this took place on British soil and so we have to take the lead.'

'I'll give it a shot. But no promises.'

'Thank you.' He held up his whisky glass. 'Your health.'

'And yours.' As Wilde drank he noticed that Templeman was looking at him as though he wasn't finished with the conversation. 'Is there something else, Dagger?'

The MI5 man nodded gravely. 'I'm afraid there is, Tom. Something rather unpleasant, but I have to tell you. You'll have heard of the Nazis' Black Book, I'm sure.'

'Of course. It's hilarious. I was disappointed not to be in it, quite frankly.'

'Me too.'

The Black Book – the *Sonderfahndungsliste G.B.* – was a Gestapo list of more than two thousand people to be arrested immediately when the Nazis invaded Britain. Everyone from politicians to journalists, broadcasters to novelists, singers to architects. Men and women who had perhaps demonstrated a distaste for Hitler's criminal gang over the years or who were thought to be influential. The book had been discovered in September, a few weeks earlier, and had become a badge of honour for those included.

One celebrated newspaper cartoonist when told he was in the book had replied that he wasn't worried – 'I had them on my list, too!'

'However,' Templeman continued, 'what you won't know is that there was a much smaller volume, an addendum to the Black Book. This one won't be receiving any publicity because it is too sensitive. There are about two hundred and fifty names in it – so a tenth the size of the Gestapo's main Black Book.'

'Am I in it?'

'I'm afraid you are, so am I.'

'Well, that's made my day, Dagger.'

'Not so fast. We believe the addendum was not a list of people to be arrested but of those singled out for instant death. Most are intelligence officers or senior military. Men and a few women who might present an immediate danger to an occupying force, the sort of people who would organise resistance and sabotage ops. There were also names of a few people who had caused grave offence to Hitler or Himmler or any of the other senior Nazis. You probably fill all categories.'

Wilde began to feel a churning in the stomach. 'Why are you telling me this now, Dagger?'

'Because one of my men in the addendum has been murdered in the past two weeks. And another has disappeared.'

'And you believe there's a link between them?'

'I've no idea, probably pure coincidence, but I'm paid to spot connections and I haven't been able to strike it from my thoughts. My instincts tend to be pretty sound, however, so I listen to them.'

'But you're not linking this to Flowthorpe?'

'Aren't I?'

'Well, that would be a thought too far, wouldn't it? I can't see any possible connection – unless you're not telling me something.'

'Let's leave it at that for the moment. I just wanted to give you a friendly warning because we're having to go around those on the list to warn them that they could, just possibly, be in danger. You're one of the first to be told, Tom, so take a few precautions while we try to work out what's going on.'

'I was given a Colt .32 ACP Hammerless as a parting gift from the OSS. I shall dust it down.'

'And there's worse. It seems Mrs Wilde is on the list, too.'

CHAPTER 7

Lydia was out and Johnny was at school when he got home. It was difficult to take it all in. Was there really a threat to Lydia and himself? It seemed implausible. Laughable even. Templeman hadn't been able to add much; it was simply a name in a slim volume, but Wilde couldn't dispel his anxiety.

What sense did it make, though? He had certainly faced real danger in the war years, but now? He was a university professor plain and simple. No one could have the slightest reason to kill him or his wife.

The Nazis and their Gestapo henchmen were a busted flush. The Black Book was a historical curiosity. If someone had killed a man who happened to be on an addendum to that list, that was surely a meaningless coincidence. Yes, another man was missing, but he could turn up safe and well at any time. Dagger Templeman was making something out of nothing.

Then again, there *were* those who believed the Nazi monster *wasn't* dead, merely hibernating in its cave. General Bill Donovan was one of those people. He had always believed that the Nazis wouldn't give up simply because they had suffered military defeat. There would be an underground guerrilla movement, perhaps involving forty thousand or more specially trained resistance fighters.

Was he right?

The problem was, men like Templeman and Wilde did not believe in coincidence. Dagger Templeman was holding something back. He believed there was some link between the Black Book and the incident at Flowthorpe, but he wasn't providing any evidence.

Wilde found himself sinking into crazed conspiracy mode. It was what came of working with a secret intelligence agency that always had to think the worst of an enemy, just to cover all the bases.

At the moment there was no proof that there was even a single attack. No one knew the truth about Flowthorpe yet and nor was

there any certainty that secret agents in the Black Book addendum were being picked off.

But supposing, just supposing, there *was* an attack on two
fronts, it would be naive not to consider a possible link. The
obvious line might be the one Templeman was taking – a collaboration between Nazi and Japanese diehards.

Wilde made coffee and settled down in the hallway with the
phone. First he booked a call to his old friend Jim Vanderberg in
the State Department in Washington, DC. His room-mate from
Chicago University many moons ago. They hadn't seen each
other since Berlin in December 1941, just before America entered
the war.

When he finally got through, the time lag between speaking and
reply made the call difficult. But Vanderberg had useful information: Donovan was presently in Germany. 'He was going to Berlin
first, then Nuremberg, Tom. I'll get the numbers for you.'

Half an hour later, Vanderberg called back. 'I'm told he's
already in Nuremberg.' He gave Wilde the number, then they
exchanged pleasantries and family news and promised to communicate more extensively by airmail. 'And I hope to be over in
London by the end of the year, Tom. Can't wait to see you and
Lydia and your beautiful boy.'

'Likewise, our love to Juliet. Bring her with you – and stay here
with us in Cambridge.'

'Sounds like a fine offer, Tom.'

Finishing off his black coffee, Wilde tried to place a call to
Germany. That was less easy but he eventually got through to
Donovan's office in the Nuremberg courthouse; having lost the
directorship of the OSS it seemed he was now to bring his legal
expertise to bear as a prosecuting attorney in the impending
trials.

'Good to hear from you, Tom. How's university life treating you?'

'Well, I gave my first lecture yesterday, Bill. That was fine.
But there have been some strange events. I could do with your
advice and assistance.' He gave a shortened version of the situation at Flowthorpe and his conversation with Lord Templeman.

'Anyway, he clearly needs to know who's behind this attack – if it *is* an attack – otherwise there may be worse to come.'

'And you naturally thought of Unit 731. What a damned sewer of a place.'

'I told Dagger all I knew, but he wants more.'

'Did you tell him about Ryoichi Naito and his link to Berlin?'

'I did because it seemed relevant. Templeman wants to know everything I can discover about possible collaboration between German and Japanese microbiologists.'

'Well, the Nazis were certainly carrying out biological experiments in their camps, but it wasn't a priority, and they were some way behind Shiro Ishii and his diabolical crew in applying their knowledge. I don't think we have any proof that the Germans got as far as devising a workable bio-weapon. You know we've got some of these dirty Nazi doctors in custody and we'll be putting the worst of them on trial in the months to come. We may find out more then, but I realise you need information sooner rather than later. Let me ask around here.'

'Thanks, Bill. And I guess there'll be a trial involving the Japanese doctors, too.'

'Well, you'd certainly hope so. But don't hold your breath.'

'That doesn't sound promising.'

'Just a whisper I've heard, Tom. Realpolitik. If the Japanese doctors have valuable information, trades might be done. We've been doing much the same with German scientists, as I'm sure you're aware. Protecting them from prosecution in return for working for us. Well, who's to say we won't do the same with the ghastly Unit 731 guys. If you want my opinion, it stinks.' A heavy sigh came down the line from Nuremberg. 'Jesus,' Donovan said, 'this thing you've told me about the possibility of a plague bomb – it's exactly why we need a centralised intelligence-gathering agency. Truman just doesn't get it.'

'He's left America naked.'

'In a blizzard. And you know what, I've got to confess I was hurt bad when Truman closed us down. He didn't even have the grace to tell me in person. Deputed his goddamned budget director, Harold Smith, to do it. His budget director of all people! But even that time-serving sonofabitch didn't have the balls to front me up – and sent his own assistant Donald Stone to do the deed. We've been betrayed by our own side. Thousands of unbelievably brave and clever men and women told to sling their hook.'

Wilde could feel the anger and disappointment radiating down the line from Germany. He didn't know what to say because he knew that Donovan was right and there were no words to lessen the sense of betrayal.

'I know, I know,' Donovan continued. 'I'm ranting. I'm an old soldier, probably over the hill, bemoaning the new generation like some damned blimp. But they're wrong and I'm right.'

'They'll learn soon enough.'

'Will they? What matters is that Truman gets his act together quickly so the hard-won expertise is still there. Anyway, that's enough about my problems. I'll put through some calls for you to our former colleagues who worked in the Far East OSS stations and maybe try to get to Sanders at Camp Detrick, if he's still there.'

'Thank you.'

The phone clicked dead. The handset felt burning hot in Wilde's fingers. Lydia arrived just as he put it down.

'Interesting call, Tom?'

'Sort of.'

'Well, I also had an interesting call this morning from Isabel Parsons at St Ursula's Hospital Medical School. She wants me to go up to town first thing in the morning. It seems a last-minute place has come up for a medical student and she thought I might be interested. Can you imagine? It could really happen.'

Wilde tried to smile, but he was worried. She had been disappointed before in her quest to become a doctor. It seemed very few medical schools were willing to accept women, and a married woman was completely out of the question.

'I can see it in your face, Tom. You think they're going to turn me down because I'm married and a mother and practically in my dotage. But Isabel has a plan. I'm not going to say anything about you or Johnny, and she assures me I'll pass for early twenties.'

Well that was true enough. 'But won't they make checks?'

'Let's hope not. I'm applying in my maiden name, Morris – Miss Lydia Morris. If I'm caught, I'll be sacked. But if not, well, I'll be a doctor and I'll be able to save lives and do something useful with my life. And if it's you and Johnny you're worried about, don't be. I've found a live-in nanny-cum-housekeeper. She's very sweet and she can cook. You'll meet her this afternoon. And then I'm catching the train to London, because I'm meeting Isabel first thing tomorrow and, all being well, I'll be interviewed.'

For a few moments they stood looking at each other, then he laughed and took her in his arms and held her tight. How the hell was he going to tell her that her life might be in danger? And did he even believe it anyway?

The new housekeeper arrived at 2.30 p.m. Her name was Sylvia Keane and she was twenty-eight, a few years younger than Lydia. She had been interviewed for the post two months earlier when Lydia was applying to St Bartholomew's Hospital. Unfortunately, Mrs Keane had not been able to supply references, as she had not done work of that nature before, but Lydia had liked her and, most importantly, had trusted her. However, the process had come to nothing as Lydia's hopes of doing a medical degree had been shut down by a cold rejection from Bart's without even the courtesy of an interview, but she had kept Sylvia's details.

'Her husband was killed on D-Day,' Lydia had informed Wilde over lunch. 'She has a small daughter, about three, I think, so she's certain to be fine with Johnny. Most importantly, she has a kind face. I hope you like her, but not too much.'

'But should you be raising her hopes before you're accepted?'

'I can't face the interview process in London unless I'm sure Johnny will be well looked after. If we're all agreed on Sylvia Keane, I'll have the freedom I need simply to be Miss Lydia Morris again.'

It seemed an absurd idea to Wilde. But that wasn't unusual for Lydia, the woman who had once stood him up at the altar before finally tying the knot a couple of years later. As with all Lydia's insane projects, there was a glimmer of hope, and it was pointless arguing with her. Anyway, perhaps she *could* become a doctor; she'd certainly put her heart into it and would be an excellent practitioner.

Lydia was upstairs packing an overnight bag when the bell rang. Wilde answered the door to a tall slender woman clutching the hand of a small child.

'You must be Sylvia Keane.'

She acknowledged that she was, indeed, the candidate for housekeeper, and responded to his words of welcome with possibly the warmest smile he had ever encountered.

'And this is Penelope,' she said.

Wilde bent down and offered his hand to the little girl. She took it shyly and they shook hands.

'Well, come in, Mrs Keane. I'll just call Lydia down and we can all have a chat and a cup of tea. How does that sound?'

'That would be lovely.'

'And may I say how sorry I was to learn of the loss of your husband. It is a great tragedy for you and your daughter.'

'I can't pretend it has been easy, but one must be philosophical about these things, I suppose. Penelope will learn that her father died saving her from Hitler. She was only two at the time and will, sadly, have no memories of him.'

Lydia arrived and they all settled in the sitting room. Lydia handed the child one of Johnny's toys, a red racing car made from Meccano, and she happily began pushing it across the floor.

Wilde realised he had to dampen expectations. 'I'm sure my wife has made it clear to you that this isn't certain yet, Mrs Keane.'

She seemed surprised. 'Oh,' she said.

'It's as good as certain,' Lydia said. 'My husband is just being his usual cautious self. Doesn't like counting chickens.'

For a moment Wilde thought that the putative housekeeper was about to cry. It was clear to him that she was setting great store by Lydia's offer of a job. He felt he really had to take some sort of control of the situation by injecting a bit of harsh reality.

'What are your circumstances at the moment, Mrs Keane?' he asked, offering her a biscuit.

'We're living in a small hotel called the Regency Arms, not far from the station. Just one room with breakfast and supper. It's not the best place to bring up a child, but it's all I could get for two pounds twelve shillings and sixpence a week. We have been left with very little money, you see.'

Wilde could tell from her accent and demeanour that she came from a middle-class background in the south of England and he could see that she was ashamed to be revealing her reduced circumstances. He felt great sympathy for her. He wondered how many other widowed young mothers of all classes were struggling to survive. An idea was formulating in his head for a sort of trial run. 'Well, look, would it be asking a lot of you to stay here for a night or two while Mrs Wilde is away in London talking to the hospital? We'd pay you for the inconvenience, of course, and we'd see how we all get on.'

Lydia immediately seized on the suggestion. 'And perhaps you could cook some supper for the men. It would be a weight off my mind because Tom's not much of a chef, and it will be one less thing for me to worry about.'

'Yes, I could do that,' Sylvia said.

'Well, Tom will be driving me to the station shortly, so you could come along, too, and pick up your toothbrushes and nighties from the hotel. How does that sound?'

'That would suit me very well. Thank you.'

At the station, Lydia was still in a state of high anticipation for what awaited her in London. Wilde walked her onto the concourse to say goodbye and wish her well while Sylvia and her daughter remained in the car. Lydia clutched her husband's hand. 'You will let me know about May, won't you? Please tell me she's all right.'

'I'll get in touch with Templeman when I get home. Call me this evening from your hotel and I'll let you know all I can find out. And, Lydia, there was one other thing I have to mention.

It will probably sound like silly alarmist nonsense to you but it seems we're in the Black Book after all.'

'Hitler's *Sonderfahndungsliste*?'

'Yes. An addendum to the main list. About two hundred and fifty names.'

'Gosh, what fun. I can't wait to tell everyone. I felt so left out!'

'The point is, Templeman told me that one of his agents on the addendum list has been murdered and another's missing. He seems concerned that there might be some kind of connection and suggested we take precautions.'

For a moment she became serious. 'Are you worried, Tom?'

Was he? He still wasn't sure. 'I don't know. Dagger Templeman's job is to take obscure threats seriously. It's what MI5 does. Of course I would imagine we'd be a long way down any list because there must be far more important people than us. Templeman's on it and he doesn't seem too worried for his own safety. I'm not going to run away and hide, but it's best to be aware, don't you think?'

'Message received.'

But he could tell she wasn't worried in the slightest. Her mind was elsewhere.

CHAPTER 8

When Johnny got back from school, he and Penelope hit it off instantly. As the elder of the two, he decided he was the boss and Penelope seemed happy to go along with all his ideas for games. Above all, Wilde supposed, she was just pleased to be in a proper house for the evening, rather than stuck in a rather wretched hotel room.

Picking up their things for the night, Wilde had not been impressed by the grandly named Regency Arms. The entrance hall had peeling wallpaper and smelt of overboiled cabbage. There was a general air of decay and despair about the place. If Sylvia was paying £2 12s 6d a week for bed and board here, she was being overcharged.

But, of course, that was the way of things all over the country. The rubble was still there, the bombed houses had not been rebuilt and water mains went unfixed. Britain was broke, as were many – perhaps most – of its inhabitants.

For supper, Sylvia cooked shepherd's pie, which was mostly potato, plus peas and sprouts. It tasted pretty good, thought Wilde. Later, when the children were in bed she stayed in the kitchen expertly knitting her daughter a little pink cardigan. Wilde offered her a glass of wine, but she declined.

'Won't you tell me a little about yourself, Mrs Keane?'

'There's not much to tell really. I was born and brought up in Surrey, an only child. Daddy was deputy manager of a local bank and Mummy was a housewife. They were respectable but not very well off.'

'Are they still alive?'

'No. Daddy was only forty when he died of a heart attack. Mummy never really recovered . . .'

He could tell that he was entering painful territory and changed the subject. 'And how did you end up in Cambridge?'

'My husband, Duncan, hailed from Ely. I wanted to be close to him. Silly really.'

'Does he have family there?'

She shook her head. It occurred to him that perhaps she had never hit it off with Duncan's parents or siblings. But that seemed unlikely, for Sylvia Keane was an easy person to like.

'Was he in the army before the war?'

'Yes, he was a career soldier, an officer of the old school.'

'And your widow's pension?' he said. 'I don't suppose it goes very far.'

She looked down at the table and shook her head despondently.

'Forgive me for prying. I know it's none of my business.'

'That's all right.' She looked up and smiled at him. 'I've got to stop feeling sorry for myself.'

'It seems to me that you have every right to feel sorry for yourself. The least any country can do is look after those who are left behind when they call on young men to sacrifice their lives for the common good.'

'I don't care about myself. It's Penelope. Living with me in a tiny hotel room is not the way a little girl should be brought up. I'm sorry, Professor Wilde, you must think I'm an awful moaner. I'm sure there are many people a great deal worse off than me.'

'Please stop saying sorry. If you are on your uppers, you have nothing to apologise for. It can happen to all of us. Anyway, it seems to me that you are managing to raise a delightful little girl in extremely difficult circumstances, and that you have a lot to congratulate yourself about.'

'I'm sorry—' She laughed. 'I mean, you're right – no more sorries.'

He thought a tear had come to her eye as she laughed. 'I only asked you about yourself because I was interested,' he said. 'So let me return the favour. I'm not sure what Lydia has told you about me, but I am an American citizen. My father is long gone but my mother is still with us. She's Irish by birth but now lives in Boston, Massachusetts. My subject is history, especially Elizabeth and the European conflicts of the late sixteenth century.'

'The Tudors? Oh, I loved the Tudors at school. They were all so dashing and romantic. All those doublets and hose . . . throwing their capes into the mud so Elizabeth's dainty feet shouldn't get soiled.'

'Actually, the Tudors were a pretty deadly bunch of gangsters if you want my honest opinion. Al Capone in cloth-of-gold, swords and daggers rather than tommy guns.'

That made her laugh again. 'You obviously know them a lot better than I do.'

The phone rang and broke into their conversation. He excused himself and went to the hall. It was Dagger Templeman. Wilde had left a message for him to call earlier in the evening.

'Any word on Unit 731, Tom?'

'I've talked to Bill Donovan. He's mightily pissed off about Truman and the OSS business, but he's going to make a couple of calls for us.'

'Well, keep me in the loop.'

'Actually, I wanted to know the news about our friend, May Hinchley. I think it was Rogers, your butler, I spoke to – did he mention it?'

'Indeed. And yes, I have been told that Miss Hinchley is making progress, but that she is not in the clear yet. Apparently recovery is a slow process for those fortunate enough to survive the damned disease. I'm afraid that's all the doctors would say.'

'Thank you, Dagger.' He understood that doctors were always cautious when giving an update on a patient. It was all too easy for someone to experience a sudden reversal and deteriorate rapidly. Best not to raise the hopes of relatives and friends. 'And the Flowthorpe situation generally?'

The sound of a long sigh came down the line, like the whisper of a breeze beneath a door. 'I'm afraid I can't really tell you a lot about that, old man.'

Wilde took it to mean that the news wasn't good. 'Perhaps I could drop in on you when Bill gets back to me.'

'Do that, Tom.'

'Also, I'd like to ask a few more questions about this Black Book thing. You didn't really give much away. Who was killed? How? When? What's the link to the missing man?'

'Good questions. There's something else, too, something I should have mentioned before. But let's not talk about it on an open phone line, eh?'

When Wilde came down in the morning, Sylvia had already given the children breakfast and had Johnny ready for school.

'Well everything seems to be under control here, Mrs Keane.'

'Could I pour you some coffee? And would you like some toast?'

'Yes, please, that would be splendid. Did you talk to Mrs Wilde about Johnny's school?'

'I said I would take him. She wrote a note for his teacher explaining who I am.'

'I'm assuming Mrs Wilde has discussed pay with you?'

'Indeed, she has, sir. By the way, Professor, do you have any idea when Mrs Wilde will hear whether or not she's to be accepted?'

'I'm afraid not. These things can obviously take time when there's a lot riding on it. We may get a clue later today, but I doubt whether there will be a decision. Either way, I'll let you know if I hear anything. And thank you for coming here at such short notice.'

'It's our pleasure. Penelope slept better than she has in weeks.'

Dr Gertrude Blake was an imposing figure, a stout woman of middle years with a loud, clear voice and formidable good looks. It occurred to Lydia that if she had taken another road through life, Dr Blake might have been an opera singer. She inhabited an untidy wood-panelled office packed with medical books, some piled up, others scattered across every available surface – desk, shelves, chairs, window ledge and much of the floor. A human skeleton dangled from a chain attached to the ceiling.

Lydia was more nervous than she had anticipated. She had already had a weak cup of coffee with her old friend from Girton, Dr Isabel Parsons.

'She looks and sounds fierce, but she's a dear,' Isabel had assured Lydia. 'Just be confident, answer questions with precision and clarity and she'll love you. But on no account admit you are married or a mother.'

Now she was meeting Dr Blake in the flesh, and the reality was even more daunting than she had feared.

'Why do you want to be a physician?' Dr Blake said without any sort of preamble.

'My father was a doctor. I always admired him.'

'*Was* a doctor?'

'He's dead, killed by a shell in the last year of the First World War. It landed in the middle of the field hospital where he was working. He was a Quaker.'

'As was our founder, Dorothy Blackmore, of course.'

'I didn't know that, Dr Blake. Anyway, I believe my father was very brave, working in terrible conditions at Passchendaele. My mother died in 1919 from the flu.'

'I won't ask you how old you are because I don't see the relevance of age, so long as you are under forty and your brain is intact. You look fit and strong, but you're clearly not a slip of a girl any more, Miss Morris. What kept you so long?'

'I wanted to be a poet. I started a little publishing company with the money I inherited.'

'An honourable calling. Do you have any background in the sciences?'

'At school, I did well at chemistry and mathematics, and I was also above average in physics, botany and biology. Perhaps I could have excelled in those subjects, but my mind was distracted by literature. I still have my reports somewhere but I'm afraid I didn't think to bring them.'

Dr Blake was sitting at her desk and Lydia was standing, clasping her hands together nervously. Her eyes kept drifting to the skeleton, which seemed to move, caught in a breeze from the half-open window.

'Sit down, Miss Morris. It strains my neck to look up at you. And never mind the school reports. I'll take your word for it.'

Lydia shuffled the books from the only available seat and plonked them at her side on the floor.

'Now then,' Dr Blake continued, 'you must realise that medicine is largely a practical discipline involving bodily fluids and unpleasant suppurations, gross deformities and pain. Does that worry you? What do you think of blood? Are you squeamish?'

'Blood doesn't worry me.'

'Not even if it's gushing from an artery like a fountain?'

'Well, I wouldn't choose to witness that, but I would cope.'

'St Ursula's is a women's hospital, of course, but when you are qualified – if you qualify – you might find yourself working elsewhere with men and their curious anatomies. How do you feel about that?'

'I am not a virgin if that's what you mean.'

Gertrude Blake stared at her hard, then her ferocious face broke into a smile. 'I suppose I must take that as a plus. Now then, Miss Morris, you come to me on the recommendation of Dr Parsons, in whose judgement I have great faith. I'm not going to ask you what you know because we will teach you everything you need to know. Nor will I give you a written test because you obviously have the Higher School Certificate and as you are a Girton girl I must assume you are capable of listening and learning and working extremely hard.'

Lydia nodded. 'Given the chance, I would do my utmost.'

'Which is important because, you see, St Ursula's may be only sixty-nine years old, but we strive to maintain the highest standards and we guard our reputation jealously.'

'I understand.' She was about to mention that she had read *Black's Medical Dictionary* from cover to cover twice, but thought better of it. Dr Blake wanted a blank canvas to work on, not someone who imagined they already knew everything.

'And have you a long-term view on which branch of medicine you would like to enter? Many of our young women specialise in gynaecology, obstetrics and paediatrics. Are those your concerns?'

'I am leaning towards general practice, but I am also very interested in psychiatry.'

'Well, you need to understand the mind for both those disciplines, but you will have to address the physical nature first, the vile body. All doctors do. Let's take you to the mortuary to see whether you blanch at the sight of mortality, then I shall introduce you to some real live patients and some of my colleagues and we'll take it from there. You should know that I value two qualities above all else: character and ability.'

Lydia had rather imagined she would be interviewed by a committee and perhaps be set a test. She knew that University College had devised such a test for women applicants in recent years.

As if reading her mind, Dr Blake said, 'You may have heard that some medical schools are introducing admission tests, but we do not believe that is the way to go. You may also be wondering who makes the decision on your future. I will be meeting with a small committee and if I think you have what it takes, I shall recommend you. And then it is for the committee to decide. In practice, they will accept my recommendation. One more question: would you be able to start immediately – on Monday?'

'Yes,' she said without hesitation or careful consideration of the practicalities of such a decision. Today was Friday, so that meant just a weekend at home. This might be her only chance, and she wasn't going to lose it.

'Dr Parsons tells me you would not require financial assistance, is that correct?'

'My parents left me financially secure.'

'Well, I am sure you would be able to afford a nice flat in Kensington, but I won't allow that. You would be required to join the other girls in our hostel.'

'Of course.'

'I should tell you that this student place has come up because of the sudden death of the girl who was to have come here. She died in a motoring accident last week, which is a great tragedy for her family. Poor girl, I selected her in June and she was to have started two days ago. Just eighteen years old.'

'I'm so sorry to hear that. All Isabel told me was that an opening had appeared.'

'Well, it would be a shame to let a place go unfilled, but there could be no delay, because we don't want anyone falling behind. There were three other girls I considered, but they have secured places elsewhere. Which leaves you, Miss Morris.'

'If you were to accept me, I wouldn't let you down.'

'Good, because if you did, I wouldn't hesitate to throw you out on your ear. And you might do well not to mention the loss of your virginity among your fellow students, or you will be deluged with requests for advice, for they will most certainly still be intact.'

Perhaps it might count as a public service to help them, Lydia wondered, though she decided against articulating the thought.

CHAPTER 9

Wilde was walking across the Old Court towards his rooms when he saw that Danny Oswick was heading in his direction around the flagstone path. He didn't really want to talk to the young man then and there, but had no way of avoiding him.

'Professor Wilde, I was hoping to catch you.'

'Good morning, Oswick. I'm afraid I'm rather busy this morning.'

'That's all right, sir, I won't keep you a moment.' He produced a book from under his arm and Wilde saw immediately that it was his own biography of Sir Robert Cecil, the book seemingly beloved of Sir Neville Catesby. 'I was wondering whether you would do me the honour of signing my copy.'

'Of course, but why not bring it to our supervision? Then I'll have a flat surface on which to write.'

'Oh, yes, indeed – I hadn't thought of that.'

'Until then, Oswick. And remember, Conyers Read is the man to study. You'll find all his works in the library.' God preserve us, thought Wilde as he turned away from the young army officer with his flamboyant moustache, Oswick was the type of undergraduate all dons dreaded – the overfamiliar ones desperately trying to make their mark. There were the other ones, too, those who tried to gain advancement by family or professional connections. In a word, nepotism. Oswick with his link to Catesby fitted in both camps. Such tactics were wasted on Wilde. His undergraduates could only succeed by letting their essays do the talking; that was all that mattered.

Wilde spent the morning reading his notes on the Jesuits in late Tudor England, the men who took their lives into their hands to tend their Catholic flocks in great secrecy at a time when the new Protestant Church held sway and slaughtered any priests coming into the country from France or Rome. It was a story of intolerance and brutality, a tale that demonstrated the dark underbelly of Elizabeth's otherwise glorious reign.

The telephone rang shortly before lunch. 'I have a call from Germany,' the switchboard operator said. 'Will you take it, sir?'

'Put him through.'

Bill Donovan was in slightly better humour than during their last call. 'I'm sorry I went on at you, Tom. But you were one of us, I thought you'd understand and I needed to get it off my chest.'

'That's OK, Bill. I feel the same way.'

'Anyway, Unit 731. I've got some interesting stuff for you. We know they worked with plague, malaria, cholera, anthrax, smallpox and various other nasties. Some ceramic bomb-shaped containers were discovered and it is assumed that they were the delivery systems when the bio-weapons were used in China. It seems that a conventional bomb made of iron or steel would have to explode with such force that the bacteria or virus or whatever was inside would probably be destroyed. With a ceramic bomb, a relatively soft detonation would splinter the shell and release the germs intact, in a cloud of droplets that would drift gently down over a wide area. That's my understanding anyway.'

'So we need to find a cache of ceramic bombs.'

'Or some kind of aerosol equipment by which the bacteria could be sprayed.'

'And any word on collaboration with Germany?'

'Now that's where it becomes really interesting. There's a guy called Kurt Blome, worked at Dachau and Buchenwald concentration camps. He's already in the custody of US Counter Intelligence Corps here in Germany and is expected to stand trial and swing for his crimes at a later date. He has told us about extensive collaboration between Germany and Japan.'

'How did they communicate?'

'Wire, mainly. Encrypted, of course. But also by submarine. Japan sent technical information, specimens of their weapons and even some of their research scientists to Germany throughout the war. It worked the other way, too. Blome says the last sub left Germany for Japan with specialist medical equipment in May this year.'

'The very last week of European hostilities!'

'Indeed. Several names came up of those involved. Our old chums Shiro Ishii and Ryoichi Naito, of course, as well as Hojo Enryo, a doctor in the Imperial Army. He was a frequent visitor to the Robert Koch research institute in Berlin. Shiro Ishii himself is fluent in German and spent at least two years in Germany before the war. On the German side, the big names included Blome and a fellow named Sigmund Rascher. Rascher is now dead, shot by his own side in Dachau in the last days of the war. I'm not entirely sure why. Anyway, there must have been others – their collaboration on biological warfare, in fact all manner of medical affairs, harks back to the beginning of the century. The Japanese learnt a lot from studying German medicine and technology. In the end, the roles were reversed and they were giving the Nazis research data from their heinous experiments at Unit 731. The point is, the links are there, and they're strong.'

'Is Blome cooperating?'

'Apparently. Desperate to save his skin. Offering us the results of his research.'

'Then can you get the CIC to interrogate him further, about any knowledge he might have regarding a plan to attack Britain?'

'Good idea. He's being held over at Frankfurt – in Kransberg Castle. I might make time to go and talk to the fellow myself. I could do with a break from all this legal stuff. I'll let you know.'

As Wilde put the phone down, there was a knock at his door. It was Bobby.

'You've got a visitor, Professor Wilde. A very tall gentleman by the name of Lord Templeman.'

Templeman here? Well, well, what a surprise. He thought His Lordship always insisted on being the mountain rather than Mohammed. 'Bring him up, Bobby.'

Thirty seconds later, Templeman appeared at the doorway, ducking his six foot seven frame under the arch. 'So this is where you work, Tom. Very cosy. I imagine you have a good view.'

'It'll be even nicer when the gardeners cast off their army fatigues and get to grips with the Old Court. It was rather scarred by a vast water tank during the war years. Lawn hasn't recovered yet and there has been little in the way of floral decoration.'

Bobby was hovering at the door. 'Can I get you gentlemen anything?'

'Well, actually, I was just thinking of lunch,' Wilde said. 'Would you care to join me in Hall, Dagger? We can find a quiet corner to talk.'

'An excellent idea.'

Wilde caught the gyp's eye. He was in the doorway, half hidden behind Templeman. 'Bobby?'

'I shall go and tell them to expect you gentlemen in a few minutes' time.'

'This is a remarkable place,' Templeman said as they took their seats at the end of high table. Few dons were there, so they were able to position themselves at a generous distance from the other diners and speak freely.

'The Hall is early Tudor, built a few years before the delightful Combination Room, which I must also show you. It is a place of secrets. The college itself is rather earlier, mid-fourteenth century – even older than your own home, I should imagine.'

Wilde rarely ate here, but usually enjoyed it – particularly on formal occasions. It was a glorious space hung with portraits of eminent members of the college, going back centuries and culminating with the present master, Sir Archibald Spence, who was not present in the flesh this day. He was, of course, just another face in a long line that would presumably carry on for many more centuries.

Murmuring voices echoed from the towering walls, along with the constant tap-tap of the shoes of the serving men, one of whom approached them to take their order. Neither of them wanted wine. Templeman asked for a gin and vermouth and Wilde opted for a small Scotch.

'So where do we start?'

'I've heard back from Bill Donovan. There was indeed a strong bio-warfare cooperation between Germany and Japan. They not only communicated by wire, but shuttled personnel by submarine throughout the war years.'

'Any suggestion that Japanese weapons were freighted to the Germans during these submarine trips?'

'Samples, certainly. No word on whether weapons were actually transported.' He filled in Templeman with the rest of the detail he had acquired from Donovan. 'And now Bill hopes to head off to Frankfurt to talk to this man Blome, so he might produce more.'

'Well, that's a great help, Tom. It's information our own secret services might not have put together in a hurry. Do give Bill my thanks when you speak to him. He has always been a marvellous friend to Britain – I doubt we could have won the war without him.'

Wilde knew it was true. Bill Donovan had persuaded President Roosevelt to ignore the defeatists like Ambassador Joe Kennedy who believed Britain could not withstand the Nazis and should be abandoned to its fate. He had also campaigned for an American version of MI6, and had founded the OSS in its image. Only to see Truman destroy their work.

'America has been utterly misguided in discarding what Bill and the rest of you built up,' Templeman continued. 'As an Englishman, I worry that we will both be left a great deal weaker and more exposed in the years to come.'

Wilde swirled his whisky. 'Time will tell. But to get back to Flowthorpe. Do you have any evidence that this incident had something to do with the Japanese and their research unit?'

Templeman shrugged. 'Pure conjecture at the moment, I'm afraid. However, it's the obvious place to look, given what we know.'

'But if the germs were supplied by Unit 731, they must have local assistance of some kind. You don't see many Japanese faces in England these days.'

'Actually, Tom, that brings me on to something else I wanted to discuss with you. Of course there has to be a local organisation, but who? British fascists almost certainly, but which ones?'

Wilde was surprised. 'British fascists? Really? They're goners, aren't they? Surely they've seen the error of their ways by now.'

'You'd think so. But who else in Britain would be collaborating with Nazis or the Japanese Imperial Army? Or both? The problem is that the British fascists are as restless as the sea, endlessly switching loyalties, fighting among themselves, forging new groupings.

We try to watch them closely but they're an elusive, tricky bunch. A real headache for both MI5 and Special Branch.'

The soup arrived and Wilde looked at it dejectedly. It was thin, grey and unappetising. He smiled an apology at Templeman. 'The fare was a great deal more interesting back in thirty-nine.'

'Don't worry, old chap. Anyone who has been to boarding school would consider this a gourmet feast.'

'You mentioned the British fascists, Dagger. They were mostly interned, weren't they?'

'Oh yes, we know who most of them are. But they are free now, and there are still thousands of them. We can't intern them all again.' Templeman tapped the oak table with his long index finger. 'Believe it or not, there are presently over fifty fascist organisations in this country. They have all sprung up like weeds since the ending of internment and the demise of the British Union of Fascists.'

'More than fifty groups? That's appalling.'

'Fifty-five at the last count, but that has probably changed again today and will probably change again by tomorrow. Most are very small, which may weaken them, but also doesn't help us because it is difficult to keep track of them. Put together, they still have a large number of members, mostly driven by their unhinged anti-Semitism. They are a many-headed serpent and they harbour deep resentment at Hitler's defeat and their own imprisonment and impotence.'

'And you think one or more of these groups could be involved?'

'I couldn't say, but it's an obvious possibility, isn't it? And there's something else: the Black Book. You know, Tom, in my spare time, I am a keen betting man – nothing I like more than a hefty wager at Newmarket or Ascot – and I tell you this, I'd bet a lot of money that this is connected to the recent Black Book killing.'

'The addendum. God, I hadn't taken your warning that seriously, Dagger. The Colt's still locked away – and Lydia as good as laughed at me when I mentioned it to her.'

'Quite understandable. I find it hard to worry about it myself. But I fear we might both be deluding ourselves.'

The soup plates were removed and more fare arrived, this time a roast platter with golden, crisp potatoes, cabbage and thin slices of beef.

'Is this just a hunch, Dagger – the connection to the Black Book?'

'An educated hunch. It's all we've got to go on at the moment.'

Wilde knew the British secret services well enough to understand that Dagger Templeman's hunch was based on some piece of evidence which he was not imparting.

He knew, too, that this visit was no social call. He was here because he wanted something, and that he, Tom Wilde, was firmly on the hook; like it or not, he was part of this now. His visit to Flowthorpe, the terrifying experience of their friend May Hinchley, and his name in the Black Book addendum had made sure of that.

'What do you want me to do?'

'It's all hands to the pump, Tom.'

'I gathered that.'

'Some of our best agents are already working on this. We have men and women inside some of the fascist groups, but not enough, and they are making painfully slow progress. So any help you can provide would be greatly appreciated.'

'Of course. I'll push Bill Donovan for whatever he can get from Germany. He's eager to assist.'

'I want a bit more than that. A person of interest has recently come into your orbit. One of your new students, believe it or not. A young army officer named Daniel Oswick.'

'Oswick?' Wilde couldn't conceal his incredulity. 'I thought he was supposed to be some kind of war hero.'

'We have new information on the man, and he worries us.'

'I'm sure you'll give me a bit more explanation than that. Why would he have come to Cambridge if he's some kind of insurgent or revolutionary?'

Templeman shrugged his angular shoulders. 'We don't know but we can guess. To acquire something he never had, perhaps – respectability. A Cambridge history degree would go jolly well with young Oswick's war record. Whitewashing his past. We believe he has big plans – as do his sponsors.'

Wilde was surprised. 'I must say I hadn't seen him in such a light. I still don't.'

'You expect them all to be lowlifes. But that's where you're wrong. The movement, if you can call it that, is full of aristocrats and senior military men, even professors. Anyway, it seems that Oswick had an important role in Mosley's lot before the war but somehow slipped under our radar.'

'Go back a bit, Dagger; tell me more about these fascist groups . . .'

'Where do I start, Tom? I can't list them all, but to name just a few off the top of my head, you've got the British People's Party, English Array, De Profundis, British Reich, National Front After Victory and one of the nastiest, the BVAL – Britons' Vigilantes Action League.' He was counting them off on his fingers. 'What's that, half a dozen? The list goes on ad nauseam. Some have supposedly closed down, but we know they're still there, just beneath the surface.'

'Are they all much of a muchness?'

'Some are talkers, others are doers. Mostly the former. Some don't even consider themselves fascists or Nazis.' He laughed. 'Eventually they have a punch-up, sometimes verbal, often physical, over some pathetic policy disagreement or personality clash and then they split apart and form yet more groupings. The thing they all seem to have in common is a visceral hatred of Jewish refugees.'

'And which group does Danny Oswick belong to?'

'Our latest information suggests he was originally a BUF fixer, collected huge sums for Mosley, but we didn't know that at the time.'

'Ah, Mosley. What's his role in these new movements?'

'He's keeping quiet, farming and writing at Crowood in Wiltshire, where he has a thousand acres. Still spouting anti-Semitic garbage, of course, but he seems to be waiting to see which way the wind blows before committing himself to any one group. Awaiting the call from a grateful nation to assume his rightful position as great dictator!'

'He must be connected to Oswick, surely?'

'It's extremely likely. The problem is we still don't know the full extent of Oswick's role with the BUF. His membership was only revealed to us in the last two weeks of the war.'

'How did that come about?'

'Well, as you can imagine, we had a couple of MI5 men embedded in the internment camps. In April, Oswick's name came up out of the blue. But by then he had acquitted himself well in the army and had a commission. So all we have been able to do is watch him from afar. He must have been one of the more clever ones to have avoided notice in the Blackshirt days.'

'What about Neville Catesby? He's been mentoring him.'

Templeman grimaced. 'That's a problem. He's always been close to Oswald Mosley – they were school friends – but we've never actually thought of him as a fascist and I don't suppose you have either.'

'No. I thought he swung more towards Stalin than Hitler.'

'We thought the same, so we reasoned that he had simply been taken in by Oswick. Well, you have been so far, haven't you?'

'I've only spoken to Oswick for about ten minutes in total and then not about politics, so I could hardly make any kind of judgement. You're not suggesting he had anything to do with the plague attack, are you?'

'I'm suggesting exactly that. Catesby, too. In fact, particularly Catesby. There's an obvious problem with him, though. He's so bloody well connected. He can call someone in Cabinet or even, I'm afraid, the intelligence services, and put a stop to any investigation at a moment's notice. We see your undergraduate Oswick as a way in.'

'There's something you're not telling me.'

Templeman slipped his hand into his inside pocket and pulled out a sheet of paper. It wasn't a written note, but in the time-honoured way of kidnappers and blackmailers, letters cut from newspapers had been pasted on.

PLAGUE *Catesby*

That was all it said.

'Good God. That really is something.'

'What do you make of it?'

'I'm stunned.'

'That's why I wanted you to keep an eye on Oswick. His connections to the fascists and his closeness to Catesby. We need to follow this up, and you're the only person I can call on who knows both men.'

'Do you have any idea who sent it?'

'Not a clue, except that it had to be sent by someone who knew about events at Flowthorpe, and also someone who knows or knows about Neville Catesby. Other than that, all I can tell you is that it arrived on my desk like that, by way of the Royal Mail, four days ago. The envelope was typed and has been sent for analysis in case it matches any on file. Nothing back so far. But the big thing is, we are pretty sure who our enemy is. I hate to do this to you, Tom, because I know you just want to get back to academia, but I need your help.'

'OK, I'll watch Oswick, though you have to keep me in the loop better. I want details of the Black Book, and I want access to Flowthorpe.'

'You're going there this afternoon. It's all arranged. Frank Broussard will introduce you to Paul Fildes, Britain's most senior biological warfare expert. A car will come here to get you at two.' Templeman consulted his watch. 'Half an hour from now.'

CHAPTER 10

The car dropped him outside The George and Dragon. Broussard was standing there in full USAF lieutenant colonel's uniform, waiting for him. The driver skirted the front of the vehicle to open the door for Wilde, but he had already done it for himself and was out, walking towards Broussard, who held out his hand to stop him.

'Stand a little way back from me and anyone else you meet. It's possible some of us are infected. I understand you're here in some official capacity this time, Professor Wilde. Good to have you back.'

'I won't say it's a pleasure, Lieutenant Colonel, given the circumstances.'

The men did not shake hands. Wilde noted that the officer was wearing long gloves.

'I'll get you protective wear, too,' Broussard said. 'Can I arrange coffee for you?'

'Perhaps in a while. I believe I'm to meet Mr Fildes.'

'Indeed. He's in a closed meeting with the doctors right now, but he'll be with us soon. Now then, let's get you dressed up like a Martian, Professor. I'm afraid it's essential if you want to talk to Miss Hinchley or any of the other patients – but mostly it's important for your own health. You don't want to inhale anyone else's breath and you don't want to be bitten by fleas. It's advisable to wear your trouser legs tucked into your socks and long gloves over the cuffs of your sleeves.' He proffered Wilde a pair of gloves.

Wilde put on the gloves and squeezed his trouser legs into his socks so they looked like plus-fours. 'Can I speak to May Hinchley first?'

'Sure thing. But be brief. I'm told she's weak.'

May Hinchley was asleep when he saw her, so it would have been cruel and senseless to wake her. But he could at least report back to Lydia that she looked peaceful and there was no evidence of swellings or pustules on her face.

The doctor at his side, a young man who barely looked out of his twenties, said, 'We have great hopes for Miss Hinchley.' Both he and Wilde were now wearing masks.

'She'll live?'

'She has a better chance than many. The fever has gone and she was clearly fit and strong and the right side of middle age. Beyond that, it would be foolish of me to promise anything. The recovery time is long.'

'May Hinchley means a great deal to my wife and me,' Wilde added.

The doctor's eyes creased up into a smile above his mask. 'She means a lot to us too, Mr Wilde.'

'Please tell her that I was here and that Lydia has been asking after her.'

'Of course.'

They left her bedside and made their way to the pub. One of Broussard's junior officers, who was not introduced, produced a flask of milky coffee from the airbase canteen and poured two cups. 'Sugar, Professor?'

'No thanks.' In fact, he didn't really want the coffee, not with milk in it anyway, but he was too polite to tell the young airman, who remained hovering at his senior officer's side. Wilde nodded to him and turned back to Broussard. 'Tell me, Lieutenant Colonel, you are obviously wondering whether the events here are connected to the nearby airbase. If this was an attack, do you think the USAF might have been the target?'

Broussard shrugged. 'It's one line of inquiry. But there are others.'

'You told me that there have been three deaths and some of your men had been affected.'

'Five deaths now, including one of my men. They're generally fitter and stronger than the villagers, who include quite a few of pensionable age. But there have been no new cases in the past twenty-four hours, so we're keeping our fingers crossed that we've got the thing beat.'

The door opened and a man in his sixties in a white coat stepped into the room. He was practically bald and what little hair he had was white. Broussard stood up but the man went straight past him and addressed Wilde. 'You're the Cambridge professor, yes?'

'Tom Wilde.' He stood up and offered his hand. 'Are you Fildes?'

The man nodded almost imperceptibly and ignored the hand. 'I'm told you're not a scientist but you're quite clever nonetheless. Well, I'll stick to laymen's terms.'

Paul Fildes clearly didn't do small talk. He had come here from the biology department at the Porton Down research establishment in Wiltshire with a two-man team whose task was to take samples and discover the precise nature of the outbreak, and its source.

'How much do you know about pathogens and biological warfare, Professor Wilde?'

'A little.'

'Well, if these pathogens have come any distance – from Japan, for instance – the time taken will be critical. I believe the Japanese have made great advances in applying stabilising coatings to the culture, but these will not be perfect. If this *Yersinia pestis* is still alive months after its production and encasement, then they have done a pretty fair job. We don't know of course how long ago the weapons were produced.'

'I think I understand.'

'Please don't interrupt me. I'm going to try to put events here into context. To do that I will tell you what we know about the Pingfang operation in Manchuria. It's a little sketchy because everything I know has been gleaned from my American contacts. I spent a considerable time at Camp Detrick during the war. You know about Detrick?'

Of course he did. He had been in the OSS. 'Some might think of it as America's version of Unit 731?'

Dr Fildes just frowned. 'Yes, I suppose you could draw a comparison between the two operations, the difference being that we didn't have the luxury of working with live experimental subjects.'

'Luxury?'

'That must sound to you like a poor choice of words. I am talking merely in scientific terms. Biological research is inevitably more accurate and expeditious when live human subjects are available. Think of our own Edward Jenner, who created the smallpox vaccine. He didn't hesitate to inject cowpox pus into an eight-year-old boy who fortunately survived and was then found to be immune to smallpox.'

'I believe the men and women at Unit 731 – Pingfang – weren't so fortunate.'

'Indeed not, they were all murdered. And so one must judge their research methods inhumane. But were their war aims and methods any worse than ours? Churchill was quite prepared to employ biological warfare against the German people on a vast scale using anthrax, though in the event he never did. And, as we now know, both Britain and America were complicit in detonating the atom bomb. The rationale of both methods of warfare? Huge loss of life.'

Wilde understood. The debate over criminal methods of research and criminal methods of warfare was not an easy one. And yet there was a difference. Wasn't there? God, he hoped there was, or what had he been fighting for?

'The Japanese operation was extremely sophisticated,' Fildes continued. 'Far more so than anything that's come out of Germany. Unit 731 began developing biological weapons before the war and the *Yersinia* pathogen was the one they seemed to favour, which obviously fits in with events here. Generally, the disease was dropped from aircraft when used against Chinese populations. It worked, up to a point. The problem was the haphazard, poorly targeted nature of the attacks.'

'What I need to know, Dr Fildes, is how certain we can be that the illness here at Flowthorpe was an attack rather than a naturally occurring event?'

Fildes looked Wilde straight in the eye. 'You're asking the right question. A naturally occurring event is an outside possibility. Anyone – airman or villager – might have brought the disease from abroad, especially if they had been to certain parts of Africa or Asia. But I don't believe that for a moment. We have had close links to those parts of the world for generations without the pathogen travelling here. So why would that occur now? No, this is an attack. I wish you well with your inquiries, Professor.'

With that, the microbiologist turned on his heel and exited the room.

Wilde turned to Broussard. 'Well, that was to the point.' *Succinct* was the word that came to mind.

'He doesn't waste words. Are you done here now, Professor?'

'No. I want to look around. I want a list of villagers and I would like to talk with some of your airmen.'

'Well, I can't allow you to do that.'

'I thought you were supposed to be assisting me.'

'But talking to servicemen would be outside the remit. They couldn't possibly discuss service matters with a civilian.'

So this was as far as cooperation went. Wilde had already marked Frank Broussard down as a time-server. And he knew it was pointless arguing with such people. The rule book was all; no deviation. 'And the villagers?'

'I have a copy of the electoral roll. Lord Templeman also has a copy, I believe, and has checked the names against known suspects.'

'What I most want to know is whether any of the names do not correspond with the patients, either living or dead. I mean, were there any strangers in the village in the days leading up to the first outbreak of the disease?'

'None recorded.'

'So everyone accounted for – either quarantined or lying in one of your makeshift wards or dead?'

'Yes, Professor.'

Broussard's junior officer put up a tentative finger. 'Actually, sir, there is the one man who still hasn't been traced . . .'

'Ah, yes, of course. It's assumed he is away visiting family or friends, or perhaps on a holiday break.'

'His name?'

'Lyngwood. Gram Lyngwood. We have called on him a number of times, but he has not been home. We had to break into his house to make sure he was not lying in bed sick, or deceased.'

'Let's go there now.'

'There's nothing to see.'

'Then it will be a very short visit.'

Lyngwood lived at number 18, The Street – one of only two roads in the village, the other being called Tree Lane. The door had not been fixed since being broken by Broussard's men, so Wilde pushed it open and allowed it to swing in the breeze.

It was an ancient cottage with a thatched roof, two doors down from May Hinchley's house and a hundred yards from The George and Dragon.

Wilde looked around the front room. A large wireless set dominated one corner and next to it there was a decent and quite new armchair. A sofa, too, and a couple of framed Victorian prints of rural scenes on one of the walls.

The fireplace was open and above it there was a mantelpiece with two pictures in silver frames, one of King George VI and his Queen, the other of a married couple that must have been taken before the First World War. It was probably Lyngwood's parents, thought Wilde, for he had been told that the man who lived here was about thirty.

'There's a small dining room and a tiny kitchen out the back.'

'I'll just wander around on my own, Lieutenant Colonel Broussard. I'm sure you have far more important things to do than escort me.'

'My orders are to stay with you.'

Wilde raised an eyebrow. 'Orders from America?'

'Let's just make this easy, shall we, Professor?'

Upstairs there were two bedrooms, a lavatory and a bathroom that had been squeezed in at the end of a short corridor. In the larger of the two bedrooms, drawers had been pulled open and were empty.

'Did your men do this?'

'No, it was like this when we came in.'

'So Mr Gram Lyngwood departed in a hurry.'

'I suppose he did. But we weren't that concerned about his movements. His absence simply meant we had one less villager – and one less patient – to worry us.'

'Have you searched outside? I take it there's a garden of sorts.'

'No, why would we have done that?'

Thoroughness, thought Wilde, but didn't say it. 'I think I'll take a quick look.'

The garden was long and narrow, about 200 feet by 40 feet. Halfway down, on the left, a large shed nestled beneath a silver birch and further on there was a small orchard of half a dozen trees, all laden with apples. Leaves were skittering in the breeze.

Wilde followed the path and came across some debris just beyond the shed. He guessed instantly what he was seeing and wondered how it could have been missed.

Shuffling his gloved hands up his sleeves, he stood back from the ceramic shards, then looked back at Broussard, who was standing in the kitchen doorway. 'You'd better come and see this, Lieutenant Colonel. I really don't think it's wise for me to touch it.'

'What is it?'

'Some sort of broken canister. There is writing on part of it which, to my untrained eye, looks very like Japanese characters.'

CHAPTER 11

'Have you spoken to any of Lyngwood's neighbours?'

'The old couple on the left between this house and Miss Hinchley's are both dead, but not of plague – they both died naturally last year. The young man on the right is a demobbed soldier, lost one of his legs at El Alamein. He's not infected and we've got him in quarantine on base. We have had no reason to interrogate him, up until now."

'Can we go and see him?'

'Of course.'

Wilde's first instinct was that the dark grey ceramic pieces were powerful – perhaps conclusive – evidence of Japanese involvement. His second thought was that the bomb – if that was what it was – hadn't been detonated but had been accidentally dropped and shattered, releasing its deadly load. The shards were not spread over a wide area, which would surely have happened if it had fallen from any great height or if there had been explosive force.

Broussard agreed with his assessment and summoned the Porton Down team, fully equipped in bio-hazard clothing, to remove the ceramic shards of the canister and examine what remained of its contents.

They had opened up the shed with great care, in case it contained more canisters or could be booby-trapped. But there was nothing of note. Garden tools, pots, daffodil bulbs and a bag of compost.

'And now we have to find Lyngwood. If this was an accident, then one must assume he hightailed it to preserve his own life because he knew the nature of the canister and also because he would be a wanted man.' Wilde was thinking out loud, trying to imagine events at this house, number 18, The Street, Flowthorpe. Either Lyngwood had been looking after the weapon for someone, or he was the one who intended to detonate it. But where? Surely this small, obscure Cambridgeshire village wasn't the intended target.

Toby Chandler looked up from his detective novel when Wilde and Broussard entered the room. He was sitting in an armchair, his remaining leg resting on an age-worn ottoman.

Wilde's eye immediately strayed to the place where Chandler's leg should have been.

'I can't stop looking at the bloody empty space either,' Chandler said, smiling. 'Excuse me if I don't get up, gentlemen.'

'Of course.' Broussard introduced Wilde and then the two visitors sat down. Chandler was occupying officers' quarters, rather more comfortable than the room in which Wilde had been confined, especially as it had a window.

'Before I went off to North Africa I got engaged,' Chandler said out of nowhere. 'I played hockey for the county and I had taken over my father's upholstery business. When I returned minus a leg, one look at her face told me everything I needed to know, and so I spared her the unpleasant task of calling off the engagement by doing so myself. The girl's gone, hockey's gone, and the business . . . . well, who's got any money for upholstery? God, I hate war.'

'I'm sorry,' Wilde said.

'We wanted to know about your neighbour,' Broussard said. 'Mr Gram Lyngwood.'

'Is he OK?'

'He's disappeared. We were wondering whether you might be able to describe him, tell us all you know about him.'

'Well, he was a neighbour, that's all. Harmless enough, I suppose, but we didn't get into any deep conversations, simply smiled and said hello when we passed each other or caught each other's eye over the garden fence.'

'And his appearance?' Wilde asked.

'He looked about thirty, I'd say, a little older than me. I rather assumed he survived the war and was trying to rebuild his life like the rest of us. I never saw him heading off to work, so I guessed he was unemployed. He had fair hair, not particularly good looking but neither was he ugly. The only unusual thing about him was that he wore a single gold earring, like a bloody pirate.

Broussard offered the man a cigarette, which he accepted.

'Did he have visitors?'

'I suppose he did. Yes, there was a bit of coming and going, usually in the evening after dark. I heard a car pull up occasionally. Oh, and there was the woman – a blonde. Shabbily glamorous if that means anything.' He smiled sheepishly. 'I saw her as I was hobbling home from The George and Dragon on my crutches and guessed she was his lady friend, but I only saw her the once, so perhaps she was a professional. Actually, I shouldn't say such things. Shouldn't ever speak ill of people unless they're called Hitler. Scrub that out, if you would.'

'We're not taking notes,' Wilde said. 'In your brief encounters with Lyngwood did he ever mention what he had done for a living in the past, or perhaps hoped to do?'

'Nothing.'

'How long have you lived in Flowthorpe, Mr Chandler?'

'All my life save my three years in the army. I inherited my house from my parents. I was born and brought up here.'

'And Lyngwood, I take it he's not a native of the village?'

'No. He arrived six or seven weeks ago. Bought the house at auction, I believe.'

'Did he ever mention where he came from?'

'London. He said he was from north London, which doesn't narrow it down much.'

'Politics?'

'God knows.'

'Religion? Did he go to church?'

'I've no idea, because I don't either. The war killed all the sky pilot stuff for me.'

'You said you sometimes exchanged pleasantries over the garden fence. What did Mr Lyngwood do in the garden?'

'Well, not much in the way of gardening. He pottered around in his shed, but I never saw him weeding or pruning. And he didn't bother with the muddy tangle of grass and moss he might like to have called a lawn.'

'Did you ever see him with a canister of any type?' Wilde held his arms out wide, about three feet apart. 'Made of some dark grey ceramic material.'

'Is that what's behind all this alarm?'

'I can't really tell you anything, I'm afraid.'

'Well, at least tell me this – when can I get out of here? It's beginning to feel like a POW camp.'

Wilde got home just before a taxi pulled up bringing Lydia from the station. He knew from her face that she had some good news. And yet, her broad grin was tinged with something else . . . doubt, perhaps.

'Well?' he demanded.

'They've taken me on. I'm going to become a doctor, Tom.'

'Are you serious?'

'Never more so. Isn't it wonderful?'

'Absolutely marvellous, darling. I'm so happy for you.'

Smiling broadly, he took her in his arms and held her tight, but his heart was sinking. He could never tell her the truth about his feelings nor try to dissuade her, but he really didn't want her going away for months and years on end. Johnny would be heartbroken, too.

He knew from his own time at boarding school that the English middle classes considered it entirely normal for parents to be separated from their children at an agonisingly young age. Five-year-olds, six-year-olds torn away from their mothers and sent into the care of strangers in cold institutions where the birch and cane ruled. It was a thing that Wilde and Lydia had decided they would never do with Johnny; he would go to a day school until at least the age of thirteen when he could decide for himself.

This was a bit like that, in that the boy would be separated from his mother, although without having to leave home and without the corporal punishment. And at least he would have his father and a maternal figure in the form of Sylvia Keane. But kindly though the woman appeared to be, she wasn't the boy's parent.

Why? That's what he couldn't understand. Why did Lydia have to take this course? What was so wrong with their family life here in Cambridge? Why hadn't she at least tried to study medicine here? He knew the answer to that last question, of course; it was because her studies would always have taken second place if she had to come home every evening.

'That's such extraordinary news,' Wilde continued when he finally broke away from the embrace. 'We'll open a bottle of claret and celebrate.'

'I'm starting on Monday. I've only come home to pack some clothes and a few essentials. Not much, though, because I'll be sharing a room in a hostel.'

'Perhaps you could find a small flat nearby.'

She shook her head. 'Not allowed. I have to muck in with the other girls.'

'Well, if you're going back to London on Monday, I'm coming with you.'

'Tom, no. I can't be seen with you. I'd be sent down if they knew I was married.'

'Don't worry. We'll separate before you get to St Ursula's. I have other work to do in town. Come on in now and spend some time with Johnny while you can. I'll tell Mrs Keane that the job's hers.'

Lydia looked hurt. She couldn't disguise it. 'I'm not going away forever, you know. You don't have to replace me.'

'I'm sorry,' he said. 'That didn't quite come out the way I meant it.'

'If you think this is about getting away from you and Johnny, you couldn't be more mistaken. It's only because I feel secure in your love that I can do this. I have to, Tom – it's burning me up. Anyway, you know I'll be back up here every spare moment I have, don't you?'

'Yes, I understand. But we'll miss you.' He managed another smile and hugged her again. 'I think we'd better open that wine sooner rather than later.'

'You read me like a book.'

Except he didn't. She was so preoccupied with the prospect of her new life that she hadn't even asked about May Hinchley. Now that wasn't like the Lydia he knew.

Wilde got out of the taxi two streets away from St Ursula's. After a family weekend which felt a bit like the Last Supper, he and Lydia had already said their goodbyes, but he held her again and kissed her and knew that she was already elsewhere. He watched from the kerb as the cab ground through the gears. She looked back with a smile and waved, and then she was gone.

Yesterday, the house had been very strange and unnaturally cheerful with the two families getting to know each other. But the worst was the evening, when Lydia had seemed like a ghost as she pottered around the house collecting clothes and other essentials, considering them one by one, packing some, discarding others. 'There won't be much room for fripperies,' she had said by way of explanation. 'I think the hostel is pretty basic.'

'Take this, though.' Wilde held out a small Beretta semi-automatic he had acquired during his work in Grosvenor Street.

'Are you serious?'

'You know how to use it. Just keep it hidden away.'

She shrugged, and packed the weapon in the bottom of her case. After that, she took the time to read Johnny his bedtime story and hugged him like a bear. And she ate with Wilde and Sylvia and spoke enthusiastically about what lay ahead for her.

But on reflection, Wilde was even more concerned than he had been before. Her body and her voice had been in the house, but her spirit had already flown.

During the taxi ride from the station, he watched her shake her head in dismay at the damage all around them. Much of the area around St Paul's and Finsbury had been devastated and though a lot of the rubble had been cleared, the gaps were painful to witness for anyone who knew and loved London. Wilde had seen it often during his time working here with the OSS. He had become accustomed to the harm inflicted through Bloomsbury, along Regent Street and in Westminster, including Parliament and the

Abbey itself, but it was new and shocking to Lydia, even though she had seen bomb damage in Cambridge: missing buildings, like missing teeth in an old man's mouth.

Now, trying to hail a taxi in the cool grey of an October Monday morning, he felt empty. Were they still a family? How would this affect their marriage and, even more importantly, Johnny's development? He was an easy-going lad, but he had always been especially close to his mother because Wilde had been away on OSS work for so much of the past three years.

Another cab arrived a couple of minutes after Lydia's had gone. He told the driver to take him on to 54 Broadway, opposite St James's Park. If the cabbie understood the significance of the address, he didn't show it.

This was the headquarters of Britain's secret intelligence service, though no passers-by would know that, for the sign on the door was that of a mundane trading company. Wilde had only learnt about the place while working with the OSS at Grosvenor Street, a brisk half-hour walk away.

He knocked at an anonymous hatch and was admitted to the curious world of the spy. A secretary who gave her name as Cook had expected him and, after relieving him of his Colt pistol, escorted him up through gloomy, utilitarian stairways and corridors, pushing past endless streams of people, mostly in military uniform. There were just too many sweaty bodies for one rather grim nine-storey building; the war had ignited a huge recruitment drive in MI6, but the building had not been expanded to accommodate them all.

At last, they arrived at Philip Eaton's office on the fourth floor.

'Ah, Tom, just in time for coffee. I've ordered you strong black, no sugar.'

'Thank you. You know, Philip, I realise you have all done remarkable work here, but the place is hideous. Grey walls for God's sake, cheap, nasty linoleum on the floors, prison furniture, every other light bulb gone. And it's still ridiculously bloody overcrowded. All of which I could put up with, but it's the lack of light that pierces the soul.'

'I agree. It's a disgrace, but the country's bankrupt so we can't expect refurbishment any time soon. Not like your chums across the pond.'

There was a knock at the door and another secretary entered with two cups of black coffee and placed them on Eaton's desk, then departed.

'Anyway, as I told you on the phone, we can't bring the German here. The war might be over, but this place stays unacknowledged.'

'So where?'

'I've booked a room at Claridge's. He's being brought there from Camp 020. So drink up and my driver will take us.' He glanced at his watch. 'Actually, the Shell is probably already there. Still, it never hurts to keep an interviewee waiting.'

The Shell. Walter Schellenberg, Himmler's right-hand man in SS head office. Wilde had interrogated him only two months earlier in his quest to find the whereabouts of Adolf Hitler and determine whether or not he had died in the Berlin bunker. The information he provided had been extremely helpful.

Now he had more questions for The Shell.

'Did you tell Dagger you were coming here today?' Eaton asked Wilde casually as he sipped his coffee.

'I said I thought it would be a good idea to talk to Schellenberg about the Black Book, yes, but I didn't mention I would be using you as an intermediary. Why, was I out of order?'

Eaton smiled unconvincingly. 'No, no. It's just that Dagger sometimes takes his need-to-know policy to extremes. I'm not the only one in MI6 who thinks he has failed to keep us fully informed on certain matters lately. Which is strange, because V Section is supposed to be all about communication between the various departments. But there you go. Don't tell him I mentioned it, old man.'

'I can't see why I would have occasion to.'

'That's the ticket.'

The two men finished their coffee and slowly made their way back down to the ground floor. Eaton's progress was painful and awkward and his stick didn't seem to help much. It seemed to Wilde that he was a great deal more shaky than he remembered him.

The secretary gave Wilde back his gun.

A driver with a black Daimler was waiting at the kerb and sped them north towards Claridge's hotel. Wilde made use of the moment to ask again about the nagging doubt that he couldn't quite clear from his mind – what had happened to the defector Boris Minsky, now supposedly known as Sergei Borisov, the SMERSH chief he had spirited out of Berlin only for him to disappear in England?

'You must have heard something, Philip?' He hoped the irritation in his voice was obvious.

'Would that I had.'

'But you're his case officer. You're responsible – and the man's disappearance leaves me in an impossible position. I brought him out in good faith, secreting him aboard a USAF transport flight. He was supposed to give secrets to the British and the Americans in return for safe asylum. Well, as far as I know he has given nothing to Washington, which leaves me wondering – are you keeping him all to yourself? That would not be good practice among allies.'

Eaton didn't lose his composure, nor indicate that he even acknowledged Wilde's disquiet. He never did. 'If your allegation – your *suggestion* – were true, then yes it would be shameful of us. But it's not. He made tracks of his own volition and I was as shocked as you were. Do I trust him? No. Do I badly want to find him? Yes. Will I let you know when we have word on his whereabouts? Most certainly. And for the moment that's all I can tell you.'

'It's not good enough.'

'I agree. And I am mortified by our inexcusable lapse.'

There was nothing more to be said. Wilde turned away from the MI6 man and gazed once more at the ruins. Even Mayfair had not gone untouched.

On arrival at the hotel, a porter showed them through to a large ground-floor room that had been set aside for the meeting. At the door, Eaton asked the serving man to bring sandwiches.

Walter Schellenberg stood up from the table when they entered. He was guarded by two soldiers who had brought him from the

Camp 020 interrogation centre at Ham Common in south-west London. He was the Western Allies' prize catch. As chief of the SD intelligence operation – the Sicherheitdienst – he knew everything there was to know about the Nazi secret services and was happy to reveal it all if it increased his chances of avoiding the noose for war crimes. For despite his protestations that he was in no way involved in Himmler's massacres, it was inconceivable that such a senior man should not have known the truth about the atrocities, especially those committed in the eastern theatre of war.

It was said that he would be giving evidence against his former masters and colleagues at the main Nuremberg trial in the coming months.

'Sit down, Herr Doctor,' Wilde said.

'Ah, Professor Wilde, it is you once more. I am so pleased to meet you again.' Schellenberg spoke good English.

'And this is Mr Eaton. He is here as an observer.' In fact, Eaton had demanded he be included; if Schellenberg revealed anything, he wanted immediate access to it. His role was not to ask questions, simply listen.

'I am pleased to meet you, sir,' Schellenberg said. He bowed his head deferentially to Eaton, then turned back to Wilde. 'But tell me, Professor, is this to do with your quest for Hitler? Was my information of any assistance?'

'We are not here to talk about that.'

Wilde asked the two soldiers to leave the room, then he, Eaton and Schellenberg sat down around the long table. 'This is about the Black Book – the *Sonderfahndungsliste G.B.* I believe you were instrumental in compiling it.'

Schellenberg nodded. He was a smooth, sickly man of thirty-five, but despite his pallor, he looked a great deal younger. 'Yes, sir, that is so. It was before the planned invasion of Britain in 1940. The intention was to arrest and hold all those considered our enemies, particularly those who might form a resistance movement. And I believe that Sir Oswald Mosley was to have been Gauleiter of Great Britain if the invasion had been successful.'

'We know all that. But there was another list too. The so-called addendum.'

'Sir, that was not my work. Heydrich ordered it at the beginning of 1942, a few months before he was assassinated.'

'But you knew about it?'

Schellenberg hesitated.

'I'll take that as a yes.'

Schellenberg nodded. 'Very well, yes, I am ashamed to say that I knew about it. But that does not mean I approved of it. It was a death list. All those named were to be killed as soon as they were located. Informally, we called it the Phenol List.'

CHAPTER 12

The word 'phenol' struck Wilde like a bullet. Until this week, he had never heard of the substance. Now he had encountered it twice – once in connection with a murder being investigated by their police surgeon friend Dr Rupert Weir, and now this. Was there a link? There had to be a link.

'Why phenol?' he demanded of Schellenberg.

'Don't you know? It was the poison used to kill the useless mouths in the Aktion T4 euthanasia programme.'

'Useless mouths?'

'Forgive me, I am so accustomed to the terminology. The old and infirm, the insane, the crippled, children born blind . . .'

'And who would have administered it?'

'Doctors, of course. Physicians. There were several centres – six, I believe – where patients were sent for termination. Often their family doctors or hospital specialists would have them despatched to these places when life seemed worthless.'

'I mean who would have administered it to those on the so-called Phenol List when you invaded Great Britain.'

'Why, as I said, doctors. There was no shortage of such men – and a few women – happy to work for the SS, even in the concentration camps. Undoubtedly some doctors took advantage of the National Socialist ascendancy believing it gave them an experimental freedom they would not otherwise have enjoyed. I believe there were those who used human beings as guinea pigs. May I ask why you are interested?'

'No,' Wilde said.

A plateful of dainty sandwiches arrived – their crusts neatly removed – and Schellenberg looked at them hungrily. 'They're all yours,' Wilde said.

'Thank you, sir.' He picked up a cheese sandwich and bit into it.

'Tell me more about phenol. Was it used outside the euthanasia programme?'

'Yes, I believe it was, much to Germany's shame. I heard that it had been used as a clean and efficient method of execution in Dachau and Buchenwald. Almost certainly elsewhere too.'

Clean and efficient execution. Otherwise known as murder. Wilde's stomach churned as he met this young man's eyes, as he watched him nonchalantly tucking into sandwiches while speaking of clean and efficient murders as matter-of-factly as he might discuss the weather. Schellenberg painted himself as an unwilling accomplice, an innocent on the sidelines. Yet he had lived the high life as a Nazi functionary and had happily served the murderers. In fact, he was one of their leaders, an SS-Brigadeführer.

The soft, youthful face, the weakness of the narrow shoulders and the attempt to transfer all culpability to others belied the truth about this dreadful man. When he had met him before, Wilde had had to resist the urge to punch him. Just like today when instead of crushing that face to a pulp, he smiled and said pleasantly, 'Do carry on, Herr Doctor.'

'Also perhaps against captured partisans and resistance fighters in the east.'

'And who do you think might be using this stuff in Britain now that the war is over? Why might the Black Book addendum – the Phenol List – have been activated? Was there, perhaps, a plan for guerrilla warfare once the main conflict was over?'

'Phenol used here in Britain?' Schellenberg sounded genuinely shocked. 'I can't think why anyone would be using it other than for ordinary industrial purposes. But, you know, it could be a matter of vengeance. It was rumoured that the list included people who were not considered a great danger, but had somehow offended one of the top men in the hierarchy of the Third Reich. Could it be possible that someone has taken it on himself to carry this out regardless of the fact that the war is over? Vengeance for defeat, perhaps?'

Wilde was well aware that there had been those in the old Nazi regime who wished him dead, Lydia too. Could the hand of retaliation reach out from beyond the grave?

Lydia's new room-mate was lying on her bed wearing only large knickers and an enormous bra. She was reading a book without a dust jacket and no visible title.

'Hello, I'm Lydia Morris.'

The reader looked up. 'Gosh, you've arrived. You're only a week late! Have you got any sugar?' She put the book down without closing it and slid her legs from the bed.

The question took Lydia aback. 'I'm sorry I didn't think to bring any.'

'What about butter? Your parents must have given you their butter ration.'

'No, I'm afraid not.'

'Well, that's just too bad. I was so looking forward to your arrival bearing treats.'

'I don't know what to say. I feel such a fool.'

'Oh, don't worry. By the way, I'm Miranda. Miranda March. Very pleased to meet you, Miss Morris, even if you didn't have the decency to bring the essentials of life. I don't suppose you know the time?'

'Just after ten thirty.'

Miranda jumped up. 'Then we'd better get our skates on. Anatomy beckons in less than half an hour. Are you scared?'

'I don't think so. Should I be?'

'One girl was sick in our first lesson. It was hilarious.'

Lydia looked around the room. There was a gas fire with a meter to be fed with shillings if either of them wanted any warmth in the middle of winter. Also a rickety table with two chairs where they would have to write up their notes, a single basin and two hard and joyless beds. She realised she had no choice between the two because the one furthest from the draughty window had already been bagged by Miranda. Lydia dumped her two suitcases on the one beneath the window and shivered in the chill of the breeze.

'Sorry,' Miranda said. 'First come first served, I'm afraid.'

'That's all right, I'll survive.'

'Will you? You have no idea how cold it gets at night and how bad the food is.' Miranda hastily fastened her damson woollen skirt around her ample girth, then grabbed her crumpled blouse from the back of one of the chairs. 'If we survive long enough to become doctors we'll probably have to treat ourselves for frostbite and malnutrition.'

It occurred to Lydia, somewhat unkindly, that Miranda did not look close to starvation. Then she had an idea. 'Actually, I do have a pot of honey. I'd very happily share it with you.'

'Really?'

'Really. Finest Cambridgeshire honey.'

'Is that where you come from? Well, that's the best news I've heard all week. I've got the curse and it gives me such awful sugar cravings. Can we crack open the jar at teatime? We can get the gas fire going, toast some bread and tuck in like bears. You know, Lydia Morris, I think we're going to get on famously. By the way, may I call you Lydia?'

'I insist on it.'

'Come on. We'd better make tracks. Punctuality is taken very seriously by the stern lady doctors of St Ursula's.'

The first thing Lydia noticed about the anatomical lab was the smell. It hit her like a fist and she knew she would never get it out of her nostrils. There was formaldehyde, of course, she recognised that. Overwhelmingly formaldehyde. But there was also the miasma of human death, of bodies kept in the cold to preserve them. Very different to meat, nothing like the butcher's shop. The blend of chemical and flesh was sickly and unpleasant and all-enveloping.

The lab was high up in the building, on the third floor, and its shutters had been thrown open to let in as much light as possible through the large windows. Lydia had expected it to be in a dark, dungeon-like basement, because that had been her own father's experience, as related to her in one of his vivid descriptions of medical school days, but she supposed they must all be different.

There were twenty autopsy tables, each encircled by six students. On each table there was a dead body, naked and shaven of all hair. Her father had said they kept the heads covered, but here they were exposed and she could see that they were mostly old men, but also a couple of old women and one or two younger ones.

Lydia had steeled herself for this moment. She had read enough to know what was expected. What she hadn't been prepared for was the 'white' coat she had been assigned; it was spotted all over the front with yellow globules of human fat. Did no one launder them? Nor was she expecting to have to slather her hands in a thick pink cream, whose purpose had not been explained to her.

A tutor, whom Lydia at first mistook for a man, sauntered over, pipe held between her teeth. She had short hair and a solid rugby player's frame, and an attitude that immediately put the new young women at their ease.

'That's Dr Belmer,' Miranda whispered in Lydia's ear. 'You'll love her.'

The doctor met Lydia's eye. 'I take it you're the new girl.' She stressed the word *girl* as though it was an obviously preposterous term to be applied to one so ancient. 'So for your benefit, having missed my introduction, I shall explain what we do here.' She took the pipe from her mouth and prodded the cadaver's chest hard with the chewed mouthpiece. 'The first thing all medical students need to know is that this is not a human being. It is the remains of a human being, of no more consequence in itself than a pail of mud, which it will, of course, eventually become. As will we all.'

She sucked once more on her pipe, unconcerned by the fact that it had recently come into contact with a corpse. 'However,' she continued, blowing out a stream of aromatic smoke, 'this former human being is a superb teaching tool. It is the most wonderful textbook in the world, and it has been given to us by its former owner. So treat it with respect. At the men's colleges, they have unpleasant senses of humour. I heard of one who sliced off a nose and added it to the genitalia of another corpse. I heard, too, of a young man who smuggled a potato into the lab and placed it deep inside the brain of a half-dissected head. He is now an eminent surgeon – the student not the corpse – but that does not excuse his dreadful behaviour.'

She turned once more to Lydia. 'Do you have a scalpel, Miss Morris?'

'No, Doctor.'

'Here, have mine.' She handed her the razor-sharp implement. 'Now make an incision in the forearm.' She used her pipe once more to indicate the precise spot. 'Then slowly peel back the skin on either side to reveal the muscle beneath.'

Lydia looked at the arm with horror. She had never stuck a blade into flesh before. But then a little voice in her head told her that wasn't quite true. Like almost every woman in the land, she had jointed a chicken and removed its skin. *Think of this as a chicken, Lydia. It's no longer a human being.*

With only the merest hesitation, she cut a thin line into the pallid, grey skin of the cadaver, then drew back the skin like peeling an orange, as though she had done this all her life.

'Not bad,' Dr Belmer conceded. 'But take it a little slower. The subject isn't going anywhere, you know.'

Liz Lightfoot looked in the mirror and wondered, not for the first time, what anyone could see in her. She wasn't ugly, but she was decidedly ordinary. And yet she knew that Tony loved her, that he would do anything for her. What a strange thing it is, she thought, the human heart.

Lucas would be back from the pub soon, and she was dreading it. Her husband's moods had worsened, and so had his boozing. In his sober moments when she tried to suggest he drink a little less, he turned on her and told her that she knew nothing, that he had seen friends shot dead at his side, that he had seen 'more stinking corpses than you've had hot dinners'. He held his fist up and he threatened her.

His darker moods were becoming more frequent, and he delighted in telling her that he had 'fucked' dozens of mam'selles and fräuleins in France and Germany and that if she didn't like it she could lump it. She was pretty sure he must have had the clap, but she couldn't keep him away from her forever, so she just prayed the army had given him penicillin and that he was OK now.

In her brief stolen moments with Tony, she warned him about her fears – terrified of passing a venereal disease on to the man she truly loved – but it made no difference to his feelings for her.

What she didn't tell Tony, because he couldn't have endured it, was the extent of her husband's encroaching madness and threatened violence.

At night, sometimes, Lucas screamed out in his sleep. He thrashed about in the bed and drenched the sheets in his sweat. She guessed it was the war that caused such nightmares, but he wouldn't talk in detail about his experiences. Alcohol was his only safety valve, and yet it wasn't safe.

So what were they to do, she and Tony? This was hopeless and it couldn't go on, not for a lifetime. Yes, Tony loved her, but he was also besotted by his baby boy, and who could blame him? He was a gorgeous little child.

The toughest part was the occasions when she and Lucas visited Tony and Sandra Hood at the farm and cooed at the baby. They had been friends for so long that there would have been no way of avoiding the shared lunches and afternoon teas and then, of course, there was the big event – the christening. It was an awful day – false and horribly awkward, with Lucas and Liz playing the roles of godparents.

Ostensibly, the get-togethers were the same as they always had been. But the truth was very different. Everything had changed. Even sweet Sandra was frazzled by her sleepless nights with the baby. If she had been wider awake, she might have spotted the change in all their relationships; so would Lucas if he hadn't been either inebriated or hungover.

And then there was Mrs Fearon across the street. Liz was sure she knew or suspected something even though she and Tony had always taken great care over their assignations. Perhaps someone else had seen them and had reported back to the Fearon bitch.

Liz and Tony came up with a series of insane solutions: just take the baby and run away, change their names. But how could Tony leave the farm? All his money was tied up in it. They thought, too, of blurting out the truth to Sandra and Lucas. But the probable consequence of Lucas's reaction was too awful to contemplate.

The idea they considered most seriously was to go to lawyers in Norwich and employ them to come up with a way forward. But that seemed such a huge step that they dithered and delayed and nothing came of it.

As if these problems were not enough, there was the other thing. Still unspoken, still gnawing away. Something lethal but obscure. The secret of the dunes. The secret they could tell no one without revealing their own adultery. She was haunted by the eyes of the man looking at her in the moonlight, but not seeing her. What would have happened to them if they had been discovered? She shuddered at the memory.

Downstairs, the door crashed open. Liz looked away from the mirror and closed her eyes. Her shoulders tensed hard; she knew the sound all too well. Lucas was home and he was stinking drunk, the bastard. He had always been a tough man and a drinker, but before the war his roughness had been leavened by a sense of humour. He had been able to make Liz laugh and, in bed, he could be surprisingly gentle.

That had all changed. The tenderness had vanished, the coarseness accentuated. The laughter was long gone.

'Woman!' His voice reverberated up through the house.

'Just coming, Luke.' That was what she had always called him, Luke not Lucas.

'Where's my fucking dinner?'

As she came downstairs, the stench of booze filled the hallway. He was reeling. A streak of vomit ran from the side of his mouth to his chin, his eyes were dull and angry.

'It's in the oven, Luke. Irish stew. I managed to get some neck of mutton. Sit down and I'll bring it to you.'

'Neck of fucking mutton! Is that what I get for saving you from the fucking Nazis?'

'I thought you liked it.'

'Where you been today, scrawny cow? You went on the bus.'

'I went into Norwich to buy some fabric to make myself a dress for winter. I saved up my clothing coupons. I'll show you later.' In truth, she had hoped to find Tony at the market, because she was sure he would be bringing in some poultry to sell; but there had been no sign of him.

'You were at the livestock market. Eddie saw you. Buying a fucking ox were you?'

'No, I told you.'

'He said you were looking for someone. Who would that be?'

'No one. I wasn't looking for anyone. I just had a day out. I've always loved the market and I needed some warm material.'

And then it began, as she knew one day it would. For no good reason, no real provocation. His hand went to her throat and lifted her off the ground. For long, desperate moments she scrabbled at his chest with her nails and thought she would be suspended there until all the breath was taken from her. Even as she thought she was dying, she was thinking of the foul stench of his beer breath and knowing, with certainty, that this all had to end, for it would be better to be dead than live like this.

But then he threw her across the hallway like a discarded toy. He was twice her size and powerful. He could carry two hundred-weight bags of coal on his back with ease. She was small and light and her head cracked into the door jamb and stunned her.

Now he was standing over her. For a moment he just looked, then he snorted with derision and kicked her in the ribs.

She wanted to scream out, but she didn't, refusing to give him the pleasure of her pain. Nor would she beg him to stop. Instead, she just curled up like a foetus and clasped her hands to her head to minimise the injury and waited for the blows to come – and they did, in a flurry of punches and kicks, until he had had enough and kicked her one more time then strolled on into the kitchen to get his dinner.

CHAPTER 13

To the people for whom she worked, Doris was just Doris the cleaning lady, but in fact she did have a surname – Welch. She didn't like to mention it because her father had once told her that the word had unpleasant connotations of failing to pay a losing bet.

It was the name she had taken when she married her husband Peter Welch in 1902. He was eighteen years old, a farm labourer and cowherd; she was seventeen and a milkmaid. But when the Great War came, he enlisted and lost a leg at Ypres. He was invalided out and the farm had apologetically said they would not be able to use him anymore. Nor was there any other work for a crippled ex-soldier and the service pension was not enough to live on.

Doris had no option but to work as a cleaner, for she had no skills other than milking cows and she had no intention of returning to that life. There was little enough work for men anyway, let alone women. Over the years she had worked for several families, but her main employers had always been Lydia and Tom Wilde. Separately before they lived together and then jointly.

They had a good relationship and she happily performed extra tasks for them, such as preparing food or looking after Johnny from time to time. It was far closer than a traditional working relationship; there was a real warmth between them all.

Doris would do anything for the Wildes.

But she was sixty now and her prematurely grey hair had turned white and her husband was nearing death with the cancer, so she had begun to wonder whether a time might come when she could retire. The problem was she had very little money put away and she wasn't at all hopeful that she would qualify for any sort of pension.

She arrived at Cornflowers at 9 a.m. as usual and was about to put the key in the door when it opened and she found herself looking up into the face of a woman she didn't recognise.

'Yes?' the woman said.

'It's a cleaning day.' She couldn't think what else to say and for a moment she wondered whether she was going senile and had turned up at the wrong house. 'Are the Professor and Mrs Wilde in?'

'Ah, you must be Doris. Do come in. I'm Mrs Keane, the new housekeeper.'

Doris was puzzled. 'I'm sorry, I didn't know there was to be a housekeeper.'

'Well, Mrs Wilde has been accepted for medical training at St Ursula's in London and has had to start straightaway, so of course she needed me. It has all happened in a great rush. Anyway, if you just get on with your work as normal I won't disturb you. I'm afraid the professor is also out and I don't know when he'll be back.'

Doris nodded and stepped into the house. She was tiny and this new woman, Mrs Keane, was tall. Despite herself, Doris felt slightly uncomfortable, as though the new housekeeper was intruding on her territory. It was a sensation she had never felt before. The woman was smiling, but Doris found it difficult to smile back.

'Perhaps you'd make coffee, Doris,' Sylvia Keane said.

Doris didn't know what to say. She often offered Lydia or Tom a cup, but it wasn't part of her duties – something she liked to do, but certainly nothing she would ever be ordered to do. In fact, there were times when one of the Wildes brewed a cuppa for *her*.

But she let it go for the moment. Clearly Mrs Keane was finding her feet and soon she'd find out the way things worked at Cornflowers. It would all turn out well in due course.

So she just nodded and carried on through to the kitchen wondering about the exchange of names. Doris was just Doris, as usual, but the new woman was Mrs Keane. Was there a hierarchy? Was the position of housekeeper grander than that of cleaning lady?

A little girl, about three years of age, followed in the new woman's wake.

'And this is my daughter Penelope. Not Penny mind, I think it's rather common to shorten such a name, don't you?'

Doris had no feelings on the subject, but she smiled and congratulated the child on being sweet and pretty, then bustled about in the kitchen looking for coffee. The tin was almost empty and she knew there was no more in the house.

'I'm sure the professor will want some coffee tomorrow morning, Mrs Keane. I don't think I should use this. It's the end of their ration and I'm not sure when any more will be available.'

'Really? But I'm here *in loco parentis* for Mrs Wilde, so I'm sure I'm entitled.'

'No, I'm sorry.' She put the lid back on the tin and placed it back in the cupboard.

'Very well, a cup of tea then.'

The tension was palpable for a minute while Doris reluctantly put the kettle on. And then Sylvia Keane touched her arm and graced her with a smile.

'Look, I'm sure you're right, Doris. Of course I can't drink the professor's coffee. Forgive me.'

'That's all right,' Doris said stiffly.

A little later, while Doris was washing up the breakfast things, Sylvia Keane appeared in the kitchen again and said, 'What time do you finish today, Doris?'

'Four thirty. Always four thirty unless they need something else doing.'

'Really? Oh, that's marvellous. Perhaps you could do me a small favour. Something private and rather important has come up and I need to go out alone for a couple of hours this afternoon. Would you mind dreadfully if I asked you to look after Penelope while I'm out, and pick up Johnny from school, of course? I'm sure I'll be back by four thirty.'

'Well, it's not terribly convenient. I have to change all the sheets and then wash them, as well as dusting and polishing upstairs. It will be rather difficult to keep an eye on your daughter, too.'

'Oh Penelope is very easy. She'll just follow you around. And I'm sure the Wildes would understand, don't you think? I'll be in your debt forever, Doris. You are a sweetie.'

Sylvia smiled that smile that had beguiled Lydia and Wilde. Doris wasn't so easily won over.

Rupert Weir removed the sheet covering the corpse while Wilde and Templeman looked on.

The face of the man was pale, but unmarked. Templeman gazed down from his six foot seven inches and nodded. 'That's him, that's Rafe Crow. He was a damned fine man, one of our very best. He didn't deserve this.'

'I'm sorry.'

'Poisoned, you say, Dr Weir?'

'Yes. A vial of phenol jabbed straight to the heart with a syringe. It would have been painful but a remarkably quick death.'

'Well, if he didn't suffer too much, I suppose we must be thankful for small mercies.'

'Rupert,' Wilde said, 'didn't you mention some thought you had that he was killed elsewhere and moved to the roadside where he was found?'

'It was the lack of any great disturbance, but also the discovery of footprints, as though two men had carried him. He must surely have been taken there either alive or dead. An assassin wouldn't just have stumbled across him in such a remote place.'

'What if they had arranged to meet there?'

Weir nodded. 'Ah, yes, I suppose that must be a possibility. That's why you two gentlemen are intelligence officers.'

'Still,' Templeman said, 'the footprints might rule that out. I'll get Special Branch onto the case. Hopefully the prints are still there and can be compared to Rafe's shoes.'

'There was something else,' Weir said. 'If you look at the left hand you'll see his ring finger is missing. Police searched for it near the body but didn't find it.'

'Could have been taken by a predator.'

'Of course, but it was severed cleanly – by a knife or clippers, not teeth.'

Wilde and Templeman went through all the details with Weir and then returned to the waiting Rolls-Royce. They sat in the back seat. In the front, the driver kept the engine running but didn't move away from the kerb.

'What now, Dagger? Any word from our missing man from Flowthorpe? Lyngwood . . . Gram Lyngwood.'

'Nothing. And we think it must be an alias, because we have no record of a man of that name. He's not on the electoral register and I can't find official paperwork for him anywhere. No birth certificate, ration book, nothing. I have talked to the tax office and the name isn't in their files – which are probably better kept and more extensive than our own. So we have to assume it's a false identity.'

'And Rafe Crow, you said he was in the Black Book addendum, the Phenol List.'

Dagger Templeman nodded. 'He was.'

'What you haven't explained to me is whether there's some kind of order to it or indication of how it was to work. I suppose it's an alphabetical list, like the main part of the Black Book?'

'Not quite. There are in fact fifteen sections, some with a dozen names, some with twenty or more. Rafe Crow and the other murdered officer, whose name I am not at liberty to reveal to you, were in the first section. I must assume they were considered highest priority targets.'

'How was the other man killed? Also phenol?'

The MI5 chief shook his head. 'Two bullets to the heart, .32 calibre. He was also investigating the neo-fascists, that's all I can tell you.'

'And where do we come on this list. I can't imagine Lydia and I were considered high priority by the SD or SS.'

Templeman winced. 'Actually you were. The curious thing was that your names had been scratched from a lower list and handwritten into the first list in black ink as though you were promoted at a later date. That's why I felt I had to mention it to you as a matter of urgency.'

Added at a date later than early 1942. September 1942, perhaps, after he fell foul of Gestapo chief Heinrich Müller.

Wilde shifted his weight and felt the metal of the Colt against his hip. 'You've got me worried now – not for myself, but for Lydia. She treats the whole thing with disdain and refuses to take any precautions.'

'Where is she exactly?'

'She's enrolled in medical school. St Ursula's in London.' Wilde explained the situation further.

Templeman expressed no surprise that a married mother in her thirties should be studying medicine. All he said was, 'Would you like me to give her a tail?'

Would he? What if she found out? She'd never forgive him. But nor would he forgive himself if anything happened to her. 'Are you doing that for others on the Phenol List?'

'One or two. But many of them have been warned and are quite capable of looking after themselves, which might explain why the Nazis saw them as such a threat.'

'OK, well let me give it a bit of thought, Dagger. I'll get back to you. What I can't understand is why this thing has been activated. Why now? I realise what they were intending back at the height of the conflict when they still harboured hopes of an invasion, but in October 1945, almost half a year after the end of the war? Who could gain from this?'

'I'm as puzzled as you, Tom. On another note, have you heard any more from Bill Donovan in Germany?'

'All I know is that he's in Frankfurt and will be making his way to Kransberg Castle this afternoon. Hopefully, this supposedly biddable Nazi, Kurt Blome, will know all there is to know about phenol and its use, as well as the Nazis' biological warfare links with Japan.'

'When you've spoken to him, call me. And I want you to get yourself back into college in professor mode and do your best to find out what you can about this young man Oswick. He was one of those on Rafe Crow's radar, as was Catesby. Make contact with Catesby again, too, if you can. We have to take that anonymous note seriously. One thing is certain . . .'

Wilde nodded. 'Something else is planned.'

'Indeed, Tom. We must assume the worst.'

Wilde was back at college when a call came through from Bill Donovan in Frankfurt.

'I've been to Kransberg Castle just north of here to meet Kurt Blome. He styled himself Deputy Health Führer of the Third Reich or something like that and tried to make out he was a big cheese, worth saving for the scientific information he can give us.'

'What sort of information?'

'Oh, much the same as we're getting from the Japanese. Testing biological weapons on concentration camp inmates, on Himmler's orders. He admitted some involvement with developing ways of storing and deploying various pathogens, including plague and malaria. But he was *only obeying orders*. The usual get-out clause.'

'You sound less than convinced, Bill.'

'After spending an unpleasant hour with the bastard I would happily have put a bullet in his head. He certainly wasn't as important or knowledgeable as he made out. He was trying to sell himself as an expert, when he actually seemed to know very little. I got the feeling he had somehow heard of Werner Braun and the other science guys being given immunity in exchange for working for America. He wants to hop on the bandwagon.'

'Did you ask him about phenol?'

'He just told me what we already know – that it was used as a cheap and quick method of euthanasia in places like Hadamar in Hesse.'

'What is that?'

'Ostensibly a psychiatric hospital. In reality they did away with the sick and the mentally ill, including thousands of children. German children – their own children. Mercy deaths, they called them. The depravity kills me, Tom.'

Wilde thought of the words Schellenberg had used: *useless mouths*. He thought of his own son, Johnny, playing innocently with the housekeeper's little girl Penelope. Who had the right to deem whether either of them was of use or not? Who had the right to condemn them to a grisly death if they failed an intelligence test or were handicapped? He felt like weeping with rage.

'Phenol was one murder method,' Donovan continued, 'but they also instituted a gas chamber at Hadamar and they had a crematorium which belched a ghastly fog of grey smoke over the town. It carried on until the end of the war. The perpetrators had no shame, no concept of right or wrong.'

'Do we have names for these killers? Could they be at loose in Britain?'

'I think not. But Blome did give me a couple of other names. He mentioned Sigmund Rascher – said he must have used phenol at Dachau, though he wasn't famous for it. Mostly he tortured men in pressurised cabins or in cold water baths on behalf of the Luftwaffe to see how downed pilots could withstand pressure changes and survive in icy waters.'

'Rascher was mentioned in connection with biological weapons research too, wasn't he?'

'Yes, but I don't know what the truth is.'

'He's dead though.'

'Well, Herr Blome doesn't believe that. He thinks his execution by the SS in Dachau in the last days of the war was all too neat and convenient. As we've both said before in other places, if you're trying to escape into obscurity it's a good idea to let the world believe you're dead.'

'That doesn't help us a great deal. If he is alive, he could be anywhere in the world. Including Britain, of course.'

'Now that's where things get interesting. He's part English. If he is alive, it's possible – perhaps probable – that he speaks the language, which would make it a great deal easier for him to slip in, perhaps posing as a refugee. Anyway, the other guy mentioned was Josef Klehr. He is an abominable piece of work, veteran of at least three camps, including Buchenwald, Dachau and Auschwitz. Now this man took great pleasure in injecting phenol into the sick, the tired or any prisoner to whom he took a dislike. They called him the *Spritze* – the squirter. He perfected his murder method, so that a killing could be done in seconds with a jab from a 20 cc syringe to the heart rather than the slightly more long-winded version of looking for a vein in the arm and shooting in there.'

'Good grief, we need to find him.'

'Already got him locked up. We caught him in Austria back in May. So he's clearly not your man. Pathetic little creep by all accounts – rose to the dizzying heights of SS-Oberscharführer which is roughly equivalent to sergeant. His reward for murdering for the Führer. He'll swing.'

'Back to Blome a minute, did he talk about the Japanese connection? Did he meet the Tokyo medical men and scientists?'

'He swears he knows nothing about that and I'm sure he's telling the truth. He was desperate to find something new he could impart to me to make himself seem valuable, so if he had been involved in such collaborations or even just known about them, he would have coughed immediately.'

'Thanks, Bill. If you hear anything else . . .'

'I'll let you know. Good hunting, Tom.'

They said their goodbyes and Wilde put down the phone. It rang again, almost immediately. This time it was Rupert Weir.

'There was something I didn't mention, Tom – about our murder victim Rafe Crow.'

'Carry on.'

'I was reporting back to the irritating Detective Inspector Shirley that we had a name for our body in the ditch. He thanked me and said he would pass it on to Special Branch as they had taken over the case.'

'Because you got in touch with them, you mean.'

'Yes, and Shirley knows it. He gave me a death stare through a fug of his dreadful cigarette smoke when I told him. I didn't mention you or Lord Templeman, of course. Anyway, while Shirley was making his feelings about me glaringly obvious, I noticed something on his desk – a petrol receipt from a garage on the Norfolk coast.'

'And I'm sure you'll explain the relevance.'

'Well, I had given it to the detective inspector in the first place. I'd found it during my initial examination of the body of Rafe Crow. It was in his jacket pocket and I noticed that it was dated October fifth – two days before the body was found, so I thought it might be important in identifying him.'

'What had the detective inspector done with it?'

'Nothing. Didn't pass it on to Special Branch or any of his own investigators. And there it was, just lying with a pile of random notes and papers on Shirley's desk. I asked him whether he had learnt anything from it. He just shrugged and said it had been checked out and was of no consequence. No one at the garage remembered a man answering the description of the corpse. He then picked it up, folded it and threw it at me like a paper aeroplane. I have it here with me. Would you like it?'

'I think I would. Thank you, Rupert.'

Sylvia Keane stepped out into the fresh autumn air. There was a suspicion of rain and so she wore her mackintosh.

She had considered the viability of taking the Wildes' car for the afternoon to get to Bedford because she was sure they wouldn't mind, but she had no ration allowance for petrol and wouldn't be able to fill it up. And there was always the danger that Doris would see her driving away and complain. So the train it would have to be. That was probably quicker anyway.

If she was late back at Cornflowers, it might be awkward. But she would have worked out a plausible story by then. She was having to learn to be plausible.

CHAPTER 14

Bit by bit, the coastal defences were being dismantled. The larger artillery batteries designed to blow enemy shipping out of the water had been among the first installations to go, along with the huge anti-aircraft guns that dotted the shoreline and backed up deep into the countryside.

Then the seemingly endless coils of vicious barbed wire were cut and up and loaded onto lorries. Would they be of use to any-one melted down? Or perhaps saved for the next war? Pillboxes and other concrete gun emplacements were broken up slowly into rubble that builders were happy to take away to use as hardcore. But the most difficult, the slowest, job was locating and removing the thousands of landmines that made various beaches unusable.

Wilde understood that this huge demolition job around the coast of Norfolk had started the previous year, many months before the end of the war, when the threat of invasion had diminished to almost zero. He knew, too, that the troops who manned these gun posts had long since been replaced by Home Guard patrols, and those too had now disappeared as men returned to their civilian roles.

He was riding his motorbike, the Rudge Special, because it was fast and because it did his soul good to speed around these East Anglian byways. But he had overestimated the likely temperature and the cold was seeping through his gauntlets into his hands and through his boots into his legs. A sea mist clouded his goggles, so he hitched them up onto his forehead. But the cold air in his eyes was too much.

There were no trunk roads and few road signs to help him find his destination; signposts had been removed soon after Dunkirk, when invasion seemed likely. Anything to disrupt and confuse the enemy.

Finally, he arrived at Skyme-next-Sea. Ahead of him, on the left of the main street, his eyes alighted on a wide whitewashed garage and forecourt with a single petrol pump. It was a 1920s building with art deco rounded edges, and it had come out of the war without losing any of its glory. The sign painted across the front above the wide workshop entrance said Skyme Motors. This was the place Rafe Crow had bought petrol during the last hours of his life.

Wilde stopped beside the pump. An attendant ambled over and eyed up the Rudge appreciatively. Wilde produced his ration book. 'Fill her up, please.'

'Good bike this,' the attendant said.

'Thank you.' Wilde looked around. 'This looks like a nice little seaside town. The day trippers will probably be back soon.'

'Only when the mines have all gone. Mind you, they've cleared most of them. Still don't like to go down there on the beach myself, though. What if they've missed one or two?'

The attendant was a man in his fifties, small, thin, almost bald, with a jagged scar down his left cheek.

'A friend of mine told me about this place,' Wilde said. 'Man by the name of Crow – Rafe Crow. He was here eleven days ago, October fifth. In fact, he mentioned he filled up here.'

'Did he now? Biker like you, was he?'

'No, he was in a car.'

'About your age?'

'A little younger, maybe thirty.'

'Someone did turn up around then. What does he look like?'

What did he look like? Difficult to describe a living man when all you have seen is a pale, flat corpse stretched out on a police surgeon's slab. 'Dark hair. About as tall as me, I think.'

'You sound a bit American, but not quite.'

'I'm half American, but I've spent a lot of my life in England.'

'We've had a lot of you Yanks around here – airmen, soldiers.'

'Anyway, my good friend Rafe Crow – do you remember him?'

'Possibly. We don't get many customers these days, to be honest, so new people stand out. Why do you want to know?'

'Just curious.'

'You know what curiosity did – killed the cat.'

Wilde gave the man his best smile. 'And I'm the cat, am I?'

'Don't worry, anyone who rides a Rudge Special is safe with me. I had one before the war. Loved her almost as much as the wife – but don't tell her that.'

'What happened to her?'

'Wife or bike?'

Wilde laughed. He knew he had met a comedian and realised this might be his lucky day. A shared love of motorbikes meant you were part of the club.

'Actually, the old Rudge ended up on the scrap heap, slid away from under me on a wet road and smashed into a tree. I ended up in hospital with a broken ankle and this.' He touched the scar on his cheek. 'Stupid mistake for someone who did a bit of race-riding in his time.'

'I'm sorry.'

'My fault, not the bike's. I'd let the tyres get slick.' For a moment he seemed lost in a reverie of his beloved motorbike, but then he smiled at Wilde. 'Now I mention it, your own bike there could do with a new pair of tyres, but you'll be lucky to find a set with the rubber shortage. Anyway, you were asking about your friend Mr Crow.'

'Did you chat to him at all. Did he say anything to you?'

'Like what?'

Wilde shrugged. 'I don't know. Like where he was heading. I want to see the same places he did.'

'What, the sand dunes? The barbed wire, the cold grey sea and the seals?'

'Is that all there is around here?'

The attendant laughed. 'Not selling the place that well, am I? Some folks like to gawp at the old lighthouse.' He removed the nozzle from the Rudge's tank, replaced it in its hook then screwed back the motorbike's petrol cap. 'Four gallons dead. That'll be eight bob.'

Wilde gave him a ten shilling note along with his ration book and told him to keep the change.

'That's very generous of you, sir.' He ran a hand lovingly along the sleek lines of the motorbike. 'You've kept her in pretty good nick. Actually now that I think of it there is something I remember about your friend Mr Crow's visit – assuming it was him. It was a couple of days after the coastguard robbery.'

Wilde gave a puzzled frown. Was this something he should know about? 'I'm sorry,' he said. 'What robbery?'

'Well, you wouldn't have of heard of it unless you live locally. No one dead, not much missing. But it was big news around here because we don't get hold-ups as a rule. Anyway, what happened was the coastguard up the road was robbed one evening. Two masked men with guns came into their station, tied up both the officers and robbed them. Been little talk of anything else hereabouts, but didn't merit a measly paragraph in the national newspapers.'

'Strange target for a robbery. Couldn't have got away with much.'

'Aye, you're right there. Just their wallets and watches. A few quid, less than a fiver in all, some food coupons and pictures of their children. Worst thing was, they made Joe Tuggett take off his wedding band and hand it over. Threatened to cut his finger off to get it if he didn't slip it off sharpish.'

'Were their families there?'

'No. Bailey's never married and old Tuggett lost his wife a few years back. His children have long since left.'

'And apart from that threat and the guns, was there any violence?'

'Well, they weren't injured, but they were pushed about a bit, and scared enough. Tell you what, mister, you seem mighty interested in all this. Who might you be, if you don't mind my asking?'

Wilde decided to come clean – up to a point – and trust this man. 'OK. My friend Rafe Crow went missing after coming here.' No need to tell this man he was dead. 'I'm tracing his last known movements before he vanished. I can't explain exactly who I am, but suffice to say I'm with the security services.'

'Well, in the not so recent past I would have reported you as a possible German spy. But I don't suppose anyone's interested in invading us just at the moment. What's your name?'

'Tom Wilde. I live in Cambridge. Could I give you my phone number in case you ever hear of anything unusual in the area?'

'Well, *unusual* covers a lot of ground. I won't pry anymore, though, because I reckon you Yanks did us a good turn when you lent us those ships and joined the war, so any way I can repay the favour is fine by me. My name's Wax, Barnaby Wax. And this is my garage.'

'It's a remarkable building.'

'I know. Wasted out here in the wilds. The war didn't do a lot for business.'

Wilde shook the man's hand. 'Now perhaps you could point me in the direction of the coastguard station. You've got me interested.'

'Just up the road.' He nodded his head northwards out of the village. 'Can't miss it, Mr Wilde.'

There were no cliffs here, so the coastguard station was on flat land halfway between the road and the shoreline. It was a broad, low, comfortable-looking building, rendered and painted white. A tall pole bearing the ensign loomed over the sea frontage, the flag fluttering in the breeze. Nearby, there were two other buildings, which had the appearance of storerooms, and further on, near the sea, there was a boathouse. The whole compound was encircled by a white wall, less for protection than to show that this was an official establishment and to be taken seriously.

Wilde parked the Rudge on its stand and strode up to the main entrance. A man in naval-style uniform with a peaked white cap and badge was just coming out and stopped when their eyes met.

'Can I help you?'

'My name's Tom Wilde. I'm looking for Messrs Bailey and Tuggett, the coastguards. Are you one of them?'

'You are on HM property. Please explain exactly who you are.'

'I'm here on official business.'

'Then you'll have papers to show me. Are you from the Admiralty?'

'No, I'm working with military intelligence. This is about the attack your men endured a couple of weeks back.'

'Ah, yes, that was rather humiliating. Look, without seeing papers, I still don't really know who you are and I'm not at all sure that Mr Tuggett and I should be talking to you, because we have already told the local constabulary and our superiors in the Admiralty all we know.'

'I understand.' Wilde smiled, trying to put the man at ease. Clearly the incident had shaken him up more than Barnaby Wax at the garage had suspected. 'It's not a good feeling being held at gunpoint. But I just want to ask you a few supplementary questions.'

'I'm not happy about this.'

'Do you have a telephone here? You could call Lord Templeman at Military Intelligence. He would vouch for me.'

'Very well. Give me his number, then wait out here. First I'll talk to the Admiralty, then your Lord Templeman if they give me clearance.'

Wilde wrote out the number for the the man he assumed to be Bailey then watched as he disappeared into the building. Ten minutes later he emerged and nodded.

'All right. Fire away.'

'I believe there were two gunmen, both masked. What do you think they were after?'

'Well, they got our money and watches, and Mr Tuggett's ring. Apart from that they absconded with a beautiful late-Victorian telescope.'

'Did they tie you up?'

'Very tight. Gagged and blindfolded too.'

'How long until you were freed?'

'The attack was soon after dark. About seven, I think. We were freed in the morning at six thirty when the cleaner came in. The gags were rather alarming. Mr Tuggett and I both feared we would suffocate during the night.'

'I'm sorry. It must have been extremely disturbing.'

'That's something of an understatement.'

'Did you wonder why they picked on you? I don't imagine coastguard stations are subjected to such raids often.'

'There will always be desperate men, I suppose. The pity of it is that Mr Tuggett's ring can't be replaced, and my wallet contained a picture of my brother, who died at sea in 'forty-two.'

'But you understand what I mean? In one sense they sound like professional thieves, but you are not an obvious target for such people.'

'I suppose not.'

'Why you, then?'

Bailey paused, then nodded slowly. 'I didn't mention it before but I have been thinking in recent days and couldn't help wondering what was really behind it.'

'You and Mr Tuggett must have been out of action for something like eleven hours. If something happened at sea on this stretch of coastline, you wouldn't have observed it.'

'Exactly. At first we considered ourselves fortunate that there were no alarms. It was a quiet, calm night – no one in trouble at sea. It would all have been a great deal worse if the raid had happened in bad weather with a ship in distress. This is a blind spot – the next station along the coast has no view of this shoreline and inshore waters to a distance of about six miles. But in the past couple of days it has occurred to me to wonder whether that might have been the point of the raid. Hobble us while something was being smuggled ashore. Not that smuggling's our responsibility – that's Customs these days. Our mission in the mid-twentieth century is simply observation and search and rescue. But, of course, if we ever saw anything untoward we would report it to the correct authority'

'You didn't hear of any unusual activity on the shore that night, or any other night recently for that matter?'

'No.'

'Thank you, Mr Bailey. By the way, did you meet a man called Rafe Crow at about the time of the raid – or a day or two later?'

'We were interviewed by two police officers and a man in plain clothes. I'm afraid I don't recall their names.'

'You have been very helpful. Do you think I might have a word with Mr Tuggett?'

'He's not here at the moment.'

'One more thing: what is the state of the beaches in this area? Have the landmines all been cleared?'

'Most of this stretch, yes. Certainly the seafront in town. Any areas of beach waiting to be cleared are surrounded by rolls of barbed wire and are clearly marked with danger signs. All the mines were planted above the high tide mark, of course.'

CHAPTER 15

Wilde hugged his arms around his chest as he walked along the shore, southwards from the coastguard station. He had no idea what he was looking for, yet he was sure that this area had some significance in the death of Rafe Crow and his investigations as an MI5 officer.

Before the war this coastline would have been extremely attractive, with a swathe of soft, fine sand, but now, in autumn, and with the detritus of war still evident, it was a bleak place. The ugly concrete of pillboxes scarred the foreshore and every so often he skirted an area where landmines were still to be dealt with. Definitely not the sort of place to walk your dog of a morning.

And yet, despite the unsightliness and the possibility of danger, a few brave souls had ventured out, including a couple with their pets, sensibly kept on leash. He tried to engage them in conversation, asking them about the coastguard robbery and whether they had heard or seen anything on the day in question. He was given a few theories, but no hard facts or evidence. As to Rafe Crow, no one had seen or heard of a man answering his description.

After twenty minutes, he came to Skyme itself. He couldn't decide whether it should be termed a village or a town. Although it was out of season, he could imagine that it must have been a pleasant destination in summer and would be again. Today, though, the North Sea chilled the air and it felt as though winter could not be far away.

A strand divided the shore from the town. At the southern end, just on the beach, a woman was perched on a rock, bent low, her head in her hands, shrouding her face. At first he thought she was old, but as he approached he realised she was quite young, probably early twenties, and that she was weeping.

For a few moments he held back, but then his instinct to help made him approach her in case she needed assistance. He touched her shoulder gently. 'I don't mean to intrude, but I was wondering if I could help in any way.'

She shifted her face sharply away from him so that he could not see her, but he had already noted the violent bruise on her cheek. He saw, too, that there was bruising on her arms and leg.

'Are you hurt? Would you like me to call an ambulance or find a doctor?'

She shook her head, slowly, as though that simple act was painful in itself. Wilde wasn't sure what to do; it wasn't in his nature to pass on by when another human being was in distress.

'Let me go and find help for you.'

She didn't reply, merely shrank into herself and wept.

The bruises suggested she had been attacked rather than the result of an accident, and her reluctance to ask for assistance pointed towards a domestic incident. A husband beating his wife. Though it made no sense, he was aware that the injured party, the woman, often felt shame and thus shunned interference or help from outsiders. Commonplace enough, but he still couldn't just do nothing.

Lightly, he touched her on the shoulder again. 'I'll come back,' he said, then walked across the strand into the little town. He looked around for someone who might be of assistance, a policeman perhaps or a kindly woman, but no one was in evidence. The only person he could think of was the one person he had met – Barnaby Wax, proprietor of the Skyme Garage.

He found him tucking into sandwiches and a cup of tea.

'Mr Wax, I'm sorry to interrupt, but I need some help.' He explained what he had seen.

The garage owner left his tea things on the table in the little oil-reeking room that served as his office and stood up. 'That can wait,' he said. Together they walked back to the beach. 'Ah,' Wax said uncomfortably. 'It's my niece, Liz. Poor bloody lass. Her husband did it, I'll wager. He's come back from the war an angry, hard-drinking man.'

'What can we do?'

'Leave it to me, Mr Wilde. I'll look after her. Thanks for alerting me.'

Wilde fetched the motorbike and rode south, along the coast road past the rising dunes. He wasn't at all sure what he was looking for, just hoping for inspiration. But nothing came. It was a strange, mysterious coast that seemed to be full of secrets.

After an hour, he turned back. At Skyme, he took a side road inland to head the quickest way to Cambridge. It had been an interesting outing, but he wasn't quite sure what he had learnt. It was certainly possible – perhaps likely – that the coastguard robbery had been a decoy operation to prevent the officers observing something happening along the coast.

It didn't take a huge amount of brainpower to wonder whether that *something* was the landing of canisters full of pathogens. Why else would Rafe Crow have ventured out east to Skyme? He must have had word that something had happened – or was happening – here. Perhaps he had heard a report of the coastguard raid and put two and two together.

But that supposition, however logical, did not take Wilde any further in discovering who was behind it and where the biological weapons – the BWs – had been taken. One had ended up in Flowthorpe, of course, yet there had to be others.

Didn't there?

The day was gloomy now and a low mist gave the road an autumnal sheen that made it slippery. He really should have come in the car rather than on the Rudge. He switched on the headlight, but all he could think about was the state of his tyres. Barnaby Wax had been right; they were in a bad way. He hadn't changed them since before the war.

Behind him, the headlights of a black car loomed, then the vehicle swept past him. On a dry road, the Rudge would have left it for dead, but he had already been riding for almost four hours and he wasn't in the mood to risk his life in a race.

The car streaked onwards. Wilde used its tail lights as a guide to the unmarked road, following the vehicle until it disappeared into the foggy wooded countryside, and then he gave it no more thought. Simply slowed down and settled back for the long haul home.

Three minutes later, it happened.

He didn't see it coming, but some unknowable sense had already made him brace for the impact. He was deep in the woods, on an isolated stretch. Had he been going fast, he might have been decapitated. He had heard of such incidents in the waste-land that was now Germany. Renegade and unreformable Nazis strung wires across roads to take the heads off jeep drivers and motorbike riders. There had been several such incidents, until the Americans began to take serious precautions by adapting their vehicles with protective bars.

The wire caught him at the brow, snapping his head backwards as it latched onto his goggles and leather flying helmet, ripping them both from the top of his head, jerking him from the saddle.

Somehow he managed to keep hold of the handlebars as the bike reared up beneath him and the soles of his boots scraped along the pitted tarmac. His hand was still on the throttle, but in gripping it to stay on, he accelerated and the bike flew out of control, weaving from side to side like a crazed snake, then finally spinning away from him.

He was flung hard to the left, hurtling into the ditch, his shoulder slamming into the base of a tree.

The impact took his breath away. His next sensation was the not-unpleasant scent of leaf mould and earth and the bitter worm-wood of his own blood. He tried to assess what had happened to him. His head was uninjured, but what of his neck? He had felt it snap back as if it would break. The thought did not last long for he was able to move and turn and he had more immediate con-cerns for his health. With the presence of mind of a man who has known danger and fear in his life, he rolled over and dragged the little Colt .32 from his pocket. If his neck was damaged, well, it wasn't slowing him up.

By staying on the Rudge he had put some distance between himself and his attackers – a hundred yards or more. He arched his neck. It was painful, but not broken.

With no time to assess other injuries, he crawled to the lip of the ditch, spitting out blood and dust. The mist was swirling and the woods let in very little of the late daylight. He could hear voices. Two men, speaking German. Or was it three? The words were unintelligible.

They were coming his way. He loosed off a high shot from the pistol. The crack rent the air like the smack of wood on wood. There was little chance of him hitting one of them, but that wasn't the point. He wanted to let them know he was alive and armed, let them know he would fight to the death, take one or more of them with him if they came too close.

Wilde was lying flat in the shallow ditch. A whiff of fox urine assailed his nostrils. His eyes peered into the gloom, searching them out, trying to gauge the best way to deal with this. Suddenly, he made out three shapes in the mist, crouching low in an arc, coming his way, and then they were gone again.

What now? What if they separated and came at him from three directions? He wouldn't stand a chance. He had to get away from here. Scrambling around to the back of the tree, he fired off another speculative shot, then ran, stumbling across roots and brambles, trying to get deeper into the darkening woods.

He was losing his sense of direction, keeping low. He was surprised that no shots followed him. They hadn't fired at him once. Did they want to take him alive?

After five minutes, he reckoned he must have distanced himself by the best part of half a mile. He was at the edge of the woods now, close to a field of weeds and mud. It was less misty here and there was still a trace of daylight. He settled down in a hollow behind bracken and waited for dark, the gun clenched tightly in his right hand.

CHAPTER 16

Inside the farmhouse, a dog was barking. Wilde circled the building with stealth, peering through windows. He saw a man on his knees laying a fire, but no one else. The dog, a collie, was at the man's side, howling furiously. The man – who was grey and old – tried to calm the animal.

Wilde went to the side door and knocked. No one used the front door in these old farm cottages.

There was no answer, so he knocked again, louder. When there was still no answer, he opened the door and called out. 'Hello?' Nothing. Tentatively, Wilde walked through to the room where the man was making the fire, adding kindling to the flames. Evidently, the old man was deaf, but the dog wasn't. It was crouched in attack mode, its teeth bared, growling.

The man turned and gasped in surprise. Wilde put up his palms and smiled to indicate that he meant no harm. The man was even older than he had expected, probably late eighties or even ninety, bent and small. He pointed at his ears to explain what Wilde had deduced. 'I'm deaf as a post,' he said in a voice that didn't need to be quite so loud.

Wilde looked around for paper and saw a pad and pencil next to a telephone on a small round table. Why did a man who was deaf need a phone? Was someone else here, someone upstairs or outside?

My name is Tom Wilde, he wrote quickly in clear letters. *I have had an accident. Do you have a car?*

'Horse,' the man replied. 'Horse and cart.'

Can I use your telephone?

'That'll be a florin.'

Fair enough. Wilde dug into his jacket pocket and fished about for change. He pulled out a two-shilling piece and handed it to the man.

'Thank you.' He pointed to his chest and grinned toothlessly. 'I'm Charlie Bagshawe.' Then he patted his dog. 'It's all right, Joey, settle down.' The dog sank to the floor and lay calmly at his master's side, his eyes still on the intruder, ready to pounce.

What's the address here? Wilde wrote.

'Bagshawe Farm, Church Lane, Haring Green.'

Wilde picked up the phone and got through to the operator. He placed a call to Latimer Hall. A few moments later, Dagger Templeman came on the line and Wilde briefly explained to him what had happened.

'Give me your address and wait there. A couple of our men are in Norwich and I should be able to make contact with them. I'll get one or both of them along to you as soon as possible. I think they'll be more use to you than the local plod. Are you OK for an hour or two, Tom?'

'Well, I've got nowhere else to go so hopefully my host won't mind. His name's Charlie Bagshawe and he's deaf.'

'But you've still got your pistol. Give me the phone number, and hold tight.'

Wilde soon discovered that Charlie Bagshawe was a fine man, a recent widower who had farmed this land all his life. He had been born in this cottage, as had his father and grandfather before him.

Despite the difficulty of communicating with a deaf man, their conversation rattled along, because Charlie was intelligent and glad of the company. He had already had his supper, but asked Wilde if he would like some leftover vegetable soup and bread. Wilde accepted gratefully, but first he asked if he could close the curtains on the downstairs windows.

'No one will look in around here. The only time I close them is when it's bitter cold outside, to keep in a little of the warmth.'

Please, if you don't mind, Wilde wrote.

'As you wish, Mr Wilde. You're the guest.'

He closed the curtains with great care. He had no idea what had happened to the three men who had ambushed him, but he wasn't taking chances.

The soup went down well, then Farmer Bagshawe produced an old bottle of whisky. He blew the dust off and pulled the cork. 'You look like a whisky man. Don't drink it myself. My missus didn't like to have booze in the house. I don't really know why I kept this one. Act of defiance maybe, show that I wasn't totally under the sweet lady's thumb, God bless her.' He chuckled and poured Wilde a couple of fingers in a tumbler. 'I hope it's all right.'

Whisky doesn't go off.

They conversed by talking and writing for an hour and a half until finally Wilde heard a car growling up the road and stopping outside.

Two whiskies had mellowed him after the drama and had eased some of the ache in his neck and shoulder. His tongue went to the cut on the inside of his lip as he remembered being hurled from the Rudge. He knew it was dark outside, but he pulled back the kitchen curtain an inch. The car was still running, its headlights blazing into the fog. It was black and big, the sort of vehicle Templeman chose. But the car that passed him on the road . . . that had been black and big, too. He hadn't noted the marque.

He saw the shape of a man in a suit walking towards the house. No face, it was too dark for that. There was a knock at the door.

It was just what one of Templeman's agents would do, but it didn't feel right. *You answer it, please,* he wrote and held up the message to Bagshawe. Better for the guest to hear the old man's voice first.

Charlie Bagshawe went to the door, his dog at his heels as though welded to him. The animal was growling again, just as it had when Wilde first appeared.

'Who is it?' Bagshawe called without opening.

'Is Mr Wilde there? Professor Wilde?' The voice sounded English, but perhaps not.

Bagshawe couldn't hear the reply, but he put his hand on the doorknob, then turned back to Wilde for confirmation that he was doing the right thing. Wilde put up his hand, deferring a decision.

But the door wasn't locked and it burst open.

Wilde's hand was already on the grip of the Colt and he pulled it instantly from his pocket. The newcomer stepped forward. He wore a balaclava with slit eyes and had a hypodermic syringe in each hand. Behind him there was someone else, another masked man, with a pistol.

The speed of what happened next was bewildering. Wilde loosed off two shots, his instinct and OSS training telling him the man with the pistol in the background was the immediate threat and must be eliminated. Take down the most heavily armed foe.

But that was wrong.

His bullets both struck home, one in the chest, one in the gun arm. The man stumbled and crumpled, but Wilde had lost split seconds. What caught him blind was the rapid movement of the other man, the one with the needles. That was the one he should have shot.

It was a strange blur. He saw the dog's jaws clamped around the right forearm of the needle man, but he couldn't see the left hand, except that it seemed to be striking downward. Charlie Bagshawe was staggering backwards, his old legs buckling beneath him at the shock of the onslaught. Wilde's eyes were shifting from the falling gunman to the needle man and their eyes met.

The eyes in the slits of the balaclava were intense but curiously distant. Wilde lunged forward at him, the Colt raised again, but the needle man had wrenched his arm clear of the dog's jaws and was now holding up the animal as a shield. In one swift movement, he hurled the dog at Wilde.

He feinted sideways like a boxer in the ring, his finger hovering on the trigger. Again he hesitated; why would he shoot a dog? It was just long enough for the needle man. As Joey fell awkwardly, yelping at Wilde's feet, Wilde moved sideways and raised the pistol again. But now the door was closed and the needle man was gone.

Charlie Bagshawe was on the ground, convulsing.

Wilde dropped to his knees at the old man's side. His mind was racing. There had been three of them in the fog. He had shot one, the needle man had vanished. Where was the third?

But most vitally, what was he to do about the old man? He saw now that a hypodermic needle was protruding from his chest. Suddenly, the old man stopped convulsing and went limp. Joey the collie was there, whimpering, licking his master's pale, dead face.

From outside, Wilde heard the roar of an engine and a screech of tyres on unmade road. He flung open the door and saw the black car in a tight turning circle, with two men inside in the front seats.

A third man, the one he had shot, was at his feet, writhing in pain.

CHAPTER 17

The second car arrived a few minutes later. Wilde, who had tried in vain to bring Charlie Bagshawe around, viewed the vehicle with apprehension, then relief when he became sure it was not the car that had sped away with the needle man and driver.

He stood over the gunman he had shot. The man was groaning in agony, clutching at his chest, begging for morphine in a mixture of German and English. '*Morphium, bitte*. Please . . .' He was a thin, powerful-looking man in his thirties, unshaven and coarse-featured. Wilde had the man's pistol in his hand, his own Colt stowed in his pocket.

As the car stopped, he bent down and placed the German's pistol on the ground, then stood up and raised his palms to show that he was no threat. He recognised one of the two occupants of the car as a man he had seen in the company of Lord Templeman at Latimer Hall, and the tension washed away.

By midnight, Wilde was back in Cambridge and the gunman was in hospital being operated on under armed guard. It had been a long, gruelling evening. The local police had been informed and attended the scene, but it had been made clear to them that it was a security matter and that they would not be leading the investigation. However, they would be responsible for finding the relatives of Charlie Bagshawe and informing them of his sad death.

They would also take custody of the old man's dog and, if the family wouldn't take it, try to find a decent home for the animal.

The gunman, meanwhile had been conveyed to hospital by ambulance. A late evening call drew the prognosis that his survival was still in the balance, depending on whether the bullet to the chest had hit any vital organs. Even though he couldn't possibly escape, two guards with guns had been assigned to ensure that no one came near him.

Wilde wanted to talk to Templeman, but the MI5 driver said he was under instructions to take him home and collect him in the morning to discuss the events. He also promised Wilde that the recovery of his motorbike would be organised on his behalf.

Opening the front door of Cornflowers, he found that Sylvia Keane was still up, in her nightgown, her face creased with anxiety.

'Oh, Professor, I was so worried, I couldn't sleep. Are you all right? You look as though you've been dragged through a hedge.'

'Something like that – a little road accident, Mrs Keane. But I'm fine, just a sore neck. I'll be even better when I have a glass of whisky in my hand.'

'You must tell me all about it.'

'Tomorrow maybe. How is Johnny? Any word from my wife?'

'Johnny's well. He was asking about you and Mrs Wilde. I said you'd see him in the morning. I gave him his tea and allowed him and Penelope to play for an hour.'

'That's good, thank you.'

'I think Mrs Wilde might have tried to call you, but I was bathing Penelope and I didn't get to the telephone in time.'

'Don't worry. Well, it sounds as though you've done a fine day's work here, Mrs Keane, so why don't you get yourself off to bed and I'll just have my drink and read a little.'

'Yes, sir, of course. Goodnight, Professor.'

'Goodnight, Mrs Keane.'

Wilde settled down with the newspaper and found himself wondering: how had the three men known he was on the coast of Norfolk?

'We know who he is,' Templeman said when they met in his study at 9 a.m. 'We've identified him as Georg Sosinka. He identifies himself as a *feldwebel* in the Wehrmacht, or what we would call an army sergeant. Though it's possible he was actually SS. I'm told that many SS men have been trying to pass themselves off as regular soldiers. Anyway, we have records on him because he absconded from a POW camp at Epsom in Surrey three months ago. He made his escape in the company of a fellow prisoner named Paul Kagerer, so it seems likely that he will be one of the two men still at large.'

'Is Sosinka talking?'

'He was fortunate that the bullet missed the heart and he'll survive, but he's still sedated. We'll give him the third degree as soon as the doctors allow us. We're pretty certain that neither he nor Kagerer speaks much English. So the voice you heard, the man with the needles, is still unidentified.'

'If Sosinka and Kagerer absconded from Epsom in July, what the hell have they been up to since then?'

'Someone must have been protecting them.'

'The third man – the one with the needles. He's the important one. He said my name and he sounded English . . . but not quite. What now, Dagger?'

'We take the Black Book threat very seriously. You're going to have to keep yourself armed at all times and so am I. And, just as importantly, I'm going to give your wife a round-the-clock shadow. Don't worry, she won't know we're there. But we'll keep her safe. I'll send someone over to fetch a photograph if that's all right.'

Wilde nodded. Lydia might not like it, but it was a necessary precaution.

The head porter, Scobie, doffed his bowler hat then delved into the mail cubbyholes. 'Letter for you, Professor. Delivered by hand this very morning.'

Wilde accepted the missive and shoved it, unopened, into his pocket. It was in a fine quality envelope and had the feel of an invitation; the last thing he wanted at the moment was another drinks party.

He needed a coffee badly because there hadn't been any left at home. Here at college, though, Bobby produced the goods as always.

Sitting at his desk, he took out the letter and cut it open, sliding out a card with italic script. It was from Sir Neville Catesby and was an invitation to a shooting party at Harbinger House this coming weekend. Wilde wasn't in the slightest bit interested in shooting, but he immediately called Templeman and asked his opinion.

'I'd like you to go, Tom.'

'It seems to me that I must have been a bit of an afterthought. Invitations don't usually come this close to the event.'

'But you shoot.'

'Only my enemies, not pheasants.'

'Very funny. What guns have you got?'

'None. I really don't like shooting.'

'You can borrow my old Dicksons – a Scottish round-action pair. They're not Purdeys but they're not at all bad. I really want to know who's there, you see. In particular, I want you to get close to Neville Catesby. See if you can provoke him into revealing his true self. Anyway, the food should be pretty good.'

Wilde wasn't keen, but he took Templeman's point. No harm would be done. Anyway, he doubted whether Lydia would be able to get home on her first weekend so there was nothing to be lost in spending a night or two away. Mrs Keane seemed to have everything under control with the children.

'All right,' he said, 'I'll do it. But I don't have the clothes.'

'You'll need plus twos or fours, jacket, waistcoat and I'm sure you have some stout shoes. Anyway, don't worry – I've a couple of good friends about your height and weight, so I'll fix all that for you. Come to Latimer Hall before you go and we'll get you fitted up and you can practise with the Dicksons on a few clays.'

Wilde replaced the telephone receiver and wandered to the window. It was a gloomy day with a light drizzle, but he badly needed some air, so he grabbed his aged trench coat and the old felt hat that he rarely wore and wandered down the stairs. As he stepped through the archway he saw a newly familiar figure striding away on the far side of Old Court. The young officer turned student Danny Oswick was heading towards the entrance gatehouse with intent. Without consciously making a decision, Wilde found himself following his undergraduate. What did he do with his days outside college? Who did he meet? Like everyone else on this chilly, damp autumn day, Wilde pulled his hat over his brow and hunched into his coat. The Colt was there in his pocket. He wasn't going anywhere without that.

Oswick was wearing his gown over his jacket and had his hands in his pockets as he strode jauntily southwards along Trumpington Street. Wilde kept a good distance behind, a little less than a hundred yards. It was easy to follow the young man, because he didn't turn around. There were a lot of people about and Wilde melted into the crowd.

Almost a mile down the road, Oswick removed his gown and shoved it unceremoniously into a leather shoulder bag he was carrying. Soon afterwards, he turned right into a street of modest houses. Fewer people were around, so Wilde dropped back further.

The rain had intensified, teeming down his neck. He followed Oswick through the backstreets until the young man stopped outside a small terraced house in Colstead Road, took a key from his pocket and entered, closing the door after him. Wilde walked on past, glancing sideways at the house number – 43 – and the window. It was no more than a glimpse, but he saw Oswick embracing a fair-haired woman.

Lydia was rocked by the arduousness of the work. It was many years since she had last studied – at Girton College – and she had forgotten the rigour required. Yes, she had read Black's from cover to cover, but that was a long way from this. If Black's was the skeleton of medical knowledge, this was the muscle, organs, sinews, nerves, glands and blood vessels. There was so much new terminology to be memorised. Every minuscule part of the body had its role and had a word attached to it. As she struggled through the great medical tomes in the St Ursula's library, she felt her heart sink.

Her room-mate, Miranda, was the one person who cheered her up. She wasn't going to fret about the work. 'It'll all come together eventually, Lydia, you'll see. We can't learn it all in our first few weeks. Now, you should put the textbooks aside and read some of this.' She held up the book she had been devouring when Lydia arrived.

'What is it?'

Miranda grinned and put a finger to her mouth. 'Don't tell a word, but it's quite illegal.' She lowered her voice. '*Lady Chatterley's Lover*. Have you heard of it?'

THE ENGLISH FÜHRER | 134

'Vaguely. It's a bit naughty, isn't it?'

'I should say so. It's an uncensored copy smuggled in from the continent. Every other word has four letters. But it's glorious, Lydia, it really is. Everyone says it's a dirty book, but I don't think it is. It's passion and joy – and it makes sex seem like fun rather than sin. Now I've read about it, I can't wait to try it.'

Lydia just smiled. She wasn't quite sure how to respond. A thought struck her. 'I did peek at a copy of *Fanny Hill* once. Have you heard of it?'

'Of course. Have you got a copy? I'd love to read it. We could swap.'

'Sadly not. I found it in a friend's house.'

'Well, then you'll just have to steal it for me. And steal some sugar while you're about it.'

Lydia returned to her studies. Whatever Miranda said, she knew she was going to have to work harder than she had ever worked in her life. Even though Dr Gertrude Blake was not often in evidence, she felt her eyes bearing down on her, as though she expected her to fail, and she couldn't allow that.

Dame Gertrude – that was what all the young women called her behind her back – had summoned her to her office that morning to ask her how she was settling in.

'Very well, thank you, Dr Blake.'

'I'm told you didn't faint at anatomy, so that's something. How are you getting on with your room-mate, Miss March?'

'Like a house on fire, I think.'

'She's a bright girl, but she'll need to keep her nose to the grind-stone if she's to succeed at St Ursula's. I deliberately had you put with her hoping that you'd bring a touch of maturity into her orbit. Show her how much work is needed.'

Lydia nodded, but the truth was she was wondering whether she could cope with her own work, let alone play mother hen to another student. This was a responsibility she really didn't need. 'Of course, I'll do my best,' she said. 'But I think you might be underestimating her a little bit. She does a lot of reading.'

'Yes, but *what* is she reading exactly? She comes from a good Midlands family, but I'm not certain how much she really wants to be a physician. Both her parents are doctors and I have a feeling that she was pushed in this direction rather than having any strong vocation. I'm not sure I would have given her a place, but there were others on the committee who knew her mother and were adamant she should be admitted. I found myself in the rare position of being overruled. That said, I should very much like to be proved wrong in my assessment of Miss March, which is where you come in, Miss Morris, for I believe you have quite a wise head on you, as well as some experience of the world. Keep the girl in line for me, would you?'

Lydia smiled. What could she say? If she had wanted to be a nursemaid, she would have stayed home with Johnny.

'Well, that's all, Miss Morris. Come to me if you ever have any concerns. My door is always open.'

Why, Lydia wondered, did Dame Gertrude put such emphasis on the *Miss* when she called her Miss Morris?

Such matters were not at the forefront of Lydia's mind at the moment, however. She most certainly did have a concern, but it wasn't one that she would ever take to Dame Gertrude. It was Johnny and Tom and the difficulty in communicating with them. Last night, she had sneaked out to a telephone kiosk and tried to call home. But no one answered, not even the new housekeeper. It was an unpleasant sensation, a feeling of detachment from the two people she loved more than any others in the world. A feeling of homesickness, something she hadn't experienced since childhood when she was put on trains and sent away to little-known uncles and cousins in far-flung corners of the country for the holidays.

Nor was that the only thing troubling her. There was something else on her abortive trip to the phone box – a horrible feeling that she was being watched and followed.

CHAPTER 18

After observing Oswick entering a modest house in a backstreet of Cambridge, and then glimpsing him taking a blonde woman in his arms, Wilde returned to college. His curiosity had been lit but he felt disinclined to watch and wait for his undergraduate to reappear. He had other things to do – a book to get back on track and another lecture to prepare.

That was what he told himself. But once in his rooms, shuffling through his notes for the new history volume, he couldn't concentrate. Too much else was going on and he still didn't understand what it was, or his own part in it. And then the phone rang and the exchange connected him to Templeman once more.

'The German's awake,' the MI5 man said without preamble.

'Is he talking?'

'Very little. He's admitted that his name's Sosinka and that he did a runner from the Epsom POW camp, but beyond that almost nothing. It's one of those times when you almost wonder whether a little judicious torture might be in order, but sadly our consciences wouldn't allow it. Still, that won't help Herr Sosinka in the long run; he'll be charged as an accessory to the murder of the old farmer, Mr Bagshawe, and will be hanged in due course. In the meantime, we'll keep chatting to him. You never know, these people sometimes cough when they realise they'll soon be meeting their maker.'

Wilde knew what 'chatting to them meant'. He knew that MI5 didn't stop far of torture at centres like Camp 020. Sleep deprivation, glaring non-stop light, isolation, even mock execution could go a long way towards creating disorientation and, ultimately, a sense of hopelessness.

'I mentioned that Sosinka said *almost* nothing, Tom, because the bastard did have one thing to say: he said he looked forward to the day when every last *Engländer* was incinerated, along with his wife and children. And then he spat on the ground.'

'Charming chap.'

'Indeed. And what we suspected has been confirmed by the Met's laboratory: poor old Charlie Bagshawe was killed by a large dose of phenol.'

That was no surprise to Wilde. He had seen it happen with his own eyes. There was a pause in the conversation.

'Tom, are you there?'

'Sorry, just thinking about Charlie. I was only acquainted with him for two hours but he made me welcome.'

'It's a bloody tragedy.' A heavy sigh came through the wire. 'What about you? Anything else to report?'

He wasn't going to mention that he had been following Oswick. That was not a subject for the telephone. Three years in the Office of Strategic Services and participation in various intelligence missions prior to that had taught him never to assume that phones weren't tapped.

'Not for the moment, Dagger. Perhaps tomorrow.'

Two hours later, at six o'clock, as the evening began to draw in, he yawned and stretched his arms. He had pushed the book to one side and was deep into planning his next lecture. Time to go home, see Johnny and have some supper. Perhaps Lydia would try calling again.

As he passed his window, he glanced out and saw Oswick returning to his rooms, his gown once more trailing in his wake, his hair dripping wet from the rain. It was an opportunity Wilde could not resist. He donned his coat and hat again and ventured once more into the streets of Cambridge.

He arrived at Colstead Road and stood fifty yards from the door of number forty-three and waited. The rain was heavy and his hat did little to protect him from a drenching. He couldn't help noticing the odd stares he got from people rushing past and he felt a fool. Cold, too. What sort of idiot simply stands there in the rain? He spotted a grey-haired woman gazing out at him from behind lace curtains and avoided making eye contact with her. This might be a regulation watching brief for a seasoned MI5 agent, but it did not sit easily with a respectable Cambridge don.

After ten minutes, Wilde was just beginning to wonder whether this humiliation was all worth it and thinking it really was time to be wending his way home when the door opened and a woman in a raincoat and headscarf ducked out and broke into an awkward run along the street. Not exactly a sprint, just a little faster than walking so as to minimise the dousing. Wilde didn't get a look at her face but he immediately broke into a trot of similar speed, following her with ease while keeping a decent distance behind her.

The rain was full on in his face but in a strange way it helped him. Everyone was trying to get out of the weather as fast as they could and hurry home for their supper, no one was interested in what anyone else was doing and the woman wasn't going to turn around to see if she was being followed.

They arrived at a yard at the back of the Old Plough Inn not far from Colstead Road. A soggy paper sign strung above an open doorway proclaimed that this was the meeting place of THE NEW REALM PATRIOTS – ALL WELCOME, the words hand-painted, badly.

Without hesitation, the woman entered the brightly lit meeting room, which was clearly not part of the inn's public area, but a space set aside especially for this event. Wilde stopped. He couldn't follow her in, could he? Two men, one muscular and intimidating, the other smaller and smiling, stood inside the entrance porch on either side of the doorway. They were there to inspect newcomers and either admit them or send them on their way. They stared at Wilde with interest – or was it suspicion?

'You 18B?' the smaller man asked.

'No.' Wilde knew what he meant. He was referring to Defence Regulation 18B, under which those deemed a threat had been interned during the war; their number included many members of the British Union of Fascists.

'What's the accent, mate?'

'American.' Wilde was thinking fast. 'I was Bund.'

'Ah, good man. Come on in.'

Bund. The German American Bund – a pre-war organisation of American Nazis who supported Hitler. At one time its membership numbered in the tens of thousands but by the time the

US entered the conflict the group had fizzled out like a damp firework.

Wilde hesitated only a moment, then smiled back at the man and entered the back room of the inn. The light was garish from a single unshaded bulb hanging in the centre of the ceiling. At one end of the room there was a makeshift lectern in front of an upturned crate.

A bar had been set up at the other end of the room, where a small woman was dispensing beer from a keg. Wilde looked around; there were no more than twenty people here, including the blonde he had been following. She had removed her headscarf and shaken out her shoulder-length peroxide hair and was talking animatedly to a couple of men near the little bar.

They were a curious mix, mostly men in manual working clothes, half a dozen women of varying ages from twenty to seventy, and a group of middle-aged men who wore sports jackets and had the air of belonging to the officer or professional classes, perhaps lawyers or teachers. This latter group formed a huddle, keeping themselves apart from the working men.

Wilde felt self-conscious. He was sure he should be talking to someone – but who? And about what? Even as he was wondering whether to cut and run, the blonde approached him, smiling sweetly, carrying a drink in a half-pint glass.

'What's your poison, darling?'

'Oh, I'm not drinking.'

'You're not English.'

'Does that matter?'

'No, so long as you're with us.'

'That's what I want to find out. That's why I'm here. The sign says "All Welcome".'

'It means all patriots welcome. British patriots. People who believe in king and country and the empire, and no interlopers.'

'Interlopers?'

'You know what I mean, or if you don't then you really are in the wrong place.' She reached out and ran her index finger along the scar line where the hair no longer grew on the side of his head. 'I hope you sued the barber for that piece of work.'

'It was a bullet.'

'Now that *is* interesting. Tell me more.'

'Nothing to tell. I'm still alive.'

'Man of mystery, eh? I like that.'

She was almost good looking. Too much makeup, lips pillar-box red. Roots showing. A long silk scarf, red and gold, encircled her throat. Her smile did not quite conceal the acid lurking beneath.

'Shirin's the name,' she continued. 'Shirin Tombs. Do you ever go to the theatre?'

'Now and then, not much these past six years.'

'Well if you did, you might have seen me. Star of stage from London to Liverpool and most points in between. Did you ever see *Destination Midnight*?'

'I don't know what that is, I'm afraid.'

'It's a flick, darling. I had a good role in that.'

'If I ever see it's playing, I'll definitely go to it.'

'Don't blink, though, eh.' She smiled again and this time it seemed genuine. 'What's your name, darling?'

'Tom,' he said.

'Good name that. I had a paramour named Tom once. Very famous man, he was. Still is, actually. He was married, of course. They all are, darling.'

'Would I have heard of him?'

'Oh yes, but I'm not a telltale, so my lips are sealed. Anyway, Tom what? What's your surname?'

'Read,' he said. It was the first name that came into his mind simply because he had one of the Conyers Read books on his desk in his college set and he had been consulting it while preparing his lecture.

'Tom Read. I like that. Tell me a bit about yourself, darling. You're not working class and you don't look military and you sound vaguely American.'

'I told the men on the door. I was in the German-American Bund before the war. Very disappointed that it came to nothing.'

She nodded knowingly. 'Were you at the Stuttgart foreign convention in 'thirty-seven?'

'Sadly, I couldn't make it.' He had heard of it, of course. The Nazis of many countries coming together to be feted, feasted and encouraged by the German hierarchy.

'What of Fritz Kuhn? You must have known him. I met him in New York.'

'No, I wasn't one of his inner circle.' It was the safest thing to say. 'But I heard him speak. He was inspirational.'

'Did you think so? I wouldn't piss on the man. He was soft as cotton wool. With luck he's dead now.'

'I'm sorry you feel like that.'

'If he'd been half a man, he'd have kept the Yanks onside. Anyway, Mr Read, what you doing over here in ye olde England? And why Cambridge?'

He had two choices. Hastily construct a lie, or keep his mouth shut. He chose the second option. 'That's my business, Miss Tombs.'

The hammering of a stick on the upturned beer crate broke up their conversation, for which Wilde was grateful. One of the officer class men was standing on it, cane in hand, eyes staring fiercely at the little audience, which had now expanded to almost thirty. The doors had been shut.

'Friends, Englishmen, 18Bs, enemies of the worldwide conspiracy, welcome to this the first meeting of the New Realm Patriots.'

Wilde closed his ears to the remainder of the fifteen-minute speech. 'Speech' was the wrong word; it was a 'rant'. The speaker, who introduced himself as Commander Harding-Watts, RN retired, simply spewed a torrent of invective on everyone in the world who was *not British*, particularly the Jews, but followed by a long catalogue of other races and nationalities and skin colours he deemed to be lesser mortals. It was the same tired and pathetic refrain spouted endlessly by Hitler and Mosley and Goebbels.

It certainly pleased the little crowd, for they applauded enthusiastically. Wilde went along with them and put his hands together, for not to have done so would have marked him out as different. For his finale, and to emphasise his disapproval of the 'damnable' Labour government, Commander Harding-Watts, RN retired, thumped the lectern, and the structure collapsed.

Shirin Tombs turned to Wilde and smiled. 'Oh dear.'

'Not impressed?'

'Well, I liked the ending – the smashing up of the furniture. What about you?'

'I suppose he covered the ground adequately, but he's no orator.'

'Indeed not, Tom.'

'I noticed he said this was the first meeting of the New Realm Patriots. Aren't there any other better-established groups?' Wilde asked. 'What about Mosley? He's out of jail, isn't he?'

'Much as I still love Tom Mosley, he's a busted flush. He's too unreliable. We need strong men. Men of steel. Are you a man of steel, Tom?'

'That's for others to decide.'

'A man of action then?'

'I think so.'

'Perhaps you'd like to meet some other men of action, more serious-minded people. This lot, well, they're not going to set the world on fire, are they?'

'I guess not.'

'How can I get in touch with you?'

'You can't,' he said. 'But I could make contact with you if you gave me a good enough reason to.'

'Come on, let's get out of here and go and have a proper drink. I've had enough of this lot of hams.'

'Of all the people at the meeting, what made you approach me?' he asked her.

'Did you see the others?'

Yes, he had. He had to admit they were not an impressive bunch.

'So why did you come to the meeting, Miss Tombs? It obviously wasn't your kind of thing.'

'Shirin, darling. You call me Shirin. And it's very much my kind of thing. Right message, wrong people. Except yourself perhaps.'

'As you like.'

'It's all splintering, that's why. I wanted to see if there were any like-minds there, that's all. With the BUF we thought we were going somewhere. We had our glory days. Thousands of us marching. It wasn't quite Nuremberg, but we were getting there. Now it's fallen apart. We need to regroup with the very best people, all working together.'

'So you're recruiting. That's why you came here.'

'You're very astute, Tom Read. By the way, what's your real name?'

'That is my real name.'

They were in the snug bar at the front of the Plough. It was the sort of place where Wilde was unlikely to meet any college dons or undergraduates. College servants were another matter. He desperately hoped he didn't see any. It would be difficult to explain his presence here with this dyed-blonde fascist.

'Well, we'll use it for the moment, shall we.'

'Does that mean Shirin Tombs isn't your real name?'

'It's my stage name, darling. I keep my married name for the grocer and the butcher.'

'You're married?'

'And why exactly does that surprise you so much?'

He picked up his whisky and took a hefty draught. 'Just interested, that's all.'

'Interested in making a pass at me, is that what you mean? Fancy a bit, do you?'

'You misunderstand me.'

She laughed. 'I'm messing with you, darling. You know what, you're too much the bloody innocent to be Special Branch or MI5.'

He gave her a searching look. 'Did you think I was a spy then?'

'Well, you can't be too careful. There's a lot of them about these days. Don't know what to do with themselves now the bloody war's over and there are no German secret agents to hunt, so they spend all their time harassing us instead. Thing is, they're too pig ignorant and obvious. We can see them coming a country mile away.'

Her voice, he decided, was northern, probably Lancashire, though he was no expert on such things. He guessed her age at thirty-five, but she could have been a little younger. She was certainly a few years older than Danny Oswick. If it wasn't for the undyed roots, the over-powdered face and the glimpse of darkness in her soul, she might have been attractive. Obviously she was to Oswick, but not to Wilde.

'Don't look at me like that,' she said.

'Like what?'

'Like I'm a bloody insect you're studying, darling.'

'I'm sorry, I didn't realise I was.'

'Do you have a special skill, Tom Read? Apart from getting shot in the head?'

'I don't know what you mean.'

'I mean, what unique skill would you bring to a group of like-minded men and women. Are you good with your fists? I have a special skill, you see.'

'And what's that?'

'Oh, you may well find out one day.'

'You mean your acting skills?'

'No, I didn't mean that. Something more important. So what can *you* do for the movement?'

He shrugged helplessly. 'Well, I can box a bit. Apart from that, well, that's for me to know.' He wasn't quite sure where to take this conversation. They were like a pair of prizefighters circling each other, testing each other with jabs, sizing each other up and seeking out weaknesses. One thing he was certain about – she wasn't going to divulge secrets on initial acquaintance. He would have to meet her again if anything was to come of this foray.

That was what Templeman wanted, wasn't it? An entry to the world of Danny Oswick and the new fascists.

'All right,' he said, finishing off the Scotch. 'Let's meet again. Perhaps you'll introduce me to your men of steel.'

'We'll see. I need to talk to one or two people. Shall we meet here tomorrow, six thirty? Yes?'

'OK, I'll look forward to it.'

'They'll need to know more about you, so come with your story intact or you'll likely find yourself beaten to a pulp in a gutter. My friends don't like to be messed about.'

'I can handle myself, Mrs . . . Shirin.'

'That's all settled then, isn't it, darling. And for your information, my married name is Oswick. Mrs Daniel Oswick. Maybe I'll introduce you to my Danny. Now he really is a man of steel.'

CHAPTER 19

A brawl had broken out at the back of the inn. Dozens of working men had marched along the street singing 'The Red Flag' before storming the meeting of the New Realm Patriots and setting about the commander and his friends with fists and cudgels. The fight had spilled out on to the street. Blood ran down cheeks and arms, dripping in the rain.

Wilde couldn't afford to be involved. He watched momentarily from the pub doorway as the bigger of the two doormen punched one of the protesters in the nose, then staggered backwards as a cricket bat smacked full force into his temple.

'Not good,' Wilde said, turning to Shirin Oswick.

She was laughing. 'I thought you said you could look after yourself, Tom.'

'This isn't going to get us anywhere, though, is it.'

'Oh, I don't know. It worked for the Brownshirts.'

'But the Brownshirts tended to win their fights through brute strength and force of numbers. This lot are on to a hiding for nothing.'

'You're probably right, but I love a punch-up. Gets me in the mood, if you know what I mean.'

He rather thought he did know what she meant, but he wasn't going to pursue the point. 'Until tomorrow,' he said, then turned away from her and from the fight. Without looking back, he hurried through the downpour eastwards along the maze of lanes and alleys back towards college.

Only when he was several streets away did he slow down and turn around. The coast was clear; he wasn't being followed.

As he shook off the rain in the arched entrance to his staircase, he looked up and saw that a visitor was sitting at the top of the steps outside his room. 'Oswick, what are you doing here?'

'My supervision, Professor.' He looked at his wristwatch ostentatiously. 'I thought you said seven o'clock.'

He had quite forgotten. 'Good God, I'm sorry, Oswick. It slipped my mind. I have no excuse.' He realised he was more than half an hour late.

'Gosh, sir, it really doesn't matter. I have nothing else to do and I managed to read a little while I was waiting.'

'Shall we postpone it until tomorrow?'

'That's up to you, sir. I'm available now if you are.'

'Very well, if you're sure, come on in. Hopefully we can stoke up the fire and get you a cup of tea.'

'Thank you, sir. That would be spiffing.' Oswick endowed Wilde with an engaging smile that lifted his moustache at the corners.

Was this young man really married to Shirin, the shabby blonde with a taste for a fist fight and reckless right-wing politics? Wilde estimated she must be seven or eight years his senior, not that that counted for anything.

There were still a few embers in the fire. Wilde threw on some coal and used the bellows to get it going. Bobby had gone home for the night, but his door was open, so Wilde got the kettle on and quickly brewed a pot of tea. Perhaps the young man would have preferred whisky – Wilde certainly would – but it would be indecent to start off their master–scholar relationship on such an informal footing.

As to the fact that the young man was married, that was not uncommon among the new intake of undergraduates, many of whom were seasoned fighting men with war brides and one or two babies and toddlers in their rooms. And if Oswick wished to keep his own marital status private, that was his business.

'So, Oswick, have you had any more thoughts since my lecture on "Espionage and the Elizabethan Theatre"?'

'I find the whole concept intriguing, sir. Clearly, as you said, spies must be actors. They are playing a role, concealing their true identity.'

'Which as you note is merely repeating what I said. As a scholar, you need to take the idea further. What, for instance, does it say about Elizabethan society generally?'

'I suppose it was a time of great division and distrust. The Catholics did not trust the Protestants and vice versa. And the predominantly Protestant English felt themselves under huge pressure from the Catholic powers of Europe. In such societies, neighbours distrust and denounce neighbours. Everyone has a watchful eye, mostly for self-protection but also to do down their perceived enemies.'

'Good, that takes us on a little further.'

And so the hour progressed. They spoke of the Tudor theatre which was, in itself, revolutionary, and the suspicion in which it was held by many close to Queen Elizabeth. What they did not address was twentieth-century politics or the war – or Danny Oswick's personal situation.

Wilde gave the young man an essay to work on, along with a comprehensive reading list for the remainder of the Michaelmas term and they arranged a further supervision for two weeks' time. He watched from the window as Oswick walked the path around Old Court, skirting the forbidden scrubby lawns. Wilde wondered how this was going to play out. How could he meet his wife and not be exposed? What if she brought him along – what would he say then? Cambridge was too small a town for such double-dealing.

This was an insanely bad idea. He needed to talk to Templeman about it, sooner rather than later.

'You know, Tom, I thought the war would simplify things. We'd beat the Nazis and the world would settle down to eternal peace. Now it all seems so damnably complicated.'

Templeman was in an unusually reflective mood, slowly pacing around his study, brandy glass in hand. More than merely thoughtful, he seemed troubled.

'Well things are better than they were, surely.'

'Are they, Tom? Are they? Are these the sunlit uplands? How can there be sunshine with so much bitterness? The rage on all sides of those whose loved ones were killed by bomb, bullet, fire, water and gas didn't just vanish like smoke because peace treaties were signed.'

Of course he was right.

'Think of the despair of the millions displaced around Europe,' Templeman continued. 'Think of the disappointment and disillusionment of peoples who thought they were liberated only to find their freedom snatched away by the Red Army? We went to war to save Poland from aggressors, but have we saved them? I see storms brewing on all sides and I have serious doubts concerning the intentions of Comrade Stalin.'

'You're not alone in that, Dagger.'

'And what's to become of the empire? How long can we hold onto India? All the colonies know that we have been terribly weakened by the war and they will seize their opportunity. If we don't concede independence, they will rebel against us, and we certainly don't have the money or the manpower to fight wars of containment in every single pink bit on the Mercator. I'm sorry, I'm sounding off.'

Wilde sipped his own whisky. The mellow spirit and Templeman's diatribe were really rather soothing. In fact, as an American, he thought it would be no bad thing if the British colonies sought independence. 'Sound off as much as you like, Dagger. Fine by me.'

'No, I'm going to shut up. Your problems are equally complex and much more immediate. I should never have involved you in the matter of Oswick. I've put you in a corner and I can see that it could compromise your position as a Fellow of your college should it ever come to light that you have been spying on an undergraduate. It was an absolutely wretched idea of mine.'

'What do I do?'

'You mustn't meet the young man's wife again. Just stand her up – I'll get other men on the case.'

'Wouldn't you be interested to know what she has to say for herself, and who she might be involved with politically?'

'Well, of course, I would. At the moment, her name means nothing to me. I'll double-check, but I don't believe we have anything in our files on the woman. But you said yourself that Oswick might arrive at the pub with her. What then?'

'It's a chance I'll take.'

'Are you sure?'

'Not totally. But you want to discover the truth about Danny and Shirin Oswick, and so do I.'

Templeman, still uncharacteristically distracted, wandered over to a bookshelf and idly ran his right forefinger over the spines of several ancient volumes.

'Was there something else, Dagger?'

He turned. 'I'm afraid there was, and it's not pleasant. Would you mind awfully if we talked about Philip Eaton again?'

'Why, has something happened?'

'Yes, it has. A minute ago you were saying how uncomfortable you felt about spying on one of your own undergraduates. Well, I feel much the same way about spying on one of our own secret service men.'

Wilde was astonished. 'You've been spying on Philip Eaton? Surely that can't be within your remit.'

'My remit is communication within the discrete divisions of the security services. When I see the link breaking down I have to look into it. I was not satisfied with Eaton's explanation regarding the defection and disappearance of Comrade Minsky, so it was my duty to instigate inquiries, and that included keeping a watch on Eaton.'

'What were you hoping to find?'

'I wasn't hoping to find anything. This was a standard operation. But I confess I have been worried about Eaton for some time, and I rather suspect you have had your own doubts for even longer than me. Am I right?'

Was he right? Yes, and no. Eaton was undoubtedly an effective MI6 operator. By all accounts he had done good work on the Iberian desk during the Spanish Civil War, and he had earned his promotion to the top echelons of the organisation. Also, he had certainly helped Wilde on more than one occasion. In the war against the Axis powers he had excelled. There could be no doubting his visceral loathing of Hitler and all his demons.

But yes, there had been doubts about his loyalty in other matters, he couldn't deny that. The disappearance of the SMERSH defector

Sergei Borisov, real name Boris Minsky, was the most immediate worry. How *had* he managed to lose the bloody Russian?

Wilde nodded. 'Very well, I admit I've been concerned about Minsky. Eaton's explanation might sound plausible, but it doesn't really add up.'

'And that's the point, Tom. That's what's been eating away at me. And now my worst fears have been realised. You see, we think we've found Boris Minsky.'

'Good God, where?'

'In Chelsea. Entering Philip Eaton's house at three thirty in the morning. We don't have a photograph of the Russian but the man our agents saw seems to answers the description. Rotund, which is in itself a giveaway in these days when everyone is thin. Not tall . . .'

'Bald?'

'Probably. He was wearing a hat and what might have been a very bad wig. The problem is I don't know how to proceed with this information.'

'Good God, you've shocked me, Dagger. To the core.'

'I'm shocked, too. And I feel very uncomfortable about the whole situation.'

'I take it Borisov – or Minsky – is in custody.'

'No, he stayed in the house for just over an hour. In that time, one of my agents called me. I made a mistake – I told them to continue watching the house and, if Minsky left, to follow him. I wanted to know where he went. Well, he got as far as the Soviet Embassy and disappeared inside. He hasn't been seen since. We've lost the bastard again.'

'But you've discovered something. You now know that Minsky's defection was a fake. He's still working for SMERSH.'

'Yes, that seems likely.'

'Then you're going to have to arrest Philip Eaton.'

'Am I? What if this is a perfectly sound mission he's involved in? What if Minsky's playing a triple cross on Eaton's orders? Or what if Eaton is feeding misinformation to the Soviets via Minsky? You know these MI6 boys work in extremely devious and mysterious ways. I can't afford to barge in wearing my size fourteens and mess the whole thing up.'

'But you don't think that's the case, do you, Dagger?'

'I don't know, Tom. I really don't know. Forgive me for burdening you with this because I know you've got a hell of a lot on your plate. The problem is I can't discuss this with anyone in the service because once I do it becomes official and the wheels roll on regardless. Worse than that, the more people who know, the higher the likelihood that word will get through to Moscow. That's why I've put you on the spot, because I need an opinion, someone I can trust who is outside the service. And that means you. I suspect you know Eaton as well as any man alive.'

Wilde simply shrugged. 'I'm glad you feel you can trust me, but I doubt whether any man knows the heart of Philip Eaton.'

'Is that all?'

'Well, I do believe he's done some great service for this country in its fight with fascism. But put that to one side for a moment. Just because a man has fought to the death against one enemy does not mean he will fight *all* enemies with such fervour.'

'You're saying he has a soft spot for the Reds?'

'It's possible. There are plenty of fellow travellers in the West. Have you ever heard of Horace Dill?'

'Professor Dill? Of course. Been dead a few years now.'

Wilde had been with him at the very end. Held his hand as he slipped away. 'It was just at the start of the war. You know that Horace was a committed communist?'

'He was always on Five's radar, but he seemed harmless enough. Had an idealistic view of Comrades Lenin and Trotsky, as I recall.'

'You might have underestimated him. I always had a powerful impression that he was more than just a sympathiser, that he worked assiduously to further the communist cause in this country, perhaps even recruiting promising young men. People like Philip Eaton.'

'Are you suggesting that MI6 has a Soviet spy in its midst?'

'Isn't that what you were suggesting? I have always felt that Philip's true loyalties might lie to the far left, but of course he is much too good an operator ever to reveal his politics openly.'

Templeman nodded slowly, then allowed himself a grave little smile. 'Thank you, Tom. That is a most thought-provoking analysis. I think I know what I have to do.'

'Are you going to tell me?'

'Not yet. Perhaps in due course.'

'Go easy on him.'

'I can't promise anything.'

Wilde put down his glass, unfinished. 'It's late. I need to get going.'

'I'll walk you to my car. The driver will be waiting. Oh, and I'm afraid it's not the greatest news regarding your friend May Hinchley. Bit of a setback apparently.'

'Any more details?'

'Sadly not. But on a rather lighter note I can tell you that your motorcycle has been collected and is being put back together by my mechanic. I've told him I want it as good as new. Should be with you in two or three days.'

CHAPTER 20

Daniel Oswick checked his watch. Shirin had been gone ten minutes. That should be enough. The small sitting room here at 43 Colstead Road smelt of mould and the ceiling was low, not like his comfortable rooms at college and not like the barn with the high beam where he found his father swinging half a lifetime ago.

Sometimes at night when he lay in bed, he could still hear the creak of rope on wood as the body slowly turned with the gusting of the breeze through the high, wide doorway.

For a few moments he had stood there doing nothing, paralysed by the horror of what he was witnessing. And then he'd rushed forward and grasped his father around the legs and tried to hoist him up to take the weight off his neck. He had to cut the rope but he had no knife and the rope was out of reach.

In his soul he knew that the man he knew simply as Pa was dead, but that couldn't be. Not his perfect father. He stood there holding the legs, pushing upwards. He began shouting for help. He needed a blade and a ladder, but no one came.

Then he saw the tall stool his father must have stood on before kicking it away, plunging to his death. Gently releasing the legs, he picked up the stool and placed it beneath the hanging body so that he could stand on it and reach higher, to get at the rope. He looked around the old barn and spotted some tools in the corner near the hay wagon. They were stored haphazardly, but there had to be something here, something with an edge.

An ancient sickle lay in the dust. He picked it up in his shaking hand. The blade wasn't sharp, but it was the only implement available. Scarcely breathing in the midst of his dread, he clambered up on the stool and reached over his father's head and began hacking at the rope. He couldn't bear to look at Pa's face, but nor could he avoid it and he saw the bulging, lifeless eyes which he knew would never leave him, by night or day. Sleeping or awake, those pitiful eyes would follow him, haunt him until his own dying day.

He had only ever seen kindness in his father's face, and now there was nothing but a pale simulacrum, full of despair and sorrow.

The rope wasn't thick or strong, but it was taut and difficult to cut with the dull metal edge. It took a minute, perhaps more, and then it was severed. Oswick wanted to let the lifeless body down gently to the floor, but he misjudged the weight and it fell away from him, tumbling horribly to the straw-covered flagstones.

Oswick fell, too, and was hurt. But he ignored the pain in his ankle and knelt at his father's side, cradling the poor head, kissing the cheeks as his own hot tears cascaded onto the still-warm brow. 'Pa,' he begged. 'Please, Pa, please don't go. Please come back.'

Oswick was thirteen years old. His father had been thirty-four. It was the day Danny Oswick learnt to hate the ruling classes and swore that one day he would have his revenge on them for what they had done so casually and unthinkingly to good Joseph Oswick.

The year was 1932. They had been living on the road, begging bread from people who had none of their own. Sleeping in hedgerows and shop doorways and barns like the one in which his father died. Often as not, they got told to move on, sometimes with threats involving canes, dogs and shotguns.

The day before Joe Oswick's death, the pair of them had sneaked into the building late at night and slept well. Just before the dawn, the boy had gone in search of food. The farmhouse wasn't yet awake, and no one was out and about, so he was able to range around the yard and the outhouses for ten minutes.

It was his lucky day, or so he thought. He found a box of eggs and a couple of half-decent apples. That was real treasure in a country where so many were out of work and hungry.

Treasure. Six eggs and two apples. And his father's corpse.

Danny's childhood had been fine. He had never known his mother for she died giving birth to him, but his father had a job that any man would have dreamt of at that time: he was an under-butler at the royal palace of Sandringham in Norfolk, with ambitions one day to be a fully fledged butler.

As a home, Joseph Oswick had been granted the use of a little property in a nearby village where his own mother, a widow, came and raised Danny. The boy was acknowledged to be extremely clever but wild at times. He wasn't supposed to run free on the great royal estate, but, from the age of seven, he decided it was his own vast playground – all twenty thousand acres of it. He knew its woods and its meadows intimately, and could easily avoid the keepers, farmhands and gardeners. He was more cunning than any poacher and even the patrolling constables – there to protect the royal family – never caught him as he explored to his heart's content.

The very best of times were when King George went shooting with a party of the great men of Europe and Empire. The deafening roar of the guns, the questing of the dogs, and there, by the magnificent luncheon tent, his own father directing the waiters and waitresses and helping with the serving of the wines to the monarch and his fine guests.

Danny was eleven, doing well at school – despite his roving – with the distinct possibility of being awarded a scholarship to grammar school, when he was given a job in the big house, helping in the kitchens and with the boot-blacking for a few pennies and the occasional tip from one of the ladies when he ran messages for them. He loved the house, the other servants, the silver, the grandeur. This, he decided, would be his life. He would follow in Pa's footsteps.

And then it happened. Danny had never had an adequate explanation of why his father had been sacked, because adults didn't talk about such things. But Danny heard the conversations between his father and his grandmother. He heard the word 'marchioness', which he knew to be a title of a great lady, and he heard the word 'scandal' and much more besides, but he could never piece the jigsaw together.

All he was certain of was that Pa had lost his job because of someone else's transgression. Pa was innocent but he was thrown to the wolves.

By the end of the week, Joseph Oswick was not only unemployed but homeless too, for their cottage came with the job. They moved to a lodging house, using his small savings to pay their way. But there was no work to be had. Within weeks, Gran was dead from a stroke and Danny Oswick and his father were on the road.

For eighteen months they struggled from place to place, town to town. Occasionally, in summer, Joseph and Danny got a few days' work picking fruit or hops or helping with the barley harvests, but a proper job never materialised. Joseph had no references and so none of the big houses would take him in, not even as a footman or lowly pot-washer downstairs. Instead, they lived off the land, scrumping apples and cabbages, baking hedgehogs and any other wildlife they could find.

Pa became sick. He coughed up blood and became weak. By the time he hanged himself, he was already thin and haggard and Danny had to be the man.

But that wasn't the way the law saw it when the body was removed and an inquest held. The police and the town hall decided Danny should be taken to a children's home. Little did they know him.

Within two days, he absconded and hitched a ride on a lorry to London. He knew how to survive now, and if that meant stealing, so be it. He had natural cunning and fast feet and he was never caught. He kept himself fed and clothed and he never wanted for a decent berth in a squat. There were predators aplenty, but he was too quick and too smart for them.

He settled in the East End of London, ranging between Whitechapel, Bethnal Green and the docks at Shadwell. There was little enough money around, but there was energy and noise. He loved the anger and the sense of injustice, for they were the raw and deeply felt emotions that drove him.

In particular, he was beguiled by the roughly clad political men and women who inhabited this part of the city. They called themselves anarchists and Marxists and Trotskyites and spoke of bringing down the royals and the nobles and the landowners just as Lenin and Stalin had done in Russia. He listened to them intently and believed in a better world where the wealth of the nation was shared by all. He loved their passion and their promises. They stood for the retribution and justice he so badly desired.

But their talk soon palled, because their revolution never happened. They talked big and complained about their lot, but they didn't act. Sometimes there was a strike, but so what? Oswick didn't want walkouts by the dockers, he wanted heads on poles and the upper classes to be lined up against the wall.

In the autumn of 1934, when he was fifteen, he found an apprenticeship at a printer's. He also found good lodgings in a boarding house. And he found a friend who told him about the fascists and the Nazis and the work they had done in Italy and were beginning to do with ruthless energy and efficiency in Germany. He heard of men called Mussolini and Hitler. These were men of action. These were the true revolutionaries.

He moved from the left to the right in the blink of an eye and saw nothing strange or inconsistent in the switch. His friend took him to a speech by a man named Mosley. Oswald Mosley. A man with martial bearing and fire in his belly and power in his fists. He liked his name, too. Oswald was a good name, not dissimilar to Oswick. And he, too, had moved from left to right, from socialism to fascism.

His friend's name was Shirin Tombs and she was an actress, eight years older than him. She called him her 'posh boy' because she said he spoke like a toff. There was nothing between them, not then, because she had another lover, as she confided in Danny one day.

'If I tell you, you don't breathe a word, Posh Boy. Not to anyone, right?'

'Go on, who is it? A famous actor?'

She grinned at him. Her hair was dark then, undyed. 'It's him, the man, Oswald Mosley.'

'No.'

'Yes, I'm his mistress. We're that close I call him Tom, like his family and closest friends do. I think he loves me, though he doesn't say so.'

'You're shagging Oswald Mosley?'

'Not bad, eh, for a girl from Oldham, Lancashire.'

'I want to meet him. Can you fix that for me? I could do stuff for him.'

'I'll try. But you don't mention about me and him.'

In all his spare minutes and hours, he was selling *The Blackshirt*, the newspaper of Mosley's organisation. When at last he was introduced to the leader as a useful young person who might be of even greater use to the cause, he knew he had found his Messiah and immediately became a sworn disciple. How could he help, though? What could he do to further the interests of the BUF?

Shirin had the answer.

'You've got a good voice and a fine manner, Danny Oswick,' she said. 'All those years with the royals and their servants, God bless them all, makes you just like a gentleman yourself.'

'Don't be daft.'

'I'm serious. You could wheedle your way in with the gentry, get money off them. You sound like one of them. You'd be a perfect fundraiser.' And funds, she said, were badly needed if the British Union of Fascists was to gain power. 'You probably seen them all, Posh Boy,' she said. 'You've lived among the bleeding lot of them, the people with the money.'

It was true. He knew these people. He had watched them from close quarters for most of his life. He knew the way they dressed, the way they spoke and acted. He knew their coldness and their arrogance and stupidity. He knew their weaknesses. Oh God, how he'd love to relieve them of a chunk of their money.

Mosley thought it was a good idea. He sent young Oswick off to his tailor's and outfitter's in Savile Row and Jermyn Street and very soon Posh Boy was dressed exactly like a gentleman. He carried it well, because he knew how to.

Next, he was introduced to a select few of Mosley's upper-class friends in the nobility and politics, those who were already donating to the cause because they believed in it. They, in turn, introduced Oswick to others who had expressed sympathy privately. Soon he had an entrée to the greatest houses in the land.

And he was good. He was very good. He knew how to coax and he knew how to squeeze, and when they had agreed to donate £500, he managed to get them to double it, then double it again. The money flowed in.

He collected enormous sums with a simple promise: that their way of life, their wealth and their estates would be protected from the Bolsheviks by Mosley and his Blackshirts. They would build a Britain as great as the new Germany. And their donations to this cause would never be revealed. It would be their little secret.

And in his mind, it was all an elaborate lie. The politicians and the aristocracy might think that the Blackshirts would save them from the ravening Bolshevik hordes, but they were deluded.

For when the Blackshirts became the masters, those who thought themselves the greats of the land would fall as surely as they had in Russia. For the moment, however, the BUF would use these people for the money and respectability they offered, but one day their usefulness would cease. And that was a day worth working for.

Oswick looked at his watch again. Time to get out of this grubby little two-up two-down and go and meet Shirin in the Plough. This was going to be interesting.

Wilde watched the inn from the corner of an alleyway across the street. He saw Shirin go in and she was alone. He waited, weighing up his options. Two minutes passed, three. After five minutes, he decided to risk it and followed her in.

She was sitting where they had sat yesterday. She smiled at him.

'I didn't think you'd turn up, Tom.'

'Well, I did. I see you haven't got a drink.'

'A lady doesn't buy her own drinks. Even an American gentleman should know that.'

'Let's go somewhere else,' he said. 'I don't want to be seen here.'

'Why not? Are you ashamed of me? Worried your wife will find out?'

'I have my reasons. Anyway, what makes you think I have a wife?'

She laughed. 'You look married.'

'Well, that's my business. So let's go.' He knew he sounded sharp, on edge. Because he was.

'I like it here. It's warm and cosy. Nice atmosphere.'

'I'm going. You can come with me or not. The choice is yours.'

'Are you bullying me?'

'It's a simple yes or no. You can stay here or come with me. I'm not bullying you, it's your choice.'

'All right, Mr Read – or whatever your name is – take me somewhere nice. Treat me like a lady. Perhaps we could go dancing at Dorothy's.'

'No, there's a pub a quarter of a mile from here. We'll go there.'

'Well, well, aren't you the big beast, ordering a poor little female around.'

She took her time rising from the bench and ambled slowly after him as he left the pub and waited for her. When she joined him, he noted her looking back along the street.

'You expecting someone, Shirin?'

'No, why?'

'Come on. Let's go. I haven't got all evening.'

He walked at a gentle pace which she refused to match. She grabbed his arm at the corner of the next street. 'I don't like this,' she said. 'Have you got a gun on you, Tom?'

'Well, that's a question. What if I did?'

'The thing is, I'm not sure I trust you, and so I'm not coming with you.'

'Do I scare you? You didn't seem afraid of the fighting.'

'I don't know anything about you except you say you were in the Bund. Well, you know what, darling, I don't believe you. I don't even think you're one of us. Are you a Jew? Perhaps you're a Jew. You're certainly not a pure-blood. So you can fuck off back to America, Tom whoever you are.'

He let her go, and when she was out of sight he retraced his steps back to the Plough. Sure enough, Danny Oswick, his undergraduate, was there talking animatedly with his wife.

He had been set up. But how would they have played it? Would they have tried to blackmail him or convert him to their cause? Perhaps they really believed he was one of them.

And then they were joined by another man, whom he didn't recognise. A man with a gaunt, unshaven face, scars on his forehead and the stiff manner of a professional fighting man. Was he somehow familiar, or was that just febrile thinking?

He couldn't hear them talking, but he watched them for a few moments and then slid away into the darkness and set off for home. He wasn't sure whether he had learnt anything, but his two meetings with Shirin Oswick had been disturbing and he felt uneasy. As for Danny, it wouldn't be easy to face him as a student. One way or another, the young man's college career would have to be terminated.

Something about the arrival of the second man particularly troubled him, as though he had caught a sidelong glimpse of evil and wished he hadn't.

CHAPTER 21

Johnny was tucked up in bed but was still awake when Wilde went up to his room. 'You need to go sleepy-byes, young man,' he said, ruffling the boy's hair.

'I want Mummy to come home.'

'She will soon, Johnny. But she's busy in London at the moment. We're OK, though, aren't we? Mrs Keane is looking after us. You had fish pie, didn't you? You like fish pie and peas.'

'It was all right. But I like Mummy's food better.'

'It's fun having Mrs Keane and Penelope around, though, isn't it?'

'I like Penelope but she's a bit babyish.'

'Well, she's not as grown up as you. She doesn't go to school yet.'

'Read me a story, Daddy.'

'*Peter Rabbit*?' He pulled the familiar, well-worn book down from the shelf and opened it up. Was Johnny too old for it now? Perhaps a couple of new books would be a good idea. But he discovered that Beatrix Potter was still in favour and, by the time he had finished reading, his son was asleep.

Downstairs, Mrs Keane fed him the heated-up remains of the fish pie and poured him a drink and asked him about his day. He answered her questions with the usual platitudes. And then the phone rang. It was Lydia.

'At last, contact.'

'Hello, darling. How's life in Cambridge?'

'Oh, you know, getting used to college again. Eating fish pie made by the redoubtable Mrs Keane. Don't worry about us.' He wasn't going to mention that three men had done their utmost to kill him in the vicinity of a village called Skyme in Norfolk and had murdered a fine old man called Charlie Bagshawe. Nor was he going to say anything about his secret work for Lord Templeman. 'The important thing, Lydia, is how you're getting on.'

'It's hard work. I hadn't realised quite how much there would be. I'm wondering whether I've bitten off more than I can chew.'

'You'll be fine.'

'What about May? Have you heard anything?'

'Not much progress, I'm afraid, but she's still with us. Hopefully I'll get a proper bulletin tomorrow.'

'I've been reading up on it. I think that if she's survived the fever, she'll make it.'

'That's good to know. But I do have a little news for you – just that I'll be staying at Harbinger House this weekend. Catesby has invited me to join his shooting party.'

'Are you serious? You hate shooting, and you're not that keen on bloody Catesby either.'

'Well, it's something of an opportunity. Can't really say any more at the moment.'

'Good God, Tom, I'm gone five minutes and you lose your mind. What about Johnny?'

'I'm sure Mrs Keane can cope, aren't you?'

'I suppose so.' There was a pause on the line.

It occurred to him to wonder whether his wife was worried that the new nanny or housekeeper – or whatever she was – might be coping a little too well, supplanting her in the boy's affections. Well, such anxieties were a price she would have to pay. 'You haven't really told me much about the course,' he said.

'There's too much to give details. I'll run out of change any minute. I'll give you a full report when I see you. But in the meantime, there was something I wanted to mention. I hope I'm not being paranoid, but you know you mentioned that we were in the addendum to the Black Book, the list marked down for death?'

'Yes, of course.'

'I didn't take it very seriously.'

'I noticed.'

'Well, I have a horrible feeling someone's watching me. I noticed him again this evening when I came to the telephone box. A man in his thirties in raincoat and hat, just standing outside the hostel looking for all the world like the poster for a B-movie, and now I can see him again through the kiosk windows. I've seen him several times, and other men. I have to say I'm a little worried. Tell me I'm imagining things.'

Wilde was thinking fast. What sort of amateur had Templeman assigned to Lydia's protection? Lydia wasn't supposed to suspect that she was being observed and he was worried how she would react. But he had to come clean, otherwise she would go mad with worry.

'Tom, you're not saying anything.'

'I'm sorry, I've got to make a confession. Templeman offered to assign a bodyguard to look out for you and I went along with it. That's clearly who you have seen.'

'A bodyguard?' She sounded horrified. 'Are you suggesting that I really am in some peril?'

'Templeman is taking the threat seriously, so we must, too.' How far should he go with this? He didn't want to mention the death by needle of Rafe Crow, or Schellenberg's reference to the Phenol List, and certainly not his own brush with death on a back road near the Norfolk coast.

'Tom, I know very well when you're holding something back. You have to tell me the truth.'

'I'm sure you'll be safe with Templeman's agents watching over you.'

'But without them, I'd be dead, is that what you're saying?'

'I'm saying nothing of the kind, simply that it makes sense to take the threat seriously. Look, when are you going to be able to come home for a weekend? Johnny's missing you badly, and so am I.'

'Not yet. Anyway, you'll be away this weekend and I'm still settling in. Perhaps two or three weeks' time. In the meantime, I'll write letters to Johnny every day or two. I'm afraid I've been pretty remiss in that department so far, but the work is very intense and at the end of the day I just want to relax and chat with the other girls. They're a good bunch. But you know, Tom, you've got me worried. Am I safe?'

Wilde slept in an hour longer than he intended. He had stayed up too long talking with Sylvia Keane over a drink in the sitting room.

The way she looked at him and flicked her hair, he wondered vaguely whether she was flirting with him and so he deliberately steered the conversation towards the children and domestic matters, and when she suggested another drink he declined decisively and said a perfunctory 'Goodnight' before climbing the stairs to bed.

His night was interrupted by dreams.

Dreams of needles, of festering plague buboes, of heads neatly severed from bodies by piano wires, of a blonde in high boots with dark roots that grew inch by inch like tentacles. In his sleep, his brain was trying to connect these disparate images, and failing.

When he awoke, he didn't feel refreshed. The only sound was of a brush sweeping a floor somewhere in the distance. He trundled downstairs in his dressing gown and saw that Doris was doing the housework.

'Morning, Doris.'

'Good morning, sir.'

'Is Johnny around?'

'Mrs Keane is taking him to school.'

'Ah, of course. I hadn't realised the time. Well, we're out of coffee, so I think a cup of tea's in order. How about you, Doris, would you like a cup?'

'Thank you, sir, that would be nice.'

Something about the flatness of her reply caught his attention. Was Doris a little under the weather or was there bad news. 'I meant to ask, how's Peter?'

'He's in Addenbrooke's now, Professor. It'll only be a few days, they say.'

'I'm sorry to hear that.'

She smiled wanly. 'It's been a long time coming, truth be told. Be a mercy for him when it's over.' She spoke with gentleness and acceptance, but Wilde wasn't fooled.

'Why don't you take the day off and go to the hospital? The house will survive a while without dusting and mopping. You should be at your husband's side.'

'Thank you, sir. I'll do that, but not just yet. Got the bedding to change. Anyway, visiting time isn't until two o'clock this afternoon. The matron is very strict on that.'

'Are you sure? If anything needs doing here, I'll get Mrs Keane on to it. She's a good soul and we've been very lucky to find a housekeeper at such short notice. I'm sure she wouldn't mind helping you out a bit.'

'If you say so, sir.'

His brow furrowed. 'Doris?' He had never heard an edge like that in her voice before. 'What is it?'

'Oh, it's nothing, Professor Wilde. I'm just being silly.'

'No, come on, out with it. Something's the matter.'

Before she could answer, there was a noise behind them. They both turned towards the front door. The handle was being turned. Sylvia Keane had arrived home, with her daughter in tow.

Wilde had telephoned to accept the invitation to the shooting party at Sir Neville Catesby's country estate on the day the card arrived, and he was told that it wouldn't be 'awfully formal'.

'What exactly does that mean?' Wilde had asked the man at the end of the line, who identified himself as McNally the butler.

'Oh, black tie is merely optional for dinner. During the war, Sir Neville decided it was no longer de rigueur and now he has instructed me to say that such shows of class distinction and snobbery are to be eschewed in the new egalitarian society. His words, not mine, sir. Perhaps I could ask if you have any special requirements for your stay, Professor?'

'None that I can think of.'

'And will you be arriving by motor car or will you need to be collected from the railway station?'

'Car.'

'Sir Neville wasn't certain whether you were likely to be bringing a manservant.'

Wilde found himself trying to stifle a laugh. 'No manservant, or womanservant for that matter.'

'Well, we shall look forward to attending to your every need when you arrive on Friday, sir. I am sure Sir Neville will be delighted to learn that you are coming. Will that be all, Professor Wilde?'

'That will be all, thank you.'

Now, here he was at Harbinger House, late on Friday afternoon in the last hour before dusk. Seeing the building in daylight, it wasn't quite as impressive as it had appeared when he arrived in the dark of the evening for the 'Survivors Party'. Then the lights dazzled through the glass panes and illuminated the surroundings in a crystal glow; now he could see the old plum-coloured brick and it was looking a bit sad and in need of pointing. Bricklayers would have been hard to come by during the war years. The roof, too, was in poor repair; grey and mossy. He guessed there would be leaks in places. That aside, it was a fine 250-year-old mansion in pleasant parkland and three thousand acres, mostly given over to shooting.

He pulled the green and black Riley saloon to a halt in front of the main entrance. The car looked a little underwhelming against the two Rolls-Royces, Daimler and a long black Cadillac that were already parked nearby.

Two footmen approached and bowed. One asked for the car keys to park the Riley beside the other motors and the second man took Wilde's two suitcases and gun bag and led him up the steps into the main hall.

Magically, the butler arrived almost as soon as Wilde stepped indoors. 'Good day, Professor Wilde,' he said with a deferential bow of the head. 'I'm McNally, we spoke on the telephone. I trust you had a pleasant journey.'

'Well, it's not much of a trek from Cambridge.'

'Indeed not, sir. Sir Neville has asked me to place you in the Japanese bedchamber. I trust that will be to your satisfaction.'

The Japanese bedchamber. What a remarkable coincidence given the Japanese characters on the ceramic shards at Flowthorpe. Wilde simply nodded. 'I am sure I will be extremely comfortable.'

'Sir Neville has also suggested that you might like to join him in the Billiard Room when you have refreshed yourself. Would that be well with you, sir?'

'I'm sure I'll be able to find him.'

'Thank you, sir. I will inform Sir Neville that you are here.' He snapped his fingers at the footman carrying the luggage. 'Escort Professor Wilde to his chamber and deposit his firing pieces in the Gun Room.'

Half an hour later, after washing his face and admiring the Japanese silks, tiny netsuke ornaments and decorative hangings and paintings in his chamber, Wilde made his way to the Billiard Room where he was welcomed effusively. 'Tom, I'm so pleased you were able to make it at such short notice. I just thought, why not? I like to have six guns and I realised we only had five. Do you shoot a great deal?'

'I confess I haven't shot for years, Neville.' *Not at birds anyway.*

'Well, I'm sure you'll be a crack shot. Probably show us all up. Do you like the Japanese room?'

'It's exquisite.'

'I'd thought of the Russian room for you but then I thought, no, Tom Wilde is a man of wonderful sensitivity. He'll love the delicacy of the Japanese. We're all friends again now, aren't we? I'm sure you're not a xenophobe.' Catesby seemed to suddenly realise that he wasn't alone in the room for he had been playing billiards with another man. 'Have you met Larry B. Rhein? Larry, this is Professor Tom Wilde."

'How do you do,' Wilde said, shaking hands with the man, whose name and face meant nothing to him.

'I'm well, thank you. And you, Professor Wilde?'

'Larry is of the American persuasion like you, Tom. We go back quite a way.'

'So I gather from the accent,' Wilde said, grinning. 'Texas, is it?'

'Right first time.'

'Are you military, diplomatic, what?'

'Oh, I'm a businessman, Tom. We sell hundreds of thousands of radios and we're moving into televisions. Have you watched TV?'

'For about ten minutes back in 1936. It wasn't that interesting, to be honest.'

'Well, trust me, it will be. And I think England will be a big market for us sooner rather than later. This is the future.'

'Well, you obviously know a great deal more about it than I do.' Wilde put two and two together. 'Yours is the black Cadillac, I take it.'

'Do you like it?'

'Very nice.'

'Want to know how much it cost?'

'I wouldn't dream of asking.'

'Two thousand five hundred dollars. Suede seats, drinks cabinet. It's got it all. Bought it yesterday off a dealer in London town.'

'Well, it's rather more luxurious than my little Riley.'

Rhein was about forty and was not an athletic man. His shoulders were narrow and his face was soft and weak. The billiard cue he was holding upright was at least a foot too big for him. He held it out for Wilde. 'Here you are, you take over from me. The Limey bastard is thrashing me six ways to hell. Damn crazy game. Maybe I should sell pool tables to the British, too.'

Wilde ignored the offer of the cue. 'Oh, it's not my game either.'

'Well,' Catesby said, 'I think it's about time for a couple of pre-prandial drinks anyway. Perhaps we'll play again after dinner. Or cards if you prefer. Won't you both accompany me to the drawing room? It's about time our other guests joined us. Just so you know, Tom, this is strictly a no-wives weekend. I didn't want you to think I had excluded the delightful Lydia out of malice. There is, however, a remarkable female element to the party, as you will discover anon.'

Wilde couldn't keep his eyes off Catesby's dandruff snowdrift. How could such a dapper man not notice it? God, he badly wanted to take a brush to his shoulders.

A fire was roaring in the great hall. Sofas and chairs were ranged around the hearth. Wilde immediately stiffened at the sight of the young moustachioed man standing with an arm draped over the marble chimneypiece, glass of something amber-hued in his other hand.

'Oswick,' he said with a smile he didn't feel.

'Professor Wilde, I didn't know you were going to be here.'

'Nor I you, Oswick. What a surprise.' He had been about to say, *what a pleasant surprise*, but the words stuck in his craw. 'How did you get here?'

'Train, sir.'

'Had I known, I could have given you a lift.'

'Oh, it was no trouble, Professor.'

'Well, now, young Danny is fixed with a drink,' Catesby said. 'So what can I offer you two gentlemen? Larry? Tom?'

'Sidecar for me,' the businessman said.

'Scotch.'

The butler had been hovering in the doorway and, at a signal from Catesby, set about arranging the drinks.

So that was four: Catesby, Wilde, Oswick and Larry B. Rhein. Who, Wilde wondered, would make up the other two of this curious little group. As the thought entered his brain, the door opened and the fifth member of the party arrived.

Her fair hair was scraped back in a tight bun and her face was free of any trace of makeup. Her attire was straightforward – the tunic, skirt and boots of a Red Army officer, neatly finished off by a gold star medal, which Wilde instantly recognised as her country's highest honour, Hero of the Soviet Union. At her belted waist she had a closed holster. She was accompanied by a man, also in Red Army uniform.

'And this,' Catesby said, not without a hint of pride in his voice, 'is the eagle-eyed Miss Viktoria Ulyanova, renowned for her one hundred and six confirmed kills as a sniper on the Byelorussian front and presently attached to the Soviet Embassy in London and an honoured guest of Her Majesty's government. If she can't bag a few pheasants, then which of us can?'

Having already met the others in the room, she was introduced to Wilde and they shook hands. She smiled broadly, revealing yellowish teeth that had most likely been deprived of a toothbrush and tooth powder in the country of her birth.

The man at her side was revealed as her interpreter. He took a step back, keeping himself at a respectable distance behind her.

Wilde knew all about interpreters in totalitarian regimes; as likely as not he would be NKVD, with orders to keep his charge from saying anything compromising or defecting. The interpreting was a useful additional skill. He did not introduce himself by name.

'It's a delight to meet you, comrade,' Wilde said to Viktoria Ulyanova in English, for he had no more than half a dozen words of Russian.

'Me delight, too,' she said in halting English. 'I try speak without interpreter but still learning your language. I hope you forgive errors.'

'Of course.' So this was gun number five. Catesby's secretary had not been joking when he said that black tie was optional for dinner. The group became odder by the moment. Wilde had anticipated a weekend of the great men and women of the British establishment. Perhaps a couple of Cabinet ministers, one or two earls or dukes, maybe a minor royal and a fashionable millionaire or society hostess.

He tried to engage Viktoria Ulyanova in conversation for a few minutes, but it was difficult, even with the interpreter's assistance. He guessed her age at no more than twenty-five and she obviously had a heart of granite to have killed so many men in cold blood, but in this setting she merely seemed a little shy and diffident. Finally, she nodded with a smile and turned away.

Catesby stepped close to Wilde and whispered in his ear, 'I told you there was to be a remarkable female element, did I not? Do they come any more extraordinary than Comrade Ulyanova?'

'Probably not, Neville. Where exactly did you find her?'

'A drinks party in London. She was being displayed to the world as a fine example of Soviet womanhood, an advertisement for communism and Uncle Joe, if you like – much as the redoubtable Lyudmila Pavlichenko was paraded around America for her three hundred kills. I adore meeting people who have different experiences and so I chatted to her a bit. Not too easy, of course, although I have a fair smattering of Russian from my travels, but suddenly I had a thought. What about a shooting party centred on one of the great shots of the Second World War? If she can kill dozens of Nazis from a couple of hundred yards surely she can blast a few dozen fat pheasants out of the sky.'

'You're insane, Neville. Your club will be talking about this for years to come.'

He grinned. 'I like to entertain, Tom, you know that.'

The door opened again and another man entered. 'Aha, our final gun,' Catesby said. 'But not our final dinner guest. That is a surprise that must await you.'

The newcomer was two or three inches shorter than Wilde. He had a high forehead, red hair thinning at the front and a long face. He was probably in his thirties.

'Tom, please meet Dr Edmund Bacon – Eddie to his chums.'

Once again the introductions were made. Wilde couldn't help noticing the clipped and precise nature of the new man's speech. He didn't exactly sound foreign, but nor did he sound quite English. Edinburgh perhaps?

Catesby left him with the doctor and they exchanged pleasantries about the gorgeousness of the house and their hopes for the shooting on the morrow. 'So tell me, Dr Bacon, what sort of medicine do you do? General practice? Surgery? What's your speciality?'

'I do research.'

'Just that? Researching what?'

'I have specialised in aviation. Particularly the problems of altitude sickness and decompression. I won't bore you with the details, Professor.'

Wilde smiled. He wouldn't have been at all bored by a few details about this man, for he had an unpleasant feeling that he had heard his voice before. Through the fog on a lonely stretch of Norfolk road, and through a door at a remote farmhouse, moments before a poor old farmer died.

CHAPTER 22

The six members of the shooting party took their places at table in the cosy panelled dining room. Obviously this house would have a larger dining room for great occasions, but this was the perfect size for such an intimate gathering.

Wilde was placed opposite Viktoria Ulyanova and between Catesby and Oswick. Bacon and Rhein were on either side of the Russian woman. The interpreter wasn't invited to eat and stood a pace behind her, his shoulders stiff, his demeanour watchful and emotionless.

Catesby remained standing behind his chair after his guests were seated, for he had a few words to say. 'Lady and gentlemen,' he began with unnecessary precision. 'You may be wondering why I have brought such a disparate group together this week-end. Well, this little shooting party is in the way of an experiment, if you like. After the greatest war in the history of mankind, we live in a new world. A world in which the Soviet Union and America and Great Britain will play the pre-eminent roles. But it would be wrong to think that we can simply eliminate the past, which is why I have also invited another guest, who will arrive a little later. This person cannot stay the night or, sadly, for the shooting, but I hope you will all feel it a great honour that he has agreed to grace us with his presence, if only for half an hour, for he is on his way to another engagement elsewhere. Some of you may disagree with his politics – and he will undoubtedly disagree with yours. But we must learn to live together and have debates rather than tank battles to settle our differences. As Churchill put it, jaw-jaw is better than war-war.'

There was a little ripple of applause from Oswick, Bacon and Rhein, but Wilde and the woman simply nodded in acknowledgement of the little speech.

Wilde was only half listening anyway. His thoughts were a long way from Catesby's anodyne sentiments. He was thinking of the man introduced as Dr Bacon. Had he imagined that voice as the one he had heard before? He had, after all, only heard a few words from the masked man with the needles at Bagshawe's door.

It was not irrational to think the killer might be here. After all, this was why Templeman had wanted Wilde to come to Harbinger House on this shooting weekend; because he had evidence – an anonymous paper – of a link between Catesby and recent events. Perhaps Bacon proved Templeman's suspicions accurate. He would have to be watched closely.

'And so, lady and gentlemen,' Catesby concluded, 'I entreat you to enjoy our fare this evening and pray for fine weather for tomorrow's shoot.'

The food was brought by the footmen and the butler. They started with a salad of lobster, caviar and watercress, followed by a main course of beef Wellington with lustrous rare tenderloin. The wines, including samples of Catesby's purloined champagne, were all great vintages and all of them French, a luxury that had been in short supply since the Germans occupied France in 1940. Nothing wrong with Algerian wine, Wilde reflected, but this Grand Cru burgundy was a great deal more complex and it was a sadness that he could only sip at it slowly so as to keep a clear head.

The conversation ranged far and wide, largely avoiding politics and religion, and Wilde almost began to doubt that there was any threat here. These might not be the people he would choose as friends or companions, but nor did they seem hostile. Even Dr Bacon seemed modest and quiet, nodding in agreement to various points but hardly contributing to the conversation.

It was the American businessman, Larry B. Rhein, who was the loudest. His favourite topic was money and the price of everything from petrol to coffee. He also told dirty jokes, including several about his ex-wives, which Catesby and Oswick loved.

Viktoria Ulyanova ate heartily, smiled and laughed when her fellow guests did. Her appetite suggested she had never encountered such a feast of fine produce. Every so often, with the interpreter's assistance, she tried to add a few words to the general discourse. Largely these contributions were plugs for the wonders of Josef Stalin and his five-year plans.

Before the pudding arrived, she stood up to declaim a short speech. 'I hope you will like to hear a little about my country, for I wish you to know that never in the history of mankind has so much happiness been conferred on the ordinary people than that bestowed upon us by the heroes of the Revolution, Comrades Lenin and Stalin.'

Wilde guessed that she had learnt these lines by heart and he gave her a warm smile for her effort. It seemed to him that she was a simple soul, thrown by the winds of war way beyond the norms of the life she would otherwise have lived. But if she was expecting any applause from the others, she was to be disappointed, and she sat down in silence.

'Tell us a little about your war service, Comrade Ulyanova,' Catesby said. 'That must have been great fun, shooting Germans like ducks.'

Ulyanova looked at her interpreter and said a few words in Russian. He nodded and turned to the assembled men. 'Comrade Ulyanova says that it is always a pleasure to kill fascists.'

Catesby put his hands together for a little muted applause. 'Bravo,' he said. 'What a girl, eh?'

It was then that the butler announced that the guest of honour had arrived. With a sweep, he opened the door to the dining room, and in stalked Sir Oswald Mosley, former leader of the British Union of Fascists and now back in the land of the free after being interned for much of the war under Defence Regulation 18B.

As one, the men at the table – bar Wilde – stood up and applauded his arrival. Wilde had never met Sir Oswald Mosley, but he recognised him instantly. He was tall, powerfully built but slightly ungainly, and he had that famous dark moustache that some might have thought dashing but which many more considered both comedic and sinister.

Catesby, Rhein, Oswick and Bacon lined up to be introduced. Mosley's eyes shone and he accepted the deference of those he met as his right. He obviously knew Catesby well and chatted with him for a minute, but it was surprising that he also seemed to be acquainted with Oswick, for he clapped him on the shoulder and afforded him a smile like an old friend.

Wilde decided to make the best of a bad thing by allowing himself to be introduced to the man. Yes, Mosley had been wrong in his politics and his assessment of Hitler, but the war was over so hopefully there might yet be a change of heart. After all, Mosley had already switched party on several occasions – from Conservative to Labour and finally to fascism – so perhaps he would move again, and this time back to the centre.

Because it was the done thing, Wilde shook the big man's hand, and then fervently wished to go to the bathroom to wash. In return, he received no acknowledgment that he existed from the would-be dictator, merely an indifferent nod of the head.

A place had been set for Mosley at the head of the table, so he sat down and spread himself out. Catesby stood at his side.

'Tonight,' the host said, 'we could not have a more honoured – and indeed honourable – guest. He has been treated shabbily these past few years, but he will rise again – and higher – to take his role in the pantheon of this nation and lead us on to yet greater things. Thank you, Sir Oswald, for gracing us with your presence.'

Mosley nodded, then smiled and held up his hand as if silencing a crowd. And the evening continued. He didn't speak much, but drank brandy and allowed himself to be entertained by Rhein, who was sitting at his left hand. Beyond the occasional roar of laughter at the American's endless fund of jokes, he didn't seem awfully interested in the proceedings, as if he were here under sufferance. As a favour to his friend Catesby, nothing more.

The guests couldn't take their eyes off him, but it was the look on the face of the Russian interpreter that held Wilde's attention. He clearly knew who Mosley was and understood the significance of his presence, even if Viktoria Ulyanova had never heard of him. And why should she have? Mosley would have meant nothing in the Soviet Union.

It was a strange, uncomfortable experience sitting at this table with these characters. One thing was certain: there had to be more to all this than hoping to bring people of different political outlooks together. This was deliberately provocative. But why? What on earth had possessed Catesby to invite the leader of Britain's fascists to a dinner with a hero of the Bolshevik empire? Did Catesby really think it amusing to rub the nose of one of his guests in the mire, or was there a darker motive?

And then the interpreter leant forward and spoke with some animation close to Viktoria Ulyanova's ear. She looked bewildered at first, then turned to him and seemed to ask a couple of questions in quick Russian. The interpreter reinforced his message and then, when Viktoria nodded and indicated that she understood what must be done, he stepped back a space.

The Red Army woman rose to her feet and turned away, walking purposefully towards the door while her interpreter addressed the table: 'Comrade Ulyanova wishes it to be known that she will not stay in the same room as a notorious fascist. She would happily kill him for his support of the Nazi oppressors, but that is against the laws of your land. So we will leave now and return to London.'

She was already halfway to the door and the interpreter quickly followed in her wake. And with that they were gone into the night.

What in God's name had just happened? This evening had always been a mad idea with no comprehensible motive. What could Catesby possibly have hoped to gain? It was like putting a hungry dog and an untamed tomcat in a cage and asking them to be friends.

Suddenly, Catesby and the other four men burst out laughing and then Wilde realised the horrible truth – it had all been an elaborate and unpleasant joke at the expense of Viktoria Ulyanova and every one of her twenty million Russian compatriots who had been slaughtered in the war.

And one other thing was now clear. Wilde was the only man at this table who was not a fascist or a Nazi. He was alone in a den of clawed beasts and he saw no reason to smile.

Catesby grinned at him. 'Lost your sense of humour, Wilde?'

'Ah, was Comrade Ulyanova the comic turn? Silly of me not to have realised.' What, he wondered, was his own role in the evening's cabaret? He was thinking about the Colt he had left in his suitcase upstairs and rather wishing he had it in his jacket pocket here in the dining room.

But then common sense kicked in. They weren't going to kill him here, nor could he just be made to disappear. Too messy. They knew that other people were aware that he was coming to this house – family, friends, university colleagues, members of the intelligence services. No, if there was to be an attempt on his life it would have to be subtle.

'Well, gentlemen,' Catesby said. 'On with the show.' He nodded to his butler. 'I think we're ready for pudding, McNally.'

'Actually,' Wilde said, 'I think I'll go and have a word with Comrade Ulyanova. Perhaps an apology would be in order, don't you think?'

Rhein hammered his fist on the table. 'Goddamn it, Wilde, she's a bloody Bolshevik! They're the enemy now – don't you realise that? They were *always* the real enemy but Churchill and Roosevelt were too dumb to see it.'

The comment did not merit a response.

He found her alone in the driveway, sitting in the passenger seat of a Rolls-Royce. Wilde assumed the interpreter was collecting their suitcases.

'Comrade Ulyanova, I must apologise. I'm sorry. This should never have happened.'

If she understood any of what he was saying it wasn't evident in her face, which was as hard and cold as it must have been when she lay down in her snowy foxhole in Byelorussia, lining up her rifle sights mercilessly on some young German soldier's head or heart, before taking him out with a single shot.

Moments later, the interpreter arrived to take the wheel, and Wilde repeated his apology. 'I knew nothing about it,' he said.

'That is because you are not a fascist, Professor Wilde. Don't worry, we know all about you. You have a large file. Unfortunately, we did not know about the others. Foolishly, we thought Catesby might be a friend.'

'Clearly not.'

'Return to them and enjoy the rest of your dinner, Comrade Professor. But I suggest you watch your back. They are not nice people.'

CHAPTER 23

His inclination was to drive away like the Russians, but an idiotic determination to see this through kept him at Harbinger House. He returned to the dinner and they accepted him as though nothing had happened and nothing was amiss.

Afterwards, they drank port and brandy and Mosley was asked to say a few words, but he was having none of it. Finally, without rising from his chair, he stretched out his neck and thrust forward his chin, a physical manifestation of a musical drum roll. 'I will not make a speech tonight, but there will come a time when you will hear from me. Suffice it to say that my position has not moved an inch, though the press and the politicians of this country consistently misrepresent my beliefs. What I can say is this: I will not lead one named political organisation, but you may rest assured that I will always be at the forefront of the movement to defend empire and realm against those – and we know their identities well enough – who would wish us harm.'

So he hadn't changed, and he retained his sense of drama and self-regard. Who were those who wished harm to empire and realm? That was clear too: he meant Jewry and he meant Bolshevism. The same perceived enemies he had been denouncing for a dozen years. Singing from exactly the same hymn sheet as Commander Harding-Watts, RN retired at the New Realm Patriots meeting. Well, that was a piece of information that might interest Templeman, MI5 and the government. Or perhaps they already knew.

The group – all male now – returned to the drawing room with its blazing log fire, its intricately carved marble fixtures and its parquetry floor. Mosley perched himself on the arm of a large chesterfield and quickly found himself surrounded by three acolytes – Catesby, Rhein and Bacon – hanging on his every word.

Wilde stood apart, nursing his drink as he soaked up the heat of the fire. Oswick joined him and made small talk about the term ahead, which he studiously ignored. And then Oswick became quieter. 'I was awfully sorry about all that, sir,' he said.

The words took Wilde by surprise and he turned his attention to the young man. 'Do you mean the humiliation of a decent woman?'

'Yes, Professor Wilde, I agree it was pretty frightful.'

'It was bear-baiting of the worst kind. You can hold whatever political views you wish, but that does not give you liberty to abuse your fellow human beings. What possessed you to join in the bloody laughter?'

'I don't know but I feel ashamed of myself. I got caught up in the moment, I suppose.'

'Well it was unforgivable.'

'You're right, sir. Do you think I could make some sort of amends if I wrote a letter to her at the embassy and apologised?'

Wilde noted that his undergraduate was very muted. He didn't wish the other members of the party to hear him. 'It couldn't hurt. But is this the real you talking, Oswick? Or are you just saying what you think I might like to hear as your supervisor?'

'I stand admonished, sir. I hope you will discover that I am not as bad as you think I am.'

This was a ridiculous conversation. Wilde knew the truth about Oswick and his wife; they were fascists to the core. 'What gives you the impression that I think badly of you?'

'I see it in your face, I hear it in your voice.'

Despite himself, Wilde found himself drawn into the conversation, for if Oswick's contrition was false he was a fair actor. He wanted to know more, for the way this young man was talking did not accord with what he believed of him. And yet, he knew the truth, didn't he? He had seen the young officer's wife at the New Realm Patriots meeting. He had seen Shirin and Daniel Oswick together, huddled, conspiratorial, laying a trap for him.

Wilde came out with it. 'Are you a fascist, Oswick?'

The directness of the question threw the undergraduate. He hesitated, searching for a response. 'That depends how you describe fascist, sir,' he said at last.

'Well if you don't know by now after fighting the bastards for six years, I don't suppose you ever will.'

'I believe the Germany of the thirties had strong points. Hitler gave the people back their pride and he gave them work and food. Mussolini made the trains run on time. Franco has saved Spain from anarchy.'

'Bollocks,' Wilde said. 'Total unadulterated bollocks.'

'Excuse me?'

'You heard me, Oswick.'

'Well, of course, I agree that everything went very wrong in Germany. They should never have got into a war with us or France.'

'You think that was Hitler's only flaw?'

'Of course there were others. We are all flawed. Look to the East, sir. The true horror of Stalin's rule has yet to emerge, but we already know enough to realise he committed atrocities of his own and now we are supposed to accept the Soviets as allies.'

'And Mosley over there, what do you think of him?'

'I believe he is a man of principle.'

'But what damned principles, eh? Crush the weak, favour the strong, disdain the foreigner.' Suddenly, Wilde softened. Perhaps this young man was simply naive, too easily influenced by powerful men. 'Forgive me, I didn't mean to have a go at you. I know you've fought in the war and you are entitled to your political beliefs, but I find them rather hard to stomach tonight. I'm just so bloody angry at the treatment of Viktoria Ulyanova. Look, Oswick, why don't you tell me a bit more about your background. Perhaps I might understand you a bit better.'

'My origins are humble. I never knew my mother and my father was in service.'

'In a stately home like this?'

'Actually, rather grander than this. Sandringham. He was an under-butler but he was unfairly dismissed and fell on hard times. Finally, he took his own life.'

'Then I have sympathy for you, but perhaps you still need a little guidance. You might think it is not my place to offer advice, but if you were to ask me, I would suggest you look closely at your political stance. Fascism has been found wanting and there's no future in it. You'd do well to listen to some different viewpoints if you're to fit in to the modern world and prosper.'

Before Oswick could say any more, Catesby had joined them. 'What's this, Tom, secret whispers? Not more politics, I trust?'

'Young Oswick was telling me his life story.'

'Ah, a tale of inspiration and aspiration. One to force-feed to Attlee and Dalton and their dismal crew. Men who would have us all living in slums so that the poor shouldn't feel so bad about their lot. I can't stand the British socialists – you can smell them a mile off. Give me Stalin over Attlee any day – got red blood in his veins.'

'You know, Neville, I always knew you were a bit eccentric, but no one ever mentioned your bizarre and wayward political judgement.'

Catesby grinned. 'Come, come, old fellow, don't want to ruin a splendid evening. The great man has to go now, so I thought you'd like to bid him farewell.'

'I don't really think I'm his cup of tea.'

'I'm sure you're not, but we're civilised men, so we observe the conventions of polite society. Not like bloody Hitler and his lot, eh?'

'I thought you liked Hitler. Didn't you meet him once?'

'Indeed I did. Jumped-up tedious little house painter with a ridiculous moustache. Awful breath. To tell the truth, Ozzie Mozzie's a boring fart, too. But he's *our* boring fart, not a bloody German one.'

'Well, you have strange friends.'

'Didn't you know, Mosley and I were at Winchester together. Fought many a battle with foil and épée, but the bastard always bested me. I don't give up on friends as easily as some. Anyway, don't judge a man by the company he keeps.'

'Actually, I may be wrong but I think the quote usually omits the word "don't".'

'All the world's a stage . . . I like to think of the play as a divine comedy.'

'And I think you're mixing your metaphors.'

'Why not? It's all a game.'

Yes, it rather seemed it *was* all a game to Catesby. But what were the rules? In fact, *were* there any rules? He looked at Oswick, who was both frowning and smiling, as though he thought the conversation must be amusing but he wasn't quite sure.

'How long have we known each other, Neville? Ten years is it?'

'About that, I'd say. You were new in Cambridge and I invited you to dinner. Splendid evening. Horace was there, wasn't he?'

'Indeed, he was. The thing is, we've been acquainted all that time, but I'm not sure we've ever had much of a conversation. I realise I don't know a thing about you except the public image you construct so carefully. Give me a clue, Neville. Have you ever married? Do you have a family hidden away somewhere? What do you want from the world? And, perhaps most interesting of all, whose side are you on?'

Catesby roared with laughter. 'Whose side am I on? That's a good one, Tom. And my answer is: you'll never know. Think of me as an enigma. A closed book full of mystery. Does that answer your question?'

'I'm surprised you have never entered Parliament, that's all. I could imagine you in a senior Cabinet role.'

'Oh, didn't you know? I was an MP in the twenties when Ramsay MacDonald was first in power and then crumbled. The disappointment was terrible and I came to realise there were other, better ways to wield influence.'

'By influence, I take it you mean power?'

'Is that what you think? Do I seem power mad to you?'

'I think you enjoy wielding power in your own way.' *Often at the expense of others.*

'You have a vivid imagination, Tom. As to the fairer sex, well I might have been married a few times, but then again, I might not. What do I want from the world? Life and experience. The full cup. The joy of living. What else is there? We're here one minute and the next we're not, so perhaps none of it matters. Come on, let's all say our goodbyes to Ozzie Mozzie and then we can wind down the evening and make an early start to the morning's mass slaughter. I predict an exceptional bag.'

And that, Wilde realised, was all he was going to learn about Sir Neville Catesby.

In his room, with its Japanese silk wallpaper and its array of artefacts, Wilde had initially considered staying up all night with the Colt pointing at the door waiting for an intruder, but now he wanted sleep. Perhaps his apprehension had been eased by the confusing end to the evening, when his appraisal of both Catesby and Oswick had taken a distinctly odd turn.

It occurred to him that Catesby had been playing games all along. He could be anything or nothing. No wonder Templeman was so desperate to discover the truth about him. And as for Oswick, one could almost believe him guilty of nothing but naivety. But how did that fit in with the rabid politics of his wife and their obvious attempt to entrap him?

Undressing, he slipped into the cool, luxurious red kimono that had been laid out on the bed. The room had an adjoining bathroom, which was a remarkably modern and American thing for such an old house, and so Wilde brushed his teeth and put out his razor and shaving brush for the morning. Just before climbing into the large double bed, he took the precaution of removing the Colt pistol from his suitcase to place it on the bedside table for the night.

At least that was his intention. The problem was, the gun wasn't there.

CHAPTER 24

Knowing that his gun had been taken, he couldn't sleep. His eyes ranged around the room. Among other Japanese objets d'art in this exquisite space, a long and beautiful samurai sword was hanging on the wall at the side of the bed. It slid from its black and red leather scabbard as smoothly as a snake from a hole. He weighed it in his arms and the curved steel blade shone in the electric light. He ran a finger along the sharp edge and drew a thin line of blood.

Well, he had a defensive weapon, but he still wouldn't sleep.

His thinking was clear, but decisions were hard to come by. Would it be prudent to slip away into the night, or would they be waiting for him, guarding the Riley? He could always make a getaway on foot, through the fields and woods. Looking out of the window, there was a twenty-foot drop and no safe way down, so he would have to make his way through the corridors and stairways of the house. What was he scared of? More than anything else, it was the removal of the pistol that unnerved him.

He sat on the bed against a bank of pillows, his knees bunched up, the sword in his lap. He needed sleep, but that seemed impossible. There wasn't even a lock or bolt on the inside of the chamber door.

And yet sleep still beckoned. With a good meal and some alcohol inside him, his eyes became heavier and he was close to dozing off when there was a soft knock on wood.

It was 12.30 a.m. He was instantly awake. Why would someone rap at the door in the middle of the night? Killers don't do that; they barge in and attack in a rush, or they steal in silently. Slipping off the bed, he made his way forward, clutching the long hilt of the sword with both hands, the blade inclined in a downward arc. 'Who's there?'

A strong Texan drawl. 'It's me, Larry Rhein.'

'What do you want?'

'Can I come in?'

'The door's not locked.'

Rhein turned the handle and peered around the door. His eyes opened wide at the sight of the samurai sword as he slid his unimpressive frame into the room. 'Jesus, Wilde.'

'I'm not planning to hurt you. Get in and shut the door.'

The American businessman had been the only one wearing a dinner jacket and tails, which he was still wearing. Now, however, his white tie was undone as was the stud of his wing collar. He kept his eyes on the blade.

'Well, why are you here, Rhein?'

'I'm here because I want to know what *you're* doing here.'

'Damn fool question. I'm trying to sleep, of course, and was about to nod off when you turned up.'

'I mean here, in this house. What in God's name are you up to?'

'The same as you, Rhein – I'm here for the shooting party. Stop talking in riddles and get to the point.'

Rhein went across to the bed and sat down. 'You can put the sword away. I'm unarmed and you're in no danger from me. I can't vouch for anyone else in this house.'

Wilde lowered the sword so that its point touched the carpet between his splayed bare feet. 'Speak.'

'You're not OSS anymore, so why are you here? Who sent you?'

OSS. How did Rhein know he had been in the Office of Strategic Services?

'I still don't know what you're talking about. I was invited for the weekend by Neville Catesby. He's an old Cambridge colleague and we go back a long way. What about you?'

'I'm not going to beat about the bush, Wilde. You obviously think I'm some kind of Nazi, but that's not the case. Everything's a cover. My radio business is a cover. I'm State Department.'

'Are you here as a diplomat?'

'Not exactly.'

'Then what?'

'That's a long story.'

'Well, you've got me wide awake now, so we've got all night.'

'OK, I'll give you the short version. Sir Neville Catesby and I just happen to go back a-ways. You may know that he was in

America from early 'thirty-seven to late 'thirty-eight, attached to Princeton on a visiting fellowship. But he spent a lot of his time down the road in Washington, DC and after a while I was assigned to watch him because he seemed to go out of his way to cultivate some interesting friends, including members of both the German-American Bund and the CPUSA.'

'The Nazis *and* the communists?'

'Indeed, and that's not all. He quickly became a regular on the society and diplomatic circuits. All the hostesses loved his British accent and his expensive English clothes, and he was a big hit at the embassy drinks parties. We knew he wasn't real, but we struggled to work him out. I made a point of becoming his buddy, which was easy, for he couldn't meet enough people and always kept in touch.'

Wilde had seen the same thing here in Britain. Catesby surrounded himself with politicians of all persuasions, great men and women of the arts and sciences and military. He was a collector of people. Invariably people of influence.

'There was one man we noticed in particular. A Japanese gentleman named Ryoichi Naito, who was in America doing God knew what on behalf of his government. For some reason Ryoichi was trying to procure disease samples from the Rockefeller Institute in New York. We kicked him out of the country after that, but I never forgot his link to Catesby. To use a cliché, they were chalk and cheese. Why would Catesby be interested in such a man?'

Ryoichi Naito. That name again. The man inextricably linked to the barbarity of Unit 731. The man who had offered his services as an interpreter to the Americans at the end of the war but had clearly been a spy.

'You know about Flowthorpe, right?' Rhein continued.

He didn't reply. He was giving nothing away to this man.

'I'll take that as a yes. I don't blame you for being cautious. Anyway, when I heard of the terrible events at Flowthorpe, I was on the first clipper over, and I was immediately in touch with Catesby. "Hey buddy, I'm over your side of the pond, let's meet up." His invitation to this weekend followed like night follows day.'

'This is an interesting though confusing story. I know the village of Flowthorpe, of course. But what of it? It's a pleasant little English community with a US airbase attached. We have a friend who lives there.'

'Not anymore, huh?'

'What did you say?'

'Forget it, Wilde. Play it your way. But now you know what I'm doing here at Harbinger House, that still leaves a big question that needs answering: what the hell are *you* doing here? You're not OSS anymore, because there is no OSS. And you don't work for the State Department. So who are you working for?'

Rhein was plausible, as was his story, and Wilde wanted to believe him because then they could work together. It would also be good to know that there was someone in this house who wasn't a potential enemy. At the moment, the odds stacked up badly; it would be foolish to think that the servants were not up to their necks in Catesby's business, whatever it was. And what about the unseen, the kitchen staff and God knew who else?

Still, all his OSS training and all his instincts told him to hold back. He needed evidence of trustworthiness, because he had never encountered this man before. 'I hear every word you say, Rhein, but give me some more.'

'You mean like a warrant card? Is that supposed to be a joke?'

'I'm just an old friend of Neville's and I've been asked here to shoot some birds. Nothing more, nothing less. It's not an unusual gathering in this part of the world. You were talking about some Japanese man, but the name means nothing to me. I need some sort of clue to what you're talking about, and why you're in my room.'

Rhein's demeanour changed. His hands gripped and ungripped in frustration. 'Look, I'm the one who has taken all the risks coming here and giving you the lowdown.' His anger was palpable. 'I was pretty damned sure that as an old OSS hand you were one of us, but perhaps I was wrong. So give me a bit of slack.'

He was right, of course. If he was who he said he was, then he had put himself in extreme danger. For all he knew, Wilde was as Nazi as the rest of them.

'OK,' Rhein said with a sigh. 'There is something else that might help convince you. A mutual friend in the diplomatic service, name of Jim Vanderberg.'

'You know Jim?' His oldest friend, the man who had put him in contact with Bill Donovan a few days back.

'Yes, I know him,' Rhein said. 'He has talked about you. As have others in State.'

'Well, Jim never mentioned you, Rhein.'

'Maybe calling him a friend is stretching it a bit. We're acquaintances, I guess.'

Finally, Wilde realised he had to accept the risk and nodded slowly. The name Jim Vanderberg swung it. 'OK,' he said. 'Let's say for a moment that I take you at face value. Let's just hypothesise that we're both working in the same direction. What do you propose?'

'First, I have to know who you're working for, because at the moment I'm in the dark.'

'What if it were British intelligence?'

'So you're working for, what, MI5? I won't even ask how that came about. But I guess you've had links with the Limeys for many years now.'

'Do you think this room's tapped?'

'Well, if it is they've already got all they need, so what the heck.'

Wilde put down the sword on the bed. 'I ask again – what do you propose? You must have come to this room with a strategy in mind.'

'First off, I propose that you take stock of the danger we're both in. This is not a house party. Somehow or other, they're connected to Flowthorpe, and they allowed us into their sanctum for a reason. I doubt that reason is good for our health.'

Wilde came straight out with it. 'There are almost certainly other BWs, in the form of ceramic bombs containing pathogens. We have to find them.'

'Now we're getting somewhere. Do you think they're here, on this estate?'

'It has to be a possibility.'

'Then we search the place,' Rhein said. 'The question is, how? Get the British Army in? Would your intelligence contacts agree to that?'

He doubted it. Hard evidence against Catesby was minimal in the extreme. In fact, was there *any* evidence of wrongdoing? Everything seemed entirely circumstantial: the link to Ryoichi Naito, the presence of Daniel Oswick and the neo-fascist groups espoused by his wife, the possibility that his guest Dr Edmund Bacon was the masked man from Bagshawe's farm. Added together it might make a case, but it was flimsy.

'Well, we'll reconvene in the morning. Together we can work it out. For the moment, we both need sleep. Shame you didn't bring a gun to keep under your pillow. That sword might not be a whole lot of use against a firearm.'

'I brought a pistol,' Wilde said. 'Unfortunately, I seem to have mislaid it.'

'That was careless.'

'Yes, I suppose it was.'

'God willing, I'll see you at breakfast.'

Eventually, Wilde got to sleep. He had wedged a chair under the door handle. It wouldn't stop a determined attacker, but it would make a racket if the door was pushed.

Nothing happened and he awoke surprisingly refreshed.

He got out of bed straightaway, all the while thinking about his conversation with Larry Rhein. He had to believe he was genuine; how else would he have known about the connection to Jim Vanderberg in the State Department? There was no way of making checks while they were here at Harbinger House, so he had two choices: take Rhein at face value or consider him an enemy. He went for the former option.

Dressing in the borrowed plus fours and shooting jacket, along with a knitted tie, he checked his appearance in a full-length mirror and decided he didn't look such a fool after all.

Boots on, he made his way down to the small dining room, where he found Danny Oswick and Dr Bacon. He said good morning to them, then loaded a plate with fried eggs, toast and sausages from a sideboard where the breakfast food was kept hot beneath silver cloches. One of the footmen stood beside the table and asked whether the professor would like some tea or coffee.

'Coffee, black, no sugar.'

'And would the professor like some fresh orange juice?'

'The professor would like that very much.'

He sat by Oswick, diagonally opposite the doctor. 'Did you gentlemen sleep well?'

'Like a top,' Oswick said.

'And you, Dr Bacon?'

'I slept well enough, thank you.'

'Well that's probably not good news for the pheasant population of the Harbinger estate.'

Bacon observed him blankly, as though he were talking Martian. Wilde smiled in false sympathy and then tucked into his breakfast. The coffee arrived and it was excellent, followed soon by the arrival of their host, who greeted the other three men already at breakfast. His plus fours and jacket seemed to have been fashioned directly onto his body by a Savile Row master tailor so snugly did they fit.

'And then there were four,' Catesby said, an unlit cigar held elegantly in his smooth fingers. 'What a damned shame.'

'Neville?' Wilde demanded, alarmed.

'Our other American friend has departed.'

'What do you mean?' Wilde could not conceal the rising alarm he felt.

'Just what I said, Tom. The man's gone. He upped and left in the middle of the night or the early hours. His bed hasn't even been slept in. Didn't even leave an explanatory note. Not even a word of thanks. Damnably rude, if you ask me.'

'What about his car?'

'Gone.'

'This isn't right, Neville. Something's happened to him.'

'Well, I agree it's not right. As for something happening to him, I tell you this: the chap's lost his mind. I knew him in America before the war and he seemed a decent enough fellow. I feel bloody let down, Tom. Remind me never to invite another businessman – or a Russian sniper for that matter. They're not reliable, and they're certainly not gentlemen.'

'Can I see his room?'

'What a curious request, but yes, of course, if you wish.' Catesby looked at his watch ostentatiously. 'One of the footmen will take you up. But be quick about it. I finished my breakfast half an hour ago and the beaters won't wait. The wagon is brimming with ammunition, and your guns await by the front door.'

Wilde stood up from the table, his breakfast half eaten, and was escorted up to the so-called Italian room where, he was told, Rhein was to have slept. It was untouched. No sign of a struggle, nothing. He looked at the young footman by the door and saw only a blank expression.

'Did you see Mr Rhein leaving?'

'No, sir.'

'Do you not think it strange for a man to go in the middle of the night like this?'

'Very strange, sir.'

The voice was flat, uninterested. That was all Wilde was going to get. Cold emptiness, leaving churning dread in the pit of his stomach.

CHAPTER 25

The loaders carried the guns in the horse-drawn ammunition wagon, while the four shooters loaded themselves onto the shooting brake with the dogs.

'And what a glorious day it is,' Catesby said to his companions. 'Little wisps of cloud, no rain. Let the birds fly, and none shall pass unscathed.'

'Where do your beaters come from?' Wilde wanted to know exactly who he might be dealing with.

'Oh, tenants, villagers. Anyone who wants to earn a few bob and get a bowl of hot soup.'

Wilde's loader was the butler McNally, who assured Wilde that he could do his side of the business faster than any man could shoot.

Ten minutes later, they arrived at a large field that had been allowed to lie fallow, abutting an ancient wood of oak and hazel and silver birch, the leaves now in their golden autumn finery. The wagon and shooting brake were unloaded and Catesby insisted that the shooters should all begin the day with a slug of brandy. He then ranged the four men and their personal loaders along the field, facing the woods whence the birds would fly when the beaters got to work. The order from left to right was Oswick, Wilde, Catesby and Bacon.

Catesby blew the horn to give the beaters the signal to begin the drive.

Wilde was holding the first of the two Dickson shotguns, loaded but still broken, loosely in his arms. The weapon was lightly weighted with beautiful, smooth curves – almost sensual – and after his practice with clays at Latimer Hall, he was pretty sure he could acquit himself with some sort of credit. The problem was he didn't much like the sport; he was a meat eater and would happily eat roast pheasant, but it was the killing for fun that offended him. He was aware that others would disagree fervently and say that at least a game bird had had a life in the wild and a chance of survival, unlike its cousins confined to coops. But logic didn't always come into these things and that was an argument for another day.

The noise of the beaters intensified and the first flush of birds took to the air. Wilde snapped the gun closed, raised the barrel high as two pheasants flapped noisily from the trees. He let off one barrel then the next, deliberately missing. He handed the gun to McNally, who immediately passed him the second gun.

'Mr Wilde, sir, bird to your right.'

Wilde saw it and shot. This time he hit it and watched it fluttering downwards like an enemy aircraft. Nothing for it, he would have to take it home, have it plucked, and eat the damned thing.

There might have been only four men shooting, but the air was filled with a cacophony of gunfire. Catesby on his right was firing non-stop, keeping his loader busy as he let off a dozen or more shots a minute. Oswick was also maintaining a high rate. The dogs were in their element, racing around the field and into the edge of the woods to pick up dead or dying birds and convey them to their masters.

A bird flew low from the wood above Wilde's head. He lined up the gun but McNally put a gentle hand on the barrel. 'Woodpecker, sir.'

God, he'd nearly shot a woodpecker. Not done. Woodcock, yes, woodpecker certainly not. 'Thank you, McNally.'

'My pleasure, sir.'

The shooting went on all morning. A large tent had been erected, a little way back from the game cart and the other vehicles, and food and drink was being brought for the men with guns. Some way away, a trestle table was set up with a terrine of soup for the loaders and beaters, to be served strictly in that order.

'I really think someone should go and try to call Mr Rhein,' Wilde said. 'You must have a number for him, Neville.'

'I rather think it's the other way round, Tom. He should call me, explain himself and apologise. I'm certainly not going to let the ill-mannered swine ruin our day. So let's tuck into the feast with relish. Oh, and well done with the shooting. Took a couple of pheasants, didn't you?'

'And how many did you take, Neville?'

'Not sporting to count.' He cupped his hand and whispered in Wilde's ear. 'But that doesn't stop my loader keeping a card – something over fifty, I'm told.'

It was then that things began to happen. Three beaters in the undergrowth just inside the wood were conversing and gesticulating. One of them was restraining a pair of dogs. A fourth beater was running across the field towards Catesby.

'We've found a body, sir.'

'Good God. A *human* body?'

'Yes, sir. A man.'

The corpse of Larry B. Rhein lay by a thicket of brambles, slightly to the north of the area the beaters had been covering. It seemed one of them, a young lad in his late teens, had moved away to take a piss and found it.

Rhein had a wound in the temple and a pistol at his side. He was wearing the clothes in which he had visited Wilde in the early hours.

Catesby and the other shooters stood around the body examining it. The shooting brake had been sent off to fetch the police and ambulance.

'Suicide,' Catesby said. 'The gun's just by his right hand. Took his own life, poor devil.' He went down on his haunches and touched the dead face with the back of his hand. 'Cold as the grave – must have been dead quite a few hours.'

Wilde said nothing. He knew that this was murder. And he was certain of something else: the pistol was his Colt .32 ACP Hammerless, the one taken from his room last night.

'He must have been a deeply troubled man,' Dr Bacon said. 'I did not notice that in him.'

Wilde didn't hear the words, but he heard the voice. That voice again. The man with the needles. What voice was it? It sounded English, and yet it wasn't. Had Dr Bacon killed Larry Rhein?

And then there was the gun. It would be covered in Wilde's fingerprints, for the killer would have worn gloves. It was owned legally and its identification number was registered. It would not be long before he was connected to it.

'Anyway,' Catesby was saying, 'nothing we can do for the chap now. It sounds frightfully poor taste, but life goes on and I really am damned peckish. It would be a shame to let the hot food go to waste. Shall we go and eat, gentlemen?'

'I'll wait here with the body,' Wilde said.

'As you wish.'

Oswick was at his side. 'Shall I stay with you, Professor?'

'No. Go and eat. Point the police in my direction when they arrive.'

He stood by the dead body, working out his next move. More than anything else he didn't want this crime scene disturbed. This had all been a bloody disaster and a tragedy of horrific proportions, but it was his own role in Catesby's game that consumed his thoughts.

Kill one man. Hang the other. Two men with one bullet.

McNally appeared at his side. 'Sorry business, sir.'

'Did you know Mr Rhein?'

'Never seen him before yesterday, Professor. Funny how there's some that will claw their way through fire and brimstone to survive while others think so little of their lives that they'll put a bullet in their own head. Can't understand it, sir.'

'Perhaps this wasn't suicide.'

'Really, sir? You're surely not suggesting murder?'

'I'm not suggesting anything, just thinking out loud. Where, for instance, is his car? Go and get your food, McNally.'

Fifteen minutes later two constables arrived, followed by an ambulance struggling along the muddy track. Catesby broke into his lunch to accompany the law officers to the scene.

'Not much to investigate,' he said to the men. 'A case as old as mankind, I'm afraid – a distressed fellow taking the easy way out.'

'I'm sure you're right, sir,' the elder of the two officers said.

'No.' Wilde shook his head. 'This bears proper investigation. You need to get the police surgeon along to inspect the body before it's moved and you need to inform senior detective officers so that they can come and question everyone who was in Harbinger House with Mr Rhein last night. You also need find his car, a distinctive black Cadillac. Why would he have taken it somewhere then returned here to kill himself?'

'There was a big black American car just outside the gates to Harbinger House, sir.'

'Well, that must be his. In the first instance, you will need me to accompany you to the police station – for the pistol that killed Mr Rhein was mine.'

The policemen both looked at him as though he were mad. 'But this is Sir Neville's estate, sir, and if he says it was suicide, we must take his word for it.'

'That's not for him to decide, though, is it? That will be up to the police surgeon and the coroner. If you want to keep your jobs, you'll do as I say.' He knew it had to be this way. The truth about the gun would come out in due course; better sooner rather than later. He held out his hands to be cuffed. 'In the meantime, do your duty and arrest me on suspicion of murder.'

Catesby looked bewildered. 'This is madness, Tom. Of course you didn't kill Larry.'

'I know that and I'm sure *you* know that, but I need the law to know it, too. Perhaps you'd send my things on.'

'Of course . . . good Lord, old man, this has certainly put the mockers on the day.'

CHAPTER 26

As she sipped her shandy and half listened to Sandra chatting away inanely, it occurred to Liz Lightfoot that the only way out of her marriage was to murder her husband. Lucas was a powerful man, a soldier, but like everyone else he had to sleep at night. And those sweat-drenched slumbers invariably slipped towards delirium with the assistance of copious quantities of beer and his incoherent nightmares.

When he thrashed and screamed in the early hours, haunted by dreams of blood, he was at his most vulnerable.

She had killed chickens before. Anyone could kill. It was easy. Hone the blade of the filleting knife to razor sharpness and slide it firmly and deftly across Lucas's throat. Sever the jugular and carotid. There would be a lot of blood. The hard bit was getting away with it, avoiding the rope.

The key was to work alone. That meant not saying a word to Tony. Her meetings with Tony were becoming less and less frequent and she could not abide this situation much longer. They had only been together once since that Thursday evening, over two weeks ago, when they had seen the submarine emerging from the waves.

But she had been thinking a great deal and she had come to the conclusion that even without Tony, even without a lover, something had to change. She could not throw away her life on the man she had married.

If she was to kill Lucas, she had to do it herself. She had read enough true-life murder stories in the papers and magazines to know that the way to evade justice was to never involve another soul. Never write anything down and never trust anyone with your thoughts or your plans. Even your one true love might crack under questioning or confess when the guilt became unbearable.

And now they were here all together. Two couples just like the old times, talking about inconsequentials and drinking beer. Tony and Sandra Hood, Lucas and Liz Lightfoot. Only this time there was a baby, too. Lovely little Ronnie, always smiling and gurgling.

The invitation had been a surprise. Lucas had come home early and, as always, Liz had been tense, preparing herself mentally for whatever awaited her. His bad, drunken days were becoming more frequent and even the good ones, when he had no money left for alcohol, were characterised by sullen silences and complaints about the food she had cooked. Even if he didn't hit her with his fists, he lashed her with his tongue. But she could put up with that. Her hopes rose. Surely, today, he couldn't be drunk, not at five o'clock in the afternoon?

Incredibly, he had shut the door without slamming it and even afforded her a half-smile.

'Get your coat, woman. We're going out.'

'What do you mean? Where?'

'I met Sandra in the shop this morning. We got chatting and realised we hadn't seen much of each other for a week or two. She's asked us to supper. Be nice to have a change of scenery and a pint with Tony. Let's go.'

Now they were in the Hoods' cosy farmhouse kitchen with its low ceiling and its warm range and the evening was going well, despite her initial apprehension. On arrival, it quickly became clear that neither Lucas nor Sandra had any idea about the affair.

Liz exchanged stolen glances with Tony, but nothing more. She saw the longing in his eyes, but the others didn't. Did he notice how thickly she had applied make-up to camouflage the bruises?

They had finished eating the main course. It had been a good meal because Tony had managed to get some rump steaks – something Liz hadn't eaten since before the war. Such were the benefits of dining with a farmer.

The plates had been cleared away and Lucas was downing pints at an alarming rate. He was getting louder too. Tonight would end with a beating.

On the other side of the table, the women were having a conversation of their own. 'I'm sorry about Luke,' Liz said softly so that her husband shouldn't hear. 'He's been drinking more since the army.'

'Oh don't worry about him. He's earned a pint, hasn't he?'

Liz simply shrugged and took another sip of weak shandy.

'Are you trying for a baby yet, Liz?' Sandra was cuddling little Ronnie, who was sucking vainly on a dummy.

What a question. The thought of having a child with Lucas horrified her, but they weren't taking any precautions on those rare occasions when he decided to 'slip her one', so it had to be a very real possibility. Unless, of course, she was barren. 'Well, you know how it is. We're just not having any luck at the moment.'

'Oh, it'll all be fine in due course. You wait. You'll make a great mum one day. And Lucas, what a dad he'll be.'

Liz finished her drink and decided she'd rather like something a bit stronger, something to numb the pain when they got home and he set about her. A pint of gin would suit.

'Apple pie for pudding,' Sandra said. 'With custard.'

'I love apple pie,' Liz said truthfully but without really thinking. God, this conversation was banal, and inside she was dying.

'But first,' Sandra continued, 'I've got to put Ronnie down for the night. Then it'll be the four of us, just like old times.' She stood and wandered around the table offering the baby's face to be kissed by her husband and guests, then disappeared upstairs. The sound of wailing drifted down through the old house.

'She'll be a while settling him,' Tony said, grinning.

'Well, I'm going for a piss,' Lucas said. Unsteadily, holding on to chair backs and cupboard handles, he made his way towards the back door, then stumbled out into the chilly evening air – to the privy, or simply a wall.

Liz and Tony looked at each other with hunger. 'He'll be an age,' she said. With luck, she thought, he'll trip on a paving stone, fall and crack open his skull, spill his brains in the dirt.

'Sandra will be a while, too.'

They met halfway around the table and kissed. His arms were holding her as though she was his prisoner. She broke away from him. 'Stop, Tony, this is crazy.'

'I can't stand it. We've got to tell them. Tonight.'

'No.'

'We can't go on like this.'

'Like what?'

They both turned. The voice was Sandra's. She was standing in the doorway, looking at them uncomprehendingly. For a moment, there was silence, then Tony spoke.

'I'm leaving you, Sandra. I'm in love with Liz.'

The words were so simple, such plain English. They must have been said many thousands of times over the centuries, only with different names.

The baby was in her arms, silent now. 'I couldn't get him to sleep,' she said as though she hadn't heard what her husband just said. 'He's all right when I hold him, but as soon as I put him down . . .' The words trailed off.

'Did you hear what I said?'

'No. I don't want to hear what you said. I'm going to heat up the apple pie and custard.' She plonked Ronnie in his high chair and turned towards the range.

Liz stood back from Tony, horribly aware that they were still in each other's arms, all in the presence of the woman who was still his wife and would always be the mother of his child. She broke away from him and sat down, trying to compute what to do next.

A gust of air announced Lucas's return. He was trying to do up his fly buttons, which was awkward because he had a heavy pipe wrench gripped in his right hand. 'Found this, mate. Can I borrow it?' He grinned, then clapped Tony on the back. 'All right, Tone? Your face, mate, you look as though you've trod in a cowpat.'

It was then that Sandra dropped the pie and screamed.

It was not the first time that Wilde had been held in a police interview room, but his exit was taking a great deal longer than he had anticipated. Detective Inspector Shirley had driven out from Cambridge to take charge of the case. The shooting party and all the workers associated with it looked on with fascination as he was bundled into the back of a police car and driven away. Never had such a thing been known in the history of the sport.

In the village pub and across the fences that divided backyards, there would be much gossip.

Now they were back at St Andrew's Street in Cambridge and the interview was proceeding at a crawl. Shirley was accustomed to housebreakers and small-time crooks; the murder of an American gentleman by a professor from one of the ancient colleges – and all of this at a great estate – was beyond his limited brain. He needed advice from above and so he had put through a call to the chief constable. So far no word had come back.

'For pity's sake, let me call Lord Templeman at Latimer Hall. You must have heard of him.'

'Upper-class chum of yours, is he?'

'He's a senior member of British intelligence. He will convince you of my innocence and explain what you have to do. You need to work with him.'

'All in due course. This is a murder inquiry, not *The Thirty-Nine Steps*.'

'I'm not sure you realise what you're dealing with, Inspector. We need to have teams searching that estate.'

'Don't worry, we've secured the crime scene and prints have been taken from your pistol. And, surprise surprise, the prints are yours. But you knew that, didn't you?'

'There are other matters, involving national security. I would explain it all to you, but I can't. Call Templeman and he will be better placed to put you in the picture.' *Or simply order you to free me and stand back from the investigation.*

'Templeman, Templeman, Templeman. You're like a broken record, Wilde. I'm in charge of this investigation, and I'll play it my way.'

'What about the post-mortem examination?'

'Dr Weir is in charge of that and he has agreed to expedite his work, so we'll have an initial report quite soon. But I'm not here to answer questions – you are. I want a statement from you. A confession. Save us all some time. First let's address your motive. How long have you known Mr Rhein?'

'I met him for the first time yesterday. I have absolutely no reason to kill him. But there may be others in that house with a motive. Have you questioned all the guests? The servants?'

Rupert Weir had warned Wilde about this police officer; his time-serving, bone-headed intransigence. When he took the decision to hand himself in, he believed Dagger Templeman would have him out in no time. But he hadn't reckoned with Detective Inspector Shirley being in charge of the case.

The officer ignored Wilde's entreaties. 'If you didn't have murder in mind, perhaps you'd care to explain why you considered it a good idea to take a handgun to a shooting weekend.'

As he spoke, the door to the interview room opened. The desk sergeant poked his head around. 'Call for you, Detective Inspector. Apparently it's urgent.'

'Very well.' He left Wilde, bolting the door behind him. Five minutes later, he returned, his sharp, weasel features knotted like a boy trying to make sense of an exam paper when he's done no work all year and no revision. 'It seems there has been a development, Wilde.'

'Does that mean you're going to listen to me now?'

'Dr Weir was on the line. He believes the deceased was not killed by a gunshot but by an injection of poison. He was shot post-mortem.'

Phenol. It had to be phenol. 'Then I can go?'

'Not so fast. You're still prime suspect.'

'But why would I kill a man with poison and then shoot him with a pistol that had my fingerprints all over it. Think it through, Inspector.'

'You may be held in high regard in your college, Wilde, but I would advise you not to take that tone with me.'

'For God's sake, someone stole my gun from my room. Whoever it was – and I have my suspicions – was trying to frame me.'

The detective inspector was silent and it was obvious that the cogs were grinding slowly. He was staring at Wilde with loathing and something else – bewilderment and perhaps a horrible feeling that he had, indeed, got the wrong man. 'All right,' he said at last.

'Let's call this Lord Templeman of yours and find out what he's got to say for himself. Give me his number.'

Lucas had picked up the pipe wrench in the tool shed because it was just what he needed to unscrew the outside tap in their backyard and replace the washer.

It was a heavy steel implement, two-feet long with most of the weight at the adjustable end. A useful tool for plumbers and other workers. But this evening it became an instrument of darkness.

Sandra was screaming. The dish had shattered on the stone floor. Apple and pastry were spread wide. Lucas stood there with the wrench in his hand, his eyes flicking between Sandra and the other two adults in the room – his wife Liz and his best friend Tony. They were standing close to each other.

Through the fug of alcohol, some semblance of understanding entered Lucas's brain.

'What's all this then, mate?' He was looking at Tony but he was addressing the whole room. His shoulders had gone back, the dog at bay.

The silence was broken by Sandra's sobs.

'We're in love,' Tony said. 'Liz and me. She's leaving you, Lucas.'

He shouldn't have said it, not like that and not to a man with a heavy pipe wrench gripped in his fist.

'You what?'

Liz was edging away, trying to pull Tony back out of Lucas's reach. But Tony wasn't having any of it. He was facing up to Lucas, his chin jutting.

'I'm sorry, Lucas. I didn't want it to come out like this.'

'Is this a joke?'

'No joke.'

The pipe wrench swung up and around in an arc, like a broad-sword. It smashed with terrible force into the side of Tony's head, knocking him sideways onto the table. His other temple caught the oaken edge and ricocheted back, snapping his neck. He crumpled to the floor and might already have been dead, but Lucas kept hitting him, pummelling his face and body with the wrench, spraying blood across the floor to a soundtrack of Sandra's screams and Liz's terrified sobs.

Lucas pulled back from his bloody work and held the wrench out to the side. He looked at his wife with loathing. 'You next, bitch.'

Liz was by the door. She dragged it open, and ran.

Templeman arrived at the police station half an hour after receiving the message from the officer interrogating Wilde. He immediately made his large presence felt and took control of the situation. A call to the War Office was enough to put Detective Inspector Shirley in his place.

It was almost eight o'clock in the evening. Templeman and Wilde sat in the back of the car as they were driven to Cornflowers.

'The devil take it, Tom, I no longer know what to think. Are we getting anywhere or are we going around in circles?'

'Have you confirmed the dead man's identity?'

'Yes, that was indeed Larry Rhein. Quite an operator apparently, but also something of a lone wolf. Tell me about the other guests.'

'Well Danny Oswick was there. He's a good actor. Happy to admit he's a fascist, but trying to suggest he's one of the principled ones, whatever that means. He has a bit of self-deprecatory charm. Dr Bacon, I am certain, is the man with the bloody needles. Just something in his voice. English but not quite English. It's difficult to explain – nothing that I could honestly attest to in a court of law.'

'And Neville Catesby?'

'Oh, he's playing games with us. The Japanese Room . . . was that a coincidence? I still have no idea which side he's on, though, and I'm not sure whether he does. He's on his own side and he likes creating mayhem.'

'The phenol suggests Nazis.'

'Indeed, as do the Germans he seems to be using. But you know there's something childlike about Catesby – a boy smashing up everyone else's toys, for the hell of it.'

'What constitutes winning for him?'

'Destruction, perhaps? He's a psychopath.'

'Then you're certain he's behind all this?'

'Yes, but how do we counter it? This isn't wartime, Dagger, so you can't just intern the bastard. You need solid evidence, and we have nothing.'

'I have a horrible feeling we're running out of time.'

'Give me a gun, Dagger. I'm going back there.'

'Are you serious?'

'Never more so.'

CHAPTER 27

At Cornflowers, Templeman waited in the car while Wilde changed out of the plus fours and shooting jacket into a pair of his own dark cords, water-resistant motorbike jacket, boots and picked up a torch with fresh batteries. He had a few words with Sylvia Keane, who seemed a little taken aback by his arrival.

'I wasn't really expecting to see you this evening, Professor. Has your weekend been cut short?'

'Sort of,' he replied vaguely. 'Has there been any word from Mrs Wilde?'

'No, Professor, I'm afraid not.'

'And Johnny is well?'

'Very well. He has been playing with Penelope nicely. I'm sure he missed you though.'

He went and had a quick look at the boy, but he was asleep so he didn't disturb him. For a moment he wondered what Doris had been trying to tell him. It was almost as if she had had some doubts about Sylvia Keane, but that was not something that could be addressed now. Importantly, the house seemed to be in order and Johnny was fine. Time to go.

At the front door he turned around. 'If she does call, give her our love. Ask her to call me tomorrow.'

'Of course, sir.'

'And help yourself to the rest of the wine bottle.'

'Thank you, Professor. That's very generous.'

From Cornflowers, Wilde and Templeman were driven to Latimer Hall. This was a time for checks: who exactly was Dr Edmund Bacon? What was known about him? Was he in MI5 files?

Templeman made a series of phone calls while Wilde waited with a strong coffee and some sandwiches. It was almost nine o'clock when his host finally put down the phone.

'Yes, the General Medical Council has an Edmund Bacon in their records, but I doubt it's your man, unless he's a ghost. The real Dr Bacon died in the Coventry blitz in 1940.'

'Ah, why doesn't that surprise me? Is that enough to send men in to arrest him for impersonating a medical professional?'

'Do we have proof that's what he's doing? Who is he supposed to have deceived? It's possible he simply has a PhD.'

'Point taken.'

'Do you still want to go back there, Tom?'

'I don't think I have any choice. Can your driver take me?'

'Of course. First let's get you kitted out.' He left the room before returning with a bundle of leather strapping and a weighty package wrapped in soft cloth.

'God go with you, Tom.'

'I think I'd rather rely on this.'

As the car sped away smoothly on the road out of Cambridge, he switched on the rear light and unwrapped the automatic pistol that Templeman had thrust into his hands.

It was a Browning 9 mm Hi-Power. A fair bit larger and heavier than the Colt .32 that was presently held by the police. This one didn't need to be so small and discreet, for there was no reason to conceal it from view. He had fitted the shoulder holster beneath his jacket before leaving Latimer Hall. The gun boasted a thirteen-round magazine, which pleased him; he had no intention of shooting anyone, but the extra firepower gave him a warm feeling of confidence.

Outside the night was dark, cool and dry. Not for the first time, he found himself thinking about the anonymous letter Templeman had received:

PLAGUE Catesby

That was all it said, but it spoke volumes. Templeman had made the point that whoever sent it must know about events at Flowthorpe as well as being aware of Neville Catesby.

But there was something else, wasn't there? Whoever sent it must *also* know that Lord Templeman was a senior officer in MI5 and that he was investigating the plague attack. Few people could be in possession of such knowledge, for MI5 was a secretive organisation, little known to the public at large.

It was not a long drive but the time in the car gave Wilde precious minutes to plan his movements. 'Stop here,' he said when they were a hundred yards from the Harbinger House gates.

The driver halted and let him get out. No words passed between them. The driver was a professional, attached to the ministry, and he understood operational matters.

Wilde waited until he'd gone, then approached the long drive on foot. As he anticipated, there were no lights showing in the gatehouse and the gates were wide open. The wall that surrounded the estate was no more than three feet high and constructed of flint, so it would have been pointless to try to keep anyone out, for a child could easily scale the wall. The gatehouse and gates were there for vanity's sake.

He walked straight in and used the drive to lead him towards the house, keeping to the side of the roadway, ready to move into the cover of the trees if a vehicle approached. There was just enough light to guide him without using the torch. The drive was about half a mile long and, stepping purposefully but with caution, he covered it in ten minutes.

Stopping on the lawn beneath a broad cedar, he scanned the forecourt and looked up at the old building. His Riley was still there on the gravel, where the footman had parked it, along with one other car, large and black.

This was his third visit to the house in recent days and he knew its layout. The curtains were drawn closed and the only light visible was through a chink in the drapes in the drawing room. The whole of the upstairs floors were in darkness. It had the feeling of a house that was either shut down or in the process of being evacuated.

He walked a circuitous route around to the back, to the kitchen area, which was also dark and locked and he wondered whether Catesby and the others had already departed. He could understand why they might wish to be gone from here; they must know that the place would be searched.

But where would they have gone? What other properties did Catesby have?

The door to the orangery was unlocked and he looked inside. The music and the laughter were long dead. From there, he made his way to various outhouses, including the gun room, which was empty. There was nothing to be seen, no sign of biological weapons or even human life.

There was an option, of course: break into the house. But if there was still a light on in the drawing room, that must indicate the presence of at least one or two people. He made his way back around to the front of the building.

He stopped in his tracks, beneath the cedar.

The portico light was on now and someone was walking in the night air. No, there were two of them. Wilde shrank further back into the lee of the tree and watched. It was Danny Oswick and his wife, Shirin, both caught as silhouettes in the glow from the entrance. The young man had his hands in his pockets and was hunched forward as they walked. She kept turning to him, talking quietly, her long silk scarf wafting in the breeze. Occasionally, she ran a hand through her hair and shook her head, as though annoyed by something he said or didn't say.

They walked on a little way. She stopped again, and even from a distance Wilde detected anger in her eyes. She slapped her husband's face and he stumbled back. This was not a happily married couple out for an evening stroll.

Jump them and hold them at gunpoint? Force them somewhere away from the house and subject them to hard questioning?

He watched and waited. Who else was here? Dr Edmund Bacon, perhaps? That was the one he wanted more than any other. He was certain now – it was Bacon who had killed farmer Charlie Bagshawe and Larry Rhein and MI5 agent Rafe Crow. One way or another, he had to be neutralised.

There was no safe or subtle way to do this. He walked up to Oswick and Shirin, as casually as meeting them on a street. 'I see you two know each other,' he said.

They both looked shocked. 'Professor Wilde . . .' Oswick stammered.

'Surprised to see me? Due to unforeseen circumstances I was forced to leave my car here and came to get it. Why, there it is.'

'I thought you were under arrest.'

'Oh, that was all sorted out amicably. It seems Mr Rhein wasn't killed by a bullet after all, but by some sort of toxin. Perhaps Dr Bacon didn't mention that to you. But tell me, how did you two meet? I'm surprised to see you here, Shirin.'

'Well, he's my husband, but you already knew that, didn't you?'

Wilde laughed. This was a deadly business but he had the upper hand and he was enjoying their discomfort. 'Before you ask, yes I am armed. This time I've got a proper gun, not the little Colt. Let me show you.' He slipped his right hand into his jacket and withdrew the Browning 9 mm from the shoulder holster. Oswick automatically backed off, but Shirin just sneered. Wilde jabbed the automatic in her direction. 'I have a few questions.'

'You realise we're not alone here,' Shirin said. 'You won't get away from here alive.'

'In which case, nor will you. So, is Bacon here?'

Neither of them replied.

'Not helpful. Another question then: what can you tell me about him? He seems to be going around killing people. You two are both involved with him and Catesby in something bad. Very bad. The security services know all about you, so there's no way out for you. Your best chance is to talk. Tell me all you know.'

'I've had enough of this, Danny. Let's go. He's not going to shoot us.'

'You go, Shirin. I'll stay with the professor.'

'No, fuck him. He's dead meat. Lily-livered bastard won't shoot us in cold blood.'

She clutched at her young husband's arm but he wouldn't budge. She spat on the ground, turned away and strode towards the front entrance of the building.

Seemingly from nowhere, a blaze of light dazzled Wilde. The black car lurched forward, coming straight at him.

Wilde hadn't realised the car was occupied. He turned sideways, but there wasn't time to evade the oncoming machine.

Oswick moved with him, his arms going around Wilde's upper body, pushing them both to the left. The black car missed them by a fraction of an inch, spraying up gravel like grapeshot.

He landed hard on his shoulder with Oswick on top of him. The impact took the breath from Wilde's lungs, yet he had caught a glimpse of the driver at the wheel as the car roared away down the drive. He looked like the man in the street outside the Plough when he followed Shirin. Wilde sensed, too, that there was at least one other person in the car – maybe more – but he couldn't be sure, and they were unidentifiable.

The gun was still in his hand, his index finger curled tightly on the trigger. The smell of cordite assailed his nostrils. Dear God, he had unwittingly fired it in the heart-stopping heat of the moment. He could hear the ringing memory of the explosion. The shot itself must have been muffled by the sound of the car, or the rush of blood in his head from the impact as he hit the ground, for he hadn't noticed it. Where had the bullet gone? He pushed Oswick off and, for a moment, feared that he had shot the young man.

Oswick was climbing to his knees, dazed but seemingly sound. A little way off, Shirin was on the gravel, one hand scrabbling at the stones, the other hanging loose. Her legs were dragging and she was losing her grip. She fell sideways, screaming in pain. The bullet had hit her.

'The gun went off,' Wilde said. 'Your wife, she's hurt.'

The two men went to her side. Wilde still had the gun in his hand. He had no idea who else might be about the place, and armed. Possibly no one, possibly the butler, the other servants, Catesby himself? No one seemed to be coming out to intervene, but that could change.

'Shirin,' Oswick said, trying to cradle her head. 'Where are you hit?'

'Shoulder . . . Oh God, the pain.' Even in the faint light from the wall lamp by the door in the portico, the agony was clear to see on her face.

'We'll get her to hospital in my car – Addenbrooke's. Help me put her in the back.'

'She's bleeding badly.'

'OK. We have to staunch it.'

There was a lot of blood at the top of her left arm. The obvious action was to go in the house and find bandages, but who was in there? Wilde unravelled her long scarf and bunched it into a ball to hold against the wound and stem the blood flow. She screamed again.

Together they lifted her up, but it was a struggle. The woman didn't want to be helped and was fighting to get away from both Wilde and her husband, all the time groaning and howling with the terrible pain. Wilde looked at the injury as well as he could but this needed a doctor. They had to get her to hospital without delay.

Somehow, they managed to ease her into the rear seat of the Riley, laying her on her uninjured side as gently as possible. Wilde got behind the wheel and Oswick clambered into the front passenger seat beside him, leaning over to hold the scarf against the wound and trying to reassure her that she would soon be in safe hands. The car started first time. Wilde switched on the lights, engaged gear and drove.

CHAPTER 28

Lord Templeman – Dagger to his friends but usually Richard to his family – was born into privilege.

His family was extraordinarily wealthy and so he had been coddled and cosseted from birth, with nannies, tutors and the very finest of educations, all of which he now found rather embarrassing, particularly in the new socialist post-war world.

The concept of public duty was strongly ingrained, for he was also brought up to believe that the more you had, the more you must give. If you were rich and powerful then you were obliged to spend your life earning that good fortune through service to the nation and the community at large.

He was also a man of habit. At this time every evening, he took himself for a walk around the ancient colleges of the town he had always called home. This evening, though, there was a pounding in his forehead. And when the veins in his port wine stain began to pulsate, he always thought of it as a sort of alarm bell. Well, to hell with that. A walk was a walk, nothing more.

That said, he wasn't a fool and he decided to play safe. He was, after all, on someone's death list, and if he was handing out warnings to other people whose names were entered in the addendum to the bloody Black Book, then he should exercise caution himself. And so he secreted his favourite Walther PPK in the pocket of his outsize raincoat.

It was a pleasant evening for late October and there was no one about. As he strolled along the Backs, he dismissed his earlier doubts and began to feel at peace with the world. The BW episode was bad, but they would sort it out. Wilde was a good man and he was glad to have secured his assistance.

In the near distance he could see college lights glowing and he imagined he could hear singing, probably from the Trinity chapel. Below him, the River Cam flowed on soundlessly in the dark.

He stopped a moment outside the rear entrance of St John's and breathed in the cool air. And then he felt uneasy again, unpleasantly aware just what a good target he presented. That was the problem with being six foot seven inches tall. He turned around and began to set off back home when he heard a car pull up at the kerb and then a voice he recognised.

'Templeman?'

He stopped. 'What are you doing here?'

'Oh, you know, just going home after a drink with friends.'

Templeman frowned and his hand went into his pocket to grip the Walther. But the marksman in the car already had his range. The hollow-point bullet hit him in the head and exploded his brain. Templeman was dead before he hit the ground.

A few miles away, Shirin had gone quiet in the back of the car. Oswick was talking soothingly to her, but she didn't respond, except for the occasional moan. 'I think she's blacked out,' he said.

Wilde was driving fast. He knew the way and reckoned they would be at Addenbrooke's within twenty-five minutes, perhaps quicker if the roads stayed as empty as they were.

'Keep stemming the blood flow. She should be all right if you can reduce the bleeding. No internal organs have been hit.'

'God, this is a damned mess.'

'Yes,' Wilde said. 'That's an understatement.'

'I'm so sorry. It's all my fault. I had no one to turn to.'

'What do you mean?'

'All this. I didn't know who to trust, who to confide in. I thought you were one of them. You were at the New Realm Patriots meeting . . . you told Shirin you were in the Bund.'

Wilde looked at the young man's profile in bemusement, still unable to work out who he was. 'You're not making any sense.'

'That's the problem. I'm not making any sense to myself, sir.'

'Look, what's going on, Oswick? You saved my life back there. The car was being driven straight at me.'

'The car was coming at *me* – I was saving my own life. I told you last night, Professor, I'm not the person you think I am.'

'But you *are* one of them – Catesby, Bacon, whoever else. Your own wife, for pity's sake. You're part of some filthy conspiracy.'

'I *was* one of them, before the war – before the *end* of the war. And then I walked into Belsen and the scales fell from my eyes.'

'Ah, you saw the result of the Nazis' inhumanity and changed your mind. In which case, why are you still associating with them? Why is your wife recruiting new members with you at her side?'

'I love my wife, Professor. We have different political opinions, but I won't hear a word said against her.'

'Till death do you part . . .'

'Yes I made a marriage vow. But I believe she is wrong and that she is in grave danger of being harmed by her decisions.'

'Where does all this stem from, her anger?'

'Mostly the treatment of the 18Bs during the war.'

'No, before that. What attracted her to the Blackshirts in the first place? By her own account she was a reasonably successful actress. What changed?'

'She was always angry, we both were. I told you about my father – that was what enraged me. I thought Mosley was fighting for justice.'

'Well, you misread that one. And Shirin?'

'I don't know.'

'What's her background?'

'I've never met her family. She left home young and wants nothing to do with them. They're from Lancashire and all I know is that her father works in a factory and he's a shop steward. I know she hates him, but I don't know why.'

But there was a clue there. If her father was a union man, there was every chance he was left wing. Whatever happened between them, her reaction was to go in the opposite direction. Daddy went left, Shirin turned right. It all sounded ridiculously simplistic, but that didn't mean there was no truth to it.

'She couldn't accept that I had changed,' Oswick continued. 'And I'm afraid I was too in thrall to her to argue with any great conviction. But I knew I had to stop what was happening. My problem was only how to protect Shirin.'

'That's not going to be easy.'

'They're losing confidence in me – Shirin, Catesby, the others. No, it's worse than that – they know I'm not one of them now. They've tolerated me up until now because of Shirin, but they no longer confide their secrets in me and once you lose their trust, you're done for. But you saw that, didn't you? The car was meant for me. They take no chances.'

'Who was in the car? Was it Bacon?'

'No, he left hours ago.'

'Who then?'

'I don't know. I didn't see them. Probably the German.'

'Is that the man you and Shirin talked to outside the Plough? Scars on his forehead. Evil looking.'

'You saw us there?'

'You set me up.'

'We thought you were a fascist. Shirin wanted to draw you in. I didn't really know you, sir; I was just told by Sir Neville that you were one of us. That you were the man to teach me.'

'You have been easily led.'

'You don't understand – I wanted to *expose* you.'

Wilde found himself laughing. 'Well, I had a lucky escape there, Oswick. And the German?'

'Yes, it was him. His name is Kagerer. Paul Kagerer. There was another German, too, but he's disappeared.'

Georg Sosinka. That was the other one's name. He was now in the hands of the security services, having been shot by Wilde outside the house of farmer Bagshawe. And so the circle was complete. The link between events in Norfolk, the death of Rafe Crow, and this – the Catesby conspiracy.

Templeman's instinct had been right all along.

They arrived at the hospital. Oswick said, 'I'll take it from here, Professor. It won't look good if you're seen to be involved.'

The young man was correct, but Wilde was hesitant. He had accidentally shot this woman, so he had a responsibility to her. But Oswick was her husband and his caution made sense. Could he be trusted? Wilde still wasn't sure. His wife might be the actress by profession, but they were all actors in this game of Catesby's.

'What will you say?'

'I'll say it was an accident. I was showing her an old service revolver I brought home from the war. Every house in England has such souvenirs – Lugers, Mausers, bayonets, German helmets, Hitler Youth daggers.'

'Your wife will tell them the truth, though.'

'What, and implicate herself? Shirin has faults, but she's neither stupid nor suicidal.'

'In the case of a bullet wound, the hospital will be obliged to call the police.'

'Don't worry, I'll leave my details with the staff and slip away. Doctors and nurses are not going to make a citizen's arrest.'

'Are you certain?'

'Yes. Go to your rooms – I'll be with you once I'm sure Shirin is in good hands.'

With the assistance of two porters, she was eased out of the back of the car and carried into the hospital, where nurses and a doctor immediately took control. Wilde waited a few minutes, watching through the open entrance, before leaving.

Addenbrooke's was only a few minutes' walk along Trumpington Street from the college, but he took the car anyway, and parked outside the gatehouse.

He exchanged a few words with the night porters, who were surprised to see him so late in the evening. There were no messages in his cubbyhole, so he wandered across the courts up to his rooms. Few lights were on and his rooms were cold and cheerless, for there had been no reason to light a fire in his absence. He got out the whisky bottle and poured a couple of fingers. He knocked it straight back and poured another. This had been a long and disagreeable day.

Would Oswick really follow him here, as he had promised, or were the words he uttered in the car all lies? He wished more than anything that he could call Lydia in London, but that was impossible. Instead, he put a call through to Latimer Hall and asked for Templeman.

'I'm afraid His Lordship is out on his evening constitutional, Professor. I'll tell him you called.'

'Get him to phone me here at college.'

'Of course, sir.'

He sat on the sofa nursing his drink, trying to make sense of the events of these last few days and hours. Any doubts about Neville Catesby's role and the nature of Dr Edmund Bacon, if that was his true name, had evaporated. They were at the heart of a conspiracy that involved deadly pathogens.

The death of Larry Rhein was proof. He had died because he had a clear idea what was going on and posed a threat. Most importantly of all, he had confirmed a link between Catesby and Ryoichi Naito of Japan's diabolical Unit 731 research facility.

The only doubt remaining about Catesby was his motive.

Maybe there was no motive. Simply destruction and mayhem for its own sake. The great game.

Danny Oswick arrived within half an hour. He looked deadbeat and Wilde immediately poured the young man a drink.

'This is as bad as anything I encountered during the war, Professor. This involves the woman I love and I am at a loss.'

'I think you'd better start from the beginning, Oswick. Settle down, have a drink, and tell me exactly what's going on.'

Oswick obeyed the professor. He sipped the whisky and closed his eyes, as though deep in thought. 'Well, it's true,' he said at last. 'I was a fascist. I worked for Mosley before the war, secretly collecting vast sums of money from Nazi sympathisers in the great houses of England. My knowledge of the royal household at Sandringham gave me an invaluable insight into the ways of the aristocracy and the wealthy. I knew how to address them and I knew their weaknesses. Above all, I knew that they feared Stalin a great deal more than they feared Hitler. They saw Nazism as a bulwark against Bolshevism.'

'But you must have seen the fascists' brutality too.'

He shrugged. 'Of course, but I was young and angry and I didn't care. If Reds got beaten up in the street, they were fair game. If Hitler rounded up the Bolsheviks and put them into Dachau or Sachsenhausen, so much the better.'

'You don't paint a very attractive picture of yourself.'

'I'm not trying to. I want you to know the truth. And then you might believe me.'

'Go on.'

'Well, I became close to Neville Catesby.'

'How did you meet him?'

'I was sent to Harbinger House to get him to cough up funds for the cause. We hit it off immediately. He was like a foster father to me – in fact Shirin said I was the son he wished he had had. When the war started he got me into his old regiment – which he had rejoined – and eventually singled me out for officer training. But I sort of suspected that one day he'd want something in return. He saw me as his thing, his property, and I went along with it, because I had no real father and, to be honest, I enjoyed the attention. It's a good feeling to have a mentor. You begin to believe in yourself, that you might have some value in the world.'

'And your wife?'

'Shirin was always there, too, pushing me forward, insisting that I listen to Sir Neville and follow his lead in all things. They became my family, and we owe loyalty to our families, don't we? My country right or wrong, that's what they say. Even more so, my family right or wrong.'

'But you had already met Shirin, yes?'

He nodded. 'I knew her right at the beginning. It was her influence that drew me into the BUF fold and she introduced me to Mosley.'

'When did you marry?'

'April 1939, a few months before the war, and the reception was at Harbinger House. It was all rather unconventional – Sir Neville was my best man and gave Shirin away. I think the vicar was rather confused and not at all sure whether it was legal, but Sir Neville doesn't worry about little details like that.

Some interesting names from the British fascist movement were there, then we honeymooned in Austria, all at Sir Neville's expense. It was marvellous. But when you owe someone that much, it becomes difficult to admit to yourself that perhaps you are being used.'

'But Belsen persuaded you.'

'Yes, Bergen-Belsen. I still wake in the early hours with the smell of the place in my nostrils. I still see the lifeless heaps of white flesh, the walking skeletons, the horror. The moment I entered that hellish place, I understood what fascism had done and knew instantly that I had been terribly wrong about everything since that first BUF meeting. Belsen was the work of the devil, and the devil's name was Hitler. The SS and the Gestapo and all those raising their arms in salute, they were his demons.'

'Wasn't Catesby at Belsen, too?'

'No, he was sick and had already returned to England. I suppose he saw the newsreels, but he didn't see it first-hand.'

'Did you talk to him or Shirin about your experience?'

'Oh yes, I tried to, but they wouldn't listen. They said the conditions in the camps were the result of Allied bombing and the consequent disruption of food supplies.'

Oswick was a bright young man, the sort of student Wilde would expect to gain a first-class degree, but in some ways he was like a child – a fact which even his Kitchener moustache could not disguise. He had been taken for a fool and used mercilessly by the two most important people in his life, but he had been too naive to see it. Even now, his loyalty to Shirin remained unbroken.

Wilde changed tack. 'Do you know about the Black Book?'

'Yes.'

'And the addendum?'

He nodded. 'Catesby has a copy of it and believes it to be an important document. Just like Himmler, he said the names in there were the worst of England's enemies and would have to be annihilated if revolution was ever to come. Kill them first, before they become a problem. No person, no problem, that was his motto repeated endlessly. He often spoke highly of Stalin who apparently said much the same thing. He had met him in Moscow in the early thirties.'

'Have you actually seen the addendum?'

'No, but I have heard a great deal about it.'

'My name is in it, so is my wife's.'

'Then you must both be in mortal danger.'

Yes, thought Wilde, I think I realised that. Thank God that Dagger had put watchers on to Lydia's hostel in London.

'He always had it in for you, for some reason. Long before this all started. Did you not know that? And even more so your wife.'

'But why?'

'You must have slighted him somehow. He bears deep grudges.'

'I certainly don't recall either of us insulting him in any way.'

'That doesn't mean he didn't imagine it.'

Or could it have been simply because of his appearance in the Black Book addendum? Wilde was certain he had never offended Catesby. Perhaps there was yet another motive. Perhaps Sir Neville or someone close to him had got wind of the fact that he had been investigating the events surrounding the Flowthorpe attack. That would certainly be a reason to do away with him. But how would he have known such a thing?

Whatever the truth, the newly acquired knowledge that he was helping Templeman inquire into events at Flowthorpe might well explain the last-minute invitation to the shooting weekend. A chance to eliminate both him and Larry B. Rhein. Two enemies erased.

Oswick had moved on and was trying to explain his involvement. 'The thing is, Professor, I know you must think me a complete ass to get mixed up in all this. Well, I considered running away, simply vanishing in another city or country.'

'That might have been your best move. Why didn't you?'

'I couldn't leave Shirin and I knew she wouldn't come with me. And there was something else – I realised I had to stay to stop Catesby's plans; there was no one else on the inside, no one who really knew what was going on. My problem was that I was working alone and I didn't know how to go about it – how to make contact with the secret services. This was hardly something I could just take to the police. What I am hoping is that you trust me enough now to work with me.'

'Have you ever heard of Lord Templeman?'

'Yes, Sir Neville often mentioned him. I believe he was at the party last week. He's a senior man in MI5, isn't he?'

'So you know about MI5?'

'Of course. Everyone in the BUF did – they were the enemy.'

'Tell me, Oswick, did you ever send an anonymous note to Lord Templeman?'

Oswick hesitated, then nodded.

'And what did it say?'

'It said, "PLAGUE Catesby" in cut-out headline letters from newspapers.'

So that was that question answered. Did he trust him? He didn't really have any option. They were both in danger, so they had to be safer and more effective together. And at least young Oswick had military training and had seen combat. 'Very well. Stay at my place tonight, and in the morning we'll plan our next move.'

'First I need to find out how Shirin is.'

'You can't go back there. Use my phone.'

'Thank you.'

'There's hope for you yet, Oswick.'

He shrugged uncertainly. 'Is there? Do you know what, Professor – and I hope you'll excuse my military language – I still hate the fucking upper classes for what they did to my dad.'

CHAPTER 29

Shirin had heard them in the car. They thought she was unconscious but she heard every word. So now she knew the truth about Danny. She had had her doubts, of course, as had Neville, because he had come back from the war a changed man.

She tried to shift her position in the bed and the pain coursed through her body like electricity. The shot had come from behind while she was walking away. She had twisted at the blaze of headlights and the screech of tyres. The bullet had gone into the flesh at the side of her shoulder, and had passed straight through, missing bone, with a neat exit wound. It was an agonising injury, but she had not needed an operation and the wound had been cleaned up and bandaged; it could have been a great deal worse, the doctor said.

As Danny was waiting by her side holding her hand, he had whispered in her ear what to say and she had nodded.

When the police arrived, she had told them it was an accident involving her husband. 'Just a stupid accident, Constable. He was showing me the gun he brought home and he didn't realise it had a bullet.' What else was she supposed to say?

'Where is the weapon now, Mrs Oswick?'

'I don't know. You'll have to talk to Danny. He's very distraught.'

'We'll need to interview him. Bullet wounds – even accidents – are serious matters.'

'I'll let him know.'

'Tell him to come to the station in St Andrew's Street. He'll have to give a full statement.'

'Of course. Yes, he'll do that as soon as possible.' She apologised for making such a fuss over such a small incident and the officer said that he was just thankful that she had got off reasonably lightly.

She smiled as he took his leave. It was a shame about Danny; she had a soft spot for him despite everything. He could have been someone.

Tonight, though, she had to be with Neville. She would leave this place in the early hours when the wards slept. Pain or no pain.

CHAPTER 30

Sylvia Keane was awake when Wilde arrived home with Oswick in tow.

'We have a guest, Mrs Keane. This is one of my undergraduates, Danny Oswick, who needs somewhere to sleep for the night. He can use the sofa.'

'Of course, sir. I shall get him some blankets and a pillow.'

'Thank you.'

He made one last call to Templeman, but he still wasn't home. 'He's on a long walk, Rogers.'

'Indeed, sir. Far longer than usual.'

'No word at all?'

'No, Professor. This is most unlike His Lordship.'

'Please ask him to call me when he gets in – however late. I'm home at Cornflowers.' This was urgent. He needed Templeman more than ever because the police were out of the question and the danger was very real.

'Of course, sir.'

While Mrs Keane sorted out bedding, he resumed his conversation with Oswick in the kitchen. 'In the absence of police protection, we have to assess the risk of certain courses of action. Firstly, though, we have to consider your safety.'

'Don't worry about me, sir. I lived under enemy fire for months on end.'

'This is very different. I can't help wondering whether the best thing for you might be to do what you considered before – get on a train and go to some city you have never been and lose yourself for a week or two. You could keep in touch with me and I'll let you know when it's safe to come back to college.'

'No, sir. I feel responsible for these events and I want to help you deal with them.'

'And how are you proposing to do that?'

'That's for you to say, sir. I'm a soldier. I just take orders.'

'And that warning note you sent – "PLAGUE Catesby" – how did you know about that if you were excluded from the centre of the conspiracy?'

'It was something I overheard. I wanted to find out more.'

'Something you overheard? Catesby, I suppose, but who was he talking to?'

'A man called Gram or Graham. I hadn't met him before and I never saw him again. I was worried that I had got the wrong end of the stick, but I had to tell someone – hence the note.'

'Why didn't you go straight to Templeman?'

'I was worried that if my name was known, the authorities would go for Shirin. I couldn't allow that, so it had to be anonymous.'

'What exactly did you hear?'

'It was vague and incomplete, but the man was in a hell of a state. He said he'd dropped something and that he feared he was going to die of plague. Sir Neville told him to stop being so melodramatic and to go and make himself scarce.'

'He dropped a ceramic canister, releasing the plague pathogen in the middle of an English village. People have died. So tell me, Oswick, where are the other canisters?'

'I've told you all I know.'

'There's another question: Harbinger House had servants – a butler, at least two footmen, cooks, loaders for the shoot. Are they innocents or are they part of this thing?'

'The butler McNally isn't innocent, but that doesn't mean he's privy to details of the conspiracy, any more than I was. I think he's probably ex-BUF but I couldn't swear to it. I really don't know about the rest of them. I never saw them before. I think they were simply there for the weekend, short-term contract. All the pre-war serving staff have left.'

'Write down everything you know about all of them. We will pass their details on to Lord Templeman to be checked.'

'Of course, sir.'

'I'll get you a pen and paper.'

Wilde's doubts about Oswick were evaporating. Either he should be on stage in Drury Lane, or he was telling the truth. But how far did that take them? This was information he had to get to Templeman fast. Where the hell was he?

In the meantime, there were two immediate problems – how to stay safe against an implacable enemy and how to avoid the police. If there was any suggestion that Wilde had fired the bullet that wounded Shirin Oswick, he would not be left at liberty again; even Templeman wouldn't be able to keep him from Detective Inspector Shirley's greasy clutches.

Did Catesby know about Cornflowers? He had never been here, and his recent communications with Wilde – the invitations to the Survivors Party and the shooting weekend – had both been addressed to the college.

And then there was the third problem. Not just staying safe, but going on the offensive. They wouldn't be secure unless and until this conspiracy could be smashed – before it progressed to its ultimate aim, whatever that was.

He handed the pen and paper to Oswick. 'Everything you know – every tiny detail, however insignificant it might seem. And tomorrow, just sit tight and keep your head down. I've got to do something alone. I don't think it's advisable to go back to college – the police would find you there, as would Catesby. Do you have anywhere else you could go?'

'No.'

'Well, I think you'll be safe here, but just be wary. Catesby may not know about this place, but you have to imagine he could find out, given a little time. There's a woman and two children in the house, so I'm entrusting them to your safekeeping . . .'

In the morning, after just five hours' sleep, Wilde took the Riley and drove south-west towards Wiltshire. It was a long, tortuous but beautiful route through the autumn countryside of Bedfordshire, Buckinghamshire and Oxfordshire.

All the way, he kept thinking of Lydia in London. He felt certain that the threat posed by Catesby apart, they simply couldn't go on like this, spending so little time together and unable to communicate. The war had been bad enough with him away in London so often working for the OSS, but this was worse because it meant Johnny didn't have his mother.

His other thoughts centred on Templeman. He had stopped at Latimer Hall on the way out of Cambridge and received the same response from Rogers, the butler. 'I'm afraid we still have no word from His Lordship. I'm extremely concerned.'

'You mean he didn't return home last night?'

'Indeed not, sir.'

'Have you told the police.'

'Yes. But they have no knowledge of his whereabouts. No accidents reported. I have also put through a call to Leconfield House in London, and I'm waiting for them to get back to me. This is all extremely concerning and most unlike my master. He is not one to disappear for any length of time without leaving contact details.'

'I'll call to see what news you have.'

Hours later, in the early afternoon, he arrived in the large village of Ramsbury and asked a woman of middle years the way to Crowood House.

The woman looked at him strangely, with undisguised contempt. 'Crowood House. Why on earth would you go there? Are you a Nazi?'

'No, but I have urgent business.'

'With the Nazi?'

'You mean Oswald Mosley? Yes, I have urgent business with him.'

'Well, give him a good kicking from me.'

'To do that, I'd have to find the place.'

'I'm sure you'll work it out.' Without another word, she strode away on her shopping errand.

Clearly, Mosley's recent arrival in the parish had not met with universal approval. Eventually, he found a shopkeeper who gave him directions and ten minutes later he pulled up outside Mosley's new home, a large country house of seventeenth-century origins in the centre of a thousand-acre farm.

He rang the bell hanging outside the front door of the tall, ivy-clad building and waited. When no one came, he rang it again and finally it was answered. He instantly recognised the woman standing in front of him as Diana, the third eldest of the feted Mitford girls, now notorious as second wife to Sir Oswald Mosley and erstwhile friend of Hitler and various other senior Nazis.

Although Wilde was taller than the woman he had a strange feeling that she was looking down at him.

'The tradesman's entrance is around the back of the house,' she said and started to turn away.

'I'm not a tradesman.'

She stopped and turned back. 'Really? Then what are you?'

'I'm Thomas Wilde, a Cambridge professor. I met your husband the night before last and I would like to talk to him.'

'You sound a bit American.'

'Well, that's because I am American, though I've probably spent as many years of my life in England. Would it be possible to speak with Sir Oswald?'

'If you can find him. He's out farming somewhere, probably with his beloved shorthorns or riding around on his new tractor. Good luck, Mr Wilde.'

Wilde roamed around the outbuildings and eventually found someone who described himself as estate manager. He didn't seem certain about Mosley's whereabouts, but suggested he was either mending some fences in the far field or examining the woods with his gamekeeper to discuss coppicing.

'Could you take me?'

'Is this important?'

'It is to me.'

'Then there'll probably be a quid or two in it, won't there.'

'How does ten shillings sound for your time?'

'Better than nothing. Come on then, mister.'

Half an hour later, they found the tall, broad-chested figure of Mosley emerging from the wood with his gamekeeper before striding along the edge of a meadow where handsome red cattle grazed. Wilde handed his guide a ten-shilling note, then approached Mosley with an insincere smile.

'Sir Oswald, we met at Neville's a couple of nights ago.' He held out his hand, but it wasn't accepted.

Mosley didn't look quite as imperious as his wife, but he was close. 'Yes, so we did. What was your name?'

'Wilde, Tom Wilde.'

'Ah yes, the night of the dreadful little Bolshevik girl. What a humourless slattern. That was a very strange evening. Neville always did have a knack for the absurd. And you were Cambridge, weren't you? What are you doing down in Wiltshire?'

'I've come to visit you.'

'Long way for an unannounced social call. Did you drive or train?'

'I drove. There are things I need to talk about with you.'

With a jerk of his aristocratic chin, he dismissed his game-keeper. 'Walk with me, Wilde,' he said. 'There's a fence to fix. You look strong enough so you might as well make yourself useful.'

They strode to the far side of the field. Mosley had an awkward farmer's gait, but he made good progress. 'Carry on,' he said as they walked through the ranks of his uninterested cows. 'What's this about?'

'I want to talk to you about Sir Neville Catesby. You must have heard that there was a murder on his estate during the night.'

'Yes, I heard something of the sort. Are you a detective then? I was rather under the impression that you were a historian or something.'

'I was in the OSS during the war. And I have an interest in Catesby. There are grave doubts about him.'

'Really? What are these doubts and who harbours them?'

'MI5.'

'Ah, that bloody crew. They locked me up and they're still watching me. Traitors to a man. I'm not inclined to help the security service in any way at all. I'm a writer and a farmer now. My political days are over.'

'I fear innocent people may be killed. You can't want that.'

'Are you suggesting Neville is hatching some sort of plot?'

Wilde didn't answer, merely let the question hang in the cool autumn air.

'You do realise you are traducing one of my oldest friends?'

'You were at Winchester together.'

'He's a damned fine man. One of us. What about you, Wilde? Are you one of us? I couldn't work you out the other night, chasing after that ridiculous commie girl. Didn't you realise she was the entertainment? The cabaret? Well, *are* you one of us or aren't you?'

'That would depend on what you mean by "*us*". If you are asking whether I'm a fascist, it's a resounding no, I am not one of you. But I know that there are many seemingly patriotic English men and women who still believe in you. I can't imagine they would want harm to befall the country or its people. My question is this: do you have any idea what Neville Catesby is up to? And where exactly is he now?'

Mosley stopped and stared at Wilde. His eyes were hard and unforgiving.

'Get off my land, Wilde, or I will have you thrown off.'

CHAPTER 31

After Wilde had left for Wiltshire, the Cornflowers household went about its daily business rather quietly. The two children, Johnny and Penelope, looked at the man with the moustache with suspicious eyes and were uncharacteristically taciturn while Sylvia gave them their porridge and made a pile of toast.

'I'm sorry to intrude on your daily routine like this,' Oswick said.

'Oh, don't worry about them,' Sylvia said. 'They're just trying to work out who you are. Can I make you a cup of tea?'

'Thank you, that would be very welcome, Mrs Keane.'

'Help yourself to toast. Go easy on the margarine, but there's plenty of marmalade or Marmite.' She gave him that smile that won men so easily.

Oswick was on edge. He didn't believe for a moment that this house was safe. But for the first time, he noticed this woman.

'And please,' she continued, 'won't you call me Sylvia? I have to be a bit more formal with the Wildes, because they're my employers.'

'Thank you. And I'm Danny.'

She gave him her warmest smile, somehow combined with a line of concern in her brow. 'I'm very pleased to meet you properly, Danny. I hope you were comfortable last night.'

'Not too bad.' It had been a lot worse in foxholes on the drive eastwards into Germany.

'I'm so pleased. Now look, I know we've only just met, but could I ask an enormous favour of you. The professor meant to leave me some money for various things – some shopping I did and Johnny's money for the collection plate. Could you manage to lend me a pound or two.'

'Yes, yes, of course. How much do you need?'

'Oh that's so terribly kind. Could you manage two pounds?'

'Actually, I believe I could.'

After breakfast, he looked through the hundreds of books piled in shelves around the house and settled down in the sitting room with *Farewell, My Lovely*. The only tasks given him by Professor Wilde were to keep the household safe and to answer the phone. In particular Mr Wilde wanted him to get the phone if Templeman called and ask if he could have a meeting. Also he wanted him to arrange a call if Lydia rang.

Half an hour later he heard the key turning in the front door and his body tensed; Wilde couldn't be back so soon.

Doris wouldn't normally come in on a Sunday and she certainly knew she shouldn't have come today, but Peter had shown a little improvement in hospital and his death did not seem imminent. She couldn't mope at home without going mad and she couldn't bear to go to church and put up with all the expressions of sympathy and questions about Peter's condition, so she needed to keep busy, and this was the place for that, even with the blasted housekeeper here.

This morning though, Cornflowers felt completely alien to her. The professor had gone off somewhere early and Mrs Keane was bustling about as though she owned the place. More than that, there was a young man with a large moustache who introduced himself as Danny Oswick, one of the professor's students who had been in need of somewhere to sleep for the night.

He was a charming young man, a little tense perhaps, which might not be surprising as he was in someone else's house when the host was absent. But she liked him.

Unlike Mrs Keane.

She had been trying to work out what it was about the woman that so offended her. The children both seemed well looked after and though Johnny obviously missed his mother, he was getting on all right with the little girl and eating his breakfast properly. Doris liked to believe that she could tell when a child was distressed, and that wasn't the case here.

No, the problem lay elsewhere, somewhere hidden. What troubled her was the thought that Mrs Sylvia Keane had some secret.

'Ah I was hoping to see you, Doris,' Sylvia said as she prepared to set off to church with the children. 'I hate to be an awful nuisance again, but do you think I could leave Penelope and Johnny with you for a couple of hours after church. I still haven't quite sorted out all my affairs you see.'

'I'm sorry, Mrs Keane, I can't help you.'

'Perhaps just an hour?'

'No, Mrs Keane, the Wildes are paying *you* to look after Johnny, so he's your responsibility. I have to visit my husband in hospital.'

Sylvia smiled sweetly at Doris. She was now certain where she stood with the cleaner; they were not going to be friends, and that made things rather awkward.

For a brief moment, Wilde's hand went towards his jacket and the shoulder holster that nestled within, but his hand carried on upwards and he rubbed his chin instead. No good would come of threatening Mosley with a gun.

'Of course I'll go,' he said. 'But you should be aware that MI5 has gathered a lot of information already – and you are firmly in the frame.'

'What frame? What are you talking about, man?'

'You know quite well what this is about. That became clear when you turned up at Harbinger House. But you have a chance now to save your skin. Reveal what you know.'

Mosley rose to his full height. He was carrying a heavy walking stick and for a moment Wilde wondered whether he was going to beat him. Instead, he waved it at his gamekeeper and estate manager and summoned them over.

'Get this man off my property,' he said. 'And thrash him if he resists.'

Wilde sighed and smiled at the two men. 'No need for that, gentlemen. I'll walk with you. Perhaps one of you would like to accompany your master. Apparently, he's got a fence to mend.'

Within a quarter of an hour he was off the property and setting off on the long haul back to Cambridge. His first instinct was that this had been a completely wasted trip, but then he realised that he had learnt something important by coming to Crowood

House. It was clear now that Mosley knew nothing about the conspiracy.

If he was part of Catesby's plans, he wasn't aware of it, because he was no actor; that had always been part of Mosley's problem – no subtlety. He wore his heart on his sleeve.

Which also meant that neither Catesby nor his murderous weapons were concealed here. So where were they?

Another thought struck Wilde. If Catesby wasn't planning to put Oswald Mosley in power, who else would he want?

There was only one name that came to mind: Sir Neville Catesby himself. The English Führer.

It was just after nine in the evening when he arrived home. Oswick seemed remarkably pleased to see him.

'Any word from Templeman?'

'Nothing, sir. But Mrs Wilde called. She said she'd try to slip out to a phone box and call you at eleven.'

Well, that was something at least, but the lack of communication from Templeman was alarming. Dagger always kept in close contact with his secretary or butler. He would certainly have returned Wilde's calls in the normal course of events. It was impossible to come to any other conclusion: something had happened to him.

'There was one other call, Professor, from a Mr Barnaby Wax of Skyme-next-Sea. He said he was calling from a garage but that you could call him at home if you were back late. He gave me the number. I'm afraid he didn't tell me what it was about.'

Barnaby Wax. The proprietor of Skyme Motors in a seaside village in Norfolk, and the man who had told him about the attack on the coastguard station. What on earth could he want?

Wilde dialled the number Oswick gave him. The phone rang and rang. He was just about to give up when it was answered. 'Hello, Wax here.'

'Hello, Mr Wax, Tom Wilde here. You rang, I think.'

'Ah, I'm glad you called. I have a very strange situation to tell you about. You recall you met my niece on the beach and she was distraught.'

'Yes, I remember that.'

'Well, something's happened. Actually quite a lot has happened and she's very keen to talk to you. Not on the telephone, though. In person. From what I can gather she might be of some use to you in your inquiries, but I'll have to leave that to her.'

'Can't you give me more of a clue?'

'She said she saw something out at sea. She's in a bad way, I'm afraid, and I couldn't get much more out of her. But she is convinced she knows something important.'

'I'll be with you first thing in the morning.'

'Come to the garage.'

Outside the little churchyard, Ernest Wainwright found himself yawning. It was 10.55 p.m., and that meant his eight-hour shift was almost up. Bert Hollings would be replacing him any minute.

This was cushy work, watching the young woman in the photograph every time she left the medical students' hostel. Pretty thing, he thought. A bit like his sister. God knows why anyone would want to hurt her, but that was not information to which he was privy. He had been told to protect her, and protect her he would. He was good at his job. He'd watched embassies, senior politicians, spies. And he'd lost none of them.

There had been incidents, of course, attempts to get past him, but his watchful eye and the pistol in his shoulder holster had always done the business. Not that he had had to shoot anyone yet, but he'd made a couple of arrests at gunpoint.

He yawned again and wondered if Jill would be up. She usually stayed awake for these late shifts, and that pleased him, because he fancied a bit tonight. Maybe it was the sight of all these young lady doctors coming in and out of the hostel, some of them in their white coats, others in their civvies going off to the pub, probably to meet their blokes. It was enough to stir any man's blood.

The young woman in the photograph – all he knew was that her name was Lydia Morris – had been to the telephone box early on in his stint, five o'clock, and he'd made a note of her excursion in his book. He hadn't seen her since. Probably studying her medical texts or perhaps she'd turned in for the night. She surprised him because she didn't seem quite as young as the other lasses. Very attractive though, in a slightly bohemian sort of way.

He looked up at her room on the third floor, wondering if she had gone to sleep. No, the light was still on.

Ah, Bert Hollings was on his way, in his bowler hat. Always wore a bowler, did Bert. Not an item of apparel that had ever appealed to Ernest Wainwright. He raised his hand in greeting, and Wainwright nodded back. He liked it when his replacement was punctual because that meant he'd be home in good time.

No, what was he thinking, that wasn't Bert, just some passer-by in a bowler hat and overcoat. He stepped back a pace to let him go on his way, but the bloke was smiling at him. Instinctively, Wainwright's hand went inside his jacket and reached for the butt of the pistol.

'I'm stand-in,' the man in the bowler hat said.

The voice was strange, slightly alien. Wainwright's hand didn't move. He kept it on the pistol, still inside the holster. 'No one told me about no stand-in. What's happened to Bert?'

'He's sick. Last-minute change.'

Wainwright relaxed a fraction, and that was his fatal error, for the bowler-hat man's left hand struck out and grasped the wrist of Wainwright's gun hand, holding it firm, while his mouth went to his ear. 'This won't hurt a bit,' he whispered, then his right hand plunged the long needle of a hypodermic syringe deep into his side, puncturing his liver and squirting the thick, scorching hot juice into him.

Their eyes met and held, then Ernest Wainwright spasmed violently and he slumped in the killer's arms.

Sigmund Rascher, aka Edmund Bacon, held the convulsing, dying body upright, not wanting him to fall. A passer-by stopped. 'Everything all right, mate?'

'My friend's drunk.'

'Too much lemonade, eh? Need any help?'

'We'll be all right.'

'As you like. Get him home safe, yeah.'

The passer-by walked on. Rascher looked around and saw that he was alone. Someone was just entering the phone box along the street, but they were too far away to be of concern, and so he dragged the twitching corpse into the churchyard that bordered the pavement behind a low wall and hedge. They were away from the lamplight, and out of sight of anyone who came along. The other corpse, the one whose name he now knew to be Bert, was a little way back along the road, dumped in the rubble of a bombed-out school.

Rascher removed his bowler hat – the one he had taken from his first victim – and placed it on the corpse's chest. Then, when he was satisfied that the body wouldn't be found in a hurry, he returned to the pavement and stood for a few moments gazing up at the hostel. Half a dozen lights were on, but it was one of two on the third floor that interested him most. If that was her, it must mean she was still awake. But was that her room? It was going to be simple enough to find out. The woman might have had a guard watching over her from outside, but places like this had no security on the inside.

He made his way into the entrance hall. There was no lock on the door and no doorkeeper to question him. There was a desk, however, with a book on it. Quickly he flicked through the pages, looking for a name: Lydia Wilde.

Nothing there, the closest thing to it was a Lydia Morris. Was she using her maiden name or an alias? He had no option but to try.

The staircase was dark, so he took out his torch as he climbed the cold stone steps. Ten steps to the first floor, ten more to the second, ten more to the third. He swept the light along the corridor. There were four doors. The first one he opened was a store cupboard, which he quickly closed. The second had two names on it – Miranda March and Lydia Morris. So there would be two of them here; that made things interesting.

He twisted the door handle and it opened. The room was lit by two bedside lamps and a single yellow bulb, unshaded, hanging from the centre of the room. A girl or young woman was sitting on the side of her bed at the far end of the space. She was wearing a nightgown and slippers and seemed more interested in her book than the opening of the door. But then she looked up and shied away, a horrified expression on her face.

'Who are you? Get out.'

'Lydia. I've come to see Lydia.'

'She's not here – go away.' Miranda had grabbed hold of her bedside lamp and was hunched up against the wall.

'I'm her husband, Tom Wilde. I need to talk to her. Where is she?'

'What are you talking about. That's not her name and she's not married. Now please leave us. You've got the wrong place.'

For a moment he held back, computing what she had said. Perhaps *this* girl was Lydia – but no, she looked too young. And why was the surname wrong? 'I'm sorry,' he said. 'I didn't mean to alarm you. When will Lydia be back?'

'She's gone to make a phone call. Now please, leave me alone. Men aren't allowed in the hostel.'

'I think I'll just wait here for her.'

Wilde had rarely been more pleased to receive a phone call. 'Lydia, darling, is that really you?'

'Oh, thank God, Tom, I keep missing you. How are you? How's Johnny?'

'We're both fine, but an awful lot has been going on here. What about you?'

'It's hard work. Bloody hard work. I'm sorry to keep moaning, but I really didn't know what I was letting myself in for. We had anatomy again and I noticed that the body had a gold ring on its wedding finger. I hadn't noticed it before. Suddenly, it became a real person rather than a waxwork dummy. I felt faint and had to leave the room.'

'Were you in trouble?'

'No, Dr Belmer was very kind. She said it was the worst thing and she was sorry, it should have been removed beforehand.'

'Lydia, I can't go into everything now, but I want to be sure you're safe. I take it you're still guarded by Templeman's men.'

'Yes, I see them all the time. I'm always surprised when none of the other girls notices them. Actually, now that I say that, my man wasn't in his usual place just now when I popped out to the phone box.'

'Do you have the Beretta?'

'Not with me. It's too heavy to carry around. I leave it under the mattress. Why?'

'I really think we're both in grave danger, that's why. I'd very much like to take you and Johnny to a safe house, or even a hotel in a strange town. What would you say to that?'

'I'd be sacked, Tom. Dame Gertrude would take my place away and I'd never get it back.'

'Carry the gun with you then. Keep your eyes open. Be ready.'

'I can't take a gun to lectures.'

'Find a way. Look, I want to meet you in London. Early tomorrow evening. Can you get out? We could go to Rules or Simpsons.'

'Rules. I need some rich, hearty food. Seven o'clock. I'll tell Miranda I'm meeting a cousin and she'll cover for me. Bring sugar and jam and anything sweet you can find to bribe her with.'

'OK. If I'm a little late, hang on. I've got a lot on tomorrow. Before you go, there's something else I want to mention.'

'You better hurry up – my pennies are running out.'

Even though he was sure the nanny/housekeeper was in bed fast asleep, he lowered his voice. 'Did you have any doubts at all about Mrs Keane?'

'No, why?'

'Doris seems to have taken against her.'

'That's most un-Dorislike.'

'Quite.'

'Has she said why?'

'No.'

'But Johnny's OK?'

'Yes, he's fine. Personally I don't have any problem trusting her, but you have a much better instinct for these things. It was you, for instance, that put me right about Neville Catesby.'

'Well, I suppose we shouldn't be surprised if Doris has lost her bearings a bit. Her Peter must be awfully close to death.'

'I'm sure you're right,' Wilde said, but he was speaking to thin air. The line had gone dead.

CHAPTER 32

Lydia hadn't had time to send her love to Johnny or Tom. Of course, Tom would take it for granted and he'd tell the boy all about Mummy anyway, but she had wanted to say the words. Words were important. You never took love for granted, you had to *tell* people they were loved.

She replaced the receiver and stepped out of the kiosk. For a moment, she stood looking across the street to the rather drab and ugly Victorian hostel and wondered about it all. There was an emotional cost to this venture; there were always consequences to every action. It was too much, wasn't it? Her marriage might not survive; she would miss a huge chunk of her little boy's childhood.

Lydia had always been aware that her life was made up of a succession of compulsions and she knew it was a weakness. She set her mind on things and had to follow them through, and then, at the end, would often wonder why she had bothered. Typical had been her decision to start a poetry publishing company. She was immensely proud of her early achievements but there was a problem – no one in modern Britain was in the slightest bit interested in reading poetry, let alone buying it. She was lucky if the collections she published managed sales in double figures.

And so, eventually, the office she set up gathered dust and she lost interest.

It occurred to her that perhaps she was a little manic depressive.

The thing was, she had money, left by her parents following their early deaths in the First World War and the great flu pandemic, and she had a wonderful house to call home. Those benefits had given her the freedom to follow her dreams. And they weren't all negative.

But this time she was worried that she had embarked on one dream too many.

A silhouette crossed the window of her room. That would be Miranda getting ready for bed. In their first few days together she had grown to like, even love, the younger girl. She knew that with her warmth and attention to detail she would one day make a superb doctor, despite Dame Gertrude's doubts. Would she, Lydia, be able to match her?

Huddling into her thick woollen coat, she walked over to the hostel entrance. Looking back furtively, she was rather surprised that her watcher still wasn't in his usual place.

There were three of them altogether and they took their watch in turns throughout the night and day. She didn't know their names and hadn't said hello to any of them, but in her mind she thought of them as Bill Brewer, Jan Stewer and Peter Gurney – characters from the Widdecombe Fair song. Jan Stewer should be there tonight because she had seen him earlier when she made her first call home. She knew his shift was 3 p.m. to 11 p.m., so he should be finishing. But he wouldn't have left until Peter Gurney arrived. Perhaps he'd gone for a piss. That had to be allowable. Or maybe Lord Templeman had decided there was no threat after all and had called off his watchdogs.

She knew the staircase by heart now, so she didn't need a light to climb to the third floor. At the door she stopped, her hand just about to turn the knob. There were voices inside. One of them was Miranda, the other a man. Good God, had the girl got herself a boyfriend? She had certainly never mentioned one.

She put her ear to the door and heard something that chilled her to the bone.

'I think I'll just wait here for her.'

Wait here for her. He could only mean one person, and it was a voice she did not recognise.

For a few moments she stood with her fingers on the handle and listened to the silence of the house and her own breathing, blanking out the distant sounds of the city. Her very being was crystallised in this moment and this place and she knew terror.

And then there was a noise. A series of sounds.

Something hard hitting the ground, something breaking, grunts and moans. Lydia turned the handle and threw open the door. A man was sprawled on the ground by Miranda's bed, trying to pull himself up, grabbing hold of her blankets with the long talon-like fingers of his left hand. She was crouching against the wall, clutching a pillow and the remains of a bedside lamp. Her eyes flicked upwards and caught sight of Lydia, then down again as she smashed the lamp into the man's broad forehead and shoulder. Swatting at him like a wasp. Again and again.

After the briefest of hesitations as she tried to gauge what was happening, Lydia threw herself forward and grasped the man by his feet, dragging him away from the bed. He already seemed stunned from the wooden lamp stand, but his fall, face first, onto the floorboards doubled the blow. He emitted a low groan as his chin cracked against the wood.

Lydia noticed that he had something in his right hand – a hypodermic syringe, with a long needle. She lunged forward again, this time grasping his right wrist with both her hands, but he had a firm hold and wouldn't release the needle.

She found herself kneeling on him, but he was regaining his composure. He was bigger and easily shook her off. As he did so, Lydia lost her grip on the wrist. He was turning, twisting, holding the hypodermic up and rotating the spike towards her chest. She was trapped by his weight, her left arm pinioned and only her right hand free.

With what little strength she had, she balled her hand into a fist and crunched it into his face. But even as she did so, the needle was coming at her and she couldn't stop it. The man yelled with pain as her fist connected with his nose, but that didn't impede the needle's deadly trajectory. For a moment, Lydia felt certain the spike had penetrated her chest, but she felt no pain. Is that what happened when death was upon you? Did the agony simply vanish. She had heard of men in battle being shot but not even realising they had been hit.

And then she saw that the needle had ripped into the lapel of her thick coat and deflected, missing her flesh. His hand still gripped it as he pushed the plunger, sure that the spike was in her flesh, but she was able to wrench the syringe from his hand and throw it aside.

Miranda was behind the man now. She had somehow looped a dressing gown cord around his neck and was tightening it. Blood was dripping from his nose where Lydia had flattened it.

He was bigger than the women, but Lydia could tell that he wasn't the most powerful of men. That said, he was strong enough. He turned on Miranda, his wide face red and angry. His hands tore hers from the cord.

As he moved, Lydia was able to slip away from under him. She scrambled to the far side of the room and picked up the needle. A drop of tinted gel-like fluid hung from the tip. The man was up now, coming towards her with murderous eyes, his face bloody, but Miranda leapt on his back and pummelled him with her fists. He shook her off. For a moment, his eyes rested on the hypodermic and his brain seemed to take in the fact that the plunger had been pushed, the contents emptied. Realisation seemed to dawn on him that he had failed, that the needle had not gone into his intended victim and that he wasn't going to win this battle.

'*Scheisse,*' he said, or that was what it sounded like to Lydia who had a reasonable command of everyday German. *Shit.*

And then he was at the open door and was gone. They heard his footsteps clattering down the stone staircase, and then nothing. Lydia dropped the needle to the floor and ran to the door, closing it and pushing home the bolt. She and Miranda looked at each other wide-eyed and then they fell into each other's arms, half crying, half laughing.

'Who *was* that?' Miranda said.

'I've never seen him before,' Lydia said truthfully. But she had a fair idea what they had been dealing with. The question was, what to do now? They clearly had to call the police, but there was no phone in the building. Tom would know what to do, but she daren't go out to the phone box. Not just yet. In a little while perhaps.

She went to the window and saw him crossing the street, holding his hand to his bloody nose. But then she lost sight of him. Was he still there, waiting?

'And what's in that hypodermic?' Miranda said. 'It looks evil . . . you know, Lydia, I have a horrible feeling he was after *you*.'

Of course he was, but she couldn't tell her friend that. It would require too much explanation, and her cover as unmarried Miss Lydia Morris would be blown. 'I can't see why anyone would want to hurt me,' she said. 'But if he was after me, all I can think is that you saved my life, Miranda.'

'Take me with you,' Oswick said. 'We can work together. I told you, I'm a good soldier – I can take orders.'

'I think you should stay here again, look after Mrs Keane and the children. If it all goes well, I should be back by early afternoon.'

'Don't you think my presence here might actually pose a danger? Catesby wants to kill me.'

It was a fair point. And in truth, the young man might be useful. 'Very well. Let's go. We'll leave a note for Mrs K.'

It was 2.30 a.m. The night was silent and the roads would be empty. Wilde couldn't sleep anyway. His whole being was alive with anticipation and dread. He had tried to call Lord Templeman one more time, with the same result.

'What is London saying?' Wilde asked the butler. 'There's something very badly wrong here.'

'Two officers from the service are on their way up here to take control.'

'Tell them I'll try to get along and meet them tomorrow. Give them my telephone number.'

'Of course, Professor.'

The drive was easy. The Riley was cold and rattled and the head-lights cast eerie shadows on the empty roads, but they made it to Skyme just before 6 a.m. and went straight to the garage. On the way, Wilde and Oswick had talked in great detail about what was known. Both men understood there must be a target. The question was twofold: What was it? And when would it happen? They both had suggestions, but no conclusive answers.

Wilde had brought a vacuum flask of hot tea, milky with sugar. He always took his coffee black without sugar, but sometimes, especially a morning like this when he had no access to coffee, he liked the kick of a couple of spoonfuls.

Barnaby Wax arrived at 6.30 a.m. with a large bacon sandwich. 'Ah, there's two of you – you'll have to share. I thought you might be hungry, Mr Wilde.'

'Thanks, Mr Wax. This is Danny Oswick. He's working with me.'

'Nice to meet you, young man. Four wheels today, eh, Mr Wilde? You must be getting old like me.'

'I had a bit of an accident, but the Rudge will survive.'

'Look, before my niece arrives, I have to fill you in on a few things. It's all a great tragedy but I'm afraid her husband is in jail awaiting trial for murder, and the man he killed was her lover, Tony Hood. An absolutely desperate story and not the sort of thing you expect around sleepy Skyme. Poor Liz can barely speak, so you'll have to go very easy with her.'

'My God, what a dreadful thing to happen. I'm sorry.'

'Yes, well, her husband's a brute and may just about escape the rope given his war service and the provocation of an unfaithful wife. He found out about the affair when they were all having dinner together. Beat the poor man to death with a heavy pipe wrench. Might have killed Liz too, but she ran away and he ran out of steam. The truth is she should never have married the bastard in the first place. Everyone in the family knew that, not that it's worth saying now.'

'Don't worry, we'll go easy on her. When can we see her?'

'She's coming here in about half an hour, so eat up your bacon sandwich.'

CHAPTER 33

Wilde was surprised by Liz Lightfoot. He had seen her on the beach weeping, but he hadn't managed a good look at her face. Hearing the story of the love affair and the murder from Barnaby Wax, he imagined her as a silver screen seductress. Now he saw the truth.

She had a fine figure, perhaps a little on the slender side, but that wasn't unusual in these days of hard rationing. She had tried to cover her bruises with makeup, but they were still visible. He liked her appearance and he could understand how she could engender strong emotions in the men in her life.

'Mr Wilde? You came up to me on the beach after Luke beat me last week. I was in a bad way but you tried to help.'

'Luke?'

'Lucas – my husband. He's banged up now.' She spoke forthrightly without tears.

'Your uncle told me what's happened.' He realised he hadn't introduced his companion. 'And this is Danny Oswick – we're working together.'

She looked at the young man, and recoiled as though his appearance startled her. 'Hello,' she said briefly.

'Nice to meet you.'

She hurriedly turned back to Wilde. 'We should have run away, me and Tone, but we couldn't because of his baby. What could we do? We were trapped. I knew what Luke would do if he found out and I was halfway right. I'm only surprised he didn't kill me too.'

'Your uncle says he's a violent man.'

'Well, yes, he's always been rough. But in the old days, he was manageable, if you know what I mean. Then the war and the booze did for his brain and I knew he'd kill us. The thing is, me and Tone were crazy for each other and we couldn't stay apart.'

For the first time Wilde heard a catch in her voice.

'Come inside, Liz,' Wax said. 'The kettle's on, we'll all have a nice cuppa and you can talk to these two gentlemen in your own time and explain why you wanted them to come here.'

'Oh that's simple, it's because of what I saw.' She turned to Wilde. 'Uncle Barnaby had told me about you last week, said you were investigating something around this coast. I put two and two together and reckoned it had to have something to do with what Tony and I saw.'

'And what was that?' Wilde asked gently.

'I'm getting to it. Couldn't tell anyone before because I'd have had to explain what I was doing on the dunes after dark, and that would have been a death sentence. I can speak freely now Luke's locked up. What are you, Mr Wilde, some sort of copper?'

'Not exactly, but I'll explain my interest.'

They went inside the garage and made their way to Barnaby Wax's cosy little office. The whole place smelt pleasingly of grease and cigarette smoke. Wilde had always liked garages. Wax had put out three chairs and apologised because he didn't realise Oswick would be there.

'Don't worry, Mr Wax, I'll stand.'

'No you won't, son, you'll sit yourself down and I'll perch on the desk.'

'You mentioned the dunes?' Wilde wanted to keep focus.

'Yes, the dunes. We used to go there on Tone's motorbike. I'll take you there if you can drive me. I'll show you exactly where we were and point out what we saw. It was October the third, the night of the raid on the coastguards up the road . . .'

'Take your time, Liz, take your time,' her uncle said.

'Well, things had got complicated between Tony and me by then. He wouldn't leave his baby because he was too nice a fellow. That's why I loved him, I suppose. He was the kindest man alive and I truly believe we were in love from childhood. But our timing was all to cock and we both ended up with the wrong partner. Then the war came and Tone used to come around to my place and help me fix things.' She paused a moment, brushing her cheek. 'Well, one thing led to another and the rest is history, as they say. Sandra – that's his wife – never suspected a thing, probably because she's too nice and trusting. But we knew it was going to get messy and, of course, we couldn't see so much of each other when Luke was demobbed and came home. So we went to the dunes once a week because we could be together and no one would see us except the seals. It was getting more difficult and colder as the nights drew in, though.'

'And then, the evening of the coastguard incident?'

'We saw something out at sea. It was like an enormous submarine, rising from the waves, maybe a couple of miles out, maybe five, I really don't know. I can't judge those sort of distances across water. Just came from nowhere. Huge great thing, more like a frigate or a destroyer than a sub—'

'And that's what don't make sense to me,' Wax interrupted. 'Because it's so shallow around here. Doesn't get much deeper than twenty fathoms mostly. And a lot of it's nowhere near that. I don't see how a submarine could navigate the shoals. That's why I wasn't sure Liz had really seen what she thought she had.'

'But I saw it, Uncle! I promise you, I saw it – we both did.'

'I'm not saying you didn't see some sort of large vessel, just saying it couldn't have been a sub.'

'Just let her tell her story, Barnaby.'

'Sorry. I won't interrupt again.'

'If it *was* a sub,' Wilde said, 'it's quite possible it had arrived in the dark on the surface and submerged to just below the surface – periscope depth – to await its contact.'

Wax nodded. 'Could just about be possible.'

'I'm no expert but I suppose twenty fathoms would accommodate a submarine if it's just staying still, engines dead. Go on, Liz. May I call you Liz? And please, I'm Tom.'

'Well, then we saw men on the beach. Two of them. We were desperate to get away, but then we saw a third man, with a van, behind the dunes and we realised we couldn't escape without being seen and so we just hid in the marram grass and peeked out occasionally. They also had a boat – a small launch with an outboard motor – although we couldn't work out where it had come from because we hadn't noticed it before. Maybe they had arrived in it or maybe it had been there all the time. One of the men on the beach set off in it and a while later it reached the submarine.

Something must have been transferred from the sub, some sort of cargo. We knew it must be illegal and we knew the men must be dangerous. They weren't smuggling brandy, not from a submarine. Anyway, the boat returned to shore and the two men unloaded the cargo – all in wooden crates.'

'How long did this go on for?'

'About an hour, maybe a little less. I was terrified that Luke would get home before me. I would have been dead. But I was lucky that night, because he stayed in the pub till closing time.'

'What was happening on the dunes?'

'Well, it was slow going unloading the cargo. They took great care as though it was extremely delicate. And then the crates were carried off the beach along a path through the dunes – not more than thirty yards from where we were hiding – and I suppose they were put in the van. At one point I was certain the man loading the van had seen us, but he hadn't. Tony and I were terrified but what could we do?'

'Carry on, Liz.'

'Then one of the men from the beach went off in the van with the driver while the other disappeared in the launch. It was such a relief when they were gone.'

'What happened to the submarine?'

'It just sailed away – motored, I mean – into the distance and vanished in the dark. Tony and I waited a while until we were certain no one was still about, then we talked about what we had seen and we both agreed we could never tell a soul. We felt bad about that, but we couldn't afford to have Sandra and Luke finding out about us.'

'But now you can talk?'

'Yes. And you see the worst part of it was we recognised the two men on the beach.' Liz glanced at her uncle, as if for affirmation.

He nodded. 'Go on, Liz.'

'They were Germans and they'd been working on a local farm, or that's what we thought. We supposed they were POWs. They came into Skyme to the little shop now and then, but we didn't really see much of them and never talked to them. The only way we knew they were Germans was because the shop-keeper told us.'

'I'd like to see this farm,' Wilde said.

'Yes, I can take you there. But I wouldn't go in with you. I don't like the place.'

'Do you know the name of the farmer?'

'Well, it was old Sparks's place until six or seven years ago. Then he died and someone else bought it.'

Wilde turned to Barnaby Wax. 'Do you know anything about this farm?'

'Just what Liz says. At first we thought he must have left it to a relative, but then I heard his relatives weren't interested and they'd sold it. We never found out who the buyer was. No one seemed to move in permanently but occasionally people would come and go. Then the two German workers turned up three or four months ago. Actually, I'm pretty sure it was July. Whoever has been running Sparks Farm these past few years, they have never taken part in the life of Skyme or the surrounding area. And they certainly haven't looked after the farm properly, that's for sure. Fields are fallow, woods uncoppiced, hedges untrimmed, no livestock to be seen.'

Wilde turned his attention back to Liz. 'You mentioned the third man, the van driver. Did you know him?'

'Never seen him before. Didn't get a great view of him or hear his voice. Probably not as tall as you, Mr Wilde. Other than that I can't say. There was moonlight but he was too far away to get a good look.' Her eyes flicked between Wilde and Oswick, and rested on the younger man.

Lydia realised quite quickly that she had to give Miranda some sort of explanation – and then it all flooded out. She admitted she was a married woman with a child, that her name was Wilde not Morris and that she was at St Ursula's under false pretences.

'I'm sorry, Miranda, I had to lie to you. This means so much to me. My father was a doctor and I desperately want to be one, too. I want to do something useful with my life.'

'But that doesn't explain why that man was trying to kill you, Lydia.'

No, clearly it didn't. But that was the part she hadn't tried to explain yet. And she wasn't really sure how much she could say.

'There are other secret things in my life, mostly involving my husband.'

Miranda's eyes lit up. 'Don't tell me he's a spy! Is he?'

'Let's put it this way, like many academics, Tom spent much of the war working for intelligence. He made enemies and I suppose that, by extension, I must also have become a target. There is more to it, but I'm really not at liberty to reveal everything.'

'Gosh, how exciting. What a life you lead. I thought Cambridge was supposed to be a rather sleepy place where people read books in peace and quiet and talked about philosophy. I love spy stories. Give me *The Riddle of the Sands*, Hannay and Ashenden and *Rogue Male*. I love them all. Oh, Lydia, I want to marry your husband.'

'Well, you can't, he's mine. Anyway, this isn't a novel, Miranda. This is real.'

'So what do we do now? I suppose we have to call the police. Someone tried to kill you – and me for that matter.'

'If we call the police the truth will all come out and I'll be sacked. Please, won't you let me get in touch with Tom – my husband – first? He'll know what to do.' Wouldn't he? Something had already gone horribly wrong, because she was supposed to be under round-the-clock protection. What exactly could Tom do to prevent a further attack?

Miranda picked up the needle and examined it. 'What do you think was in this thing? I suppose we should get it tested.'

'Please, can you just wait. I'll call Tom as soon as we're sure that the coast is clear. He's supposed to be coming up to see me tomorrow anyway.'

'Can I meet him?'

'Perhaps. So long as you promise to keep your hands off him.'

'In the meantime, we must still be in danger, though.'

Lydia reached under her mattress and pulled out the Beretta semi-automatic Tom had given her. 'Does this help calm your nerves?'

The three of them walked the dunes together – Wilde, Oswick and Liz Lightfoot. Barnaby Wax had stayed at the garage because he had to open up and serve his customers. The sky was grey and dark and a bitter wind swept in from the sea. It felt like rain was in the offing.

'It was a fair bit warmer here that night,' Liz said. She took them to the hollow at the top of the dunes where they had sheltered for their lovemaking and, later, as a hiding place from the men on the beach. She pointed into the far distance, just below the horizon. 'It was way out there. We reckoned it was a few miles away.'

She took them down to the beach and showed them the exact place where the boat came ashore. Wilde picked up pieces of driftwood and fragments of barbed wire as if they might hold some secret, then tossed them away again.

From the beach, they walked the path that the men had taken through the dunes. He couldn't help noticing that she kept looking at Oswick and wondered whether she was attracted to him. What was he thinking? Of course she wasn't attracted to Oswick – she was in mourning for the love of her life.

The Riley was parked on the road where Liz had said the van was parked that night. There was nothing more to see here. 'Perhaps you could show us Sparks Farm.'

'It's just inland, no more than half a mile from here. You could walk from here. I don't want to go there.'

'What is it about the place that worries you?'

She smiled sheepishly. 'Stupid really. As kids we always said it was haunted. A child had died there back in the twenties. Jumping up and down on a wooden plank covering an old well. The plank was rotten and broke and the poor boy fell down the well to his death. Everyone says he haunts the place.'

The only spectres Wilde was worried about were the two Germans that Liz had seen on the beach. Had one of them been

Georg Sosinka, the man he had shot and wounded at Bagshawe's farm? Was the other one Paul Kagerer, his fellow absconder from the PoW camp at Epsom three months ago? Their disappearance from the camp certainly coincided with the arrival of the two supposed farmworkers here.

In normal circumstances, his instinct would be to call Lord Templeman and get him to organise a raid on the place. But he had tried Latimer Hall one last time before leaving the garage and there was still no sign of the man. Nor had the two intelligence officers sent up from London arrived.

'What do you think, Oswick? Shall we take a surreptitious look?'

'I'm up for it if you are, sir.'

'Let's go then. You stay here with the car, Liz. If we don't come back, go to your uncle's garage and get him to call out the police. And tell him to make sure they draw guns from the firearms cabinet.'

'Are you really in danger?'

'I hope not, but we are armed.'

They went a roundabout way towards the farmhouse, avoiding the main entrance and short driveway. It was not an impressive place. The wall from the front gate only extended a few yards on either side, then gave way to hedging, which was long since overgrown and turned into a ragged tangle of hornbeam and blackthorn. There were gaps and it was easy to make their way unseen into a paddock that was close to the house.

The house itself was in poor condition. Slates were missing from the roof and a downpipe was hanging loose from the guttering. No vehicles were parked on the forecourt and there was a complete absence of life, either animal or human.

'I think it's deserted, Professor.'

Wilde thought so, too, but it was better to be certain before letting their guard down. 'Draw your gun, Oswick. We're going inside.'

CHAPTER 34

The front door was unlocked. There was no sound and nobody in. A smell of damp assaulted the nostrils of the two men. The whole place was dirty and neglected. Coming into a boot room, Wilde walked into a mass of cobwebs and had to claw them from his face. Whatever else the two Germans had been doing while they were here, they hadn't engaged in basic housekeeping.

In the space that must once have served as a sitting room, there was evidence of recent habitation. Here, the smell of damp mingled with the familiar scent of a dead fire in the hearth and stale tobacco smoke. On the floor, half hidden beneath a threadbare armchair he spotted a slim volume and bent down to pick it up. On the spine he read the title *The Will to Power* and curled his lip grimly. Bastardised Nietzsche. He supposed it made sense given who might have been in residence lately. 'Someone has been here in the past twenty-four hours. We've just missed them. Come on, let's take a really good look around the place – inside and out. Keep your gun handy.'

The only thing of value was a beautiful old telescope placed by the window looking out over the fields. Was this the instrument that the coastguards said had been stolen when they were raided? Almost certainly.

The house had clearly had no maintenance for many years. Even old Sparks must have let the place go to rack and ruin and the new owner had done nothing to improve things. Wilde instructed Oswick to go outside and check the barn and other outhouses while he cautiously ascended the rotting wooden staircase to look at the first floor. There were three dismal bedrooms, an inside lavatory but no bathroom. Not much had changed here since Victorian times; it was no surprise that the farmer's relatives had not been keen to take it on. Evidence of leaks was everywhere; pooled rainwater, streaks down walls, patches of open sky where the ceiling had fallen. Wilde could imagine it would be cheaper to tear the whole house down and start again rather than restore it.

Who had bought it then? Neville Catesby, almost certainly. He had not acquired it as a farm, though, nor as a seaside holiday home. His only purpose was to use it as a base to receive smuggled weapons and as a hideout for his two German henchmen. Its proximity to the coast was no coincidence. Whatever was happening, it had been a long time in the planning.

Each of the three bedrooms contained a single iron bedstead with thin mattresses. Two of them looked as though they had been slept in recently. The bed in the larger and slightly better room – it was the only one without obvious leaks – looked a little less rudimentary and had pillows, rumpled sheets and blankets.

Wilde heard his name shouted from below and returned downstairs, his Browning Hi-Power clenched tight in his right hand. Oswick was approaching through the kitchen door holding a handkerchief to his nose. He looked as if he were about to vomit.

'What is it, Oswick?'

The young man struggled to gain enough clean air to speak. 'Two bodies, sir. One of them ... dear God ... I think it's Lyngwood. He's barely recognisable, but he's got that earring he wore.'

Gram Lyngwood. The occupant of number eighteen, The Street, Flowthorpe. The man with a broken ceramic canister of plague pathogen in his back garden. The man who had fled the scene. The man that Oswick had overheard talking about plague with Neville Catesby.

'I saw some bad things in the war, sir. The worst was at Belsen. That rotting corpse ... it brings it all back.'

'I understand.'

He followed Oswick out to the barn. The two bodies had been dumped behind an old wooden cart. They were invisible from the doorway but easily discovered by anyone searching the building. However, they could have lain here undiscovered for months or years but for the evidence of Liz Lightfoot. No one would ever have had cause to come here. No one but the killers themselves.

Wilde's heart sank. One of the bodies – that of Lyngwood – was in a repulsive state, the face and neck suppurating and in an advanced state of decay. The stench was overpowering and sickening.

But it was the other body that made him want to weep. The tall and distinguished form of Lord Templeman, Dagger to his friends, was unmistakable. He was stretched out on his back, one arm folded at the elbow in rigor mortis, upright, the fingers open as though about to catch a cricket ball, the other arm twisted beneath his back. An entry wound close to the right eye suggested he had been killed by a shot to the head.

And then, looking closer, he saw that the back of his head was shattered and his brain was spilling out. The effect of an expanding bullet, commonly known as a dum-dum. He never stood a chance.

Wilde gazed upon the man with ineffable sadness at the loss of a fine human being. Even in death, he had nobility.

There was no telephone at the farm; probably never had been for no line was in evidence. Old Sparks had not entered the twentieth century with all its gadgets.

'Go back to Liz and the car, take her to the garage and make a call from Wax's phone.' Wilde quickly scribbled out the number for Latimer Hall. 'It will be answered by Templeman's butler, Rogers, or his secretary. I'm hoping that two intelligence officers have arrived and will be awaiting information. Get one of them on the line and tell him exactly what we've found and where we are. Is that clear?'

'Yes, sir.'

'Good. Tell the MI5 officers that you will be waiting for them here. Explain to them that you are working with me. I don't know which men have been sent but they are probably quite senior and I might be acquainted with them through my recent work with the OSS. So give them my name. If they seem unsure, then refer them to Templeman's butler Rogers or his secretary who both know me well. If they ask about *your* role, explain that you will debrief them in full when they arrive, but that you have an inside track on a group that is threatening the state, and that that group was being investigated by Lord Templeman. When you have spoken to them, bring the car straight back here. Do not wait around in Skyme and do not answer any questions.'

Oswick nodded. He looked concerned.

'Oh, and whatever you do, don't call the police and don't tell Liz what we've discovered – she's spooked enough as it is. She'll suspect something's up but she mustn't know the truth. Go easy on her, but remember that this is national security. Same with Mr Wax, you use his phone but don't allow him to overhear you – understood?'

'You say I will be waiting here, sir – does that mean we will be splitting up?'

'Yes. One of us has to stay here to ensure the place is not disturbed before Templeman's men arrive and to show the intelligence officers what we have found. And that can't be me because I have to go to London. I will, however, be here until you return with the car, because I'm not convinced we've found everything yet.'

Oswick hesitated, his brow creased.

'Is something not clear?'

'It's just . . . well, I'm worried about Shirin. I should have called the hospital.'

Of course he was worried. However dark her soul, she was still his wife. 'You'll see her soon enough. With a gunshot wound, quiet rest has to be the best thing for her at the moment. She's not going anywhere.'

Oswick nodded but Wilde could tell he wasn't convinced.

'Could I call the hospital from the garage?'

'No. Just do what I asked. As soon as the intelligence men are here you take them to the bodies and explain the whole background. Tell them I am certain that ceramic canisters were brought ashore and concealed here. We must assume they have now been taken elsewhere – probably close to the intended target, wherever that may be.

'When you have briefed them in full and answered all their questions, you can make your way home as far as I'm concerned, though the MI5 men might well have other ideas.'

'But—'

'No buts, Oswick, you said you could take orders like a soldier. You also said you want to assist the forces of law and order to make amends for your flirtation with the forces of darkness. Well, this is your chance. I admit this isn't easy, but it's critical because you have become intimate with dangerous people and they must be dealt with. Time is running out.'

He walked him to the end of the short driveway, then returned to the barn. He had an unpleasant task to perform. Searching through the clothing of two dead men, one of them in an advanced state of putrefaction.

One of the first things he discovered was that both of them had their ring finger missing.

Oswick arrived back at the farm forty minutes later. He looked exhausted.

'How did it go?'

'Difficult. I spoke to a woman named Bentall, who wouldn't give any information about herself except to say she worked in the ministry. She seemed highly sceptical of everything I told her. I almost found myself shouting down the line at her.'

'But they're coming here, yes?'

'Yes, they're coming here – reluctantly. I don't think Bentall believes that Lord Templeman is dead. When I mentioned your name she said something like "Jesus, not that damned Yank!"'

Wilde's laughter had an edge. He had encountered Freya Bentall at a couple of meetings in London when the Office of Strategic Services was being set up in the middle of the war and the British intelligence services were asked to help; they didn't hit it off. The MI5 officer had decided that the OSS were amateurs and was reluctant to offer any assistance with their training programme. 'Some bloody history professor wants to be a spy, God help us all. Hitler will be quaking in his boots.' She had said it just loud enough for Wilde to hear.

In the event, MI5 had not been much involved with the OSS. That was left to an MI6 training team, and it had worked well. 'Don't fret about Bentall. She might not like me, but she's extremely professional and she'll see things differently when she gets here. Tell her I'll call her at Latimer Hall either tonight or tomorrow morning.'

'I'll do that.'

'You look wiped out, Oswick.'

'We didn't get much sleep last night if you recall, sir.'

'There are beds upstairs. Why don't you kip down for a couple of hours?'

'I'm not sure I can sleep knowing about the bodies in the barn.'

'Well, go back to Cornflowers when you can get away and I'll be in touch. You know the danger, so keep alert.'

Wilde took the Riley and drove back to the garage in Skyme. Barnaby Wax was pleased to see him but deeply puzzled. 'What's going on, Tom? Where's your young friend?'

'He's staying at the farm. If I could tell you any more than that, I would, but I can't. This involves national security. If you want to help, you could stretch rationing regulations and fill me up – I have to get to London.'

'You'll owe me one.'

'I'm already indebted to you. One day I'll tell you everything, if I can. For the moment, perhaps you could direct me to Liz's house. I have one last question for her.'

'It's only five minutes' walk from here.' He pointed northwards along the street. 'Turn left just before the church and you'll find yourself in St Withold's Street. She's third house along on the left. A little semi. She should be there – she said she was going home. Leave the Riley here and I'll fill her up.'

Finding the house was easy. She opened the door almost immediately and invited him in.

'Thank you, but I didn't want to trouble you. I just need to ask you something.'

'Well, come in and have a cup of tea anyway. You look like you need one, Mr Wilde.'

'No, I can't wait, I've got a long drive.'

'Fire away then. But I've already told you everything I know.'

'It's about my companion, Danny Oswick. I saw the way you looked at him when we arrived – as though his face was familiar. Have you seen him before somewhere?'

For the first time, she smiled. 'The thing is, he's so like my poor Tony. The same lovely eyes and hair. Actually he's much better looking than Tone and he's got a moustache, but his eyes sent a chill down my spine.'

'But you definitely haven't seen him around here before?'

'No.'

Wilde smiled, too. 'Thank you, that's put my mind at rest.'

'Why, did you suspect him of something?'

Did he? No, he had faith in Oswick now. But it always made sense to check. He shook his head. 'Fear not, Danny's a good man. And thank you for contacting me, Liz. I must tell you that you have done a remarkable thing today. I can't give you all the facts, but suffice it to say your brave testimony is extremely important.'

'I knew it was something bad. If only I could have told you sooner . . . I wish it hadn't taken Tony's death.'

CHAPTER 35

He arrived outside 54 Broadway in the late afternoon. Without being asked, Barnaby Wax had not only filled the tank but had stowed three jerrycans full of petrol in the car. Wilde parked around the corner near a bombsite, then walked back and presented himself at the modest doorway that disguised the true purpose of the building.

The secretary who had relieved him of his pistol on his last visit recognised him instantly.

'Professor Wilde,' she said. 'How can I help you?'

'I have to talk to Mr Eaton.'

'I'm pretty sure he's not here but I will check for you. Are you armed?'

He knew the drill and handed over the Browning 9 mm.

'Thank you. Just wait in the side room.' She indicated a doorway. The room was cold and empty save for two wooden chairs and a table. A newspaper, *The Times*, was the only distraction available for those waiting for appointments, but he was too tired to read it.

Five minutes later, the secretary appeared. 'Mr Eaton is not here. I called him at home and he apologised for his absence from work but said he would receive you if you could make your way there. I believe he's in a rather bad way.'

'The leg?'

'More than that actually. Poor chap's been diagnosed with Parkinson's.'

'That explains a lot. Thank you.'

'I take it you have his address.'

'Indeed.'

Philip Eaton's house in Chelsea was only a ten-minute drive. Eaton, stick in hand, was waiting for him by the front door and Wilde could see straightaway that he was struggling with his health. He had deteriorated dramatically in the days since they met Walter Schellenberg together and discovered the secrets of the addendum to the Black Book.

'Come in, Tom. I'm afraid I've been in a bit of a state these past couple of days. Takes all my energy just to get out of bed and dress.'

'I'm sorry to hear that, Philip.' It was obvious now, the Parkinson's. Eaton was deteriorating fast.

'Actually, you don't look so hot yourself.'

'It's been a long day.' *And night before that.*

They settled into his wonderfully comfortable sitting room and Eaton groaned as he eased himself down on the sofa, his legs and hand trembling.

'You really need to get yourself some help, Philip.'

'Oh, I have a woman who comes in every morning. She assists me and I trust her. I don't really want anyone else nosing around. Have to go through the whole security checks rigmarole. Even then, you never know who you're really getting. Your woman, the delightful and hard-working Doris, you've had her for ages and trust her, don't you? I'm sure you'd have to think long and hard before taking anyone else on after the work you've been doing these past few years.'

'Yes, I suppose I would,' he lied. Perhaps their employment of Mrs Sylvia Keane had been a bit hasty, but it had been necessary.

'I've got some good coffee. Do you think you could do the honours, old boy? You'll find the percolator in the kitchen. My coffee is supplied ready ground, which takes away some of the freshness, but saves me a lot of bother. It's in an airtight tin by the perc.'

Ten minutes later, Wilde took his first sip. 'God I needed that.'

'Glad to be of assistance, as always. Now, what can I do for you. I doubt you've driven down from Cambridge simply for a cup of coffee.'

Wilde grimaced.

'Your face tells me it's bad news.'

He nodded slowly. 'Yes, the worst.' There was no way to sugar the pill. 'Dagger's dead, murdered.' He spoke the words quietly and firmly, yet even as he uttered them, he felt a swine, for his eyes were searching Eaton's haggard face, looking for a reaction. He wanted to convince himself that Dagger Templeman's death was in no way connected to the recent hostility – or at the very least breakdown in trust – between the two intelligence officers.

Eaton did not disappoint. Although he was already slumped back on the sofa, he physically sank yet further. His recoil and the widening of his eyes were genuine. That shock could not have been feigned. Spies might be actors, but this was real life and death, not Shakespearean drama.

'Dagger dead? Is this true, Tom?'

He nodded. 'I'm sorry, Philip.'

'How, for God's sake?'

'He was shot in the head. I discovered his body myself.'

'Dear God, where did this happen? Who did it, for Christ's sake? Please tell me this is nothing to do with the incident at Flowthorpe.'

'I fear it is *everything* to do with it. These people take no prisoners.'

'Do you know who's behind it yet?'

'Oh yes.'

'Well?'

'Catesby.'

'Are you serious? Neville Catesby?'

'Deadly serious, Philip. But we'll talk about that in due course. First, I want to talk about your relationship with Dagger Templeman. Things had evidently become a little strained between the two of you.'

'What? Why are you bringing that up now?'

'Because I have to.'

'This is ridiculous. I told you everything there was to know – he simply wasn't communicating with us and I wondered what the hell was going on because communication was his job. I was as bewildered as anyone.'

'Surely you had some theory, though? What did your instinct tell you? There's no one more attuned to the story behind the story than you, Philip.'

'My theory? I just thought it was typical of Five. There has always been a schoolboy rivalry between MI5 and MI6. Five envies us because we're rather more glamorous and we deal with the whole wide world whereas they are somewhat parochial – hardly more than a secret police force. The Gestapo without knuckledusters, if you like. They have certainly never *understood* us, so yes, there was friction between us.'

'Very well. You say his job was to communicate. Curiously, he thought you were the one falling down in that department. He thought there were matters of import that you were keeping from him.'

'Did he talk to you about me?'

'He did. He wanted to know my opinion of you.'

'And what did you say?'

'I told him you had done great work for Britain.'

'But? There's always a but.'

'But I was perturbed at the disappearance of Boris Minsky. He felt the same way.'

'I don't like to speak ill of the dead, but this all sounds like paranoia.'

To tell or not to tell? If he was giving away secrets that MI5 would rather keep hidden, well to hell with it. How secret could it have been if Templeman had told him this thing? He decided he had no choice. He had to get some semblance of truth out of Eaton, because the matter affected him, too.

'There was more to it than paranoia or interdepartmental rivalry, Philip. I'm sorry to be so blunt, especially at a time like this, but the truth is Dagger had lost trust you.'

'That's outrageous. A bloody calumny.'

'I hope so, Philip, I truly hope so. But that's what I want to satisfy myself about. You see, Dagger had you under surveillance and his shadows witnessed something that caused him great concern. They saw a man believed to be Boris Minsky coming here to this house at three thirty in the morning. He stayed with you for an hour and then they tailed him to the Soviet Embassy.'

There was a chilling silence in the room. 'Is that why you've come here, Tom?' Eaton said at last. 'To accuse me? Do you think I was involved in Dagger's murder?'

'I'm here because I am investigating a deadly threat to this nation and I have to follow every lead, however slender. These are the facts: Dagger Templeman was investigating the BW incident at Flowthorpe, and he was investigating you. Is there a link between these two matters? I certainly hope not, but I have to ask questions.'

'Well, you've asked the question and the answer is no. Are you satisfied?'

'Not entirely. Let me go off at a tangent a moment. There is no doubt in my mind that Sir Neville Catesby and others are planning an atrocity using biological warfare pathogens brought here by submarine from Unit 731 in Manchuria. They killed Templeman because he was leading the inquiry, they killed an American named Larry B. Rhein because he knew all about Catesby's links to Unit 731, they killed an MI5 agent named Rafe Crow and they murdered a blameless old farmer named Bagshawe. Oh, and they tried to have me put away by framing me with Rhein's murder.'

'What's that got to do with Minsky or me?'

'Who stands to gain from a devastating attack on Britain? The Soviets, perhaps? A child could see that your apparent double-dealing with a senior SMERSH agent – and your falling-out with Dagger Templeman – need investigating.'

Eaton shifted forward, struggling to get up from the sofa. 'Damn this bloody coffee,' he said, 'I need a proper drink.'

'Brandy?'

'Neat, and very large. Help yourself to Scotch.'

Wilde went over to the sideboard and poured two drinks from Eaton's decanters. He handed the brandy to Eaton.

For a couple of minutes, they sat drinking in silence.

'Well?' Wilde demanded at last. 'Are you going to tell me your side of the story? Do you admit Minsky was here, and that he hasn't been missing at all?'

'Dear God, Tom, you know that's not how things work. Dagger Templeman was Five through and through. They're so bloody straightforward. But in realpolitik, things are anything but straightforward. In Six, we deal with double and triple bluffs.'

You know that. We taught OSS everything. We have to use brutes like Minsky, just as our American friends are hoovering up some of the dirtiest Nazis to work for them.'

'That doesn't sound like an explanation of what Minsky was doing here, or why he immediately reported back to his embassy.'

'Well, it's all you're getting, old boy. Except for one thing: you should know by now that I would never betray my country. Minsky might think I would, but he is deluded and I want to keep him that way. On the other hand, I know exactly what he's up to and I stand to gain a great deal of information about Soviet penetration of Britain. It is a tale of deep infiltration of our secret service, the government, civil service and industry. This has absolutely nothing to do with Flowthorpe.'

Wilde threw back the whisky. It burnt his throat and he knew it wouldn't help him stay awake, but he was too tired to care.

'Satisfied now?' Eaton said defiantly.

All Wilde could do was shrug. Knowing Eaton, his explanation was as plausible as he was going to get. And who knew, perhaps it was true.

'I'll have to be, because I need your help. Alongside Templeman's body there was another corpse – a man supposedly named Gram Lyngwood, though that could easily be an alias. He was living at Flowthorpe at the time of the pathogen release. He was new to the village. In his garden, I found ceramic shards from a broken canister. It had Japanese characters on it and was clearly the plague bomb that caused sickness in the village. I believe it was dropped and shattered accidentally. Why it was at Flowthorpe we have no idea. Was it supposed to be an attack on the nearby US airbase? Possibly. Or there could be another more obvious explanation, which you can work out for yourself.'

'You said you needed my help?'

'We've got nothing on Lyngwood. Whether Templeman discovered anything before he was killed I have no idea. Of course I have other contacts in the British secret services but I am not aware of anyone who would help me on this. If you could find out the truth about the man, it might just bring some clarity. We also need to find Catesby, who has gone AWOL, presumably with his cargo of bacteria. I know little about English law, but I'm sure the properties he owns must be in the Land Registry. The only ones I know about are Harbinger House and, almost certainly, a dilapidated farm in Skyme-next-Sea on the Norfolk coast, where I discovered the bodies. He could be anywhere, but there must be at least an outside chance that he's at one of his properties.'

'Lyngwood will be tricky, but I agree your other idea is worth a look. I'll get one of the girls at 54 Broadway on to the Land Registry straightaway. Hopefully that'll be easier. I'll call you this evening.'

Wilde got up and moved towards the door, but then turned back and offered his hand to Eaton. 'Thank you,' he said.

'I'm not sure I should be shaking the hand of a man who has just accused me of treason, but what the hell.'

'I had to pose the questions. It was as difficult for me as it was for you.'

'But you still don't trust me, do you?'

Wilde's hand hovered. Finally, Eaton reached out and took it. 'Good luck, Tom. I fear you might need it.'

'Don't call too early. I have another matter to attend to in London.'

CHAPTER 36

Rules restaurant in Covent Garden had somehow preserved its subtle air of elegance throughout the worst of the bombing. The smoky atmosphere, the immaculate white linen, the discretion of the waiters, the cartoons of great patrons on the walls, all spoke of a history stretching back almost a hundred and fifty years. This was where princes and politicians came and mingled with the ancient landed gentry, the literati, and the great names of theatre-land. They gossiped and scandalised over fine wines, quiet service, venison, ptarmigan and grouse.

Wilde was already at a table in a corner cubicle reading the menu through exhausted eyes when Lydia arrived with Miranda in tow. Surprised by the presence of the younger woman, he immediately stood up and simply nodded to Lydia rather than taking her in his arms.

'It's all right, Tom, this is Miranda. You can kiss me – she knows I'm a married woman.'

They embraced, holding each other rather longer than they might normally have done in a public place. Her warmth infused him with the first hint of humanity he had experienced in days. Under other circumstances, he would have suggested they forego the meal and find a hotel room.

Miranda stood there watching, beguiled.

Wilde turned to her, smiled and shook her by the hand. 'Very pleased to meet you, Miranda.'

'And you, Professor.'

'Please, I'm Tom. Anyway, let's all sit down, order some food and wine. I'm famished.'

'Actually, you look a sight.'

'Thank you, darling. Now then, I'm going for the lamb. You'll find that the pies are delicious, Miranda.'

'No, I've been here before with Mummy and Daddy and I know exactly what I want – the steak and kidney pudding and then I want treacle sponge if they have it.'

Lydia could hold it in no longer. She gripped his arm. 'Something has happened, Tom, something terrible. Miranda and I were nearly killed.'

He looked down at her small hand clasping him, then met her eyes. They told him that this was serious and true. 'My God, Lydia . . .' He looked to her side, to the girl. 'Miranda?

She nodded.

'When? What happened?'

'Last night. I called you in the early hours, but you weren't home. Where were you, Tom? I've been desperate.' She pulled the needle from her coat pocket. 'He tried to kill us – with this.'

'Lydia, you were supposed to be protected. Templeman assured me.'

'That's what I thought.'

'Sit down. Tell me everything.'

'This man – this horrible man – got into our room while I was calling you. I came back just as he was going for Miranda. Together we managed to fight the bastard off, but not before he thought he'd jabbed me. Fortunately, the needle got stuck in my coat. We gave him a bit of a beating.'

'Did you call the police?'

'If I had done that everything would have come out and I'd have been sacked by Dame Gertrude. So no, I decided to contact you instead and get your advice. I waited for hours to go to the phone because I was terrified the needle man would still be lurking. And when I finally drummed up the courage to go out and call you, you weren't there. You have been extremely elusive. Where have you been all night and all day, Tom?'

He had no intention of filling her in on the details of the past three days, especially not in the company of the other young woman. 'To hell with Dame Gertrude and St Ursula's, you should have sought help. There's a killer on the loose.'

'Actually, there has been a great deal of police activity outside the hostel.'

'Any idea why?'

'The rumour was that there had been a murder,' Miranda said. 'That the police had discovered a body in the churchyard.'

'Then we heard that there had been *two* murders,' Lydia put in. 'They found a second body up the road in a bombsite. I have a horrible feeling they must be Jan Stewer and Peter Gurney . . .'

'Who?'

'I gave names to my three watchers. You know the old Widdecombe song.'

'No, that one's passed me by.'

'But what do we do, Tom? If I'm correct, those two men died because of me.'

Wilde was thinking fast. His tiredness had simply washed away. Perhaps she was right not to have contacted the police. 'Let me talk to MI5 about it.' His overriding concern now was the fact that they had known where she was. How could Catesby and his henchmen have known such a thing? 'No one but Templeman and me knew you were at St Ursula's. You haven't told anyone else have you, Lydia?'

'Only Isabel Parsons, who recommended me in the first place.'

'And Mrs Keane, of course. Perhaps she told Doris.'

'They wouldn't have told anyone . . . would they?

Wilde had other ideas. This had to have come from within MI5. And as Templeman had said himself, Catesby had contacts everywhere.

'You can talk to Lord Templeman, can't you?'

'Not at the moment.' He wasn't about to tell them that Dagger had been hideously murdered.

Lydia patted Miranda's hand. 'I'm sorry, none of these names mean anything to you.'

'Don't worry about me, Lydia. I'm just thrilled to be part of it all.'

'I have to get back to Cambridge this evening.' He was fast coming to the conclusion that he had to take Lydia too. If it wasn't safe for her last night, why would it be any more secure tonight? 'I should go now.'

'Aren't you going to eat with us?'

'I've lost my appetite.'

'When did you last eat, Tom?'

When was it? Half a bacon sandwich for breakfast at a garage on the chilly eastern coast of Norfolk. If he was to see out the rest of the evening, he had to get some food in him. 'OK,' he said. 'One course.'

The next half-hour passed in a surreal blur, a horror story that chilled him to the bone and seemed to thrill the young student, in equal measure. After finishing their food and a glass of wine, Miranda disappeared to the lavatories. Lydia edged closer to her husband. 'What I don't understand, Tom, is why I'm a target. Is this really something to do with Himmler's Black Book?'

'I'm not sure. But I know that Neville Catesby is behind it.'

'Didn't I tell you that bastard was a piece of work? But why does he want to kill me?'

'Because he knows I'm investigating him and is worried how much I know and what I might have told you. He sees anyone who might know anything as a threat.'

'The irony being that you've actually told me bugger all.'

'True. But whose fault is that? You haven't been easy to get hold of. When we're on our own for a couple of hours I'll tell you the whole story. Sadly, it hasn't ended yet.'

'And what, pray, was that horrible man trying to inject into me? Do you have any information on that?'

'Phenol. It's what the Nazis used to kill the senile, the insane and the crippled in their euthanasia programme. One jab into the bloodstream and you're dead in seconds or minutes. You're very fortunate to have survived your encounter with Dr Bacon.'

'Dr Bacon? So you actually have a name for the bastard?'

'That's not his real name but that's what he's calling himself. Tell me about Miranda. She's delightful, but why have you brought her along?'

'To keep her onside. She's promised not to tell Dame Gertrude – Dr Blake. Anyway, she wanted to meet you.'

'She seems to think this is all a huge adventure. Look, how would you both feel about coming back to Cambridge tonight. I don't think you're safe here.'

They saw that Miranda was approaching from the Ladies'.

'And how would we be safer at home? Neville Catesby must be able to find out where we live.'

'Where then? A hotel near St Ursula's perhaps?'

'I don't know. Look, if you're worried about me, what about Johnny? Is he safe at home? How about Dagger's place – Latimer Hall? He must have excellent security. Couldn't we stay there?'

'No.' He lowered his voice so the approaching Miranda shouldn't hear. 'Dagger's dead, Lydia. He's been murdered.'

Miranda was sitting down. 'Are you whispering about me? Are you sneaking to your lovely husband about my risqué reading habits?'

'Something like that,' Wilde said, forcing himself to smile.

Lydia wasn't smiling. The blood had drained from her face and her eyes were wide in horror.

'In that case, bring on the wicked pudding.'

'I'm afraid we're going now, Miranda,' Lydia said. 'We're going to Cambridge and we'd very much like you to come with us. We'll be picking up my son and finding somewhere safe to stay until this is all over. You have seen the would-be killer, so you're a witness and may not be safe. Will you come with us?'

Wilde looked at her bemused. This was a sudden change of heart.

'Don't look at me like that, Tom – I've got an idea. Doris.'

'Has she got enough room?'

'We'll manage.'

'Cambridge?' Miranda said. 'You know we've got a lecture first thing tomorrow.'

'And we'll catch up. Don't worry. You're brilliant, Miranda and your place at St Ursula's is secure. I'm not so sure about mine, though.'

'I don't suppose I should . . .'

'We can't force you, Miranda.'

'All right then, it's an adventure . . .'

'And we'll get the waiter to wrap up some treacle sponge.'

'God, this really is better than a novel.'

Lydia sat in the front beside Wilde. Miranda had to recline across the back seat, with her knees bent to accommodate one of the jerrycans. The evening traffic was light and they made good progress out of London, but then the weather worsened – high winds making the driving hard.

'Talk to me, Lydia – keep me awake.'

'Do you want me to drive?'

'How much sleep did you get last night?'

'None.'

'We're in the same boat then. Come on, talk. Tell me something interesting that you've learnt, or describe the characters you've met.'

'Well you know Miranda now.'

A voice from the back. 'I can hear you, you know, so be careful what you say about me.'

They stopped once to fill up, leaving a jerrycan at the side of the road to gain more room for Miranda, and finally made Cambridge just after ten.

Wilde realised he had no idea where Doris lived. 'What's the address, Lydia?'

'Oh, a couple of roads from us. Just carry on towards home and I'll direct you. Suddenly I feel awful doing this, what with Peter being so sick, but I know she'll help if she can.'

Ten minutes later, they pulled up outside Doris's small terrace house. The wind had eased a bit, but there were still violent gusts. Wilde stayed in the car while Lydia went and knocked on her cleaner's door. He wound down the window so he could hear them. Doris was in her dressing gown and from her sleepy eyes seemed to have been woken up. He saw Lydia hug her, then she came back to the car.

'She's fine. There are two single beds in her spare room and Miranda and I can have those. You can sleep on the couch downstairs.'

'No, I'm going to leave the car here and walk home. One of us has to be there.'

'Can't you bring Johnny here?'

'He'll be asleep. And there are three strangers in our house. I have to be there and I'll have the pistol at hand. It's certainly possible that Danny Oswick will be in danger, and the same goes for anyone else in the house. You get some sleep and then come around in the morning.'

He got out of the car and thanked Doris for her assistance.

'Any time, Professor Wilde. I'm always here to help.'

'And perhaps we'll talk about that other matter you mentioned tomorrow, when we're all a bit more wide awake, yes?' He was aware that he still hadn't heard her feelings about Sylvia Keane.

'Oh I don't want to make a fuss . . .'

'I know you don't, Doris. But we trust your instincts.'

He hugged Lydia, took his leave of Miranda and left the three women to become properly acquainted and settle down for the night. Knowing they were safe was a weight off his mind.

Walking home slowly, he watched his surroundings every step of the way. When he reached the corner of the street, he stopped and gazed for a couple of minutes at Cornflowers, just fifty yards away. Lights were on, but there was no sign of disturbance. Nor were there any unfamiliar cars in evidence, and the pavements were deserted.

He approached the house and waited at the front door. It was a strange feeling being outside his own home when others were inside – people he had known for only a few days. On the way up from town he had found himself overcome with guilt at having left his son in the care of this woman about whom, honestly, they knew very little.

But what could he have done in the circumstances? And was it any different to the actions of so many parents in consigning their offspring to the care of nannies, governesses and boarding schools? When his own parents sent him off to board, they could know nothing about the qualities and morals of all the teachers and housemasters and matrons with whom he would spend the next five years. One man was actively sadistic and clearly took pleasure in beating his charges. Others were remarkable people, imbued with kindness and a desire to help the pupils get the best possible education. But it was always a lottery.

He turned the key in the door and pushed it open. As he did so he heard the scraping of a chair from the kitchen and he called out. 'Hello? Oswick? Mrs Keane?'

CHAPTER 37

Every time she tried to move, she was in pain, but her discomfort was so great that she couldn't remain still and nor could she sleep. Her forehead was burning up.

Neville Catesby sat on the side of the bed watching her, soothing her brow with a damp flannel. He needed her. He had lost one pilot, he couldn't lose two.

He held out his hand with two tablets. 'Take the aspirin.'

She did what she was told and then he handed her a glass of water to help the pills down.

'I know what you're thinking,' Shirin said. 'But you're wrong – I'm going to be all right. Can't Siggy do anything? He's a doctor.'

'He's already gone. Anyway, I wouldn't trust Sigmund Rascher with my cat, if I had one.' He stood up, then leant over and kissed her cheek. 'I have to go downstairs now.'

'Hold me, Neville.'

'Try to sleep.'

He went down to the kitchen where three other men were talking politics. They all jumped up at his approach, but he waved them to sit down. He could feel their nerves and their excitement. He felt it himself. It was electric. This was really going to happen, and it would work.

Wilde had asked him about the true Neville Catesby. *Give me a clue, Neville. Have you ever married? Do you have a family hidden away somewhere? What do you want from the world? And, perhaps most interesting of all, whose side are you on?*

If he, Catesby, was an enigma to the world, to himself there was no complication. In his own mind, his aims had always been clear and he had been willing to play a long game to achieve them. When it was in his best interests, he would sow confusion. Obfuscation was a weapon. No one needed to know his heart. But now such elusiveness was no longer needed. Soon it would all be over and he would achieve his goal.

He knew what he wanted and he would get it. His destiny.

Nothing and no one could stop him now.

He poured himself a drink. Through all the tribulations of his younger days he had struggled merely to survive and had come to understand, through Darwin, that this was the essence of all life.

Until . . .

Until in a blinding moment of inspiration he realised that the struggle for *survival* was false. It was the struggle to *dominate* that was at the very core of existence. All life, however primitive, understood that or fell by the wayside.

If you only sought survival, you would be a slave, subjugated to the will of the powerful.

To achieve power, you had to be as ruthless as the tiger.

One simple act could change the world. History taught you that. The assassination of Julius Caesar turned the Republic of Rome into a dictatorship, the storming of the Bastille sparked the French Revolution, the burning of the Reichstag secured Hitler's rule. There were countless other examples from the murder of the princes in the Tower to the storming of the Winter Palace.

One simple act. That was all that was needed.

He had known this for a long time, but it was the war that brought home the realisation that it could be done. He had learnt from the dictators, past and present, how a handful of unsentimental and determined men could control the lives of millions.

Why, though? Why did he want this? Most would consider his life charmed enough, so why would he need more? He had wealth and position. The great leaders of the twentieth century received him; his fellows in college feted him; his military comrades considered him brave and soldierly, a fine and dependable companion when the artillery roared; his friends in his London club thought him an eccentric with a sharp but amusing tongue.

None of them knew him, for he would never allow them into the inner sanctum of his soul.

To understand him, they would have to know his life, and that would be revealed to no one.

Deserted by his 'bolter' mother when he was three. Cast off to the most brutal prep school in England at the age of six; bullied and abused without mercy from the ages of eight to thirteen; laughed at with scorn by the only woman he ever loved at the age of twenty-one.

And through it all, he witnessed the humiliation and abject fall from grace of his father, a man he came to despise as the world mocked.

Nature, 'red in tooth and claw', had nothing to teach mankind about cruelty.

And now, the final act was drawing close. The endgame. What better moment in history than when the victors of a great war believed themselves invincible? When their guard was down. Every fighter knew that was when complacency entered the reckoning and the sucker punch won the day

Catesby reflected on his chosen few. How would they perform?

It was a shame they had lost Sosinka, but losses were unavoidable in times of conflict. Kagerer and Sosinka were both hardened fighting men, veterans of the Dirlewanger SS Brigade, the toughest and most brutal outfit in the Third Reich. No subtlety with men like Kagerer and Sosinka, not like Sigmund Rascher.

But for all his flaws and undoubted weaknesses, Rascher would always do his bidding. Herr Doktor Rascher, former Luftwaffe Medical Officer, now known as Edmund Bacon, had run a special SS laboratory in Dachau concentration camp, where he enjoyed performing experiments on prisoners without observing the niceties of caring whether they lived or died.

Always proud of what he had done, he laughed at the more gruesome elements of his story.

His aim had been to work out how the pilots and crew of the Luftwaffe whose planes were hit by Allied fire could survive if they had to freefall or parachute from extreme height.

To this end, Dachau prisoners – POWs or Jews or criminals – were locked in an airtight vacuum chamber, and subjected to the very low pressures and oxygen levels associated with high altitude. The chances of survival for those subjected to the experiments were extremely slim.

When they died, he cut them open to examine their organs, then when he had completed his inspection and written up his notes, he sent them off to the crematorium without a second thought. They were human beings but to Sigmund Rascher they were of no consequence except for what could be learnt from their wretched bodies.

Scores of men died in agony, suffering uncontrollable spasms. But that meant nothing to Rascher; he knew them only as VPs, short for *Versuchspersonen* – experimental persons. He promised the prisoners that if they cooperated and survived the tests they would be freed from Dachau, but the pledge was never kept.

And when necessary, the table in the Block 5 laboratory always held a vial of phenol and a hypodermic syringe for those who proved difficult. The prisoners knew exactly what the needle meant.

Not content with high-altitude tests, Rascher turned his attention to the problem of pilots who crashed into freezing winter seas. He commissioned the building of a large tank, which was filled with ice water.

He forced his VPs into the tank and subjected them to extreme cold, pain and terror. Standing beside them with his stopwatch, he would measure the length of time until they died of heart failure. Perhaps five hours.

Others were kept in the ice water until their temperature had dropped to 25 degrees, they were almost dead but not quite, so that various methods of thawing them could be tried. Some were placed in hot baths or under heat lamps and yet more were put in bed between the bodies of two naked women prisoners – brought from the women's concentration camp, Ravensbrück. The idea had been suggested by Himmler himself.

Curiously, Rascher discovered that using a single woman was more effective in warming the frozen body than two, because inhibitions were lowered. In some cases, as the man thawed out they engaged in sexual intercourse.

Rascher was in his mid-thirties with a large forehead, thinning hair and a broad, bland face. He was well versed in English, his grandmother having been an upper middle-class British woman named Frances Whitfield. He was good at languages – French and Italian – but felt most at home in the English-speaking world. As a young man in his twenties, he even had hopes of marrying an American heiress, Grace Richards, whose father edited the prestigious *New York Tribune*; the fact that she was thirty-eight years his senior did not deter the young Sigmund, but the affair came to nothing.

Causing pain and death were not Sigmund's only weaknesses: he also loved women, children, cigarettes and dancing. After a string of affairs – including his ancient heiress – he married the singer Nini Diehl, a close friend of Himmler. The couple used their connection shamelessly to gain privileges for themselves.

Catesby despised him, but for the moment he needed him. He was useful. To achieve anything, one had to simply hold one's nose and deal with the Raschers of the world.

They had met in Munich in 1937, through Catesby's long-standing friendship with Nini Diehl. He had no interest in Rascher but he realised that Nini's link to Himmler might one day be useful, so he humoured her husband.

Eight years later, Rascher was desperate to save his skin and made contact with Catesby through his sister Sigrid, who lived in Switzerland. If the English gentleman could organise safe passage to England, he would be in his debt forever.

His 'execution' by SS officers in Dachau was easily faked, by which time Rascher was already across the border in Zurich. From there, with his English language skills, it was a simple hop to England. Now he was repaying Sir Neville Catesby and keeping himself safe as a hired killer. A task that perfectly suited his amorality. And perfectly served Catesby's purpose.

And Danny Oswick? Originally, Catesby had seen much of himself in the boy – the same experience, the same hunger for retribution. He had become soft, but he had still served his purpose.

Shirin Oswick was another matter. He had always enjoyed her body and actually felt fondness for her. She was unlikely to survive, of course, but that was war.

The endgame was upon them, and one way or another, she would have to play her part. He had been awaiting this moment for more than twenty years.

Sylvia Keane looked startled, standing there in the hallway, then relieved when she realised who it was. 'Oh, Professor Wilde, you gave me a bit of a fright.'

'I'm sorry. Are you alone, Mrs Keane? No Danny Oswick?'

'Just me and the children. I wasn't sure where you both were after you left in the middle of the night. There's been a telephone call for you – a Mr Eaton – just a short while ago.'

He loosened his grip on the butt of the large Browning concealed in the shoulder holster under his coat. 'Thank you. And is everything all right?'

'Well, I think Johnny is a bit upset. He doesn't seem to know what's going on. I gave them a nice chop and boiled potatoes for their supper and it was a struggle to get him to eat it. And then when he went to bed he took a long time to get to sleep. I think I heard him crying.'

'I'll go and look at him.'

'Can I get you a drink, Professor?'

'That would be very kind. A whisky if we have any left.'

Johnny was sound asleep, his face a picture of innocence, his breathing quiet and soft. Wilde touched the boy's face lightly with the back of his hand, then planted a kiss on his brow.

Downstairs, he asked for privacy while he made his phone call. Sylvia left him with his drink and returned to the kitchen where she shut the door behind her.

Eaton answered the call at the fourth ring.

'Hello, Tom.'

'Any joy?'

'Very little, I'm afraid. No list of houses for you from the Land Registry and nothing on your corpse, Mr Lyngwood. All I can tell you is that there is general panic and alarm throughout the security services – and the Cabinet itself for that matter – over the death of Dagger Templeman. I have put your evidence into the pot, so you can expect MI5 to turn up on your doorstep sooner rather than later. They are taking what you have told me about Neville Catesby very seriously and they are looking for him high and low. Every known fascist in the country – and there are probably thousands of them – will be getting a knock on the door in the coming hours.'

'Good. Hopefully they'll find him.'

'I do know from personal experience, having been there to dinner, that Catesby has a house in Mayfair. That will have been among the first locations already visited by MI5 or the Special Branch boys, so he won't be there. As to that other matter, I should have been more open with you, given our history.'

'You mean our Russian friend?'

'Careful, Tom. No details over the phone, but I will say this: it involves science. Something we have but they want. My task is to ensure they don't get it. If you make it down to the smoke, I'll fill you in, but I'll tell you this much – our man is giving me more information than I could possibly have hoped for. He is a goldmine.'

As he put down the phone, Wilde realised that Eaton was talking about atomic secrets which, of course, Stalin would be desperate to get his bloodstained hands on. Where better than the place Eaton had shown Wilde barely two months ago – the little town of Godmanchester, twenty miles from Cambridge. Ten German nuclear scientists were held there, their every word recorded secretly by British intelligence. How useful might they be to the Soviet Union?

As for Eaton's curious relationship with Boris Minsky, the sharp observation of the sixteenth-century essayist Michel de Montaigne sprang to mind. 'When I play with my cat, how do I know that she is not playing with me?'

Likewise, when you agree to spy, how can you be sure who you're spying for?

His mind was drifting. He realised that he simply couldn't carry on tonight. No more calls, no more discussions, no more thinking. He had to sleep. Quickly, he downed his whisky and said goodnight to Sylvia Keane.

'Just before you go, sir,' she said, 'I have to say that I have been a little concerned that something is going on with you and your student Mr Oswick. There seems to be a frightful lot of coming and going, which makes me feel rather unsettled. Is everything all right . . . I mean, is there anything I should be told about?'

It was a fair question given that he and Oswick had disappeared in the early hours, but not one to which he could give a complete answer. What could he say to her? That he was worried that this house might be unsafe for his wife, but that it was fine for her and her daughter and his own son? Should he be moving Mrs Keane and Penelope and Johnny out to a hotel? These were dilemmas and he couldn't give her a sensible reply.

'I'm afraid there are things I can't discuss with you at the moment, Mrs Keane, but let's talk in the morning when I am more wide awake. Just so you know, I will be sleeping down here because I need to be near the telephone. You can be sure, however, that you and the children are perfectly safe.'

If it was a lie, it was a necessary one. Anyway, he would be here and he would have the Browning 9 mm close at hand.

'Oh, and there is every likelihood that Mrs Wilde will be home for a flying visit first thing in the morning.'

He had never slept more soundly. If a tank had driven through the wall, it would have struggled to wake him. It was Danny Oswick shaking him that put paid to his sleep.

'God, what time is it?'

'Seven forty-five.'

'I take it you've just arrived.'

'Five minutes ago. Sylvia let me in. The children are running riot.'

At least everyone was alive. Wilde struggled up from the couch. The Hi-Power was on the floor at his side. He desperately hoped that neither Mrs Keane nor the children had seen it. 'Has anyone else been in here?'

'I don't think so.'

'Good. Don't mention the gun.'

'I'm sorry to wake you, but I have news. I've been held and questioned by Freya Bentall and various other operatives since they arrived at Skyme. I told them everything I knew and showed them the bodies, but that didn't stop them interrogating me like a criminal.'

'That's their job, Oswick.'

'And then they brought me back to Latimer Hall, where Miss Bentall has set up an office. At least they fed me and allowed me to sleep for five or six hours. Now, she wants you there. She's quite a woman'

'That's one way of putting it.' Actually, he had been told by Guy Liddell, director of counter-intelligence, that she was the best intelligence officer in MI5, albeit the only female one. Her interrogation skills were legendary and it was said she could detect a lie at a thousand paces. What she lacked in charm, she more than made up for in ferocious diligence.

'Can I use the phone, sir? I still haven't had a chance to contact the hospital.'

'Did you mention your wife to Bentall? Particularly, did you mention that she was shot?'

Oswick looked slightly shamefaced. 'I haven't mentioned her. It seemed like a can of worms that I didn't want to open. I'm not at all sure Miss Bentall trusts me.'

'Don't worry about that. I doubt Bentall trusts her own parents. Go on, call the hospital while I get ready.'

He went upstairs to the bedroom that he and Lydia hadn't shared in recent days. The bed looked cold, sad and unused. Hurriedly, he washed, shaved and dressed in clean clothes, then went downstairs where Sylvia Keane was waiting with a steaming cup of tea.

'I thought you might need this, Professor.'

'You're a mind-reader, Mrs Keane. Thank you.'

Johnny jumped down from the table where he was eating toast and grabbed his father's legs as though he would never let them go. All Wilde could do was squat down and hug him properly.

'Where have you been, Daddy?'

'Working.'

'But why didn't I see you yesterday?'

'I got home late. But I saw you, Johnny, and I kissed you. And do you know what? Mummy will be home to see you very soon. Before you go to school.'

'If she's here, I don't want to go to school.'

'Well, that will be up to her. Anyway, darling, I've got to go out now because I'm meeting someone. Eat your toast up and be good for Mrs Keane. Yes?'

Johnny hesitated, then nodded. 'All right, Daddy.'

'Good boy.' He planted another kiss on his face and tousled his hair. Downing the tea in one, he joined Oswick in the hall. The student was just putting down the phone. 'Well?'

'She's not there. Apparently she left within hours of the wound being dressed. Just upped and walked out. What am I going to do, Professor?'

A car and driver were waiting for them and they both clambered into the back seat. They spoke in hushed voices; drivers weren't just drivers in the security service – they were ears.

'The hospital told me they shouldn't really be talking to me but that they had called the police. They had to, it seems, because Shirin's injury involved a bullet wound and it was possible a crime had been committed. There's been no sign of her.'

'I'm sorry. That's not good news. You're going to have to tell Freya Bentall the full story though. It won't do either of us any good to hold back now.'

CHAPTER 38

They were dropped off at the entrance to the hall. Lord Templeman's butler was waiting to greet them. Wilde could see that the loyal retainer was close to tears. 'I can't adequately express my sorrow, Rogers. Your master was a truly great man. He did this work for his country and for no other reason.'

'Indeed, sir.' Just two words, but the depth of emotion in the breaking voice was all too evident.

Wilde very much wanted to put his arms around the man, but he knew that the gesture would not be welcomed. Rogers came from a pre-war generation that eschewed displays of sentiment, considering it weakness.

They were taken indoors and were asked to wait in an anteroom. Miss Bentall would call for them when she was ready.

Freya Bentall had the acuity and somewhat severe manner of a top-class lawyer, which was hardly surprising considering she had been called to the Bar in her twenties after service with MI5 in the First World War. She was now in her late forties and, it was generally agreed, had had a good second war.

'This is a bad business, Mr Wilde,' she said when he entered the room alone. 'I am still unclear, though, what part you have been playing in the affair.'

No small talk. No reminiscences of the last time they met.

'I'll give you a full rundown,' he said. 'But first there is something you should know, something that my undergraduate Mr Oswick foolishly omitted to tell you.'

'Are you talking about his wife by any chance?'

'You knew about her then?'

'Shouldn't I have?'

'Dagger didn't – until I told him.'

'Well, fortunately I have his written notes. Contrary to what some people believed, Lord Templeman was not lax about such things.'

'What you might not know is that I inadvertently shot and wounded Mrs Shirin Oswick. We took her to Addenbrooke's Hospital, but after treatment, she vanished in the middle of the night. Apparently the police are looking for her.'

'You're right, I didn't know that. A breakdown in communications. Are you going to tell me why you shot the unfortunate lady?'

'Did Dagger's notes mention that she's a fascist?'

'Yes.'

'And you know also that her husband, Danny, was also an important member of the BUF until he had a Damascene conversion in Bergen-Belsen?'

'Yes, he told me. I am inclined to believe him, but I will reserve judgement for the moment. Anyway, to return to the shooting of Mrs Oswick.'

'After a discussion with Dagger Templeman, I had returned to Harbinger House the evening after the death of Larry Rhein. I saw the Oswicks there, deep in conversation and confronted them at gunpoint. A car came at me, possibly driven by the escaped POW, Kagerer, or perhaps a man who calls himself – falsely – Edmund Bacon. Oswick threw me to the ground and saved both our lives. The gun went off accidentally and Mrs Oswick was wounded in the left shoulder. We took her to hospital.'

'Thank you. I have information on Kagerer, but tell me what you know about this other man Bacon.'

The interrogation continued for a full hour. Wilde went through everything with complete honesty. Finally, Bentall asked him if he would like a coffee, and he said he would. While they were waiting for it to appear, her tone mellowed and became more conversational. 'You must be worried about your family, and with reason. I think we have to get them to a place of safety. When we're finished, I will send a car and bring them here. There is plenty of room and I have advised Rogers that I will do this. Latimer Hall will become a fortress until this matter is resolved.'

'Thank you. That seems a good idea.'

'And I want you to continue your work but reporting to me. Will you do that?'

'If you keep me in the loop.'

'Very well. I will tell you a few things you may not know. Firstly, the would-be assassin – Bacon, I imagine – killed two of our agents outside the St Ursula's hostel before attacking your wife and Miss March. They were damned fine men, two of our best. He did it with phenol, which I know was the poison that killed Crow and the farmer, Bagshawe, and was supposed to have done for your wife. Which begs the question: why was this rather obscure method used?'

'It's effective, quick, silent.'

'But it didn't work against Mrs Wilde, nor against you at Bagshawe's farm. Why not just shoot you?'

'I really can't find an answer to that.' He realised, however, that Freya Bentall had a point; why *did* they use phenol? There were elements to this affair – too many elements – that simply didn't add up.

'Let me tell you something else. We have discovered the real identity of the other body you found yesterday – the man you identified as Gram Lyngwood. His real name was Graham Stone. It was pure chance. One of my men recognised him from his time working undercover in the thirties. He was a fully paid-up member of the British Union of Fascists and during the war he was interned under Defence Regulation 18B.'

'That doesn't surprise me.'

'He had worked at Porton Down in the chemical warfare laboratory. Phosgene and mustard gas, that sort of thing.'

'But that's not what we are talking about . . . is it?'

'No, it's not. The biology department wasn't set up until the war. The thing is, though, he would have had expertise in the handling of sensitive lethal substances. It's no great leap to think of him working on pathogens – preparation or maintenance of BWs. Lyngwood – sorry, Stone – was dismissed from Porton Down in late 1938 when his political leanings were discovered. And as we both know, he was living near a US airbase, the relevance of which must be obvious to a child.'

'Delivery systems. We know that the Japanese dropped their pathogens from planes.'

'There are plenty of planes at Flowthorpe, Mr Wilde.'

'But there would have been tight security. Anyway, the place is plague-ridden now.'

'And so they'll have acquired an aircraft elsewhere, I imagine.'

That might not be difficult, he thought, given that there had never been so many planes scattered around the countryside. Wartime airfields would be decommissioned in due course, as would the planes, but for the moment there were still thousands of them – both British and American. The question was: which airfield would the conspirators use?

'We need to find Catesby. He's the key to this. Does he have a pilot? And just as importantly, what is the target?'

'Look, Mr Wilde,' Bentall said, 'would you wait outside for a few minutes. I have a couple of calls to make. I need to know how far we can go in alerting the public. This is a Cabinet-level decision.'

'Of course.' Wilde was certain that this would have to be kept under wraps; the prospect of panic in the face of a twentieth-century plague was something no government could counte-nance. He went back to the anteroom and nodded to Oswick, who had his nose in a book.

'Everything all right, Professor?'

'Not exactly. What are you reading?'

'This? I found it.'

'Is that Nietzsche – the book from the Skyme farm?'

'I'm sorry, I got bored waiting for Miss Bentall and her com-panion so I sat down and read it for a while. And then I just stuck it in my pocket.'

'Let me see.'

The Will to Power. Not a book Wilde had ever had any desire to read, but just the sort of thing Neville Catesby might like. He flicked through the pages. On the last, blank sheet, he saw a scratched note: '*Neville, a little light reading for you. It explains everything we both know. FB.*'

How come he hadn't seen this before, at the farm? Because he hadn't been looking, that's why. Anyway, people usually inscribed gift books at the beginning, not the end. He showed it to Oswick. 'Did you see this?'

'No. I hadn't got that far.'

'FB.'

'Dear God, Professor, you don't think . . .'

'What?'

'Miss Bentall.' He lowered his voice. 'Freya Bentall. FB.'

That was an insane thought. Wasn't it? Of course, Neville Catesby had extensive contacts, including the secret services, but Freya Bentall surely didn't share any of his values. She was incorruptible. She would not have had any cause to give Catesby this book.

'I'll hold on to this, Oswick.'

'As you wish, sir.'

A few moments later, the door opened and Freya Bentall summoned Wilde back into her office.

'We have to keep the lid on this by order of the Home Secretary.'

'What does that mean precisely?'

'I can't involve police forces. This is purely MI5 – and you. Nothing must alarm the public, especially not today of all days. It's Dalton's first Budget. They don't want to deflect from his headlines.'

He handed her the book. 'I thought you should see this, Miss Bentall.'

'What is it? We don't have time for games.'

'It was found at the farm near Skyme. Look inside the back cover.'

She sighed irritably, bent back the spine and read the message. Then she looked up and met Wilde's eyes. 'And naturally you thought of me.'

'Not for a moment. I thought of Frank Broussard.'

'And who might that be, pray?'

'US Air Force officer. Lieutenant-Colonel Frank Broussard, Flowthorpe airbase.'

CHAPTER 39

Even as he told Freya Bentall about Broussard, one thing became abundantly clear. He had suspected that someone within MI5 must have alerted Catesby to the fact that he was helping Templeman investigate the Flowthorpe attack and a possible connection to fascist groups. Not so. Frank Broussard must have been Catesby's informant. That was why Wilde had come under attack.

It was a crazy notion, but the more he considered the matter, the more certain he became that Broussard was the culprit. But who exactly *was* Frank Broussard, what was his background – and why was a USAF officer involved with a group of fascist terrorists?

'No delay, Mr Wilde. Take Oswick and two of my men and arrest him.' Freya Bentall spoke with the measured tones of a lawyer, but her anger and the urgency of the moment were clear. 'And do it with discretion.'

'How can I do that?'

'You're the Cambridge don, work it out, but I don't want any comeback from Washington, DC. By the way, your family will be here when you return and in the meantime I shall see what I can discover about Lieutenant Colonel Broussard. I sincerely hope you're right about this, otherwise the White House will not be best pleased with us.'

Security around Flowthorpe had been eased since Wilde's last visit. The British Army was still manning roadblocks at the two roads leading into the village and airbase, but the surrounding fields and woods were no longer patrolled. With no new cases reported in the past nine days it was believed the outbreak had been contained.

Bentall had called ahead and the soldiers at the checkpoint moved out of the way as the two cars – one with Wilde and Oswick, the other with the two MI5 men – drove into the village. Wilde looked at the field hospital tents and wondered about May Hinchley's condition. He prayed he would be able to give Lydia good news about her friend.

The airbase itself had not been informed of the impending arrival of Wilde and so the American checkpoint was less easy to pass. Wilde did not explain their mission to the eager young airman, merely said they needed to talk to Lieutenant Colonel Broussard. A call was put through to his office.

The airman shook his head. 'He's not here, sir. We believe he's off-base.'

'Did he leave information about his destination?'

'It doesn't seem so, Mr Wilde. But his second-in-command, Captain Williams, says he is happy to talk to you. Do you know the administration block?'

'Yes.'

'Then drive on through.'

Captain Williams was as much in the dark as the men on the checkpoint regarding Broussard's whereabouts. 'We were supposed to be having our regular Tuesday morning briefing, Mr Wilde, but he didn't turn up. I put a call through to his quarters, but there was no reply. May I ask why you want to see him? Perhaps I could help.'

'It's a security matter, regarding the recent incident here. That's all I can tell you, I'm afraid.'

'Of course. Message received and understood.'

'But if you have any idea where he might have gone,' Wilde said, 'it would be of great assistance to us. We need him urgently.'

'If I knew, I would of course tell you, but I honestly have no idea. It's a puzzle, Mr Wilde.'

'What have been his habits during his time here at Flowthorpe? Does he have any friends or interests off-base to your knowledge?'

'I don't have any information on that. I was posted here only last month and the lieutenant colonel and I have had few dealings outside military matters.'

'OK. Well. I'm going to leave the two plain-clothes officers here in case he turns up. Perhaps you could provide a room and coffee for them.'

'Of course. I shall see to that personally.'

Wilde moved towards the door, then turned back with a smile. 'He seems a fine man, your CO. I guess he's a pilot.'

'Indeed, bombers. Mostly B-17s. He flew thirty-five daytime missions over Germany. It's an honour to know him.'

'There's something you might not know, Professor,' Oswick said on the way back towards Cambridge.

'I'm sure there's plenty I don't know, but were you thinking of something in particular?' Wilde was distracted. He was having trouble believing Broussard was linked to Catesby. Yes, the book was signed 'FB', but there had to be a great many people with those initials. Then again, there was other circumstantial evidence, chief of which was the fact that there had been at least one biological warfare canister secreted close to his base. Also that someone must have informed Catesby that he, Wilde, was part of the investigation; an invitation to the shooting party had followed on closely from his visit here.

'I mean about Shirin, my wife. She's quite a capable pilot.'

Wilde's brain switched back to the present. 'What did you say?'

'I said Shirin flies planes.'

Her special skill. At that first meeting, when they sneaked out of the New Realm Patriots rally and retired to the bar, she had boasted to Wilde about her special skill and when he asked what it was, she had said, enigmatically, that he might find out one day.

Today, he had found out. Flying planes was her special skill. Dropping biological bombs, perhaps.

'Tell me more.'

'Well, that's just it. She learnt to fly way back in the early thirties. It's just something I hadn't thought to mention before. Talking to the captain about Broussard's flying exploits brought it to mind.'

Wilde, who was at the wheel, stopped the car and turned to Oswick. 'Has she been flying recently?'

'Well, yes, I think she has. She says she likes to keep her hand in, but I know she just loves being up there in the blue yonder. Often goes off on her own saying she's going to cadge a plane.'

'You don't have your own airplane?'

'No, of course not. We don't have that sort of money. But she has always been able to find people who will lend theirs. My wife can be remarkably charming when she sets her mind to it, and as you've seen for yourself, she's a very attractive woman. Many people remember her from her stage days.'

'People like Catesby?'

'Yes, people like him – but I don't know if he has a plane.'

Wilde was pretty sure that Neville Catesby would have the wherewithal to acquire any plane he chose. The question now was where did he keep it?

'When your wife goes flying, which airfield does she use?'

The two men had eaten a sparse breakfast of fatty bacon, toast and sweet tea, and now they were back in their shared hotel room. It was a middling sort of establishment between St Pancras and Regent's Park in north London. Not luxurious, simply clean and anonymous. They had had an uncomfortable night in single beds and now it was time to take their leave of each other.

'This is for the Führer and the German people,' Sigmund Rascher said, thrusting out his arm in a Hitler salute.

Paul Kagerer flapped his hand without conviction and grunted something unintelligible. For most of his life he had been a criminal and he had never had a great deal of time for the German people as such. It was German police who caught him for robbery and rape, German lawyers who prosecuted him, German judges who jailed him, and German warders who beat him and kept him confined in solitary.

Still, he liked Hitler and Reichsführer-SS Himmler, for they had decreed his release to join the Dirlewanger SS Brigade. Along with Oskar Dirlewanger and some of their comrades-in-arms, including Georg Sosinka, the two Nazi leaders were the only Germans for whom he had any time. He certainly didn't like this so-called Dr Bacon who, despite his command of English, was clearly as German as he was.

'What is your real name, Herr Bacon?' he asked him. 'Before we part I should at least know that.'

'Better you don't.'

Oh well, it didn't matter. He'd never see the man again after today. As to this task, Kagerer knew he was not expected to survive, but he would. He had no intention of dying here in this grim smoke-filled city. It had been much the same with Dirlewanger's SS outfit, almost all of them freed criminals. No one had expected or indeed wanted any of them to survive, but they had slaughtered their way across Warsaw, Byelorussia, Hungary and other parts of Eastern Europe and he had come out of that alive, as had Georg. What had become of him? Was he alive or dead? How ridiculous to survive the Eastern Front and then get shot by some insignificant college professor in a remote British farmhouse.

Today, Paul Kagerer would carry out his task to the letter, then disappear. All he had been told was that the weapon in the bag he was given contained germs, but he had a good idea what it was because he had seen the corpse of the man at the farm, Gram Lyngwood. He had seen a great many bodies in his time, but that was probably the most unpleasant.

And so, when he activated the contents, he would move fast and would be out of this town into the fresh air of the countryside where he would collect the final instalment of his fee. From there, he had already worked out his escape route and had booked a cheap ticket aboard a cargo ship from Tilbury Docks.

He would stay alive whatever the cost, to drink large quantities of schnapps and consort with many whores. There had been plenty of women in the East, some willing to do his bidding for a cigarette, others not so easy to persuade, but they all succumbed one way or another. America would be the place for him. He had heard that any man could disappear in that vast land, and the money he had been offered, five thousand dollars along with a forged passport, would set him up. Money talked in the States and no one would ever know his past life.

Stepping out on to the street with his case, his homburg caught a gust of wind and flew away, revealing the scars that criss-crossed his brow. He chased after the hat, caught it, dusted it down and replaced it on his head.

Sigmund Rascher's nose was red and broken. It still throbbed from the punch delivered by the woman in the hostel. In his own mind, he was a man of taste and discernment. He loathed having to consort with lower-class criminal elements like Paul Kagerer and the other one, Georg Sosinka, but he had to follow orders, as he had always done. If Sir Neville Catesby said that these savages were essential to the operation, then who was he to argue? Catesby was a leader of men, a person you could look up to and admire, every centimetre a führer.

Rascher had always known that he, too, was destined for great things. His elegant British grandmother Frances had ensured he was fluent in her native tongue. 'A civilised man must be conversant in the ways of the greatest empire builders the world has ever known,' she insisted as she put him through his paces. His mother had wanted him to be a concert pianist, but he wanted to be a physician like his father, only more distinguished. Surely, his remarkable work on aviation science at the Dachau KZ had secured his place in the annals of medicine.

It was not just his expertise as a researcher that had helped him reach such a pre-eminent position in the Third Reich, there were his connections, too.

In his working life, he had done his best to cultivate the coming men. Heinrich Himmler had been the greatest catch and that was thanks to his wife's friendship – some said relationship – with the great Reichsführer.

And then there was Sir Neville Catesby. Without his assistance, he would be just another war refugee – or perhaps fugitive. Catesby had promised him that he would find a place in England. He would provide the money to fund an exclusive practice in Harley Street and, as Dr Edmund Bacon, he would make a fortune diagnosing cancer with copper chloride and treating it with a secret plant extract.

When the new regime came into being, he would be entrusted with a high office of state.

And yes, he knew exactly what he was commissioned to do this day and he would carry out his mission with pleasure; death held no mysteries for Dr Sigmund Rascher.

As he limped out into the street, having injured his knee in the unsatisfactory tussle with the two young women, he sincerely hoped that they would be among his victims.

Wilde's first task back at Latimer Hall was to spend ten minutes with Lydia and Johnny, half of which was occupied in long hugs. 'Was Doris all right with you staying?'

'To be honest, I think she was glad of the company. She likes to be useful. But she is awfully strange with Mrs Keane. They really don't seem to have hit it off, which surprises me, because she really is very good with Johnny and you find her charming, don't you?'

'I thought so when I met her.'

'Sounds like you're having doubts.'

'Just Doris's misgivings, that's all. Anyway, how did you sleep?'

'I didn't. I stayed awake with my hand an inch from the gun. Will this all be over soon, Tom? I'm not sure I can take much more.'

He shrugged, because he couldn't lie to her. 'All we can do is hope.' He hugged them again and made his way to Freya Bentall's office. She received him alone.

'So you haven't got Broussard,' she said. 'I suspect that at least half confirms our suspicions. Where do we think he's gone?'

'To Catesby, wherever that might be. Or an airfield.'

'I've found out a bit more about Frank Broussard. He slipped through the net back home.'

'And I have discovered from Oswick something that he really should have mentioned before – his wife is a trained pilot.'

'That's extremely interesting.'

'Whether she can fly with a wounded shoulder is another matter. But they still have Broussard. Apparently he flew bombers, a fact I don't much like.'

'In which case,' Bentall said, 'they would have at least two pilots. But maybe there are more. The plan is to drop these damn things from the sky, like the Japanese did in China.'

'Almost certainly,' he said. 'But I doubt there are more pilots. This conspiracy has been kept tight and compact.'

'So what now? What are they planning? Where do we go from here?'

'Oswick told me that Shirin sometimes frequented a small airfield at Pasterton a few miles to the east of Cambridge. I thought I'd go and take a look.'

'Yes, do that. You've nothing to lose. By the way, it was a pleasure to meet your delightful wife. God alone knows what she sees in you, Mr Wilde.'

'You'll have to ask her.'

'As to that other woman, Mrs Keane, there's something not quite right about her. Something doesn't add up.'

'Are you serious?'

'I'm almost always serious, Mr Wilde. Didn't you know that about me?'

'Did Mrs Keane say something to you?'

'It's what she didn't say. Most lies are the unspoken ones. You'll learn that one day.'

For the moment, there were more pressing matters. Something had been itching away at the back of his mind for over an hour. Something Freya Bentall had mentioned in passing before he went to Flowthorpe. Only now, face to face with her again, did the words register.

'I've just had a thought . . . it's not good.'

'Yes?'

'Something you said . . . you mentioned that it's Budget Day.'

'Well, yes, it is. Dalton's first.'

Budget Day.

She had said that the government didn't want anything to distract the country from Hugh Dalton's big day – his first Budget. Today was the new Labour chancellor's post-war financial statement, the event that was designed to set the path for Britain's economic recovery from the devastation of the past six years.

'I think I see where you're going with this, Mr Wilde.'

The House of Commons would be packed and the whole government and opposition would be there. Attlee and Churchill, Bevan and Bevin, Eden and Butler, and all the other great men and women who had led the country through war.

Not only MPs, but the lords, and senior members of the press would be in Parliament today, almost certainly the governor of the Bank of England too. And all within a stone's throw of Buckingham Palace and Whitehall – Downing Street, the major offices of state. Almost the whole British Establishment in one place at one time.

What better time or place for an enemy to rain down death and havoc? Wilde looked at his watch. It was 10.20 a.m.

'Dear God.' Freya Bentall's face had fallen.

'When does it start?'

'About 3 p.m.'

'We have less than five hours.'

There was no point in Wilde and Oswick staying together. If the target was Westminster, then it made sense for one of them to be there.

Oswick was the obvious choice. If they were wrong about the likelihood of this being an attack from the air, then Oswick would be the one who could recognise all the players at ground level. He knew these people, had been considered one of them.

'I'm going with him,' Freya Bentall said. 'I have to be in London.'

Wilde nodded. He was pretty sure she still harboured doubts about Oswick and wanted to keep her eye on him. It was in her nature to never take chances.

Wilde headed east on his own. Finding the plane or planes was clearly the imperative task. Half an hour later, he pulled into a large clearing and took in the scope of Pasterton Airfield. It was little more than a broad flat meadow with a couple of huts, the sort of place used by amateur fliers, certainly nowhere near as sophisticated or well equipped as a military aerodrome. The runway was grass.

There was a small tarmac area near the huts, where a mechanic in overalls was doing some work on a plane, but the remaining half-dozen privately owned light aircraft were dispersed around a wide area – the continuation of wartime practice designed to limit damage if the enemy bombed the place.

Knocking at the doors of both huts, Wilde got no reply, so he let himself in and looked around. No one there.

He walked around to the single-engined biplane being worked on and hailed the mechanic, who had his nose down examining the engine compartment. 'Can I talk to you a moment, please?'

The mechanic grunted, then climbed down, wrench in hand. 'Yes?' he said without enthusiasm.

'I'm looking for Mrs Oswick, Shirin Oswick – or Tombs. Do you know her?'

'Well, I used to know Shirin Tombs. Is she married now? But you're out of luck. Look around, mate, I'm the only one here.'

'She flies here a lot, I believe.'

He laughed. 'Oh, that was before the war. She was always begging a joyride, that one.'

'Is that your plane you're working on?'

'Well, I wouldn't work on anyone else's. Why?'

'Just wondered whether Shirin ever flew her?'

'My lovely Tiger Moth? God no, wouldn't let the cow near it.' He laughed again. 'Sorry, that's a bit unfair. She may be a scrounger, but she's a good flier. Actually, she did come around three or four weeks back, asking me if the old girl was airworthy yet and begging some flying time. Said she had some sort of privileged access to fuel, which is always welcome, but I gave her the bum's rush. Don't know if anyone else said yes. Problem is most of the amateur boys around the country can't get their planes up at all. And a lot more of them died in Hurricanes and Lancasters in the bloody war.'

The man's voice broke and for a moment it seemed that he would weep.

'I'm sorry to intrude,' Wilde said. 'I can see how much it means to you.'

He shook his head as though dispensing with the emotion. 'Of course I joined the RAF – we all did, everyone with any flying experience – but I was too long in the tooth for combat duties, apparently. They put me down as a trainer, but you never had long enough with the poor bastards. As soon as they had had a few hours, they were sent off to fight. All you wanted to do was help them survive. Every one that died, I blamed myself.'

'I understand. Believe me.'

The man wiped away a tear. 'God, you've really got me going, mister. You a Yank?'

'Yes.'

'Well, thanks for coming to help us.'

'I was already in England.'

'Anyway, you didn't come here to talk about the war. You wanted to know about Shirin Tombs.'

'Does she use any other airfields.'

'Pretty sure she turned up at Swannell now and then in the old days. Little bit south of here in Suffolk. Why, what's this about? You a bailiff chasing her for a debt or somesuch?'

'Nothing so interesting, I'm afraid.'

'Well, good luck, mate. But I doubt she'll be flying today. Feel that bloody wind, eh.'

CHAPTER 40

Danny Oswick had faced enemy fire during the eastward drive from Normandy into Germany, but never had he felt this taut and despairing. War was an impersonal construct. You didn't know the man you were shooting at and he didn't know you. But this was different – he knew the enemy all too well, and one of them was a mentor who at one time had seemed like a father to him, the other his own wife.

He had known for months that Catesby had to be brought down, but he had hoped to save Shirin by bringing her around to his way of thinking. If only she would listen.

That had not been possible. He had never understood quite how committed she was to the cause of fascism and, indeed, to Catesby himself. Perhaps he should have known. After all, it was her fervour that had drawn him into the BUF in the first place. Since resigning his commission and returning to their small home in Cambridge, he had tried on many occasions to change her mind with gentle persuasion, but she had just grown angry, telling him he was betraying everything they had stood for and flatly refusing to move her position an inch.

Even now, when the world was learning the brutal truth about the Hitler regime, particularly the death camps and slaughter squads in Poland and beyond . . . even now she could not be dissuaded.

The MI5 operative driving them to London was motoring at top speed and didn't converse. His name was Greenstreet and he was a powerful-looking man who reminded Oswick of some of the barrel-chested men who used their fists and cudgels for the BUF when the socialists came calling on their meetings.

Oswick sat in the back with Freya Bentall and they talked the whole way. In fact, it was Oswick who did the talking and Bentall who asked the questions. He told her his life story, from Sandringham to his father's suicide, to the East End of London and the flirtation with various political factions until Shirin and Mosley and Catesby changed everything.

And then Belsen, which changed everything again, turning all his beliefs to dust.

'And what do you want next in your life, Danny?'

He wasn't stupid; he knew she was calling him by his first name and making small talk about his life to put him at ease and thus vulnerable to slips, but he didn't really care because he understood why she should mistrust him. Anyway, there were no slips to be made once you told the truth. He shrugged. 'I suppose it's out of the question now but if it was possible I'd like to stay at Cambridge and do my history degree.'

'And your chosen period?'

'Well, I love the sixteenth century, but there's a lot to be said for the thirties.'

'Does that count as history, or current affairs?'

'History. Ancient history, I hope.'

The car was close to the heart of London. What, he wondered, was he supposed to do when they arrived at MI5 headquarters or wherever else they were going? Give descriptions of those he knew, such as Dr Bacon and the German SS man, he supposed. But what then?

Even as these thoughts swirled around his head, he gazed out of the window at the city he had once called home. There were holes where bombs had removed houses and other buildings, but compared to the pictures he had seen of Berlin, perhaps Londoners had not had it quite so bad.

Just after they had traversed the Marylebone Road, he saw him. At first he thought his eyes must be deceiving him, but no, the man limping along Devonshire Place southwards was Dr Edmund Bacon.

Oswick reached out and gripped Bentall's arm. 'That's him,' he said.

She looked at the hand on her arm with surprise. 'What's that, Danny?'

'That's Bacon – Edmund Bacon. Him over there carrying the large bag, limping.'

'Are you serious?'

'Never more so.'

'Then we'll play it nice and easy. Don't want any accidents. Has he seen you?'

'No, I'm sure not.'

She tapped the driver on the shoulder. 'Greenstreet, did you hear that?'

'Yes, ma'am.'

'Slow down and get behind him, about ten or twenty yards. Stop the car quietly and you and I will get out. Give me your pistol. He's not moving fast. You will pinion him from behind and you will not allow the bag to fall, do you understand?'

'Yes, ma'am.' He handed the gun back across the seat to Bentall.

'And me?' Oswick said.

'You stay in the car until we've overpowered him. Don't make a sound. Greenstreet will get in the back with him and you will sit alongside me in the front. There is a very good chance that the contents of the bag are both fragile and lethal, so I want no alarms or excursions. Are we all clear on that?'

Latimer Hall had a sombre air. As a widower, Lord Templeman had lived alone here with his servants, messengers and secretary. He always preferred to be here than at MI5's London offices, which had tended to change location from time to time in recent years. He ensured he had good secure telephone lines and he had two drivers who could take messages by hand to and from London or elsewhere when required.

His only living blood relative was his pregnant daughter, Samantha, who arrived by midday from Oxford. She was alone because her husband was away on military duty in the Far East.

Once in Latimer Hall, there was little for her to do but accept condolences from the staff, particularly Rogers, the butler, who seemed to have been with her father forever. They shed a tear together but that was the furthest they would go in casting off the formal mistress–servant convention.

'I can promise you, Rogers, that this house will not be sold by me and that your job and that of the other servants is secure. My husband and I and our child will almost certainly move here, for I have always loved this house.'

'Thank you, ma'am. Perhaps I may be permitted to pass on that reassurance to the staff.'

'Indeed.'

'I have to tell you, ma'am, that we have some guests, brought here on the orders of Miss Bentall. I believe they are in some danger, possibly as a result of the matter that your late father was investigating. I have put them in the sitting room.'

'Then perhaps you would introduce me to these visitors.'

Lydia was in the sitting room with Miranda March, the Keanes and Johnny. Sylvia Keane had asked whether she might be permitted to know what was going on, because this sudden move to another house was alarming to say the least and Mr Wilde had not been terribly forthcoming.

'I think you know that my husband was an intelligence officer until very recently, Mrs Keane. I'm afraid it's come back to bite him. Beyond that, I'm really not in a position to comment, I'm afraid.'

Mrs Keane was not happy with the reply, but there was little she could say.

They were silent for a while. A footman brought them tea and biscuits. Lydia became lost in conversation with Miranda, talking about St Ursula's and what the reaction would be to their absence. But as they talked, she was aware that Mrs Keane was looking at her strangely and decided that she must be feeling left out. It was only polite that they should change the subject and draw her into the conversation.

But there was something else going on. It wasn't simply that Sylvia Keane felt excluded, or that she was feeling the tension of events beyond her control, but something seemed to have changed in her. That initial warmth that had drawn Lydia to the woman and made her seem the ideal person to look after the house had been curiously absent all morning. There was a distance about her, a tension not seen before.

Lydia fixed her best smile. 'I do understand how dreadfully hard this must all be for you, Mrs Keane. I suppose I'm more used to it, but I imagine it brings back painful memories.'

'You know nothing about me or my memories, Mrs Wilde.'

The words were so sharp, so out of keeping and spoken so coldly that they rocked Lydia to the core. For a moment she simply didn't know what to say, turned to Miranda whose eyes were wide in disbelief, then back to the housekeeper. 'I'm sorry, Mrs Keane, have I said something to offend you?'

Before any answer could come, the door opened and a tall and rather beautiful young woman entered the room with the butler, who introduced her to the two women and their children as Lord Templeman's daughter, the Honourable Mrs Samantha Chambers.

Lydia felt as though she should curtsey, but she merely shook hands with the woman, offered her condolences and noticed that she was clearly in the latter stages of pregnancy.

'Eight months, Mrs Wilde,' the woman said, noticing Lydia's eyes on her belly. 'The thought that Daddy will never see his grandchild is quite simply unbearable.'

'I'm sorry. He was a wonderful man, a great friend to my husband, Tom.'

But even as she uttered the ritual words and spoke yet more fondly of Dagger Templeman, her thoughts were elsewhere.

What had she done to upset Sylvia Keane? And then her thoughts went further: did she really want this woman alone in the house with her son?

Swannell Airfield was larger than Pasterton, with a couple of dozen planes parked. But Wilde couldn't see any human life. There was a large administration block but it was locked. This was hopeless. Somewhere there had to be a plane or planes which Shirin Oswick and Frank Broussard would fly to London to drop their deadly load.

He got back in the car and drove westward. His last option was simply to go back to Harbinger House. The likelihood of Catesby or any of the others being there was slender in the extreme, but perhaps there were clues to be found – something the police or security services had missed. It was, after all, a vast estate.

Parking in front of the old house, he saw that the windows were shuttered and no other vehicles were in evidence. He got out of the car, the Browning Hi-Power in his right hand, and walked around the outside of the house, past the orangery where a few days ago the champagne had flowed while a string quartet had played Beethoven and academics mingled and gossiped with politicians, writers and artists.

The dazzling lights were dead. The whole place was cold and deserted and it seemed impossible to think that it had so recently been full of life and laughter.

But Wilde wasn't done. This was an estate of more than three thousand acres, much of it arable, but also pasture and woodland. Who knew what might lie in the distant parts he had not seen and which he doubted the police had searched with any thoroughness?

All he could be certain about was that Catesby and his co-conspirators were somewhere and time was running out.

Freya Bentall had never resorted to physical violence in her interrogations, though there had been moments when she had been pretty sure it would be effective.

Today was different. She was in a room on the second floor of MI5's new headquarters, Leconfield House in Curzon Street, Mayfair. The offices made an interesting change from Wormwood Scrubs prison where they had been based for much of the war and there was still an air of impermanence about the place. Files lay around in boxes waiting to be transferred into cabinets, secretaries and telephonists struggled to make sense of the new exchange.

Here in this room, there were just the three of them: the man Oswick knew as Edmund Bacon, Greenstreet and herself. Oswick was being interrogated elsewhere in the building in case any clues could be discovered that she had missed.

Meanwhile, Bacon's heavy bag and its contents had been sent off for analysis at Porton Down. All Bentall knew was that it contained three ceramic ovoids, a little like bombs, but pointed at both ends. They bore Japanese characters, almost certainly like the one that had been found at Flowthorpe. The bag contained one other thing – a gas mask.

'Bacon's not your real name. What is it?'

'I have nothing to say to you.'

'Do I detect a slight accent? Are you German?'

'That is for you to determine.'

'Where were you going to detonate your device, Mr Bacon?'

'I have nothing to say to you.'

Freya Bentall nodded to Greenstreet. He looked surprised, probably because of her reputation for non-violence. His eyes questioned her and she nodded again.

Greenstreet was standing at Bacon's side. His right arm drew back and smacked the man's temple with vicious force, knocking the German and his chair to the floor.

'Pick him up, Mr Greenstreet.'

The MI5 agent pulled the wooden chair upright, grabbed Bacon under the arms and dumped him back where he had been before.

Bacon hadn't even cried out. The blow had stunned him and his head was lolling. His eyes were closed but his mouth was open and limp.

'Let's try again shall we, Mr Bacon. I don't like doing this any more than you, but I'm afraid we simply don't have time for subtleties today. I can promise you, however, that this will get worse before it gets better. So save yourself a great deal of distress and tell me, what is your real name?'

He was blinking now, and grimacing from the delayed onset of pain. 'Rascher . . .'

'Just that? Rascher?'

'Herr Doktor Sigmund Rascher.'

'A real doctor? Well, well. And you're German, yes?'

He nodded.

'And you have to date murdered at least four people by injecting them with phenol.'

Once again he didn't answer.

She let it go. What mattered came next. 'And so to the third question ... where were you going to detonate your biological device.'

'Your Houses of Parliament.'

'Inside or outside?'

'I don't know. As close as I could get. If we can get inside, we will do so.'

'We?'

'I.'

'You said "we". How many of you are there?'

'Just me.'

She nodded to Greenstreet, who immediately gripped Rascher's throat, lifted him up, choked him for half a minute and threw him across the room. The German landed in a heap and clutched his elbow, groaning.

'This is going to get bad, Herr Doktor,' Bentall said as Greenstreet picked him up and put him back on his chair. 'Very, very bad. Now, how many of you?'

'Two. Me and Kagerer. Paul Kagerer.'

She recognised the name from Templeman's notes and had heard it from Oswick, who had given her a description of the man. Kagerer was one of two who had absconded from the POW camp in Epsom; the other was presently in custody having refused to talk; perhaps he, too, should have been given to Greenstreet to apply a little persuasive pressure. 'And how were you going to get access to Parliament.'

'We hoped to just walk in. If we were turned away then we would simply detonate the canisters in Parliament Square. We were told that either way would have been effective.'

'Where is Kagerer now?'

He knew what was coming. 'Please, I beg you – I don't know. We were to make our own ways so that if one was caught, the other would still get through.'

Greenstreet drew back his fist and Rascher recoiled from the anticipated blow. Bentall shook her head and put up her palm to hold her colleague in check.

'Describe him.'

'He is lean but strong. He has scarring on his forehead. When last I saw him he was wearing a homburg hat.'

'And you, how did you hope to get out of this alive. You know what happened to the man at Flowthorpe, Graham Stone, don't you? Did you think the gas mask would protect you?'

'Of course. That was my hope.'

'And what exactly is in the two canisters in your bag?'

'Pathogens. That's all I know.'

'Plague? Malaria? Anthrax? Cholera?'

He shrugged. 'If I knew exactly I would tell you. All I know is that there are different pathogens in each canister. I was told there was to be a cocktail.'

'Who told you that?'

He hesitated only momentarily. 'Catesby. Sir Neville Catesby.'

'Why would there be a cocktail?'

'To make it more deadly. The plan is to kill everyone.'

CHAPTER 41

Wilde heard the drone of an engine before he saw the aircraft. Having trudged for an hour without seeing a soul, he had passed along a tangled path through a dense wood at the heart of the great estate – and a long way from the field where they had shot pheasant. Now, as he stopped at the edge, where daylight dappled through the golden autumn leaves, his eyes fell on a pair of single-engined fighter planes.

He recognised their distinctive shape immediately. They weren't simply fighters, they were dive-bombers – the notorious Stuka JU87A, made by Junkers. Even before the start of the world war, these shrieking harpies had rained down terror on the people of Spain in steep predatory swoops, releasing their bomb loads at the very last moment for maximum accuracy.

These ones still bore Luftwaffe and Condor Legion markings and they were standing at the end of a runway in a large clearing, concealed on all sides by woodland. The pilot was already in the closest one and Wilde knew instantly that it was Frank Broussard, even with his flying helmet and goggles. Lieutenant Colonel Broussard of the United States Air Force.

So he really was part of this. An American traitor about to take off in a Nazi dive-bomber as part of a band of Nazi insurrectionists. Every country had its share of fascists, and Broussard must surely have been part of the German-American Bund, but how had his involvement not been spotted? How had he not been weeded out before reaching such a senior position in the American armed forces? Not for the first time, Wilde reflected on the inadvisableness of shutting down the OSS. America had its FBI, but it needed more than that in this complex twentieth-century world.

And then he spotted a second person. Someone was underneath the further of the two planes, making a final adjustment to a large bomb attached to the fuselage.

Not just 'someone': Shirin Oswick.

Like Broussard, she was wearing flying gear, and her wounded arm was in a sling. Her peroxide hair was hidden beneath a flying helmet, goggles perched on her forehead.

The propellers of both planes were turning. Ready to be gunned up for take-off. Wilde pulled the Browning Hi-Power from beneath his jacket. As he did so, his left sleeve fell back revealing his wristwatch. It was 3.18 p.m.

The Right Honourable Hugh Dalton, MP, Chancellor of the Exchequer, rose at precisely 3.18 p.m. and the packed House fell silent. This was important. Britain's economy had been wrecked by the war, and the population, sick of privation and rationing, was depending on Dalton to wave a magic wand and produce the recovery that Labour had promised in the general election. Everyone knew the Budget would not be easy and that Dalton would be on his feet for the best part of two hours delivering it.

He began by explaining how difficult his task had been made, but how necessary.

'In the war years, menaced as we were by the most powerful and brutal enemy that this country has ever had to face in all her long history, all sections of the nation played their full part.

'The burdens borne by the general body of the taxpayers were light indeed compared with burdens of another sort which fell, in battle and in blitz, upon our fighting men on all fronts, by land and sea and air, upon our merchant seamen and upon great numbers of civilians in this country. Yet measured by the standards of pre-war taxation these burdens of wartime taxation were indeed heavy, and they were most patiently and most patriotically borne by all.'

He paused momentarily so that all might reflect on the sacrifices he described.

'Now, as we turn the first page of a new chapter,' he continued, 'there is a most widespread and natural desire for tax reduction. There is likewise a desire for increased expenditure upon the social services – upon housing, health and education and many other social objects. Over the years immediately ahead, within the five-year lifetime of this Parliament, I hope we shall be able to go far to satisfy both these desires.'

Words of hope declaimed to a people hungry for peace and an improved standard of living. The House murmured its approval.

Sixty miles away, Wilde was weighing up his options. He guessed that the chancellor would already be delivering his Budget speech. If these two-seater planes were to take off now they would be over Westminster within a little over half an hour. Broussard and Shirin the pilots, both of them seasoned fliers.

Once airborne, he guessed it would not be safe to shoot them down for fear of breaching the pathogen bombs and releasing their contents across a wide area.

This had to be dealt with now, *before* take-off.

He scanned the area, looking for the others. Where was Catesby? Where were his servants? What of Kagerer and Bacon? A chill wind whipped across the open meadow, carrying the thunderous roar of the engine in all directions.

There really wasn't any time to think. He pulled back the slide on the Browning to slip a round into the breech, then loped towards them with the pistol held out in front, at head height, in both hands. They were turning towards him, suddenly aware of his presence. He loosed off a warning shot, a sharp crack into the howl of the engine and the wind, and instantly recognised that this was no time for warnings.

First, he had to stop the closest Stuka, the one with Broussard at the controls. He needed to kill it, prevent it flying and yet protect the bomb beneath the fuselage. It could do serious harm here if punctured.

He ranged the Hi-Power at the fuselage, just behind the engine, and fired off five shots in quick succession, each one a foot or two back from the one before. His intention was to puncture the fuel tank and the fifth one hit home.

The idea was to drain the tank, but instead it exploded. A monstrous bloom of yellow and white flame shot out in all directions.

Wilde was knocked backwards by the blast. The gun flew from his hand.

Within moments, Broussard's plane was a raging conflagration. He was being incinerated alive.

Wilde was on his back but raised his head. Through the flames he saw the shadowy figure of Shirin trying to climb into the cockpit of the second Stuka. It was clearly a struggle for her with just one arm in use and she looked groggy from the effects of the blast.

He struggled to get up but he was half stunned and fell backwards, trying to make sense of the erratic movements of Shirin Oswick. As if in a dream, he realised she was abandoning her efforts to get into the remaining plane and was moving in his vague direction.

Wilde shook himself and raised himself onto his elbows again and somewhere in the fog of his brain he realised she was inching towards his pistol.

Dazed though he was, he understood the threat and tried to dive sideways to retrieve the weapon. But she was already there; she already had it in her good hand. He reached up and tried to grab it from her, but she was stumbling backwards, trying to gain some sort of stability, which was almost impossible with the left shoulder in a sling and suffering intense pain from a bullet wound. She was shaking violently, but her finger was on the trigger.

'Give me the gun,' he said. 'It's over.'

She somehow managed to get off one shot, but even at close range it flew past him. Shirin fell backwards with the recoil and screamed as her shoulder hit the ground. As she pressed her right elbow into the ground to gain purchase, she almost lost her grip on the pistol butt.

Wilde lunged forward to wrest the gun from her, but she wasn't done for and somehow now she was back on her feet. Behind them, the flames and smoke of the burning Stuka obscured the sky and the stench of burning petroleum filled the air. The conflagration leapt and danced in the high wind. He was being scorched by the intensity of the heat, but for the moment he was more worried about the woman and the pistol.

She stepped forward, holding the weapon to his forehead, a sickly sweet smile on her lips. 'Do you think this is it?' she said. 'Blowing up one plane? Do you think that's all there is? You're already too late.'

For a few moments she stood there, exulting in her triumph and the imminence of her enemy's death. A woman with badly dyed peroxide hair wearing a man's blue overalls, the legs rolled up and tied with string. What a way to go.

He kept his eyes open, waiting for death. At his side he saw that the flames from Broussard's Stuka had jumped the space to hers, which was now also on fire.

Suddenly, her head and gun hand lurched sideways. She was looking at him with a question in her eye, and then he heard the distant shot above the crackling of the flames and she crumpled to her knees and fell forward on top of him. Blood was seeping out of the side of her head where a bullet had entered and exploded. For a moment what was left of her head was on his shoulder, then it fell away to the ground.

He didn't need to check her pulse to know she was dead.

Wilde looked across to the woods and was sure he saw a puff of smoke from the dark tip of a sniper's rifle. Or was he imagining it? He dived to the ground behind the dead woman, using her body as cover, because there would be more shots; he, not Shirin Oswick, was the real target and the sniper would fire again.

Slowly, remaining flat, he wrenched the pistol from the woman's dead hand. He fired shots at the petrol tank of her plane and again there was a roar of igniting fuel, then he ranged the gun in front of him and snaked his way back in the direction of the woods whence he had come. He loosed two speculative shots towards the sniper's rifle, but if it really had been where he thought, it had now gone. He expected to hear the crack of the rifle again, but there was nothing. Just the hot whooshing of the blaze in the wind.

CHAPTER 42

Paul Kagerer had been following the man known as Dr Edmund Bacon at a distance of a hundred yards. They had been ordered to take different routes to Westminster to lessen the risk of both of them being spotted and caught, but Kagerer was damned if he was going to do that; he wanted to know exactly what Bacon was doing, for he did not trust him in the slightest degree.

And then he saw the car stop and the man and woman emerge. The woman was holding a gun and together they easily overpowered the doctor and removed his bag from him with great care as though they were fully aware what it contained and the danger it posed.

Kagerer crossed the road, so that he could watch the event unfold. The arrest was made without drama. A few passers-by stopped and watched the tussle, but then shrugged their shoulders and walked on.

Interestingly, a third person – another man – had stayed in the car. As he drew level on the far side of the road, Kagerer pulled his homburg hat down over his brow and peered into the vehicle. It was Catesby's young friend Oswick, the husband of his blonde mistress. It was right not to trust these people.

Trust your beautiful gun, Oskar Dirlewanger had always said. She is your best friend, your *only* friend, your bride.

Clutching his bag tighter, he had turned his head away, concerned that the young cuckold would turn and spot him, though that was unlikely. Oswick's eyes were fixed on the arrest of Dr Bacon. It was clear to him that he had made the correct decision when he chose to follow Bacon. Now he knew he was alone and that required a slight change of plan.

The chancellor was half an hour into his speech when Wilde found a telephone box. He had no idea whether the inferno destroying the two Stukas had also incinerated the bacteria in the bombs or whether it had simply been released into the air to spread a plague or another disease around Cambridgeshire and beyond.

Would these high winds carry it far and wide, causing more sickness and death, or would it be safely dispersed in the air? He wished he could answer this question, but he had done all he could.

It took a couple of minutes to get through to Freya Bentall at Leconfield House.

'Have you found something, Mr Wilde?'

He told her what had happened and where.

'I'll have a team there within the hour, including men from Porton Down. Good work. Are there other planes?'

'They were the only two pilots we know about, so almost certainly not. I didn't have time to look further.'

'I understand. Anyway, we've found our friend with the phenol, the so-called Dr Edmund Bacon. Real name Sigmund Rascher.'

'I'm sure I've heard that name somewhere.'

'He was at Dachau experimenting on prisoners, torturing them and killing them in the process. He covered his escape with misinformation that he had been executed by the SS. I'll tell you more when I see you. For the moment, the minutes are ticking by and we're busy looking for a second man – Paul Kagerer, one of the two SS men who escaped from Epsom. We have a good description of him from Rascher and Danny Oswick.'

'I wish I could help – I can't get down in time.'

'I don't want you down here. I want you to pick up Catesby. I have just been told that he's got another house not far from you, to the south-east of Bedford. One of our researchers found it in the Land Registry. I don't think your MI6 chum Eaton could have looked very hard. It's the delightfully named Sandalshoon Pastures at the village of Sandalshoon. It's marked down as a farmhouse with eight hundred acres.'

'I'll find it.'

After consulting the map stowed in his car, he drove fast. The journey took three-quarters of an hour along winding country roads.

Sandalshoon was a perfect English village of about three hundred souls. Many of the cottages were thatched, there was an exquisite green with a duck pond and there were two pubs, a very old church, a small school, post office, two shops – grocery and tobacconist – and a village hall. The farmhouse he was looking for – Sandalshoon Pastures – was not difficult to find, being right in the centre of the village, but set back from the green.

He parked fifty yards from the entrance, then walked up to the wrought-iron gate, which was open to allow cars in and out. Looking in, he saw that two cars were parked on the forecourt of a decent-sized and very fine Georgian-fronted house, the sort of symmetrical building erected by well-to-do farmers and landowners who were going up in society at the end of the eighteenth century.

Wilde weighed his options. On the way here he had found himself consumed with rage, but his head was taking back control from his heart and he was aware that no good could come of him charging in shooting. For one thing, he was short of ammunition. By his estimation he had just two rounds left of the original thirteen in the magazine of the Hi-Power and he had brought no spares. These bullets would have to count.

He didn't have to wait long to find out who was here: Catesby and his so-called butler McNally were standing near the cars, deep in conversation. McNally had what looked like a hunting rifle slung over his left shoulder. Was that the weapon that had been used to try to kill him but took out Shirin Oswick instead? Perhaps it had also killed Dagger Templeman.

Unaware of his presence, the two men walked with purpose across the driveway then disappeared down a path at the side of the house.

Wilde waited in the shadow of a tall old lime tree with a broad array of overhanging branches, heavy with autumn leaves. After a minute, he stepped out of the shade and followed them. Slowly and cautiously.

The pathway at the far side of the house divided the main building from a large outhouse, which had clearly once been a barn. Whether this was still a working farm was not obvious at first glance. Ahead of him, he saw a concrete paved yard and, beyond that, an even larger barn-like structure – but far more modern with a high corrugated roof.

There was no sign of the two men he was pursuing.

His breathing was heavy and the gun weighed on his outstretched arms, but he tried to step silently. For the first time that day he began to feel real fear. Even when Shirin Oswick held the pistol to his skull, his emotion was one of resignation rather than fear. Somehow this was different. He had two bullets and there were at least two men – probably more. Greater even than the threat to his own life, he feared failure.

He emerged at the far end of the side path. His grip on the Hi-Power butt was tight, perhaps too tight. *Loosen up, Tom. Control, focus, precision.* For a moment, he closed his eyes. Think of Viktoria Ulyanova, a young girl out on the snowy fields of Byelorussia, facing an implacable enemy through the gunsight of a sniper's long-range rifle. She would have known that her heartbeat must stay slow and steady, that her eye must not waver or her trigger finger tremble.

Wilde turned the corner, sweeping the pistol from side to side, his mind more alert than it had ever been, ready to fire on anyone reaching for a weapon.

But he was alone. There was no sign of Catesby or McNally or anyone else. For a minute he simply stood there, scanning the yard, the buildings, the trees and fields beyond, computing their possible movements. Had they stepped inside the main house through a back door? Were they in one of the two barns? It occurred to him that the larger of the two outhouses might serve as an aircraft hangar. Was there another airstrip here?

He listened for voices, but all he heard was the wind and the distant rumble of some farm vehicle, a tractor perhaps. Inching his way along the rear of the building, he saw no one through the windows and no lights were on. The house was cold and dead. Another shell of a place like Catesby's dilapidated farm at Skyme.

This old house was merely a staging post on a trail of terror. All he could think now was that the two men were in one of the barns, and so like a soldier clearing a street house by house in an occupied city, he would have to search the buildings and hope that he hadn't already been spotted.

And that was when he felt the cold steel of a gun muzzle on the back of his neck.

CHAPTER 43

The gunman was McNally, the butler at the Harbinger House shooting party and the one who had served him as loader. Perhaps, too, the one who removed his pistol from his room and used it to finish off Larry Rhein after the phenol had done its work.

'I'm afraid you will have to come with me, Mr Wilde. But first I'd be grateful if you would place your pistol on the ground at your feet.'

Wilde almost laughed at the courteous deference of the man, as though Wilde were still the master and McNally the servant. But as it was, he had no option but to do as he was told. He couldn't see McNally or the gun that was held to his head, but the stealth with which he had been approached and the calmness of the man's voice left him in no doubt that this man was a professional and that a false move would be his last. As he bent down and allowed his fingers to uncurl and release their grip on the weapon, he could still feel McNally's firearm hard against the back of his head.

'Thank you, sir,' McNally said, kicking the Hi-Power away. 'Now please walk to the back door.'

The door swung open as he approached and Catesby stepped out. He stared at Wilde as though he were a strange alien creature. He shook his head. 'What do you say, McNally? What do we do with him?'

'Put him down like a dog, I suppose, sir. But that is for you to say, of course.'

'Let's think about it.' Catesby glanced at his wristwatch. 'How about a last drink, Professor Wilde? Whisky's your tipple, I recall.'

'It's a bit early in the day for me, but given the circumstances I won't say no.'

'Well, come inside. It'll be brief, I'm afraid, because if you're here, Freya Bentall's hounds can't be far behind.'

They had clearly spotted him even before they came down the side of the house. And when he was examining the rear of the building they must have concealed themselves. Still, he was right about one thing: the house was bleak and unlived-in. The sitting room they took him to had an open fireplace but no fire. It was a smart house that would make a fine home for a family, but there was a whiff of neglect. The one nod to luxurious living was a splendid gold-framed mirror over the mantelpiece.

'I won't ask you to sit down,' Catesby said, pouring a single tumbler of whisky and handing it to Wilde.

'Why are you doing this?' Wilde asked, taking the drink, all the time aware of the gun held at his head.

'Oh, why do you think, man?'

'For power?'

'How clever you are. You always were, Tom. Second cleverest man in Cambridge by my reckoning. But not quite clever enough.'

'You know I destroyed the planes?'

'And I forgive you. They were a gift to me from my very good friend General Franco, having been left in Spain by the Condor Legion. I suppose you think you have won the battle. Well, I'm afraid you're quite wrong. Others are on their way to Parliament. Within one square mile, you have Whitehall, Westminster and the Palace. You saw at Flowthorpe what one of these biological weapons can do in a similar acreage. Just think what half a dozen will achieve, especially in a confined city space.'

Wilde didn't bother to comment. There was no point.

'In the next few days, they will all have taken to their beds breathing their last from a variety of unpleasant diseases. Hospitals will be overflowing. People will be falling in the street. And each and every one of them will pass on their sickness to others.'

No word about the death of Shirin Oswick, or Frank Broussard. They were acceptable casualties of his one-man war. He was a psychopath and there could be no reasoning with him, and yet Wilde wanted to know. 'If these diseases are as infectious as you hope, then you will turn this country into a desert. Who will you rule over? In fact, how will you and Mr McNally stay disease free yourselves?'

'We won't be here. We are about to go on a long journey, but we will return. Don't worry yourself with the details, Tom. It's all worked out.'

'How will you prevent it crossing the Channel and spreading like wildfire through the continent and beyond? The oceans didn't protect Europe from the Black Death. You can't travel to Mars.'

Not for the first time, Wilde felt an insane and inappropriate urge to sweep the dandruff from Catesby's shoulders and back. There was certainly no point in arguing with the man. How had he strayed so far from his life as a man of the world and academic? Was that the way all revolutionaries began their struggle? Like Lenin in his Zurich hovel or Hitler in his Munich lodging house, plotting and manipulating, waiting for their moment. 'And you, Mr McNally, what do you have to gain? What has he promised you?'

'Don't worry about me, Mr Wilde. I'm exceedingly good at looking after myself.'

Wilde smiled. 'Do tell me, Neville. This must have been a long time in the planning. Would I be right in thinking you were assisted by your old friend Ryoichi Naito?'

'You *have* done your homework, Tom. Well done.'

'And the submarine?'

'One of the few I-400 class subs the Japanese built. A remarkable piece of engineering. They can even stow light aircraft and have a range of over thirty-seven thousand nautical miles, which means they can reach anywhere in the world. They were originally designed as a way of attacking the west coast of America, but I thought why waste it on the Yanks?'

'And where is this sub now?'

'Oh, long gone to Davy Jones's locker. The captain and his crew did the honourable thing and committed a version of hara-kiri. Deep in the North Sea, never to be found. Now drink up, old man.'

Wilde took a sip of the Scotch. He was in no hurry. There was nothing more to say. He was about to die, so he might as well enjoy his last taste of life.

'You know, McNally,' Catesby said. 'We don't need to kill him.'

'As you say, sir.'

'He can't harm us now. Let him die in a fever with the rest of them. To which end, I'd be obliged if you would put him in the hole.'

The gun prodded into the back of his head. Wilde didn't believe for a moment that they were going to let him live; it wasn't their style. Catesby just wanted him out of this room, didn't want to witness the bloody deed.

As he walked to his slaughter, his eye caught his reflection in the gilded mirror over the mantelpiece. His last glimpse.

But there was something else. Another face, or at least part of a face, but wholly recognisable for all that. Neither of the others would be able to see it because they were looking in the opposite direction, but they would know that he was there, almost concealed behind the door to the dining room.

It was Boris Minsky, more recently known as Sergei Borisov.

Some instinct told Wilde to avoid meeting the eyes, to look away, to say nothing.

That familiar bald head and pudgy face were unmistakable. Colonel General Boris Minsky – one of the most senior officers in SMERSH, the Soviet counter-intelligence agency, until Wilde got him out of Berlin in the late summer, supposedly to save him from the threat of liquidation by the organisation's chief man, Viktor Abakumov, or his bitter rival Lavrentiy Beria of the NKVD.

Minsky had said that he had been answerable to Abakumov but when Beria began taking an interest it seemed wise to defer to him, too. And that, he insisted, was when things became difficult. If you try to please two masters you will satisfy neither of them.

His story had seemed perfectly plausible, given the recent history of the Soviet Union and the Stalinist purges. Reason enough to help him escape from the Soviet sector of Berlin.

The deal was that in return for asylum, Minsky would furnish the British and Americans with a mass of secrets about Soviet infiltration of the West. Well, if he was here in this house with Catesby and McNally, it raised a lot of difficult questions.

What the hell *was* going on? Wilde knew that Minsky was supposed to be disenchanted with communism ... but that was a long way from embracing the fascism of these people.

One thing was certain: Wilde wasn't supposed to know that Minsky was here. And so, he would go along with the charade.

The 'hole' was a space beneath the stairs. It was pitch black and cramped. All he could do was sit against the wall with his knees bunched up. He heard furniture being moved outside and deduced that they were piling it against the locked and bolted door so that he really couldn't escape.

Perhaps Catesby had meant it when he said they should leave him alive. Or perhaps they would burn the house around him. Or were they so confident that he would catch some foul disease and die that they simply didn't care?

He settled down in the dark, for he had no alternative. He heard their voices – though not Minsky's heavy Russian accent – and then after a few minutes, there was only silence.

After a while, when it was clear that the three men had gone, he tried pushing against the little angled door, but could get no movement. He drank the remnants of the whisky slowly and waited.

Freya Bentall's men arrived an hour later.

CHAPTER 44

There were four of them – three boys and a girl, all aged ten or eleven. They called themselves the Rubble Gang, because they spent their days on bombsites when they played truant. This was one of those days and they all knew they'd get a hiding when they got home.

They were tough and fearless. They'd been here in Hackney throughout the V1 and V2 bombing campaigns and all of them had had near misses, and they laughed them off. It didn't do to get sentimental about little things like flying bombs. If one hit you, well you wouldn't know about it. And if it hit someone else, bad luck them.

This was a good day for treasure hunting. They found a few live rounds of ammunition and a couple of shell cases from the ack-ack gun. Plenty of shrapnel, of course. There was always plenty of shrapnel.

But the strangest things of all were the three grey bomb-like things they found that were made of something like china.

'*What* are these?' said Dennis. 'Never seen nothing like them.' He threw it like a rugby ball to Little Kenny, who caught it with ease and tossed it back.

'Give me one,' said Jeanie. 'I'll take it home for mum. She can get Uncle Fred to saw the ends off and make a vase.'

'Daft cow,' said Malcolm. 'Let's launch the buggers and see what happens.'

Laughing and cheering they clambered up over the rubble to the first floor of what used to be a grocery store with flats above. They edged across to the remains of the landing, which was now open to the elements.

'Ready,' Mal said, holding the bomb thing over the edge.

'What if it's got TNT in it?' Dennis said. 'We'll be blown to smithereens.'

'You chicken, Den?'

'You know I'm not.'

'Steady,' Mal continued. He paused a few seconds. 'Go!' He opened his hands and let the object fall. It hit the bricks and stones below and shattered with a cracking sound, but no explosion. Something like a puff of smoke came out, but that could have been dust from the rubble.

'Is that it?' Little Kenny said. 'Give me one.' He tried to grab the one Jeannie was holding, but she was bigger and stronger than him and kept possession.

With a whoop, she flung it as far as she could. The bomb flew about thirty feet and crashed into pieces, but again there was a disappointing lack of a bang. Just a spray of dust or smoke or liquid, it was hard to tell.

'These are weird,' said Den, who was cradling the last of the three. 'My brother might know what they are – let's show him the last one.'

'Bollocks to that,' said Mal grabbing it. He put it down on the floor, grabbed a brick and smashed it. They all gathered around to look inside.

'Eeurgh,' said Den. 'It's full of gunge.'

Twenty-five miles to the east, Paul Kagerer stood by the bunk in his tiny cabin and looked through the porthole at the grey waters of the Thames Estuary.

It was dusk and the freighter would be leaving for America at any moment, carrying a variety of goods – including high quality shoes from Northampton, certain specialist foodstuffs such as mustard and marmalade from East Anglia, and ladies' undergarments from Nottingham.

Britain didn't have much in the way of goods to export but every little thing was important if the country's economy was to get back on its feet in the manner prescribed by Chancellor of the Exchequer Hugh Dalton.

Kagerer was here because he had decided to forego the money that Catesby had promised him in exchange for conveying the canisters to the House of Commons. Even though a certain member of Parliament was supposed to be on hand to ensure access to the visitors' gallery. Well, let the man wait forever.

The thing was, he knew he would never get away alive. Seeing the detention of Dr Bacon had made that clear, and so his decision was easily made. The area around Parliament would be crawling with police by now. In the end it had dawned on him that he and Bacon weren't supposed to survive, that the money wouldn't be there anyway.

The advance they had handed him – a hundred pounds – was more than adequate for his berth on this small and uncomfortable freighter. And if his passport under an assumed name might not pass muster under close examination, it would be enough in such a ship.

He shrugged his lean, scarred shoulders. There would be plenty of opportunities to get rich in America. Maybe he would become a gangster, a German Al Capone, or he could join the New York police. That would provide opportunities.

Below him, he could feel the rumble of the engines, then the shouts of the men as they reeled in the mooring lines. He lay back on his narrow bunk bed, closed his eyes and wondered how long it would take the British police to find the gifts he had left on the bombsite. Not that he cared much. A whole new world beckoned.

'We found a stash of the pathogen bombs at Sandalshoon,' Freya Bentall said. 'Fifteen of them, which means they originally had plans for an even greater attack. What isn't known is how many got through. However, we haven't yet found any evidence of one being detonated in the vicinity of Westminster.'

'Is it possible Kagerer lost his nerve?'

'We can but hope. The chancellor's speech finished two hours ago but we probably won't know for a day or two. If MPs and civil servants start falling like flies, then we've lost and we'll just have to contain it as best we can. But Porton Down agrees that the Stuka bombs were Catesby's best hope of causing large-scale damage. Airborne detonations would have turned the pathogen into aerosol-style droplets which could have spread disease over a wide area. On the plus side, the initial thought of our experts is that in burning the Stukas you would have almost certainly killed the pathogens in the bomb, so well done you.'

He grunted because he didn't feel that he had done at all well. He had been outwitted at Sandalshoon, and then Catesby and friends had escaped. Now, here he was in Freya Bentall's office at Leconfield House, having been freed unharmed by her agents. In truth, he couldn't understand how he was alive. Why would Catesby have not simply had him shot? He hadn't been slow to kill others in pursuit of his deranged aims and he seemed to care nothing about the deaths of those close to him.

And then – even more perplexing – there was the question of Boris Minsky. Wilde had gone through the whole thing with Bentall and neither of them could come up with a satisfactory explanation.

Until a light came on in her brown eyes.

'It's possible, of course, that the two mysteries – your survival and the appearance of Comrade Minsky – are linked, Mr Wilde. Had you thought of that?'

'Go on.'

She ran a hand through her hair. 'Don't you see where I'm going with this?'

Did he? 'I think you'd better explain, Miss Bentall.'

She sighed then gritted her teeth as though forcing herself to impart unpleasant news. 'I'm afraid I am feeling a bit queasy at the thoughts entering my head. They are taking me in directions I would rather avoid.'

Like a match being struck, a spark of possible understanding came to him, too. 'You mean . . .'

'I mean I am beginning to wonder whether certain friends are actually not so friendly after all. You can understand why I don't want to go there, because the ramifications are all too obvious – and terrifying.'

Suddenly, like a cascade, things began to fall into place: Oswick being enrolled as his student in his college, the Black Book, the phenol, the collaboration of Hitler's allies in Japan, the neo-fascist meeting with Shirin, Oswald Mosley for dinner, the despicable humiliation of the Russian sniper, the Luftwaffe dive-bombers.

What did these events all have in common? They all presented a picture of fascism and gave certain proof of a fascist conspiracy.

Or, at least, that was what they were designed to do.

The appearance of Comrade Minsky, however, did not feed into that narrative.

Nor did Wilde's own survival. There was no reason to keep him alive.

Except there was, wasn't there?

What if his survival had always been central to the plan? What if he had had to be kept alive so that he might act as witness, because he had been designated as the man who would tell the world that this merciless attack on the British Establishment was the work of diehard Nazis?

When in fact it wasn't. When this was all orchestrated by Moscow. Even down to providing their own heroine Viktoria Ulyanova to be humiliated.

It all made sense now. And he would never have known it save for the sliver of a face in a mirror.

Boris Minsky was part of it all, perhaps behind it. It was the reason he was here in England, the reason he had begged to be extracted from Berlin.

Wilde felt a wave of shame envelop him. He had been used as a patsy all along, and he hadn't suspected a thing. God, what a fool! He had been taken for a ride. Even the attempted murder of his wife in her hostel was designed to enrage him. As if he would ever need anything to intensify his loathing of the Nazis and all they stood for.

Catesby and Minsky had even recruited real-live Nazis for their conspiracy, men and a woman who believed they were working to avenge Germany's defeat. They, too, had been taken for a ride. That was why the deaths of Shirin and Broussard meant nothing. They had always been expendable.

'I feel such an almighty ass.'

'None of us saw it, Mr Wilde.'

'But I was at the centre. I was the useful idiot. They played me. They had so many chances to kill me and all the while I congratulated myself on staying alive. But they were the ones who *kept* me alive. They even killed Shirin Oswick to save *my* life. And to think I was dumb enough to write it off as a lousy shot.'

Freya Bentall came around from her side of the desk and put a comforting arm around his shoulders, something Wilde was certain she had never done before; she was too professional for such sentimental touches. 'You prevented those Stukas from doing their evil work, you neutralised Sosinka, you helped Danny Oswick do the decent thing – and you found poor dear Templeman. It's possible you have prevented a far greater tragedy from taking place, Tom.'

He hoped so, but he wasn't convinced. There were definitely more bombs out there. The only question was, had they got through to their intended target with Kagerer?

'For the present,' the MI5 officer continued as she retook her seat, 'I want to know where they are – Catesby, McNally and Boris Minsky.'

'Catesby said they were going on a long journey. How about Moscow?' he ventured.

'Most likely, given what we now suspect. You were right about that structure at Sandalshoon being a hangar. There was definitely a plane housed there and there is a strip of flat land that would serve as a runway, dry weather permitting. The locals are being questioned but several have already said they noted a plane flying in and out on several occasions. A single-wing twin-prop, about the right size for two or three people. It was seen flying off earlier today – half an hour before you were freed. Unfortunately, none of the villagers could put a make or marque to it, but my people tell me that a plane of that order is unlikely to have had a range of more than a thousand miles, so it would almost certainly have to refuel on the way to Moscow, assuming that's where it's heading.'

'I wish that helped us.'

'Don't worry, we'll get Catesby eventually.'

'What do we know about McNally?'

'Nothing yet. He's not on our radar, but I'm going to keep Danny Oswick here for a couple of days for further debriefing and he might be able to enlighten us; he's our best link to Catesby and I want to know everything he knows. But if Catesby does get to Moscow, he can live in abject misery in a Russian block of flats wishing he was back in Cambridge. His life now is one of permanent exile under the most miserable and brutal regime on earth. Worse than a death sentence in my book.'

Wilde had to agree. It would be grim.

The strange thing was, Catesby was not the only member of the British upper classes and academia to have embraced communism, but he had concealed it better than most. Were there others, he wondered, perhaps concealed in the great gentlemen's clubs, the Houses of Parliament, even royal palaces and the secret services? It was becoming clear that the Soviet Union had infiltrated Western Europe deeply, even before the war, and it was likely they had embedded themselves into American society, too, as predicted by Bill Donovan and Wilde himself.

Where was the Office of Strategic Services when you needed it?

'So we have a new enemy, the Soviet Union, and most people don't even know it yet. In Washington, DC they're still toasting our Red Army comrades-in-arms.'

'In an atomic world, it doesn't bode well,' Bentall said.

'Do we let the Kremlin know that we know what they did?'

'That's for others to decide.'

He arrived home at midnight, utterly exhausted. Lydia and the others had already left their refuge at Latimer Hall and were here, too, safely tucked up in bed. Wilde slipped between the sheets beside his wife. She turned to him, kissed him and held him.

'Well?' she demanded.

'I'm sorry, I really don't have the energy.'

'I don't mean that, I mean what happened in London? We were told at Latimer Hall that it was safe to come home.'

'Yes, I think we're safe. The man who attacked you with the needle is in custody.'

'Then I need to get back to St Ursula's early tomorrow and pray to God I've got away with it. Probably not, I have to say, because the murder of those two intelligence men close to the hostel would have raised questions that the college couldn't answer. My absence and that of Miranda must have been noted.'

'Can you not leave it a day or two? Stay here with me and Johnny?' He really didn't want her or her friend going to London – not with the possibility that a pandemic was on the cards and centred within a couple of miles of her medical school.

'I think I have to go. I'm sorry.'

'We'll talk about it in the morning.'

'There was something else – something rather unpleasant.' She lowered her voice even though the walls were thick and they were deep beneath the covers. 'The matter of Mrs Keane.'

'You mean Doris's misgivings?'

'More than that.' She told him about Sylvia Keane's sharp comment at Latimer Hall. 'I was just trying to be understanding, being a good employer apologising for all the drama and I thought it must bring back bad memories for her, of the time she lost her husband. She bit out her reply and told me I knew nothing about her feelings. But it wasn't just the words – it was the cold, scornful way she spoke them.'

Wilde was shocked; it was not something that he would have expected from the well-mannered and seemingly warm Mrs Sylvia Keane.

The most unlikely of people concealed darkness in their soul.

'What do you propose we do?'

'I don't know. I'll have to have words with her, but I'm really not sure that Johnny should be in her care'

There was something else that still nagged at Wilde's sleepy brain, something he couldn't even address right now: how did the man who tried to kill Lydia at the hostel even know that she was there?

CHAPTER 45

Lydia had not been looking forward to her little talk with Sylvia Keane. She decided the event would take place after she had driven Miranda to the station and dropped Johnny off at school, hopefully while Tom was still asleep upstairs. She had organised all this; it was her responsibility to deal with it.

That was not the way things worked out.

Driving home from the school, she spotted Mrs Keane further down the road, tightly clutching Penelope's hand. She hadn't said anything about going out. Was she leaving? If so, why did she not have their suitcase?

Mrs Keane hadn't spotted her, so instead of parking the car, she drove on slowly, following Sylvia Keane and her daughter from a distance. She was intrigued. Doris had told her about Mrs Keane's unexplained disappearances.

As they approached the centre of town, the tall, slender figure of the housekeeper picked up Penelope in her arms and broke into a run. Lydia immediately understood why: a bus was about to leave and she wanted to catch it. The mother and daughter jumped on at the last moment and found a seat at the front.

The bus pulled away and Lydia had a decision to make: to follow it, or not. The word 'Bedford' was emblazoned on a sign at the rear of the vehicle, but there were bound to be other stops on the way. Lydia's curiosity got the better of her and she drove on in pursuit of the bus.

There were plenty of stops and the journey dragged on, but Sylvia Keane and her child did not disembark. Lydia was getting worried. Could she afford this amount of time? Would she run out of petrol? Tom would get up and wonder where everyone had gone; what would he think?

And then, at last, it stopped in the centre of the town of Bedford and Mrs Keane and Penelope finally emerged. Lydia continued to follow them as they walked northwards from the town centre.

A few minutes later they arrived at their destination.

The town's prison.

Wilde woke late after nine and a half hours of sleep. From a long way away a bell was ringing and he thought it must be the Sunday tolling from the nearby church, but quickly realised it was neither Sunday nor bells but the telephone. He badly wanted to slide back down between the sheets but instead he forced himself to clamber out of bed, throw on his dressing gown and drag himself downstairs.

No one else was about, which surprised him. He picked up the phone.

'Hello?'

'Tom, is that you? I hear that things have been pretty rough over there.'

He recognised Bill Donovan's voice instantly. 'Yes, Bill, it's me, and yes, things have been rough. How did you hear about it? There's supposed to be a news blackout.'

'Oh, you know me. Always did like to keep my ear to the ground.'

'Good to hear you still have your old communications systems in place.'

'Can't let it go, Tom. Once you've been in this world you can't get out, can you? Is it true that the bastards got through Brit defences and managed to attack Westminster?'

'We're not certain.'

'And to think we reckoned the Nazi serpent was a spent force! Seems the tail still thrashes.'

'If it was them. But what if it wasn't?'

'Well, who else is there?'

'You tell me, Bill. Remember what we were talking about – where the next threat might feasibly come from?'

'Are you serious?'

'More than just serious, I'm certain. And I know you'll recall the name Boris Minsky.'

'Of course, practically second-in-command of SMERSH until his defection. In fact, you were the man who helped him out. Jesus . . .'

A few seconds of crackly silence followed.

'Bill, are you still there?'

'Trying to digest what you just told me. Boris goddamned Minsky, eh?'

Wilde had a vague feeling that he shouldn't be having a conversation like this on an unencrypted line, but he was too tired to care. 'I have no doubt it was his call all along. The Nazi thing was an elaborate false flag.'

'It's all making sense now. I had a garbled message from my old buddy Larry Rhein . . .'

Good grief, another piece of the jigsaw was slotting into place. 'So that's why he was here. You sent him over, didn't you? Couldn't just wait on the sidelines, you had to give me backup.'

'Was I wrong?'

'No, of course you weren't, but you might have told me.'

'Easier to play-act when you don't know the truth.'

'God, I was desperately sad for Larry. You must have heard the bastards tried to put me in the frame for shooting him.'

'Yes, I heard that and didn't believe it for a moment. He was one of my very best men, Tom. He told me he had inveigled himself into Catesby's place. Piece of work that guy. You know I met Catesby in DC a few years back. That's to say, he made a point of making my acquaintance. I think he does that with everyone he considers even vaguely of consequence. Others might take him for a social climber, I took him for a spy and kept him at barge pole's length.'

'That's him. Larry had a similar experience with him back then.'

'And he killed Larry. Jesus, will the killing never cease? To think he survived the war to be knocked down by this dirty crew. Where are they now?'

'On their way to Moscow probably. A small plane based near Bedford is believed to have flown eastwards with them on board.'

'How many?'

'Three. Catesby, Minsky and a man called McNally who was posing as Catesby's butler but is a professional killer. I'm not sure which one's the pilot.'

'Hmm, that's made me think. A paragraph came through on the wires last night – unknown aircraft crashed in bad weather on Sylt, the North Frisian island off the coast bordering Deutschland and Denmark. Two bodies recovered.'

'It would be good to think it was them.'

'I'll try to get identities for you.'

'Suggest they look for a mass of dandruff on his expensive flying suit.'

Donovan's laughter reverberated down the line. 'But what do you think is behind all this? Why would Stalin go along with it? What did he have to gain?'

'The destruction of the British Establishment,' Wilde said with feeling.

'But how would that benefit the Soviets?' He immediately answered his own question. 'You, heroic and trustworthy Tom Wilde, would have told the world that it was the Nazi rump and Mosley, seeking to gain power. Stalin would have stepped forward to save Britain from Mosley's clutches – and bring a bit of Bolshevik sanity to Olde England.'

'Which is just what they seem to be doing in Eastern Europe – Poland, Hungary, Czechoslovakia, Romania, the Baltic States and the Balkans. Protecting them from the evils of democracy. Not quite what Stalin promised at Yalta.'

'Dear God, and we still don't know what damage they've done.'

'But at least they've lost me as their witness, so if I can stay alive their lie won't work.' Wilde sighed. 'Bill, you mentioned that Larry Rhein passed on a garbled message. What was that about?'

'Ah yes, it involved your old acquaintance Philip Eaton – I hesitate to use the word "friend". He said he merited a second look, but didn't elaborate. What did he mean by that?'

Wilde's brow furrowed. From what he understood, Larry Rhein had flown over on the clipper service almost immediately on learning of the bio attack at Flowthorpe. Soon after arrival he had wangled an invitation to Catesby's shooting party. Where could Eaton have fitted into his schedule – and why?

Not that Eaton hadn't crossed Wilde's mind. How could he not have wondered about his possible role in recent events when he was the man supposed to be controlling Minsky in this country?

And then there were Templeman's doubts. No, they were more than that – they were suspicions. He had kept him at arm's length on the Flowthorpe inquiry and had even had him shadowed by MI5 agents. That was a huge vote of no-confidence from one section of the secret services to a senior operative in a sister branch.

The shadows had followed Minsky to the Soviet Embassy. Why would he have gone there if he was a bona fide defector? Well, the answer to that one was now clear, but Eaton's part was still shrouded in mist.

There was something else. Eaton had reinforced the idea that the initial threat somehow came from the Black Book addendum. He had readily facilitated the meeting with Himmler's incarcerated deputy Walter Schellenberg, who then confirmed the link to the Nazis' murder weapon of choice, phenol. Wilde recalled the words Schellenberg had used to describe the addendum: '*All those named were to be killed as soon as they were located. We called it the Phenol List.*'

If anyone had had any doubts that the enemy they were facing was the Nazis, those words would have dispelled them. The question was: did Eaton know what he was doing or had he, too, been played for a fool?

It had never been difficult imagining Eaton as an agent of Moscow. Wilde had harboured such doubts a long way back. Philip Eaton had been at Cambridge in the late 1920s when certain dons – including Wilde's late friend Professor Horace Dill – seemed to consider it part of their job to convert young men to communism. It was also known that Eaton had applied for membership of the Communist Party back then, but there was no record of him having been accepted. Was it possible that he had been recruited as a Soviet agent and so had to avoid being seen as a party member?

And who else was at Trinity at about that time? None other than Neville Catesby, lecturing.

These were not new suspicions, yet each time they entered Wilde's head Eaton had somehow proved himself loyal. And there was something else, something that straightforward MI5 men like Dagger Templeman had never understood about MI6 officers – they worked differently: cross, double-cross, triple-cross. The truth always concealed in the great game until checkmate.

Operations so complex that it became almost impossible to disentangle them.

Even now, with all this evidence stacked against him, you couldn't be certain what Philip Eaton was up to.

Wilde would have to talk with Freya Bentall sooner rather than later. But first he wanted to meet Eaton himself.

Sylvia Keane and her daughter were inside Bedford Prison for just over half an hour. When they emerged, Lydia was waiting for them, her car parked just across the street from the bleak, forbidding entrance. She opened the car door and stepped out.

'Hello, Mrs Keane.'

The housekeeper recoiled, clearly shocked to the core.

Lydia approached the mother and daughter. She was smiling. 'I noticed a tea shop just around the corner. Shall we go and have a little sit-down?'

'Wh-what are you doing here?'

'I hope you'll forgive me, but I saw you going for the bus and I followed you. Shall we have that tea? I'm sure they'll do a glass of milk and a scone for Penelope. It's my treat.'

Mrs Keane was still rigid. Her hand was holding her child's tightly and the little girl looked desperately uncomfortable and close to tears. At last the woman nodded. 'Very well.' She sighed. 'I've nothing more to lose.'

The little tea shop was busy but they found a table in a corner with two chairs and Penelope sat on her mother's lap.

A waitress immediately came and took their order.

'I'm not going to make any guesses what this is all about, Mrs Keane. You tell me as much as you wish, or nothing if you prefer. I already feel that I have probably intruded far too much by following you, but I can't just let it go, you see. I suspect you have even more troubles than you have told us.'

'I suppose you've gathered that my husband didn't die – he's in Bedford Prison. I was visiting him.'

Her voice was very quiet. Was that because she didn't want the other customers to hear, or her daughter? Lydia could understand a mother trying to protect her child.

'I confess I did wonder when I saw you going there.'

'He's serving eighteen months. The truth is he was part of a ring stealing cigarettes, alcohol and food from the Naafi and selling them on the black market. As an officer, he fell harder than the others, who were all in the ranks.'

'That must have been devastating for you.'

Lydia had thought that the child might cry, but the tears were falling from Sylvia Keane's eyes. She began sobbing uncontrollably.

'Mummy, don't cry,' Penelope said. Her mother hugged her to her breast.

'Oh, Mrs Keane, I'm so sorry,' Lydia said.

'He was dismissed from the service, no more pay, no pension. Our lives had revolved around the army, but that all ended. The other wives and their families, they all cut me and Penelope dead. In one fell swoop I lost my husband, my respectability and all the people I had considered friends.'

Lydia very much wanted to put her arm around the woman. Instead, she picked up a white linen napkin from the table and handed it to her. Mrs Keane clutched it to her eyes.

'I came to live in Cambridge so I wasn't too far from the prison but not in the same town. I couldn't allow my new neighbours to know that I had a jailbird for a husband. And yet I still love him, you see. He told me they were all at it – everyone was involved in the black market, but he got caught and they decided to make an example of him. There was even a paragraph in *The Times*. I thought I'd die with shame when I saw it.'

Lydia took her hand. 'You have nothing to be ashamed of.'

'I'm so sorry, Mrs Wilde. I owe you an apology ... the way I snapped at you yesterday was unconscionable. Please forgive me. I know it wasn't your intention, but you hit a very raw nerve.'

'Well, yes, I understand now, of course.'

'I know you won't want me to stay. I'm one of the untouchables now.'

Lydia was blindsided. Her heart went out to this woman, but there was something else, wasn't there. Doris had not been happy since Mrs Keane arrived, and she had to take precedence. She had been their cleaning lady for many years and she and Tom trusted her judgement implicitly. She was almost like family.

The waitress arrived back at the table with a tray laden with teapot, sugar, milk and a scone.

'Let me talk to my husband, Mrs Keane. In the meantime, let's have our tea and then I'll drive us all back home.'

CHAPTER 46

Tom and Lydia Wilde passed like the proverbial ships in the night. She arrived home with the car, complete with Mrs Keane and Penelope. Wilde vaguely wondered where they had all been, but he didn't have time to inquire further. After a perfunctory kiss for his wife, he said he had to get to London and perhaps they could talk later. He commandeered the vehicle for himself and drove off.

Philip Eaton took a long time to answer the knock. When at last the door to the Chelsea house opened Wilde saw a ghost of the man he had met nine years earlier.

'Ah, it's you, Tom.' He sounded almost disinterested.

'Can I come in?'

'Is this a social call? I'm afraid I've had a rough night and a worse morning, not in very good shape. My body's falling apart.'

'I heard you had Parkinson's.'

'Oh, that. I disguise it as delirium tremens.' He made no attempt to smile, let alone laugh at his poor stab at humour.

'I won't keep you long.'

Eaton stepped back to allow Wilde past him. Slowly, they made their way into the sitting room. 'I won't offer you anything if you don't mind. I'm really not up to it. Perhaps you'd get straight to the point.'

This was new territory. Even at the worst of times when he lost his arm and smashed up his leg, he was urbane, courteous and unfailingly hospitable. 'Don't worry. I just wanted an update on our friend Boris Minsky – or Borisov if you prefer. Last I heard, you were keeping close tabs on him – something about a plot to kidnap our German scientists.'

'Yes, well, things change.'

'Is that it?'

'What more can I say? It's fluid. You know the way the SIS works.'

Wilde tried to contain his anger, but it wasn't going to be easy. 'Philip, this is my reputation on the line. I secured Minsky's defection. The deal was that we would share intelligence – Britain and America. You can't leave Washington out in the cold like this. So where is he now? What have you learnt from him, and why aren't you communicating?'

'Let's just say I'm playing a long game and so I can't give you daily bulletins as I'm sure you're very well aware. And the central point is, if I have to put your nose out of joint, so be it. We need men like Minsky onside.'

'But you know where he is, right?'

'Of course. I'm keeping tabs on him. It's a complicated relationship. Catches like Boris Minsky don't come along every day, you can't rush these things. This is the closest to Beria and Uncle Joe himself that we're ever likely to get. He'll give us secrets from the very heart of the Politburo.'

'What if I were to tell you he is in Moscow?'

Eaton's brow furrowed. 'I would say you've taken leave of your senses. Why would he be in Moscow? Beria has ordered his death.'

'Because his work here is done.'

'Tom, you're talking in riddles. I can't take in any of this nonsense – you must be able to see that I'm in a bad way.'

'Yes, I can see you're uncomfortable. What I'm trying to work out is how much you really know about Boris Minsky and his work here in England.'

Eaton stiffened visibly. 'Good God, man, do we really have to go through all this again? I've told you what he's up to and it's a bluff. He's even taken covert photographs of the damned house where the scientists are held. You've been there yourself, Tom, so you know what I'm talking about. And these photographs have been developed and given to the Soviet Embassy as if he's trying to negotiate his way back into favour by giving Uncle Joe the one thing he wants more than any other – the science to build his own atomic bomb.'

'Then why is he in Moscow?'

Eaton lowered himself on to the sofa with a sigh. 'Who's told you this nonsense? Do you have someone in Moscow who's seen him?'

Wilde had had enough. This conversation was heading nowhere. Eaton's skills at deception knew no bounds; he could talk his way out of a reinforced concrete box. But perhaps not this one.

'I'll leave you to your ailments,' Wilde said. Then, suddenly aware that he might never see this man again, he softened his anger. 'You have done some good things in your life, Philip, including much for me. And for that, I thank you.'

Without another word, he turned and strode out of the house.

Lydia walked the short distance to Doris's house and knocked on the door. She appeared quickly and Lydia knew instantly that her husband, Peter, was dead.

'Oh Doris . . .'

'He died at ten past eleven last night. I was holding his hand. Now he's with God and the angels.'

It occurred to Lydia that for the first time Doris looked like a little grey-haired old lady. But she couldn't be that old, could she? Surely she was still in her fifties, perhaps sixty at the most. She took her in her arms and held her tight until Doris eased herself away.

'Come in, my dear, I'll make you a cuppa.'

There were no tears, though Lydia was sure they would arrive eventually. Doris came of an age when death was a constant in every family. Babies and young children died, mothers died in childbirth, men went off to war and died or were taken by industrial accidents or disease.

'At least it was peaceful at the end. He looked quite serene actually, and he had his faith, so I know he will be welcomed into heaven. This life was difficult for him, so he is in a better place now.'

'I hope you're right, Doris.'

'I am, dear, I have no doubts about that. You'll come to the funeral, won't you? You and the professor.'

'Of course we will.'

The kettle was boiling, so she spooned tea leaves into the pot and poured in the water to brew. Lydia had taken a seat at the small kitchen table. 'But what about you and your troubles? Is everything sorted out now?'

'We think so – we hope so.'

'I did like your young friend, Miranda. She will make a fine doctor. I've never met a woman doctor but I would certainly have confidence in her.'

'I'll tell her you said so. She'll be very pleased.'

Doris suddenly looked serious. 'You know, I think I owe you an apology, my dear. In fact, I owe you two.'

'Really?'

'Yes, I believe I did Mrs Keane a disservice in talking ill of her. It was not at all Christian of me and totally uncalled for. But I haven't really been myself lately what with Peter fading away and I suppose I felt jealous of her. I didn't understand why you didn't ask me to help with Johnny.'

'Gosh, Doris, it never occurred to us that you would be able to help in that way. We weren't looking for a babysitter but a live-in nanny or housekeeper.' She smiled and touched Doris's hand. 'It all happened in such a rush, but I should certainly have spoken to you first, for which I apologise.'

'You've nothing to apologise for – you're absolutely right. I couldn't move from here. I was just . . . I don't know . . . put out, I suppose. I feel very ashamed of myself and I'll say sorry to Mrs Keane when I see her next.'

'Let me talk to her first.'

'Of course. And the other thing is that there was something I should have told you. I have a horrible feeling that my silence might have contributed to your problems. When you were away and I was working at Cornflowers, a woman came around asking after you. Mrs Keane answered the door, but I saw the woman briefly and overheard a bit of their conversation.'

'Who was she?'

'I'm not sure. She gave a name, but my hearing's not what it once was and I didn't take it in. She was a dyed blonde with a sort of recognisable face, which made me think she must be an old friend of yours. Anyway, I was shocked to hear Mrs Keane telling her you were at St Ursula's. The professor has said often enough that we should never reveal anything to strangers, what with the line of work he has been in during the war. I should have told him or you what I overheard, but I didn't get a chance.'

So that was how the would-be killer had discovered where she was. Lydia was horrified.

'I'm sure it was an honest mistake by Mrs Keane,' Doris continued. 'She couldn't have known.'

'Still . . .'

'But I feel bad because I really should have found some way to alert you or the professor.'

Lydia forced a smile. 'Don't worry, Doris, it wasn't your fault. I should have made our special circumstances clear to Mrs Keane.'

'Oh dear, I hope she's not in trouble.'

Lydia nodded towards the teapot. 'Better pour that cuppa before it gets stewed.'

'I'm afraid I'm out of sugar. Your young friend has a bit of a sweet tooth, doesn't she?'

Lydia laughed. 'She certainly does. Now, I'll drink my tea, Doris, and then a brisk walk home, followed by a taxi to the station.'

'And Mrs Keane.'

'I'll talk to her.'

In the meantime, there was the matter of her medical degree. To hell with Tom's suggestion that she should stay away from London. She had to sort out her future once and for all.

Wilde made a point of driving through Westminster and Whitehall on his way from Chelsea. He knew there would be nothing to see, but it was somehow important to be sure that life was continuing as normal even if the threat was still there.

No extra police activity was discernible and no one was falling ill in the streets. That didn't mean there was no alarm, but it raised his hopes. And then, coming through Admiralty Arch into Trafalgar Square, he saw a young man bent double, seemingly coughing his lungs up into a handkerchief, and his heart sank.

But only momentarily. One man having a coughing fit meant nothing. You could see that on any street anywhere in the world any day of the week and not think twice about it.

On arrival at Leconfield House, he was immediately ushered into Freya Bentall's office.

'Well, you're looking rather more rested than yesterday,' she said.

'Astonishing what a night's sleep can do.'

'We have some good news. The three pathogen bombs found in Sigmund Rascher's bag were all dead. Apparently that's a known problem with these weapons – the bacteria do not survive forever. These ones must have been months old, perhaps years. They were duds.'

'That doesn't mean the ones carried by Kagerer or others were also dead, though. Not if they were the same batch as Flowthorpe.'

'Of course not, but it's a good sign. Anyway, there is no trace of Kagerer or any of his bombs. Nor has anyone at the House fallen ill. Fingers crossed, Mr Wilde.'

'Let's hope.' Wilde didn't believe in luck, but he believed in hope.

'Now tell me, Tom, to change the subject slightly, am I correct in thinking you visited Philip Eaton on your way here?'

'How would you know that? Is MI5 still watching him?'

'Very astute of you. Tell me his state of mind.'

'He was defensive, almost beaten. I have never known him in such a downbeat mood.'

'Did he mention that he had been retired?'

'No. When did that happen?'

'This morning.'

'That might explain a lot.'

'Nothing can be proved against him, but it was decided at a high level that his position was untenable. Too many unanswered questions regarding his relationship with Minsky and, indeed, with Catesby. It was suggested very forcibly that he take early retirement on health grounds and enjoy life as a man of letters and the arts. Perhaps he'll seek a fellowship at his alma mater. Trinity, wasn't it?'

'I believe so.'

'Then he'd be a near neighbour of yours.'

Wilde was not sure that that would be a good idea. If Eaton had, indeed, been recruited as a Soviet agent by a don, was it not possible that he would return the favour by recruiting a new generation of undergraduates? Perhaps a quiet word in one or two friendly ears at Trinity wouldn't go amiss.

'So what happens to our two Germans and, for that matter, young Danny Oswick?'

'Oh the Germans, yes that's interesting. Well, we can't find Kagerer, but the search will go on. As for Sosinka, he's going back to Germany. A decision has been taken against a public trial in England, because too much would come out – including you having to testify about why you had a pistol in rural Norfolk and why you shot him. Instead, he'll be held at one of the SS camps and will face a war crimes trial. We now know that he was in the notorious Dirlewanger SS Brigade, a band of merciless, feral criminals who slaughtered their way across Poland. He is implicated in enough war crimes to get the noose.'

'And the doctor – Sigmund Rascher or Edmund Bacon or whatever he's calling himself today?'

'Tricky. I feel very uneasy about it, but word has come down that your countrymen want him, and my seniors are disposed to give him to them. He is to be transferred to Camp Detrick in Maryland to reveal the findings of his scientific experiments. I'm told some of the Japanese doctors from Unit 731 will be going there, too. I'm afraid he and they are likely to be spared the rope.'

Wilde felt sick inside. Realpolitik raising its ugly head again.

'I can tell that doesn't make you happy, Tom. And for what it's worth, I agree with you. He was part of the gang who murdered Dagger Templeman and he personally killed at least three very fine MI5 men – Rafe Crow, Ernie Wainwright and Bert Hollings. Not to mention the poor innocent plague victims in Flowthorpe. I would not hesitate to shoot him.'

'And Charlie Bagshawe. And the attempted murder of my wife and an innocent young woman named Miranda March. And God knows how many prisoners he slaughtered in Dachau. A man like that can't go unpunished.'

'Tom, it's out of my hands.'

'And what about Oswick?'

'Well, he's obviously devastated by the death of his wife. He didn't agree with her at the end, but he loved her. So what does he do now? That's very much up to you. I suspect the best thing for him would be to resume his studies and try to put the past behind him. He's a bright young man. Oh, and I know it's none of my business, but someone really should tell him that that moustache does him no favours.'

Wilde found himself laughing. 'I'll do what I can on both counts.'

'He's here in this building and free to go.'

'You trust him now?'

'I do.'

'Then I'll drive him back to college.'

But first he had one more task to perform in London – a brief visit to the US embassy in Grosvenor Square to call in a favour.

Ian McNally drew up outside the house called Cornflowers. So this was where she lived. This was the final necessary act. He would succeed with the Wilde woman where Rascher had failed in London. But then what could you expect; Rascher was an amateur. And those other two Germans? Mindless, incompetent thugs.

Killing was work for professionals. It required a hand that did not tremble, feet that moved in cat-like silence, and a stillness of mind. That was how he had managed to catch Wilde unawares at Sandalshoon Pastures and it was how he had picked off Templeman with a single shot from a car when he was with Broussard at the back of St John's College.

That, too, was how he had dispatched Shirin Oswick from a hundred yards in trees when he was under strict orders to keep the professor alive. None of the targets were aware of what awaited them. Clean take-downs. One moment alive, the next gone.

Today's job was an urban kill and so he would use the garrotte. The most silent and efficient of all methods. A method of execution favoured by the Spanish Inquisition hundreds of years ago and hardly bettered since. More certain than poison, less bloody than the blade, quieter than the gun. Silence and the absence of blood were prime requisites in a residential street where police patrolled and neighbour looked out for neighbour.

Death had been McNally's life since the age of twelve. His sixteen-year-old sister was being bullied by an eighteen-year-old thug in the tenement where they lived. McNally, half his size, stood up to him and warned him to stop harassing his sister or he would kill him. The bully laughed at him, slapped his face, told him he was a wee squirt and to go fuck his mother. Two days later, he was found dead with a butcher's knife protruding from the nape of his neck.

That was the only time McNally had killed for any reason other than money. He only had one motive now: the fee. Others killed out of anger or for a cause, but for Ian McNally, cash was the thing – and Neville Catesby always paid well and on time.

He was watching Cornflowers with the eye of a professional. There was movement at a window inside the house, the shadow of a woman. That boded well.

CHAPTER 47

At Grosvenor Square, Wilde obtained chits for enough petrol to fill the jerrycans given him by Barnaby Wax at Skyme Garage, and then he and Oswick began the drive back to Cambridge.

The young man was silent at his side, lost in his thoughts. Wilde did not break into his reverie until they were halfway home.

'I don't know if Miss Bentall mentioned it, but I was with your wife when she died. There was no pain.'

Oswick nodded but maintained his silence. Clearly the MI5 officer had told him everything.

'This is very difficult for you and I won't try to lessen your grief in any way, but you know, Oswick, this was always bound to end in tragedy.'

'Yes, sir.'

'I'm sure she had many fine qualities, but she was horribly misguided and you both got in with a bad crowd. She will always retain a place in your heart but one day you will look back on this episode and it will all seem like a bad dream.'

Oswick nodded again.

'For myself, I would be honoured if you would return to college and resume your course. I truly believe you have the makings of a fine historian. Neville Catesby was right about that, at least, if nothing else.'

'I don't know what to do. I think I must be cursed . . . I lose everyone.'

'Everyone?'

'My mother died giving birth to me and my father took his own life when he was sacked. Hanged himself. Shirin became my new family, then Sir Neville was like a father to me. They're both gone and I have nothing left.'

Wilde reached out and put his hand on the young man's shoulder. 'I think I understand, really I do. But you know, many academics find that their college is like a family. Get into college life properly and you may discover the same thing.'

'It just all seems so hopeless. The world is an evil place.'

'There's bad, but there's also good. Your history studies will show you that. Work, that's the thing. Read, study, write – work. And one day, spring will be upon us and you may see that there is more to life than all this.'

They were silent for a few more miles. Wilde peered at the road ahead and his hands on the wheel. His gold wedding band caught his eye. 'There was one thing I meant to ask you about, Oswick, something you might know. Three of the victims of this conspiracy had their ring fingers removed. Would you have any idea what that was about?'

Oswick was thoughful for a few moments, then nodded. 'Yes, sir, I'm pretty sure I do.'

'Go on.'

'When we were in the army, Colonel Catesby as I then knew him, gave me one piece of advice. "Always carry a strong pair of wire cutters with you, Oswick," he said. "Not the big ones the sappers use for cutting barbed wire, but a smaller pair that will fit neatly in your pocket or your pack". I asked him why. "You'll understand soon enough," he replied. Later I discovered that it was to cut fingers off corpses so you could get their rings in a hurry. Apparently some soldiers make a lot of money that way.'

'And did you ever do it yourself?'

'No, sir. But Sir Neville did. I think that was my first doubt, even before Belsen changed my mind about him and about fascism.'

Except, of course, Catesby would call himself a communist not a fascist, and his ambition had not been to become the English Führer, but the English Stalin.

Dr Gertrude Blake's voice was stern, but there was no trace of anger. 'Now then, Miss Morris, I think you have a little explaining to do. I have already spoken with Miss March and I am not at all satisfied with her cock and bull story. Hopefully you will come up with something better.'

What could Lydia say to the St Ursula's principal? The truth? Throw herself on the woman's mercy? This was going to be difficult. And just as with her first time in this book-crowded study, she found herself under the unnerving, eyeless gaze of the skeleton that Dr Blake insisted on keeping, hanging from the ceiling.

'What can I tell you?'

'The truth would be a good start. I seem to recall I specifically asked you to keep Miranda March on the straight and narrow, *not* lead her astray.'

'I promise you, I would do nothing to deliberately undermine Miranda's work.'

'Well then, where exactly have you both been the past two nights, for you certainly weren't in the St Ursula's hostel? Nor were you at anatomy, in the library or in attendance at lectures yesterday. Moreover, the coincidence of a double murder outside the hostel in the hours before your disappearance has not gone unnoticed. Where would you like to start, Miss Morris?'

Once again, Lydia felt the words *Miss Morris* acutely. They were spoken in a way that made the listener uncomfortably aware that the speaker had doubts over their accuracy as a mode of address. She felt utterly lost. The only possible answer was a half-truth.

'I have a confession to make, Dr Blake, I have been living in sin with a man and he has been involved in secret war work. These past days and nights, this aspect of his life has come back to haunt us. Those two men who died were security service agents, and they were placed outside the hostel to protect me.'

'Carry on.'

'Their killer attacked Miss March and me. We fought him off, but it was too dangerous to stay – and so we made our way to my home in Cambridge. I know this sounds implausible – a cock and bull story, if you like – but it's actually true. The whole thing is, of course, rather more complicated than that.'

'It doesn't quite tally with Miss March's story, I'm afraid.'

'I suspect she was worried about my place at St Ursula's and was trying to protect me. We've become very good friends in the short time we have been here.'

'And these murders, you must have been interviewed by the police?'

'No, the security service, MI5. They are dealing with it. I am told the matter has been resolved and the murderer, a German man whose weapon of choice was injected phenol, is in custody.'

'Injected phenol? The very thought makes me shudder.'

'Apparently it was used by the Nazis in their euthanasia programme and as a method of execution in the concentration camps.'

'And this ghastliness has reared its ugly head in England?'

Lydia nodded.

Dr Blake simply turned away and looked out of the window for a full half-minute. Lydia felt the book-lined walls closing in; she found herself silently saying the Lord's Prayer as the seconds ticked by into eternity.

'This matter is by no means closed,' Gertrude Blake said at last. 'You will return to your studies and I expect to hear nothing but good things of your work.'

'Thank you, Dr Blake.'

'Obviously I can't say I approve of your relationship with this man, but I am aware that the war has brought about a sea change in morals, so I will let it pass. Had you been married or given birth, of course, that would have made your position here unacceptable. You understand what I'm saying, don't you?'

'Yes.' Lydia understood very well. Dame Gertrude had strong suspicions about the truth of Lydia's marital status, but they would engage in a pact of mutual silence on the matter.

'Good, then get along with you, young woman. And may I say, it sounds as though you and Miss March have been remarkably brave. I believe you will both be a credit to St Ursula's. But no more dramas, please. Go home to your man at the weekend and explain that to him. If he loves you, which I trust he does, he will understand my message.'

Wilde dropped Danny Oswick off at college with a promise that they would discuss his future at greater length in the coming days, and set off for home. More than anything, he was looking forward to a bit of normality – reading, writing his long-delayed history of the Elizabethan priests, informing young minds and spending a great deal more time with Johnny.

The fact that the pathogens in Rascher's bombs were dead eased his fears for Lydia should she return to London in the next day or two. But he did wonder whether she might have had a change of heart about her need to become a doctor of medicine. Perhaps that decision would be taken by others, leaving her no choice in the matter. He knew what *he* wanted, and that was the return of his wife.

He pulled the remarkably reliable green and black Riley into his street and slammed on the brake. The front door of the house was open and a child was running out, screaming. It was Penelope, Mrs Keane's three-year-old daughter, followed almost immediately by Johnny.

Without hesitation, Wilde jumped out of the car and scooped up the little girl before she ran into the street.

'He's hurt Mummy!' the child cried. 'The man's hurt Mummy!'

Wilde put her down on the doorstep. 'Johnny, stay here with Penelope.'

'Yes, Daddy – the man's upstairs.'

'Wait here, both of you,' he said in what he hoped would be a quiet and calming voice. 'Stay here, yes?'

Penelope nodded frantically. Johnny smiled uncertainly and put his arm around the little girl's shoulders.

At first Wilde heard nothing, then a scraping of feet and a low grunt. From upstairs somewhere. He pulled off his shoes and climbed the staircase on silent, stockinged feet. Whatever was happening, the element of surprise might just be on his side. His hand went to his jacket, but then he remembered he had no gun. He had been relieved of the Browning Hi-Power at Sandalshoon and it had not been recovered. All he had were his bare hands, his boxer's fists.

Sylvia Keane was lying flat on her front on her bed. McNally had his knee on her back and was pulling at a cord wrapped around her neck. Tightening it with a wooden peg, choking the life out of the woman.

He turned and saw Wilde, but he was too slow. The piledriver punch was aimed at the side of his head, but instead it became an uppercut, cracking into his chin, snapping his head back. His hands fell from the cord as he lurched sideways.

Wilde hit him again. And again. Pummelling his temple and face, grappling him to the floor. He may not have been the stronger man, but he was the better fighter, skilled from many hours in the boxing ring and sparring at the gym.

When he knew he had the man beaten, he delivered one last blow to knock him cold, then left his inert body on the floor and turned his attention to Sylvia Keane.

She was alive.

CHAPTER 48

Wilde and Lydia had three visits to make. They could have gone individually, but they decided to do all three as a family, with Johnny and Penelope coming along, too. The first, of course, was to Addenbrooke's where Penelope's mother was recovering from the attack by Ian McNally, who was now in police custody.

Sylvia Keane had an angry red ring around her throat where the cord had cut into her, and her voice was soft and hoarse and barely intelligible. She had been advised not to talk, but the doctors believed she would regain the power of speech. Otherwise she was well and would be released from hospital the next morning.

'We're desperately sorry for everything that's happened,' Lydia said. 'We believe I was the man's intended target.'

The injured woman tried to nod, but the pain made her wince.

'And we would very much like you to stay at Cornflowers. Don't try to talk, just raise a hand if that sounds all right with you.'

Penelope had already climbed onto the bed and was hugging her mother as though she would never let her go. Sylvia Keane managed a smile and both Lydia and Wilde were delighted to see that the warmth which had first attracted them to the woman was back. She raised a hand.

'Then that's wonderful news,' Lydia said. 'And we would both like to say how pleased we are that you felt able to confide in us about your plight. We can only imagine how painful these last few months have been for you – and rest assured we believe that no blame attaches to you, and you should never feel shame for the actions of others. The people you once thought of as friends should look to their own consciences.'

They stayed with her for an hour, explaining much of what had happened, then took their leave of her and drove to Flowthorpe, which had now been declared disease-free.

May Hinchley had known they were coming and welcomed them all with tea and cake, even though it was only lunchtime.

Lydia handed her a bottle of wine, as she had intended to do when she tried to visit before.

There were hugs and tears and the children were allowed to run riot in the house and around May's wonderful little garden.

'Well, I suppose I can say I survived the plague,' she said as the three adults sipped their tea. 'Not many people in England can make a boast like that. But I did lose two elderly friends, so it's not really something to make light of.'

'You look well, though, May,' Lydia said as she and Tom rose to take their leave. 'Maybe a little leaner . . .'

'Not so broad in the beam? Maybe I'll find a man yet. Never too thin, darling, isn't that what they say?'

'I'm not sure that's true.'

'When will I see you if you're going to be in London all the time?'

'Oh, I'll be home as often as I can. And I want plenty of visits at St Ursula's.'

Finally, with the children gathered up, they made the long drive eastwards to Skyme on the coast of Norfolk.

Barnaby Wax grinned at the sight of the jerrycans filled with petrol. 'I knew you were a man of your word, Tom.' He nodded to Lydia and the children. 'And this your brood, is it?'

'My wife, Lydia, and son Johnny. The little girl is Penelope, daughter of a friend.'

'It's a pleasure to meet you, Lydia,' Wax said as they shook hands. 'God knows what you're doing with this ugly reprobate.'

'Oh, he has his uses.'

'Anyway, come inside and have some coffee.'

'How many gallons of black market petrol did you exchange for that?'

Wax grinned at Lydia. 'Something of a cynic your old man, isn't he? But first, I have an interesting bit of news, Tom. It seems my lovely niece Liz is up the duff. Don't know what to think, myself, but she seems happy. She's convinced herself it's Tony's. I suppose women know these things.'

'I'd like to say hello. Is she at home?'

'No, you'll find her on the beach. She goes down there every day. Poor lass just looks out to sea for hours on end, as though waiting for something . . . or someone.'

Monday morning. The call came through from Bill Donovan confirming that the two bodies recovered from the plane crash on the island of Sylt were, indeed, those of Sir Neville Catesby and Boris Minsky.

'They're no loss to the world,' Wilde said.

'Perhaps the whole business will make Truman think a bit harder about what he's done in dismantling the OSS,' Donovan said.

'We can only hope.'

'And the plague?'

'Panic over. As of Friday, it's all clear. No infections in London. We were lucky . . . this time.'

'There will be other threats. Sunlit uplands? In your dreams, Mr Churchill. Hitler might be done for but how can a world of A-bombs, biological warfare and chemical weapons be sunny and safe? Anyway, keep in touch, Tom. We'll be needing you again when Truman is forced by circumstances to see the light.'

'I'm an academic now, Bill. One hundred per cent. Young minds to educate, a book to write.'

Donovan laughed. 'Good luck with that, buddy.'

Wilde laughed, too, said goodbye and replaced the receiver. Lydia was standing at the bottom of the stairs. 'Ready?' he said. 'Just give me one minute and I'll drive you to the station.'

She didn't say anything, just stood there with her head bowed.

'Lydia? What is it?'

Tears were streaming down her face but she was making no sound. He reached out and took her face in his hands and kissed it all over. 'Come on, you'll miss the train.'

'I'm not going, Tom.'

'Of course you are. We'll see you soon.'

'No. I've been thinking of nothing else and I'm not going. I can't leave you and Johnny.'

'It's homesickness, Lydia. We've all felt it.'

Her tears turned to choking sobs. 'No, it's more than that. This is my life. Here. With you.'

He stood back from her and clasped her hands. 'Are you serious?'

'Never more so. And there's something else. I think I can be more use here. I want to start a charity with some of the money I was bequeathed. It will be called "Mothers Left Behind". Not just war widows but anyone with children facing difficulty – people like Mrs Keane, for instance. In fact, my plan is to employ her if she's interested.'

'What a remarkable idea.'

'I think so. Oh, Tom, I've been so selfish. Becoming a doctor was a stupid dream.'

He pulled her to him. 'No it wasn't. It was a wonderful dream – and it's going to come true, because you're going to see it through. You can't imagine how proud I am of you.'

'Tom?'

'And one day Johnny will feel the same pride. So you go back to St Ursula's, Lydia Morris. Mrs Keane can look after us and set up your charity. One way or another, we'll work it all out. There are telephones and trains and we'll see you all the time once you've settled in.'

He realised he was almost crying, too, which was ridiculous because he never cried. Tears had been beaten out of him at boarding school.

'I don't know. You've confused me now.'

'Trust me. We're a team, Lydia. You and me, forever.'

HISTORICAL NOTES

The evil of Unit 731

When the vast biological research unit was being constructed – seventy buildings on a 1500-acre site near Harbin, Manchuria – curious locals were told it was to be a timber mill.

With grisly humour, the researchers later dehumanised the victims of their experiments – including children – by referring to them as 'logs'.

The experiments were beyond comprehension in their barbaric depravity: pregnant women infected with disease, then cut open alive – often without anaesthetic – to examine the foetuses; blood transfusions in which the subject's blood was replaced with animal blood; limbs amputated and switched around. Prisoners were Russians, Chinese, Koreans and Mongolians. None survived.

Unit 731 had been set up by army doctor General Shiro Ishii in 1936 with permission of the Japanese army general staff and Emperor Hirohito.

The knowledge of biological weapons gathered allowed their forces to drop pathogens on Chinese towns and villages, killing an unknown number of civilians.

At the end of the war, the United States secretly granted the Japanese doctors immunity from prosecution in exchange for details of their findings – to be used in their own bio-warfare research – but the Russians did hold a trial of 12 less important officers and laboratory workers, who were all given prison terms.

Shiro Ishii was never prosecuted and survived until 1959, when he died of cancer. It is said he converted to Catholicism but there seems to be no evidence that he ever expressed remorse for his bloodthirsty activities.

Who was in the Black Book?

This booklet contained 2,820 enemies of Nazism and was drawn up by SS intelligence chief Walter Schellenberg in 1940. It was officially called the Sonderfahndungsliste GB (Most Wanted List

Great Britain) and was intended as a guide for Nazi task forces to immediately arrest those named in the event of a successful invasion of Britain.

The book was discovered by the Allies in Berlin in 1945, after the war ended, and became a source of pride and some amusement for those who were included.

Among them were Lady Astor (the first female MP), Clement Attlee, Robert Baden-Powell (founder of the Scouts), newspaper publisher Lord Beaverbrook, Bishop George Bell, nuclear physicist Patrick Blackett, Vera Brittain, Neville Chamberlain, Winston Churchill, Noel Coward, Anthony Eden, sculptor Jacob Epstein, E M Forster, Sigmund Freud, Margery Fry (penal reform campaigner), Charles de Gaulle, Aldous Huxley, cartoonist David Low, suffragist Sylvia Pankhurst, author J B Priestley, singer Paul Robeson, actress Sybil Thorndike, author H G Wells, Virginia Woolf. Many of the others named were Jewish refugees.

Those included might have smiled but there was nothing humorous about the intent behind the list: a similar black book used in Hitler's invasion of Poland had led to many murders of the country's elite.

The truth about Dr Sigmund Rascher

He was a creepy, cruel and ambitious man. Born in Munich in 1909, his father was also a doctor and his maternal grandmother was a well-to-do Englishwoman named Frances Whitfield.

He joined the Nazi party in 1933, the year he enrolled in medical school. Never very successful with women, he eventually married the singer Nini Diehl, several years his senior and an acquaintance of SS chief Heinrich Himmler (perhaps his former lover).

Together, the Raschers perpetuated a fraud by claiming they had discovered a method for older women to become pregnant. This was at a time when the Nazis were desperate to increase the birth rate and the couple were even used in publicity pictures with the children Nini was said to have had after the age of 48. In fact the Raschers had kidnapped four babies and pretended they were their own children.

Rascher offered his services to use human guinea pigs in cancer research at Dachau concentration camp and later performed altitude and freezing experiments on inmates, many of whom died.

Conveniently for a man who would probably have faced the noose for war crimes, he was said to have been executed by the SS at Dachau a few days before the end of the war, supposedly for his child-kidnap fraud which had embarrassed Himmler.

It has been claimed that Rascher was meticulous in his research and that his findings on hypothermia were accepted as scientific fact until the 1990s.

ACKNOWLEDGEMENTS

Huge thanks to everyone who has helped me write this book; my brilliant brother, Brian, for his assistance with details of firearms; my wife Naomi for her help with research and editing – and keeping my nose to the grindstone when the going gets tough; my friends Dr Jane Ewing and Dr Philip Buttery for helping me find research sources. And everyone at Bonnier Zaffre – the designers, the editorial assistants, and the fabulous sales, marketing and publicity teams, but particularly my incredibly talented editor Ben Willis.

Four people generously gave me their time and expertise regarding various technical issues around biological warfare, toxicology, maritime matters and the history of medical schools – so my unbounded gratitude goes out to: Professor Nick Beeching, Emeritus Professor of Tropical and Infectious Diseases at the Liverpool School of Tropical Medicine; Dr Stephen Morley consultant chemical pathologist and forensic toxicologist of University Hospitals of Leicester; Jon Warren, sea captain on semi-submersible ships and marine warranty surveyor; Dr Sophie Almond, whose PhD subject at Leicester University focused on the experiences and careers of women doctors from 1879 to 1948, and now working at Ofqual. Any errors are mine, not theirs.

Last but not least, my thanks go to my agent, Teresa Chris, whose wisdom and humour always help me through the dark hours.

If you enjoyed *The English Führer*,
why not join the
RORY CLEMENTS READERS' CLUB

When you sign up you'll receive a free copy of
an exclusive short story, plus news about upcoming books,
sneak previews, and exclusive behind-the-scenes material.
To join, simply visit:
bit.ly/RoryClementsClub

Keep reading for a letter from the author . . .

Hello!

I want to tell you a little bit about the background to *The English Führer*.

The history books tell us that the Second World War finished on 8th May, 1945 in Europe and three months later in the Far East. But that's not the whole story. Fascism didn't just die with the defeat of Hitler and the Axis powers.

In Britain, many of those seen as having Nazi sympathies – such as British Union of Fascists leader Sir Oswald Mosley – had been interned during the war under Defence Regulation 18B. But when peace came they were released. And plenty of them continued to campaign for their beliefs.

In his book *Blackshirt*, the intelligence expert Stephen Dorril reveals that from 1945 onwards, there were still thousands of fascists and anti-semites in the country and that more than 50 new fascist parties and organisations came into existence. He mentions one 18B reunion dinner at a London hotel, where Mosley was the surprise guest. When he arrived 'hundreds of hands shot up in the Fascist salute'.

Nor was fascism the only threat. As the euphoria of the war's end began to wear off, it became clear that the Red Army's 'liberation' of countries in Eastern Europe merely replaced one totalitarian occupying force with another.

Britain and America were woefully equipped to deal with the new threat posed by Stalin, for they had little in the way of an intelligence operation in Moscow – while the Kremlin had infiltrated our own secret services with high-ranking traitors such as Philby, Burgess, Maclean and Blunt.

This is the tricky new world that my protagonist Professor Tom Wilde must try to negotiate and make sense of in *The English Führer*. It is a world exhausted by war, desperate for peace – and extremely vulnerable because few have any appetite for further conflict.

If you would like to hear more about my books, you can visit my website www.roryclements.co.uk where you can join the Rory Clements Readers' Club (www.bit.ly/RoryClementsClub). It only takes a few moments to sign up, there are no catches or costs.

Bonnier Zaffre will keep your data private and confidential, and it will never be passed on to a third party. We won't spam you with loads of emails, just get in touch now and again with news about my books, and you can unsubscribe any time you want.

And if you would like to get involved in a wider conversation about my books, please do review *The English Führer* on Amazon, on Goodreads, on any other e-store, on your own blog and social media accounts, or talk about it with friends, family or reader groups! Sharing your thoughts helps other readers, and I always enjoy hearing about what people experience from my writing.

Thank you again for reading *The English Führer*.

With best wishes,

Rory Clements

THE TOM WILDE A-Z OF SECRETS
AND SPIES

Abwehr. The German military intelligence service was headed by Admiral Wilhelm Canaris before and during most of the war, but he was distrusted by Himmler and Heydrich. Canaris was a deeply conflicted man. Having originally been a Nazi, he recoiled from their excesses and antisemitism and came to despise Hitler. However, he loved Germany and no evidence was found that he actively worked against the Führer. That did not save him. In July 1944, three days after the bomb plot against Hitler, Canaris was arrested and was executed in the last weeks of the war, being humiliated by being led naked to the gallows. He had spent his final hours reading a biography of the Holy Roman Emperor Frederick II.

Burglary. MI6 was always willing to use criminal methods to obtain intelligence. As far back as 1918, a training manual advised agents to acquire the services of a skilful burglar. 'He must be reliable, willing to undergo imprisonment if caught, without giving the show away, and should be handsomely rewarded.' By 1947, Q Branch (as in the James Bond films) was producing special torches with dim red beams for burglaries and developing methods to break into combination safes. Consulates and embassies were seen as fair game for these safe-cracking forays.

Counter-Intelligence Corps. This American intelligence agency had wide-ranging duties, including protecting the atomic Manhattan project, investigating Nazis in post-war Germany, administering captured towns and cracking down on black marketeers. Its agents ran Operation Paperclip in which German scientists were taken to America to keep them out of Soviet hands. Among its best-known operatives were Henry Kissinger and author J.D.Salinger.

Defence Regulation 18b. On May 23rd 1940, British citizens considered a threat to national security were arrested without warning and interned without trial by MI5 under Defence Regulation 18b. Particularly targeted were members of right-wing organisations such as the British Union of Fascists. Its leader Sir Oswald Mosley and his wife Diana were among the first to be held, and over the next three months a total of 1,000 were brought in. By 1943, this number was reduced to 500, but those who had been interned suffered lasting damage to their reputation and many struggled to find work after the war. Many also tried to reorganise fascist parties, but with little success.

Enigma. The Enigma machine was a cipher device used by the German military before and during WWII to communicate secretly on the battlefield, in the air and at sea. It scrambled the letters of the alphabet so effectively that it should never have been broken. But it was – first by a Polish mathematician as early as 1932 and later at Bletchley Park during the war by the brilliant minds in Hut 6 and Hut 8 (led by Alan Turing). By 1941, they were breaking 4,000 Nazi signals every day, including ones to and from Hitler – a huge task considering that the Enigma settings were changed every 24 hours, so had to be broken anew on a daily basis. It is believed their efforts shortened the war considerably.

Five. Slang for MI5, Britain's counter-intelligence organisation, also known as The Security Service. When WWII began, the service was moved from Thames House to Wormwood Scrubs Prison because the rapidly-expanding workforce needed far more space (there were only 36 officers at the start of the war and this increased to hundreds). For the first time, female office staff were allowed to wear trousers – because the nature of the prison gangways made them visible from lower floors. In October 1940, most members of MI5 moved again to the much more amenable surroundings of Blenheim Palace.

Gehlen. Blue-eyed and brilliant – and a clever self-publicist – Reinhard Gehlen was Hitler's chief of military intelligence in the East during the Nazis' invasion of the Soviet Union. In this role he amassed a huge amount of secret information about the Red Army and the politics of the Soviet Union, which he brought back to the West. After the war, he offered this data to the Americans – who were bereft of an intelligence-gathering service behind the Iron Curtain – and eventually became head of West German intelligence until 1968. But he was less than scrupulous in building up his new spy agency, happily recruiting former SS and Gestapo members, including many war criminals.

Halina Szymańska. One of the most important spies of WWII, she had a powerful link to German intelligence chief Wilhelm Canaris, with whom she may have had an affair. Aged 33 at the outbreak of war, she was the wife of Polish diplomat Antoni Szymański. After Poland fell, Canaris helped her escape to Switzerland with her three daughters, and she began working for MI6 and the OSS. Described by one MI6 officer as 'very attractive and formidable', she is said to have had meetings with Canaris in Vichy France and to have had dinner with him in Berne, Switzerland. Among the vital intelligence she passed on to the British and Americans was Hitler's planned invasion of the Soviet Union in summer 1941. She died in 1989 and is buried in Ealing cemetery, London.

Intrepid. Sir William Stephenson, codenamed Intrepid, was Britain's senior intelligence coordinator in North America during the war and is one of many spies cited as Fleming's model for James Bond (see *Knight*, below). When Soviet envoy Igor Gouzenko defected to Canada in 1945 Stephenson is said to have been one of only a few people who took his testimony seriously – and fought hard to convince America and Britain that their secret services and the atomic bomb project had been infiltrated by Soviet agents.

Jane Archer. MI5's only female officer in WWII (there were other female staff but not of officer rank) and was considered a brilliant interrogator. However, she was sacked in 1940 for accusing new director Jasper Harker of incompetence (he, too, was downgraded a few months later). Jane was then taken on by MI6. Unfortunately her new boss in Section IX (dealing with Communist counter-intelligence) was the Soviet spy Kim Philby. Recognising her as a threat to his safety, he managed to keep her away from any work which might have enabled her to expose him. He was not unmasked until 1963. Jane, a lawyer by training, returned to MI5 after the war and eventually retired to Devon, dying aged 84 in 1982.

Knight. Many have been called the inspiration for James Bond (see *Intrepid*, above) – but Maxwell Knight might be one of the front runners. He organised spies for MI5 from the 1920s through to the 1950s and was responsible for some of their greatest successes, infiltrating both communist groups and Nazi organisations, and was unusual for the time in employing women agents. He also lived a double life – as a naturalist, presenting hundreds of BBC radio and TV programmes.

London Cage. This was a row of impressive houses in Kensington Palace Gardens which, in 1940, became a controversial interrogation centre for captured Germans. It later emerged that some of the techniques amounted to torture under the Geneva Convention. For instance, standing for up to 26 hours, being threatened with execution, being forced to kneel while being beaten and being refused toilet breaks. Four men committed suicide while held there. That said, the Cage did provide a great deal of intelligence from captured SS officers that assisted the Allied war effort.

MI6. The Secret Intelligence Service, otherwise known as MI6, was (and is) Britain's foreign intelligence gathering service. It was based at 54 Broadway, a nine-storey building in Westminster, though you'd never know its true purpose from the outside, because it was hidden behind a door which advertised it as a fire extinguisher company. Kim Philby called it dingy and one visitor recalled that when he visited 'C', Sir Hugh Sinclair, he came in through a room full of old lavatories and baths before entering an office 'that was quite out of this world. There was a mother-of-pearl pistol on a round table in the middle, a cigar box, a Turkish carpet with so deep a pile that you nearly got lost in it and a handsome desk behind which sat C.'

NKVD. The secret police of the Soviet Union from 1934 to 1946. Its function was to protect the state and, in doing this, it was responsible for millions of people being murdered or sent to slave labour camps 'as enemies of the state'. The communist secret police had started in 1917 as the Cheka and went through many different incarnations, including the KGB, where Vladimir Putin learnt his ruthless trade. Its present title is the FSB, which is believed responsible for assassinations by novichok poison and other means.

Office of Strategic Services. This was the US wartime spy agency, forerunner of CIA and loosely based on Britain's MI6. On President Roosevelt's orders it was set up in 1942 and run by lawyer and WWI hero Bill Donovan with a mission to collect intelligence, support resistance movements and conduct special operations such as sabotage. Donovan recruited the brightest, including Allen Dulles who would go on to become director of the CIA. Another notable operative was the celebrated food writer Julia Child. She solved the problem of sharks inadvertently setting off underwater mines by devising a shark repellent in her kitchen. This was sprinkled around explosives – and succeeded in keeping the sharks away.

Philby. Almost certainly the most deadly of the five Cambridge spies (the others were Anthony Blunt, Donald Maclean, Guy Burgess and John Cairncross), Kim Philby was responsible for the deaths of countless Western agents – certainly thousands – by revealing their identities and movements to his Soviet spymasters. And yet he had a tender side, caring for a pet baby fox and feeding it whisky in a bowl. He defected to Moscow in 1963. Even then, he could not change his treacherous ways – betraying his fellow exiled traitor Donald Maclean by sleeping with his wife.

Quisling. A term widely used for a traitor. In fact the word comes from Vidkun Quisling, a Norwegian fascist who was appointed prime minister when the Nazis invaded his country. His puppet government collaborated with the Germans and deported Jews to almost certain death. Quisling is said to have been bullied at school because of his regional accent. After the war he was found guilty of murder and treason and was executed by firing squad, his name doomed forever to be associated with treachery.

Read. My protagonist Tom Wilde was inspired by two real-life Americans who, like him, have strong connections to Britain. The first is Conyers Read, an American historian who studied at Oxford and wrote the definitive biography of Elizabethan spymaster Sir Francis Walsingham. Read was later involved in setting up the Office of Strategic Services, the wartime forerunner of the CIA. The other American was James Jesus Angleton, who studied at Malvern College, an English public school, and later became chief of CIA counter-intelligence. He was a friend of Kim Philby and, like everyone else, was betrayed by him. Tom Wilde has similarities to these two men, but he is neither of them. He is very much his own man.

Sabotage. When we think of sabotage we tend to imagine high-tech interventions, ambushes and blowing up railway lines. In fact, the enemy can be dealt costly blows using much simpler methods – which is why America's Office of Strategic Services went to great lengths to teach resistance groups how to cause maximum damage with minimum risk: for instance, slashing tyres of troop carriers, using candles to burn down enemy buildings, putting pollutants into fuel tanks. Even blocking an enemy's sewage system by soaking a sponge in thick starch, squeezing it into a tight ball, wrapping in string, then allowing it to dry before removing the string and flushing the small hard ball down the toilet. It will slowly expand, bung up the works and cause mayhem in Gestapo HQ.

Trevor-Roper. The historian Hugh Trevor-Roper served in MI6 during the war and in 1945 was sent into the ruins of post-war

Germany to discover Hitler's fate. He worked fast, interviewing people who had been in the Bunker and came to the conclusion that Hitler had died by his own hand. Thirty-eight years later, Professor Trevor-Roper was a director of *The Sunday Times* newspaper. The supposed diaries of Hitler had found their way into the newspaper's hands for a large sum of money and Trevor-Roper declared them genuine. Two weeks later a forensic scientist proved conclusively that the diaries were a forgery.

Uranium. In January 1942, President Roosevelt ordered the development of an atomic bomb – because he knew the Nazis were also working on one. The essential ingredient was uranium, and the world's greatest and richest supply was held at the Shinkolobwe mine in Belgian Congo (now the DRC). Much had already been taken to New York by the mine owners for safekeeping but over 1,000 tons was still at the mine. A race began to get it out of the ground and transported to America. With the help of the OSS secret service, who protected the supplies, it was carried 1,500 miles by rail and riverboat to the coast and from there by fast boat and plane to America, all in utmost secrecy because next-door Angola was awash with Nazi spies. Two boats were sunk (one by German submarine) but overall the project was a huge success and the ore was kept out of German hands.

Venlo Incident. This was one of the most devastating defeats for Britain's Secret Intelligence Service in WWII. Having been contacted by 'the German Resistance' with a plan to oust Hitler, two MI6 officers travelled to Venlo on the Dutch border with Germany in November 1939 to meet them. Instead they were met by heavily-armed SS men in plainclothes, who dragged them over the border into Germany. Inexcusably, one of the two MI6 men – Major Richard Stevens – had been carrying in his pocket a list of secret agents in Europe. These had to be hurriedly brought to safety before the Germans could get them.

Wolkoff. Among the Russian emigres in Britain in the 1930s was the upper-class Wolkoff family, who escaped the Bolshevik revolution by settling in London and running the Russian Tea Rooms in Kensington. Anna Wolkoff, their daughter, was a dressmaker for Princess Marina, Wallis Simpson and Pamela Mitford. But Anna was a fascist antisemite and met members of the Nazi High Command in Germany. In May 1940, she was arrested and charged with trying to pass on secrets from the US embassy in London to the enemy – including correspondence between Churchill and Roosevelt – and was sentenced to ten years prison. Her British citizenship was revoked.

X: Harald Kurtz (codename agent X), was the son of a wealthy German Nazi and grandson of a Yorkshire baronet. Kurtz, a lage man who despised the Hitler Youth and refused to join, was persuaded by MI5 to spy on fascists and German agents in Britain – which he did successfully – in return for British citizenship. After the war he worked as a translator at the Nuremberg trials. But his wartime experiences had taken their toll and he became a lonely alcoholic, living at Oxford University, writing histories and playing draughts with the college porters.

Yezhov. The murderous Nikolai Yezhov was head of the NKVD (Soviet secret police) during the purges of the late 1930s and was said to take pleasure in humiliating and torturing his victims. Standing a shade under 5ft tall, he was known as the 'bloody dwarf' and is quoted as saying 'better that ten innocents should suffer than one traitor escape'. Well, after overseeing the killings of 700,000 people, even he didn't escape: when he fell from favour with Stalin in 1940, Yezhov was dragged screaming and crying to a basement cell where he was executed with a shot to the head. Curiously, in his private life he had been regarded as charming and amusing.

Zigzag. Eddie Chapman, codenamed Zigzag, was perhaps the most intriguing double agent of WWII. A career criminal, he was on Jersey escaping a charge of safebreaking when the Germans invaded the island. He offered his services as an agent to German intelligence, was given training – and was parachuted back into Britain to sabotage an aircraft factory. But he immediately gave himself up to MI5 and they decided to use him as a double agent, faking an attack on the aircraft factory and sending him back to the Germans in the vain hope that he would assassinate Hitler. After D-Day, his German contact returned him to Britain to report back on the accuracy of the V1 bombs. He told him they were hitting their targets when, in fact they were falling short. His colourful career – including several beautiful mistresses – continued after the war. He got back into crime, acquired a Rolls-Royce and a castle and remained good friends with his German 'handler' Baron Stephan von Gröning.

CHAPTER 1

MUNICH, JUNE 1935

On the day they found the English girl's body, Sebastian Wolff was otherwise engaged.

His problems began at lunchtime in one of his favourite beer joints, the Tirolkeller, around the corner from police HQ in the old town. His girlfriend Hexie was supposed to be meeting him there because it was his thirty-fifth birthday and they were going to head off to a secluded beach in woodland on the far bank of Lake Starnberger. Complete privacy there. No need for swimsuits or modesty. He checked his wristwatch. One-thirty and he was still alone.

So where was she?

Hoffmann must have kept her at the shop, which was pretty typical of him. The pompous, drunken shit thought he was a cut above the rest of the world. And what did he do that made him think so highly of himself? Fawn over the boss, hold his little Leica and take snaps all day, hoping at least one might be in focus. Hardly a job for a man, in Seb's book. A child can hold a box and press a button.

Across the echoing beer hall, half a dozen young men in leather shorts were becoming tiresome, baiting a little guy in spectacles and suit, telling him that Jews were not welcome and that he should fuck off back to Jewland, wherever that was. He was protesting that he wasn't Jewish, but that just fed their scorn and aggression.

They were clearly country lads in town for the day. Farm boys with several litres of Augustiner brew inside them. They were spoiling for a fight, their mocking voices drowning out the house zither player's vain efforts and everyone else's conversation.

Seb wasn't worried about the likelihood of a full-scale brawl. A year ago, in the weeks before the bloody events at Bad Wiessee and elsewhere, he would have expected it to kick off. But today? Not a chance. Nobody dared riot in Munich these days. Peace reigned in the utopia of Adolf's golden dawn and everyone was happy. Even the brownshirts had put away their clubs and knuckle-dusters.

'You been stood up, detective?'

He turned and smiled at the waitress, her ample bosom spilling out of her dirndl, her double armful of beer jugs perfectly balanced and spilling not a drop. 'Looks like it, Gudrun.'

'Silly girl, that Hexie. I'll have you any day.'

'Ah, you're out of my league.'

'Try me.'

He kissed her sweaty, rouge-free cheek. 'Another time, Gudrun. I'm going to see if I can meet Hexie halfway. If I miss her and she turns up here, tell her to wait and I'll be back in ten minutes, traffic permitting.'

'Don't go anywhere near Königsplatz, Seb. They've sealed it all off again for the big development. God knows what they're doing this time.'

'Thanks.'

'And get those youngsters to settle down before you go, will you?'

'For you, darling, almost anything.'

The inn's black cat snaked sinuously through his legs. He handed Gudrun the empty, which she somehow managed to balance among the full steins, then he reached down and stroked the beast, before wandering over to the farm boys. They were all in their fanciest shorts, probably chamois and handed down from father to son through the generations. Were they ever washed? Hundreds of years of sweat, piss and other secretions.

They turned their attention to him, their bleary eyes suspicious. As one, they pushed out their chests and eyed him up like prize-fighters, but he merely smiled. 'Keep it down, boys.'

One of them, the biggest, grimmest, one, pushed his face into Seb's but he didn't back off.

'Who do you think you're talking to, mister?'

Seb drew his service pistol and shoved the muzzle into the young man's ugly nose. The farmboy recoiled as though he'd actually been shot, which he hadn't, and his gamsbart hat flew off. Seb gave them all another smile, took out his badge and flashed it at them.

'Another peep out of you lot and there's a nice cell waiting just around the corner in Ettstrase.'

Suddenly they went quiet. The big lad bent down and picked up his hat.

You could hear the zither again. Such was the power of a badge denoting membership of the criminal police – the Kripo – or anything else vaguely official-looking in the third year of the Third Reich. With the big gangsters in charge of the country, the little villains had lost their confidence. A shame, though, thought Seb, the heaviest, loudest one could have done with a bloody nose and he would have been more than happy to oblige. Instead he merely tapped his chest with the Walther. 'Enjoy the rest of your day, boys. Quietly.'

As Seb left, the little man they had been tormenting approached him. 'It's a lie what they were saying, I am not a Jew.'

He looked at the man coldly. He was a weasel. Seb said nothing and continued out into the open air where he took a deep breath. He was thirty-five, it was a fine June day and it felt good to be alive.

Looking both ways down the street, his eyes rested momentarily on the fruit and vegetable stall where the old one-legged veteran who had been trading there for as long as anyone could recall was doing steady business, selling new potatoes to a couple of grandmothers and a fat little brownshirt.

In the other direction, a group of tourists – American by the cut of their clothes – were staring up at the high bulb-topped towers of Munich's most famous church, the Frauenkirche. You could always tell the Americans; they were so well fed and so loud. They were here in Bavaria for 'health and culture', as advertised on the travel bureau posters and in the New York newspapers.

Gudrun was right. The traffic really did look heavy. Cars were crawling and the driver of an almost stationary brewery dray pulled by four weary horses was cracking his whip at the cars and cursing them.

Seb's own pride and joy – a Lancia Augusta cabriolet – was parked outside the inn. Three years ago, the little beauty would likely have been stolen or smashed up by one of the SA gangs that roamed the city, but these days, following the death of their leader, Roehm, in Stadelheim jail after the Wiessee raid, the brownshirts had been castrated like the dogs they were, and the streets were mostly safe.

The Lancia was painted red and Seb loved it almost as much as Hexie, though she thought he loved the car even more. Not that he had ever told Hexie that he loved her. Didn't want the fräulein getting ideas above her station. He left the car and set off at a brisk walk. Pointless trying to drive.

The cause of the snarl-up was Adolf's grand plan for König-splatz, turning it into yet another oversized parade ground and shrine to Nazidom, as if there wasn't enough stamping and marching around the city in metal-heeled boots. On and off for months now, the building work had been having a knock-on effect throughout the city centre. Roads were dug up and two temples were being constructed to house the remains of the putsch martyrs of '23.

White-gloved traffic cops were causing even more havoc with their frantic arm-waving as they tried to divert vans and cars in directions they didn't want to go.

No matter. It was a pleasant day for a stroll and it was less than two kilometres to Heinrich Hoffmann's photographic studio in Schwabing.

He made his way to Lenbachplatz, then across to Barerstrasse and strode north by way of Karolinenplatz, which was teeming with builders' vehicles and SS guys. The road west, past the Brown House and on to Königsplatz, was completely cut off. There was noise and dust everywhere.

Hexie wasn't at the Hoffmann studio. The other girl, the one who had replaced Evie Braun and whose name escaped Seb, told him she had had to dash to the Osteria Bavaria with a package of prints for Hoffmann. Seb thanked her and wandered off along Schellingstrasse.

A crowd had gathered on the pavements and across the road outside the restaurant. That could mean only one thing: word had got out that Adolf was driving down from his mountain retreat at Obersalzberg to lunch there.

Even as the thought struck him, the leader's cavalcade appeared; three large black Mercedes open-tops, bristling with SS and with Adolf himself in the rear of the middle car, sitting beside his chief bodyguard and adjutant, the enormous giraffe of a man Wilhelm Brückner.

Seb stopped and stared. The crowd began to scream and, as one, thrust their arms out in rigid salutes. Two young women – they couldn't have been out of their teen years – tore open their blouses and thrust their pert breasts in the direction of their hero. Two grinning SS men immediately placed themselves in front of the girls to protect their modesty and their leader's dignity.

If Hitler had seen the amateur strip show, he didn't give any indication, merely flapping his hand at his worshippers in a rather languid version of his celebrated salute. The cars pulled to a halt and the crowd was held back by a squad of heavily-armed SS men.

As the car door opened, the familiar figure of Hexie Schuler emerged from the front door of the osteria and, seeing the new arrival, shrank back into the wall. Seb caught her eye and she grimaced at him as if to say, 'what have I walked into?'

After alighting from the Mercedes with his dog on a short lead held in his left hand, Adolf spent a minute flapping his pasty right mitt at the crowd – rather like a performing sealion – then turned sharply and ducked into the doorway of his favourite Italian restaurant, dragging his handsome Alsatian behind him and brushing past Hexie as though she didn't exist.

Seb and Hexie had just embraced and she had just wished him a happy birthday when he felt his upper left arm being pulled and turned to find himself face to face with an expressionless man with thinning hair and pock-marked cheeks. He was about thirty and wore a grubby grey suit, soup-stained tie and battered fedora. Seb knew instantly that he was Bavarian Political Police – the sort of slimy drudge known in Berlin and other parts of Germany as Gestapo. He had seen him around the Police Presidium in Ettstrasse occasionally and he knew he wasn't part of the regular non-political criminal corps.

Nearby, the crowd was being urged to disperse by SS men, but they were still milling around as though hoping that Adolf might re-emerge any moment to take a bow and perhaps give an arm-flapping encore. The girls who had exposed themselves were buttoning up their blouses and flirting with the SS men who had shielded them from the leader's eyes. Something told Seb that the girls and the guys would be meeting up again later in the day to become better acquainted.

'I hate that place,' Hexie said, ignoring the political cop and nodding towards the Osteria Bavaria. 'The awful Englishwoman was there with Hoffmann. You know, the tall blonde one with fingers like Munich white sausage.'

'Her name's Mitford. She's always there.'

The man's grip was tightening and Seb turned on him, right arm up with fist clenched to do some damage to his unpleasant face. 'Yes?' he said irritably. 'Can I help you?'

'Bavarian Political Police. You didn't salute the Führer. Everyone else did, but not you.'

'Forgive me, I was distracted by the girls' tits.'

'What did you say?'

'You heard me, now take your hand off me.'

'You disgust me. You don't look like a filthy Jew, so what are you – a bolshevik?'

'I said remove your hand.'

'You think you can talk to a BPP officer like that?'

'I will talk to you exactly how I please. Now go away and annoy someone else before I draw blood.'

'How dare you talk to me like that? You're a damned Red, yes? A dangerous element.'

'You'll soon discover how dangerous I am.'

'What is your name?'

Seb pulled out his badge. 'Wolff. You can see it there. Inspector Sebastian Wolff. Murder team, Police Presidium, Ettstrasse 2. Criminals think I'm a dangerous element, but not law-abiding citizens. Are we done now?'

'Ah, you're a cop, eh? I thought I'd seen you before. Well, that won't protect you. I'm taking you to BPP headquarters.' The man dropped a cigarette stub to the ground and stamped on it.

Hexie pushed herself between Seb and the little greasebag. 'This is ridiculous. Crawl back into your disgusting hole, you vile slug.'

Words that Seb couldn't have said better, but they didn't help. Herr BPP wasn't going to back down now, not confronted with an irate woman. That would be humiliating. 'Give me *your* name, too.'

'My name is none of your business. Just know this: I am employed by the Führer's best friend Heinrich Hoffmann and they are in the restaurant together at this very moment. If anything happens to me, you'll be rat food. Capisce?'

And that really annoyed Herr BPP. Which is how Sebastian Wolff ended up in the Dachau concentration camp. *Thanks, Hexie*, he thought as Herr BPP summoned the assistance of uniformed SS officers and pushed him into the back of a car. *You always did have a mouth on you.*

'What is your name?'

Seb pulled out his badge. 'Wolff. You can see it there. Inspector Sebastian Wolff. Murder team, Police Presidium, Ettstrasse 2. Criminals think I'm a dangerous element, but not law-abiding citizens. Are we done now?'

'Ah, you're a cop, eh? I thought I'd seen you before. Well, that won't protect you. I'm taking you to BPP headquarters.' The man dropped a cigarette stub to the ground and stamped on it.

Hexie pushed herself between Seb and the little greasebag. 'This is ridiculous. Crawl back into your disgusting hole, you vile slug.'

Words that Seb couldn't have said better, but they didn't help. Herr BPP wasn't going to back down now, not confronted with an irate woman. That would be humiliating. 'Give me *your* name, too.'

'My name is none of your business. Just know this: I am employed by the Führer's best friend Heinrich Hoffmann and they are in the restaurant together at this very moment. If anything happens to me, you'll be rat food. Capisce?'

And that really annoyed Herr BPP. Which is how Sebastian Wolff ended up in the Dachau concentration camp. *Thanks, Hexie*, he thought as Herr BPP summoned the assistance of uniformed SS officers and pushed him into the back of a car. *You always did have a mouth on you.*